LAME FATE

UGLY SWANS

LAME FATE

UGLY SWANS

ARKADY AND BORIS STRUGATSKY

A NEW TRANSLATION BY MAYA VINOKOUR

Published by Chicago Review Press Incorporated
814 North Franklin Street
Chicago, IL 60610
ISBN 978-1-64160-071-2

AD VERBUM

Published with the support of the Institute for Literary Translation, Russia

Library of Congress Cataloging-in-Publication Data

Names: Strugatskiĭ, Arkadiĭ, 1925–1991, author. | Strugatskiĭ, Boris, 1933–2012, author. | Vinokour, Maya, translator. | Strugatskiĭ, Arkadiĭ, 1925–1991. Gadkie lebedi. English (Vinokour)
Title: Lame fate ; Ugly swans / Arkady and Boris Strugatsky ; a new translation by Maya Vinokour.
Other titles: Khromaia sud'ba. English (Vinokour) | Ugly swans.
Description: Chicago : Chicago Review Press, 2020. | Summary: "Never before translated into English, LAME FATE tells the story of middle-aged author Felix Sorokin, who is asked by the Soviet Writers' Union to submit a writing sample to a new computer program that will scientifically evaluate its "objective value" as a literary work. Sorokin must choose whether to present something establishment-approved or risk sharing his unpublished masterpiece. Sorokin's masterwork is UGLY SWANS, previously published in English as a standalone work but presented here in an authoritative new translation. In it, disgraced literary celebrity Victor Banev returns to the town of his childhood to find it haunted by the mysterious "clammies," black-masked outcasts with supernatural talents who terrify the town's adult population but enthrall its teenagers, including Banev's own daughter. By turns chilling, uproarious, and moving, these intertwining stories from the most celebrated Russian science fiction writers of the Soviet era are sure to delight readers from all walks of life"— Provided by publisher.
Identifiers: LCCN 2020007839 (print) | LCCN 2020007840 (ebook) | ISBN 9781641600712 (trade paperback) | ISBN 9781641600682 (adobe pdf) | ISBN 9781641600699 (epub) | ISBN 9781641600705 (kindle edition)
Subjects: GSAFD: Science fiction. | LCGFT: Science fiction.
Classification: LCC PG3476.S78835 K4713 2020 (print) | LCC PG3476.S78835 (ebook) | DDC 891.73/44—dc23
LC record available at https://lccn.loc.gov/2020007839
LC ebook record available at https://lccn.loc.gov/2020007840

Cover design: Jonathan Hahn
Typesetting: Nord Compo

Printed in the United States of America
5 4 3 2

CONTENTS

INTRODUCTION

BY MAYA VINOKOUR

In July 2018, roboticist and computer vision researcher Anton Troynikov tweeted a series of wry observations about "things that happen in Silicon Valley and also the Soviet Union." The similarities between late capitalism and "really existing" socialism turned out to be numerous and amusing: both milieus, according to Troynikov, feature "promises of colonizing the solar system while you toil in drudgery day in, day out" and involve "being told you are constructing utopia while the system crumbles around you." Tens of thousands of Twitter users mashed the heart icon in weary recognition, ensuring a modest virality for Troynikov's salvos.

The roboticist's analogies to Brezhnev-era Russia extend well beyond the world of tech. All over the world today, "failures are bizarrely upheld as triumphs" while "otherwise extremely intelligent people just [turn] the crank because it's the only way to get ahead." Nearly thirty years after the Soviet Union fell and Francis Fukuyama trumpeted the "end of history," the Cold War victors seem to have entered a Brezhnev era of their own, complete with sclerotic bureaucracies, widespread economic dysfunction, and mass disillusionment with core ideological values.

There is balm in Gilead, however. As denizens of aging Western empires, Anglophone readers are now primed—even desperate, perhaps—for some of late socialism's best literature, with its self-deprecating irony, anguished soul-searching, and creeping consciousness of impending collapse. The science fiction of Arkady and Boris Strugatsky, in particular, offers a bracing corrective to stale utopianism and political grandiosity. By the mid-1960s, when they began composing *Ugly Swans*—and still more by the time they wrote *Lame Fate*, in the 1970s and early 1980s—the authors had lost much of the faith in scientific and social progress that had animated their earlier works. Rather than focusing on the exploits of "progressors," heroic figures exported from radiant communist futures to civilize their less fortunate brethren on other planets, the Strugatskys' late fiction skewered the "appallingly banal, bureaucratic, imperfect, and spiritually bankrupt" life they observed all around them in the Soviet Union.*

Arkady (1925–1991) and Boris (1933–2012) Strugatsky were born into the family of an art critic and party functionary, Natan Strugatsky (1892–1942), and Alexandra Litvincheva (1901–1981), a teacher of Russian literature. After their father managed, miraculously, to evade arrest during Stalin's purges (though he did suffer expulsion from the Communist Party and a professional demotion), the family ended up trapped in Leningrad during the 872-day siege the city endured in the Second World War.† In January 1942, Arkady and Natan were evacuated into Nazi-free territory via the "Road of Life," a winter-only transport route across frozen Lake Ladoga. Alexandra remained in Leningrad with Boris, who was ill at the

---

* Yvonne Howell, *Apocalyptic Realism: The Science Fiction of Arkady and Boris Strugatsky* (New York: Peter Lang, 1994), 18.

† For more detail on the biography of Natan Strugatsky, see Kirill Golovastikov and Ilya Kukulin, "Filosofiia Strugatskikh," *Arzamas*, July 17, 2015, https://arzamas.academy/materials/747.

time. Soon after making this journey, Natan died of starvation, leaving seventeen-year-old Arkady to rescue his mother and brother. In 1943, Arkady was called up into the Red Army; only in that year did he manage to extract Boris and Alexandra from Leningrad.

The family returned to the city in 1945. Boris earned an undergraduate degree in astronomy at Leningrad State University, then embarked on a doctorate, though he never defended his dissertation. By 1964, he and Arkady, a professional translator of Japanese and English, had dedicated themselves to fiction-writing full-time. As literary critic Ilya Kukulin notes, the Strugatskys distinguished themselves from their fellow Soviet writers by their extraordinary erudition and intellectual curiosity, which impelled them to read authors like George Orwell and Franz Kafka long before they became available in samizdat. Arkady's work as a translator was also a major influence on the brothers' writing, as references to Rudyard Kipling and Ryūnosuke Akutagawa in *Lame Fate* attest.*

In terms of style, the Strugatsky brothers deviated sharply from their most immediate predecessors—authors of "close-range" science fiction, which highlighted near-future Soviet technological achievements according to the mandates of socialist realism. A subgenre that blossomed in the Stalinist 1940s and early '50s following the systematic suppression or co-optation of Russian literary avant-gardes, close-range science fiction often featured leaden, interchangeable characters and scrupulously avoided critiquing Soviet society.

The Strugatskys' first novel, *The Land of Crimson Clouds* (1959), conformed to these conventions, with heroic scientists making manly sacrifices in a forbidding alien setting. Boris Strugatsky would later characterize this work as "a hideous monument" to an epoch of "delirious enthusiasm," "ecstatic stupidity," and "frenetic readiness for self-sacrifice."† Some of the protagonists of

---

* Ibid.

† Boris Strugatsky, *Kommentarii k proidennomu* [Comments on the way left behind] (St. Petersburg: Amfora, 2003), 42.

Crimson Clouds lived to fight another day in *Space Apprentice* (1962), where they continued to expound a philosophy of martyrdom to science—albeit to slightly more skeptical interlocutors. Shedding the explicit didacticism of their early works, the Strugatskys now began writing in an increasingly philosophical, critical, and personal vein. Though their narratives continued to include fantastic elements, from the absurd time machine in *Monday Starts on Saturday* (1964) to the terrifying "clammies" in *Ugly Swans*, their focus shifted from the underlying technology itself to the people who created and used it.

At first, the Strugatskys were able to publish within the strictures of Soviet censorship. Even the relatively pessimistic *Hard to Be a God*, which relates the misadventures of an undercover operative sent to the backward planet of Arkanar on a doomed civilizing mission, appeared in print in 1964. By then, the brief cultural and political "thaw" that had begun soon after Stalin's 1953 death was coming to a bitter end, its demise punctuated by First Secretary Nikita Khrushchev's public, profanity-laced clashes with representatives of the creative intelligentsia. By the second half of the 1960s, the Strugatskys were steadily falling from establishment favor. Presses and journals grew reluctant to publish their works, and by the mid-1970s they had largely withdrawn from official literary life. This enforced silence did not, however, diminish the Strugatskys' productivity or even their popularity among readers. Their unpublished works circulated widely in samizdat and turned up abroad in translation, sometimes without the authors' knowledge.*

Ugly Swans and *Lame Fate*, written at different points during this period, were not initially conceived as nested or even paired. According to Boris Strugatsky, the duo deliberately wrote *Lame*

* For more on the publication history of *Ugly Swans* and *Lame Fate* specifically, including the quotes and history discussed subsequently, see Boris Strugatsky's afterword, excerpted from his literary memoir *Kommentarii k proidennomu*.

Fate "'for the desk drawer,' knowing full well that it had no chance of being published." But when perestroika began in 1986 and a version of the book was unexpectedly slated for inclusion in the Leningrad journal *Neva*, the Strugatskys decided to uncover one of its central mysteries—the contents of main character Felix Sorokin's Blue Folder, his "favorite creation," which, like *Lame Fate* itself, was "painstakingly hidden away from everyone, possibly forever." During the decade they had spent working on the novel, the Strugatskys had vaguely identified Sorokin's secret manuscript with one of their own works, the unpublished (and, at the time, unpublishable) *Doomed City*. Now that *Lame Fate* seemed on the cusp of escaping the desk drawer, the Strugatskys agreed that mere allusions to Sorokin's "darling" would no longer suffice. After toying with the idea of interspersing chapters from *The Doomed City* with those of *Lame Fate*, they instead deployed one of their older unpublished works, by then a samizdat classic: *Ugly Swans*, another tale of a city in fatal decline.

For two novels that were neither written together nor imagined as parts of the same whole, *Lame Fate* and *Ugly Swans* are remarkably well matched. According to Boris Strugatsky himself, *Lame Fate* is explicitly concerned with the theme of aging, chronicling "the merciless onset of an old age that brings neither joy nor salvation." Though on the surface *Ugly Swans* seems more preoccupied with the young than with the old (indeed, the chilling legend of the Pied Piper of Hamelin is a recurring intertext), it is no less invested than *Lame Fate* in issues of memory, succession, and generational decline. Both narratives interrogate the value of pedagogy, understood to be the practice of imparting specific knowledge as well as the larger project of educating entire generations to help them avoid the mistakes of the past.

The Strugatskys were always more interested in exploring their heroes' inner lives than they were in constructing the fantastical worlds they inhabited, eschewing the science fiction standby of terraforming in favor of *anthropoforming*. *Lame Fate* and *Ugly Swans*, however, no longer display the cheerful confidence in man's teachability that so inspires the young protagonists of *Space Apprentice* or *Monday Starts on Saturday*. Having experienced bloody war and decades of empty sloganeering, Felix Sorokin and Victor Banev cannot muster the slightest enthusiasm for utopian questing. They turn instead to what science fiction author and critic Alexander Mirer called "the desperate question" of "how to make it so our filth is not transmitted to the next generation."*

The answer proposed in the Strugatskys' early works had been to create a cadre of nonviolent revolutionaries capable of counteracting evil and ignorance from a safe, pedagogical distance. The Strugatskys' Noon Universe series (1961–85) designated these men of reason "progressors," historical midwives tasked with easing the birth pangs of progress in the less advanced regions of the cosmos. But no sooner had the Strugatskys invented this model than they began subjecting it to critique. In *Hard to Be a God*, for instance, the good intentions of proto-progressor Anton collide with the intractability of human evil. When events on Arkanar fail to adhere to the supposedly unshakeable "basis theory of feudalism" invented on Earth, Anton discards his highly evolved ethics in favor of a more direct approach to crisis. He slowly ceases to believe that Arkanarian society can be reformed, classifying its members as either unscrupulous beasts or vulnerable moral mutants who were born too soon.† As Mark Lipovetsky has written, there is a "concealed violence" lurking within progressor discourse, which

---

* Aleksandr Zerkalov [Mirer], "Igra po sobstvennym pravilam" [Playing by their own rules], in *Izvne* | *Put' na Amal'teiu* | *Stazhiory* | *Zabytyi eksperiment* | *Shest' spichek* | *Ispytanie SKIBR* | *Chastnye predpolozheniia*, by Arkady and Boris Strugatsky (Moscow: Tekst, 1991), 16.

† For example, Anton compares the courtesan Doña Ocana to a bird, a fox, an ant, and a monkey (92–94), thinks of the villain figures Don Reba and Waga the Wheel as two dueling spiders (129), and regards even his friend Baron Pampa as animalistic (96). The only exceptions are the servant boy Uno and Anton's lover Kira, whose emotional sensitivity and strong moral compass mark her as born "a thousand years ahead of [her] time." (226) All page numbers refer to Arkady and Boris Strugatsky, *Hard to Be a God*, trans. Olena Bormashenko (Chicago: Chicago Review Press, 2014).

"inevitably makes the progressor perceive his ungrateful 'disciples' as subhuman."* As he loses faith in basis theory and his own pedagogical powers, Anton abandons his principles to take violent revenge on the underdeveloped planet.

Even after he is relieved of his duties and returned to Earth, Anton is unable to recover his evolved humanity and remains inarticulate and seemingly brutish.† Rather than strengthening his belief in the fragility and necessity of enlightenment, Anton's trials by fire render him not more but less anthropomorphic. Whatever the pedagogical practices that yield titans of reason like Anton, their effects don't seem to last, the ethical apparatuses they produce too easily corrupted by ambient immorality. Worse still, as Felix Sorokin reminds us in *Lame Fate*, these techniques and the "high-minded intentions" they engender may be corrosive in themselves, ultimately transforming even an "altruistic pacifist" into a "savage beast."

If *Hard to Be a God* merely interrogates the ethics of historical intervention and the pedagogical strategies it engenders, *Ugly Swans* discredits these constructs fully. When Victor Banev returns to his provincial hometown after falling out with the ruling elite in the capital, he barely recognizes it. The weather is permanently rainy, suspicious persons roam the streets, and the outskirts are dominated by a "leprosarium" housing the mysterious clammies. Most alarmingly, the city's children, including Banev's estranged daughter, Irma, are oddly enthralled with the clammies, who have turned them into preternaturally serious and intelligent miniature adults.

One of Irma's classmates summons Banev to what he imagines will be a meeting with delighted fans; instead, he encounters a group of hardened skeptics. The schoolchildren excoriate Banev for writing books that glorify "filthy and unpleasant types" and

---

* Mark Lipovetsky, "The Poetics of ITR Discourse: In the 1960s and Today," *Ab Imperio* 1 (2013): 124.

† Arkady and Boris Strugatsky, *Hard to Be a God*, 229–231.

fail to articulate any "positive program" for the future. Blindsided by the children's criticism, Banev parries:

> What you just don't get, apparently, is how an unshaven, hysterical, inveterate drunk can still be a great person, a person you can't help loving, a person you worship, whose hand it's an honor to shake, because he made it through a hell it's terrifying even to imagine and managed to stay human nonetheless.

Though Banev despises the political establishment and regards the clammies with suspicion, he warns the children against a naive ahistoricism that would discard the past entirely. As a survivor of historical trauma, he is not taken in by utopian visions, no matter how nominally progressive. As the suspicious kinship between the hypothetical figure he describes and his own "drunk" and "unshaven" person suggests, Banev is not indifferent to his own future fate, lame though it may be. Like his creator, Felix Sorokin, Banev has shed his youthful idealism. In its place, he has adopted not the ugly cynicism of the ruling classes but a willingness to bend rather than break under pressure.

For all his hard-won wisdom, however, Banev fails to convert the younger generation to his worldview. Irma and the other children believe they have nothing to learn from the past and are uninterested even in clearing it out of the way. When Banev accuses them of cruelty, they reply that, unlike the violent and deceptive generations before them, they do not see destruction of the old as a prerequisite to creating the new. When the new world is complete, they claim, the relics of the past will acknowledge that they are obsolete and simply disappear.

The masterminds behind this transformational project are the clammies, beings so intellectually advanced that they feed on books rather than food, can control the weather, and have dispensed with both gender and sexuality. They differ so fundamentally from ordinary mortals that they seem to belong to a different biological class—a fact confirmed by Banev's friend Golem, head physician at the leprosarium. Golem postulates that there are three kinds of people in the world: those preoccupied with the past, those living in the present, and those who live not just for but *in* the future. According to Golem, this category includes the clammies, who

> quite reasonably expect nothing from the past and see the present as little more than a bridge to the future, raw material . . . They're pretty much living in the future already—on islands of the future that formed around them in the present.

Yet the clammies are far less benign than their supporters care to admit. For one thing, whatever the children may say, their mentors are undoubtedly interested in the past. Their physical dependence on books, for instance, suggests that the world they are creating will not be altogether new. Indeed, since the texts on which the clammies subsist were produced by the formative thinkers of the old society, it is unclear how, exactly, they will avoid their predecessors' mistakes.

Ugly Swans ultimately demonstrates that Banev was right to suspect the impending revolution of cruelty. The clammies' program may be highly rational, but it does no less harm to the subjects of their experiments than the anti-intellectualism of the Arkanarian proto-fascists (or, for that matter, the undercover earthlings' own interventions) in *Hard to Be a God*. Golem compares the clammies to the Pied Piper of Hamelin, and like the Pied Piper, they enact a curative program that harms the city more than the original afflictions it was meant to treat. The city's problems may have been a source of torment, but they did not interfere with its viability. Without children, on the other hand, it will have no future.*

---

* As Dmitry Bykov writes, "Those who taught the children to feel contempt for their parents were not conquering the future but stealing it. In the Pied Piper story, there is no difference between the rat catcher and the rats: they tormented the city, whereas he simply killed it by depriving it of hope." Dmitry Bykov, "Dmitrii Bykov o Strugatskikh, Surkove i dvizhenii 'Nashi,'"

The clammies' paternalistic erasure flies in the face of the children's conviction that a new world can be built up peacefully alongside the old. It also demonstrates the impossibility of intervening in the course of history without causing radical damage to the present and even the past. As Banev puts it, "Cleanse the world around me, make it look the way I'd want it to, and it's all over for me." *Ugly Swans* thus problematizes the ethics of intervention that the Strugatskys laid out in previous works, revealing the viciousness undergirding even benign-seeming utopian projects. Moreover, where the proto-progressors of *Hard to Be a God* were consummately, even tragically, human, the clammies are only superficially anthropomorphic. The source of their cruelty is less malice than indifference, an inability to understand how the needs of essentially alien organisms might differ from their own.

Lame Fate, like *Ugly Swans*, highlights the alienness of negative human behavior, from the merely unethical to the actively evil. Aging writer Felix Sorokin generally tries to keep to himself, spending long evenings alone rereading his masterpiece—the text of *Ugly Swans*. Friends, family members, and colleagues pepper him with requests for advice and companionship, providing him with ample opportunities for observation and judgment. One of his acquaintances earns the designation of "idiot," but not in the "colloquial, mild sense." Instead, Sorokin classifies him as a "special psychological type," an "extraterrestrial" with "a completely different system of values" and "a strange and alien psychology."

There are worse creatures than the "idiot," however. On a rare excursion outside his apartment, Sorokin encounters a man he nicknames "Fulminating Pustule," evidently a former serial denunciation-writer from the Stalin era. Seemingly refuting the confident claim of the children in *Ugly Swans*, Sorokin reflects that it was a mistake to think that Fulminating Pustule and his ilk would just slink away in shame after Khrushchev publicly condemned

---

Russkii zhurnal, July 16, 2012, http://www.russ.ru/pole/2005-Dmitrij-Bykov-o-Strugackih-Surkove-i-dvizhenii-Nashi.

Stalinism in 1956. For Sorokin, Fulminating Pustule represents an unrelenting, ancient evil whose unremarkable appearance belies a terrifying alien essence. He recalls a science fictional description of a "monstrous beast" known as the *gishu*, "devourer of prehistoric elephants," who has somehow managed to survive into the present day. The *gishu*, though outwardly indistinguishable from contemporary humans, presents a unique challenge to society:

> Man could not escape it, because he didn't understand its habits, which had formed back when he did not and could not yet exist. There was only one way for man to save himself from the *gishu*: band together with his fellows and kill it.

For Sorokin, the Fulminating Pustules and idiots of the world are unstoppable precisely because ordinary human beings cannot comprehend their atavistic psychology. No pedagogy can forestall their pernicious influence; the only remedy is a coordinated assassination effort. Though Sorokin couches his ruminations in humorous terms, their underlying message is no less chilling than the progressors' "benevolent" colonialism. Certain types of people, Sorokin suggests, are subhuman and should be accorded no more mercy than the giant leeches that terrorize the colonists of Mars in *Space Apprentice*.

In his mild-mannered way, Sorokin confirms the progressors' darkest fears: some people are simply beyond pedagogical help. Left to their own devices and given favorable historical circumstances, opportunistic creatures like Fulminating Pustule will resurface. Sorokin's convictions subtly undermine the humanism he writes into *Ugly Swans*, suggesting that perhaps the clammies had the right idea after all. Once human evil is recast as fundamentally alien, the Strugatskys' ethic of intervention acquires a brutal dimension. Indeed, what good is gently nudging society toward enlightenment if certain segments of the population are essentially irredeemable? Taken to its logical limit, this line of thinking implies that human progress may be best served not through generalized anthropoforming but through the culling of problematic elements. We may infer the Strugatskys' own position on this issue from their chosen mouthpieces in *Ugly Swans*: the lovable ne'er-do-well Banev pleads for clemency, while the duplicitous health inspector Pavor opines that "Hitler had the right idea."

If Fulminating Pustule is the *gishu* of *Lame Fate*, in *Ugly Swans* that role belongs to the clammies—and to a lesser extent, to the children they have ensorcelled. In their indifference toward the feelings of their elders, the children are indeed cruel, but in an idiosyncratic sense. Neither rude nor malicious, they are simply unable to see the simple human value of the people they are striving to supplant, including Banev himself. Though they profess to love Hegel and Spengler, the children lack feeling for the past as a category. They thus reify one of the Strugatskys' worst fears: a "catastrophic loss of cultural memory" of the type occurring "in the Soviet Union within their own lifetime."*

When Banev calls upon the children to maintain an attitude of "irony and pity," he is precisely exhorting them not to discard their historical inheritance. It is not just that such an approach would be unethical—though it is also that—but that its maximalism begets destruction beyond the reach of even the most evolved pedagogy.

As they observed the late-socialist leadership's vain attempts to resuscitate a moribund Soviet mythology, the Strugatskys grew disillusioned with the notion of progress either through pedagogy or historical trials by fire. Traumas like Stalinist terror or the siege of Leningrad, *Ugly Swans* and *Lame Fate* suggest, are not worth repeating, even on the off chance that they might separate humanity's wheat from its chaff. And if even the most enlightened pedagogy contains a core of intractably alien evil, active intervention is out of the question. The best one can hope for is a bloodless compromise of the kind the clammies ultimately enact in *Ugly Swans*.

---

* Howell, *Apocalyptic Realism*, 24.

For all their pessimism, *Ugly Swans* and *Lame Fate* do not entirely foreclose the possibility of redemption. Given the long history of Russian logocentrism, it should come as no surprise that this redemption is a literary one, with the writer emerging as a kind of middle ground between the progressor and the pedagogue. As Boris Strugatsky makes clear, he and his brother wrote *Lame Fate* as an updated version of Mikhail Bulgakov's *The Master and Margarita*, with Felix Sorokin as a new Master for the "slowly unfolding, 'stagnant' 1980s."

With the experience of the Soviet 1930s and 1940s in the rear-view mirror, Bulgakov's famous dictum that "manuscripts don't burn" requires revision. Works that are consigned to the desk drawer (like *Lame Fate* itself) have a different life span than either their human authors (as "manuscripts don't burn" already implies) or published works. Texts that cannot appear in print or even be read aloud to friends may, in fact, die in the present, "burning" entirely away for whole generations of would-be readers. But theirs is less a permanent destruction than a lengthy hibernation. They are as if cryogenically frozen, awaiting more favorable circumstances in which to be revived and continue their arrested lives.

Only literary resurrection, the Strugatskys suggest, can offer an antidote to the cultural amnesia that produced the great calamities of the twentieth century. Taking a page from the cosmist Nikolai Fyodorov (1829–1903), whose long-suppressed (though highly influential) philosophy began its own resurrection during the years of the Khrushchev thaw,* the authors advocate for a future that neither ignores nor worships the past, instead preserving it in living memory.

Just as Fyodorov believed that even atomized matter retained the memory of its previous structure and could be reconstituted if only its particles were properly "read,"† so too did the

* Howell, *Apocalyptic Realism*, 19.

† For more on the Fyodorovian subtext in Soviet science fiction, see Leonid Heller [Geller], *Vselennaya za predelom dogmy: Razmyshleniia o sovetskoi fantastike*

Strugatskys, through characters like Banev and Sorokin, propose a strategic reconstitution of the past through a reading of its lost and forgotten texts. Though neither Banev nor Sorokin earn even the limited paradise of "peace" accorded to Bulgakov's Master and Margarita, both *Lame Fate* and *Ugly Swans* end on a joyful note. Newly unshackled from both the emptiness of the present and the traumatic weight of the past, the novels' two protagonists are finally set free into the future.

[The universe beyond dogma: Thoughts on Soviet science fiction] (London: Overseas Publications Interchange, 1985), 38.

LAME FATE

UGLY SWANS

Dancing candle flame!
Through fastened shutters
Autumn surges in.

—Raizan

The authors consider it their duty to warn the reader that none of the novel's characters exist in reality, whether past or present. Thus, any attempts to guess "who's who" here are completely pointless. All institutions, organizations, and establishments are likewise products of the authors' imagination.

1. FELIX SOROKIN

BLIZZARD

In the middle of January, at approximately two in the afternoon, I was sitting at the window and, instead of working on my screenplay, drinking wine and pondering several things at once. Outside, snow swirled. Cars crawled timorously along, snowdrifts piling up on the roadside. In the vacant lot beyond the sweeping veil of snow, clumps of naked trees and patches and stripes of bristly scrub stood out in vague black outline.

Moscow was being buried.

Moscow was being buried, like some godforsaken railway stop deep in rural Kazakhstan. For the last half hour, a taxi that had imprudently attempted to turn around had been stalled in the middle of the road, while I sat there imagining all the other cars that must be stalling all over our enormous city—taxis, buses, trucks, even shiny black limousines with snow tires.

My thoughts flowed as though arranged in multiple registers, lazily and languidly interrupting one another. For instance, I was thinking about building caretakers, about how, before the war, there hadn't been any snowplows—those brutish, brightly painted snow-cleaners, snow-hurlers, snow-scoopers—but only aproned, felt-booted caretakers wielding brooms and square plywood shovels. And yet, as I recall, there hadn't been nearly as much snow on the streets as there is now. Of course, it's possible that the very elements were different back then . . .

I was also thinking about all the dismal, absurd, and even suspicious things that keep happening to me lately, as if Whoever Is Supposed to Oversee My Fate had gone utterly stupid with boredom and started playing pranks. Except, because he's stupid, his pranks turn out stupid, too, so much so that they produce no feelings in anyone—including the prankster himself—except awkwardness and that type of shame that makes your toes curl inside your shoes.

And all the while, I thought constantly about my Tippa-brand typewriter with its congenitally jammed *e* key, which I'd shoved over to the right-hand side of my desk, and which held an unfinished page reading, in part:

> The tank guns are turned to the left. They're firing on the partisan positions, firing methodically, taking turns to avoid throwing off each other's aim. Squatting behind the front-most tank gun is Rudolf, tank commander and SS lieutenant. As the brains—the director—behind this orchestra of death, he gestures commands at the SS machine gunners behind him. Now and then, partisan bullets clank against the tanks, spraying mud all over the tracks and raising tiny water columns in the dark puddles.
>
> Retreat.
>
> The partisans' best-kept secret: a sliver of a trench near the swamp's edge. Two partisans—one old, one young—watch the approaching tanks, bewildered. Bang! Bang! Bang! boom the tank guns.

I'm fifty-six years old, but I've never been a partisan, nor have I ever experienced a tank attack. And yet, strictly speaking, I should have perished in the Battle of Kursk. That's what happened to our entire military academy, with the exception of Rafka Rezanov, minus both legs; Vasya Kuznetsov from the machine gun battalion; and me, a mortar gunner.

The week before our graduation, Kuznetsov and I were sent to Kuybyshev for advanced training. Back then, Whoever Is Supposed to Oversee My Fate apparently still felt some enthusiasm toward me and was curious to see what I might make of myself. And what I made of myself was this: I spent my entire youth in the army and considered it my duty to write about the army, and officers, and tank attacks, even though over the years I'd come to feel more and more that, precisely because I survived by pure chance, I was the last person who should be writing about any of it.

Such were my thoughts as I gazed out the window at our snow-battered Third Rome, and then I picked up my glass and took a good swig. Two more cars had now gotten stuck near the stalled taxi, and forlorn figures with shovels were wandering around them, backs hunched against the blizzard.

I turned to look at my bookshelves. Good Lord, I thought suddenly, feeling a chill in my heart, this must be my very last library! There won't be another one. It's too late. This is my fifth library, the fifth and the last. The first is now completely gone, except for one book, a rarity nowadays: P. V. Makarov's *General May-Mayevsky's Adjutant*. It was recently adapted into a television series, *The Adjutant of His Excellency*, which isn't bad—it's pretty good, actually—but it has next to nothing to do with the book. The events in the book feel much more serious and profound, although there are far fewer adventures and heroic feats than in the series. The author, Pavel Vasilievich Makarov, was by all accounts an important person, so it's nice to read the dedication (done in copying pencil on the back of the title page): "To Dear Comrade A. Sorokin. May this book call to mind the living figure of the adjutant to General May-Mayevsky, Deputy Commander of the Crimean Rebel Army. With heartfelt partisan greetings, P. V. Makarov. September 6, 1927, Leningrad." I can only imagine how precious this book must have been to my father, Alexander Alexandrovich Sorokin. Although, come to think of it, I don't have a clear memory of it either way. And what I most definitely can't recall is how this book managed to survive given that our home in Leningrad was bombed to bits and my first library perished in its entirety.

As for the second library, not a single book from it remains. I'd collected it in Kansk, where I taught at the military academy for two years, right up until that scandal of mine. Given the circumstances, my exit from Kansk was precipitous and directed from on high in a resolute and unavoidable manner. At the time, Clara and I just managed to pack up the books, and even shipped them, standard mail, to Irkutsk, but then we ended up only spending two days there. A week later, we were already in Korsakov, and a week after that were sailing to Petropavlovsk in a trawler. And that's why my second library never did find me in the end.

It still makes me so upset I can hardly stand it. That library had an English-language edition of *Tarzan* in four small volumes, which I bought at a bookstore on Liteiny Prospekt during a vacation to Leningrad; H. G. Wells's *The Time Machine*, plus a collection of his short stories from a supplement to the journal *Global Pathfinder*, illustrated by Fitingof; a bound set of every issue of *Around the World* from 1927 . . . I loved that kind of reading material with a passion back then. In addition to these, there were a couple of books boasting a very special fate indeed.

In '52, the Armed Forces decreed that any printed material with ideologically harmful content had to be written off and destroyed. At the time, the academy book depository contained a collection, captured in the war, that had apparently once belonged to a courtier of Puyi, the Manchurian emperor. And of course, since no one had either the desire or the ability to figure out which of the ten thousand volumes in Japanese, Chinese, Korean, English, and German were wheat and which were chaff, all of them were slated for destruction.

It was the height of summer, and very hot, and book bindings were shriveling in fiery blood-black piles, and cadets bustled around, filthy as devils in hell, and over the whole arrangement hovered weightless shreds of ash. Meanwhile, at night, we teaching officers snuck up to piles of books destined to be burned the next day—strict prohibitions be damned!—pounced on them like predators, grabbed whatever we could get our hands on, and scampered off with our spoils. I ended up with a splendid *History of Japan* in English, a *History of Criminal Investigation in the Meiji Era*, and . . . eh, what does it matter? I never had the time—neither then nor later—to really read any of it.

My third library I donated to the House of Culture in Poronaysk in '55, on my way back to the continent from Kamchatka. How did I ever work up the courage to apply for discharge? Back then I was a nobody, with no skills whatsoever—I'd learned nothing applicable to civilian life—with a petulant wife and a sickly kid, Katya, hanging like millstones around my neck . . . No, I would never have taken the risk if there'd been even a glimmer of hope for me in the army. But there wasn't even a glimmer, and at the time I was young and ambitious, frightened at the prospect of still being a lieutenant and a translator in the same old division years down the line.

It's strange, but I never write about that time in my life. Even though it's material that would interest basically any reader. It'd sell like hotcakes, that stuff, especially if it was written in that manly, modern style that I personally haven't been able to stand for a long time now but that, for some reason, everyone else seems to love. For example:

> The deck of the *Konoe Maru* was slippery. The air smelled of spoiled fish and pickled turnip. The deckhouse windows were broken and taped up with paper . . .

(The important thing here was to repeat the words *were* and *was* as often as possible. The windows *were* broken; his ugly mug *was* contorted . . .)

> Steadying the machine gun strapped across his chest, Valentin climbed into the deckhouse. "Come out, Senchō," he said

sternly. The skipper emerged. He was old and stooped, with a hairless face and sparse gray hair sprouting underneath his chin. He wore a bandanna covered in red Japanese characters; there were also characters on the right half of his blue jacket, this time in white. The skipper's feet were clad in warm split-toe socks. He walked up to us, brought his palms together, and bowed. "Ask him if he knows he's trespassing on our waters," the major ordered. I did so. The skipper answered in the negative. "Ask him if he knows that fishing is prohibited within a twenty-mile zone of the baseline," the major ordered.

(Another important element: *ordered, ordered, ordered* . . .)

I did so. The skipper answered that he knew. His lips parted, baring scanty yellow teeth. "Tell him we're impounding the vessel and arresting the crew," the major ordered. I translated his words. The skipper nodded rapidly, or maybe it was a tremor. He put his palms together once more; a nearly incomprehensible torrent of words issued from his lips. "What is he saying?" the major asked. As far as I could tell, the skipper was asking us to release his schooner. He was saying that they could not return home without fish, that they would all starve to death. He was speaking some sort of dialect, saying *ksi* instead of *ki* and *tu* instead of *tsu*—he was very difficult to understand . . .

Sometimes I feel like I could write that kind of thing for miles and miles. But that's probably not the case. You can only stretch something out for miles if you're entirely indifferent to it.

A week later, as we were saying good-bye, the skipper gave me a little volume by Kan Kikuchi, along with Edogawa's *Shadow Man*. There they are now, side by side on my shelf; the Poronaysk House of Culture never even missed them. *Shadow Man* is the first Japanese book I read from beginning to end. I like Tarō Hirai; it's not for nothing that his pseudonym is Edogawa Rampo—that is, Edgar Allan Poe.

As for the fourth library, that stayed with Clara. And good riddance to both of them. It's a mistake—a big mistake—to get into all of that right now. How many times have I vowed never to turn, even in thought, to those who believe I "humiliated and insulted" them, in Dostoyevsky's phrase! As it is, I'm already constantly in someone's debt, or failing to keep a promise, or letting people down, or ruining their plans . . . And is that not because I have imagined myself to be a Great Writer to whom everything is permitted?

And no sooner did I think about how inescapably cursed I am than the phone rang, and soon our chairman, Fyodor Mikheyevich, was asking me, with evident irritation, when I would finally make an appearance on Bannaya Street.

Felix Alexandrovich, he said, how can you be so irresponsible! This is the fourth time I've called you, he said, but it's like banging my head against the wall. No one's ordering you scribblers to pick over rotten beets in a vegetable storehouse or something. And believe me, that's happened! To scientists, PhDs even, whereas all I'm asking you to do is go down to Bannaya with ten typewritten pages, not exactly a huge burden. You're not doing this for your health, he said, and it's not some random whim. You're the one who voted to help out those scientists, those linguists or cybernetic mathematicians, or whatever . . . broke your promise . . . let us down . . . ruined plans . . . imagine yourself . . .

What choice did I have? I promised, yet again, to go there immediately, today, but the only answer was the angry, reproachful, clanging rattle of a slammed-down receiver. To help calm myself down, I hastily poured the rest of the bottle into my glass and drank it up, realizing, with desperate clarity, that what I should have bought last night was not this lousy wine but cognac. Or, better yet, pure wheat vodka.

The situation was that, last fall, our secretariat decided to grant the request of some sort of Institute for Linguistic . . . Research, I believe it was. This institute was asking all Moscow-based writers to present several pages from their manuscripts for specialized study, something about the theory of information, or linguistic entropy, or something . . . None of us really got what it was, except maybe Garik Aganyan—who supposedly *did* get it, yet couldn't explain it to the rest of us. All we managed to understand was that this institute wanted the largest possible pool of writers, and that nothing else mattered: neither the number of pages nor their content. All they needed from us was a visit to their office on Bannaya, any day of the week during business hours. No one had any objections at that stage; on the contrary, lots of people were flattered at the prospect of contributing to the advance of science. Rumor had it that, at first, people lined up on Bannaya; apparently there were even fights. And then it all petered out somehow, and now poor Fyodor Mikheyevich prods us shirkers at least once a month, shaming and vilifying us on the phone and in person.

Of course, it's hardly a virtue to stand obstinately in the way of scientific progress, but on the other hand, we're only human. For example, I'll sometimes find myself on Bannaya and suddenly remember that I'm supposed to go to the institute, only to realize that I don't have any manuscripts on me. Or I have a manuscript under my arm and am walking specifically to Bannaya, but for some strange reason I end up not on Bannaya at all but at the Club. My explanation for all these enigmatic deviations is that it's impossible to treat this scheme—like many of our secretariat's other schemes—with the seriousness it requires. At the end of the day, what possible linguistic entropy can there be among our little group concentrated on the banks of the Moscow River? And, above all, what does it have to do with me?

But there was no getting around it, and so I began searching for the folder where I'd put my drafts the week before last. I couldn't find it anywhere on the surface, and then I remembered that, at the time, I had intended to go to Bannaya after stopping by the *Foreign Invalid* with Old Drippy, to argue with Noseface about our article. But after the *Invalid*, we never made it to Bannaya—only to Pskov, the restaurant. By now there was probably no point in looking for the folder.

Luckily, I haven't lacked for drafts in a good long time. Creakily, I got up from my armchair and walked over to the very farthest section of my bookshelves, and, still creakily, sat down next to it, right on the floor. Lord, there are so many movements now that I can only perform with extreme creakiness! And not only movements of the body but of the soul, too.

(Creakily, we arise out of sleep. Creakily, we renew our garments. Creakily shall we apply the counsels of life. Creakily shall we hear the tread of the element of Fire, but we shall already be prepared to master the undulations of the flame. Creakily. The Upanishads, I think . . . or not quite. Or maybe it's not the Upanishads at all.)

Creakily, I opened the door of the lowermost cabinet. Into my lap tumbled folders, school notebooks in colorful oilskin covers, and yellowed, densely filled pages held together with rusty paper clips. I picked up a folder at random—one so old its corners had broken off and only one dirty tie-string remained. Its cover bore many half-erased notes, most of them illegible. I managed to discern an ancient phone number—six digits plus a letter—and a string of Japanese characters in green ink: *Seinen jidai no saku*, or Youthful Writings. I hadn't opened this folder in something like fifteen years. Everything in it was very old, from my Kamchatka days or even earlier, dating to my time in Kansk, or Kazan, or the special training academy—sheets torn out of ruled notebooks, homemade notebooks sewn together with coarse thread, individual sheets of rough, yellowish paper that may have been used for wrapping or perhaps were just unimaginably old. And all of it handwritten, not a single typed line.

A gloomy Negro emerged from the study, pushing a wheelchair occupied by a human ruin. The boss shut the door tight behind him.

What Negro? What ruins? None of it rang any bells.

"By the way, did you notice whether any of the Bolsheviks were Chinese?" The boss asked suddenly.

"Chinese Bolsheviks? Hmm . . . Yes, I think there were some. They may have been Chinese, or Korean, or Mongolian. Asian, at any rate . . ."

Oh, right, right! Now I remember! I'd written some sort of political satire . . . but I can't remember anything else.

The fortress fell, but the garrison was victorious.

Right.

"I zee 'un! I zee 'un!" roared Rabbits-Eggs, now that he had found a visible foe . . . Another shot from the darkness above . . .

Aha, right, that was my translation of Kipling's *Stalky & Co.* Nineteen fifty-three. Kamchatka. I'm sitting there in HQ and translating Kipling, because what else is a translator to do in the absence of a visible foe?

"Rabbits-Eggs" sounds pretty funny in Russian. But before you start smirking, consider that if Kipling had meant what you think, he would have written "Rabbit's Balls." Yes, I remember really struggling with that translation, but it was excellent practice. There's no better practice for a translator than a brilliant work describing a totally unfamiliar world perfectly embedded in a specific space and time . . .

Ah, and here's "Night-Watch Episode." Also '53, also Kamchatka.

Berkutov, who was stationed at the guardhouse entrance, never could remember afterward why he suddenly tensed up and gripped his weapon more tightly, straining his ears at the vague murmur of the warm July night. It was just that, besides the rustling of leaves, the noise of his own footsteps, and the somnolent creaking of branches, he could suddenly hear . . .

And so on. In short, the enemy crept up on the watchman under cover of night, attacked him, and he, unable to fight them off, provoked fire from his comrades.

When it came to my literary views back then, I was a great moralist—and not just any moralist but an inspired eulogist of military regulations. Which is why, comrade soldiers, the most important part of this particular "Night-Watch Episode" was this:

> "How could Linko, who knows the code so well, have allowed such a basic violation of garrison and watchman statutes? And what about you, Berkutov? Wasn't it scatterbrained of you not to notice where Simakov went? And what about the rest of us? How did we fail to notice that Simakov wasn't with us when we were called to arms?"

How strange to reread all this today! It's like being told in fond tones about the time you were three and just couldn't hold it, so you pooped your pants in company. Except that when I wrote "Night-Watch Episode," I wasn't three but all of twenty-eight. But I was desperate to see my name in print, to feel like a real writer, to make clear I'd been marked as a "favorite of Apollo and the Muses"! And how bitter was my disappointment when *Suvorov's Onslaught*, may God bless and keep it, rejected my manuscript with the polite excuse that such "night-watch episodes" were not typical for our army! Wonderful words. I've spent about two hundred hours on night watch in my life, and only once did I hear anything in addition to the rustling of leaves, the noise of my own footsteps, and the somnolent creaking of branches. Once, someone disturbingly pushy began shoving his way through the barbed wire, without reacting in any way to my desperate cries of "Halt! Halt, who goes there? Halt, or I'll shoot!" My superiors, who showed up at the sound of shooting, discovered a goat tangled in the barbed wire. It'd been killed on the spot. In the heat of the moment, I was threatened with court-martial, but then it all blew over . . .

No, I won't let them autopsy my "Night-Watch Episode." Let it slumber here. I was struck once again by the stupidity of using our writing for this linguistic entropy thing if they didn't care what they analyzed—whether it was "Night-Watch Episode" or the piece about the wheelchair with the human ruin.

I put aside my YOUTHFUL WRITINGS and picked up another folder. This one looked quite recent, with well-preserved, neatly tied red strings. On the cover was a white label reading FRAGMENTS, UNPUBLISHED, STORY IDEAS, OUTLINES.

I opened the folder and immediately found "Narcissus," a story I wrote in '57. That one I remember quite well. These were the players: Doctor Lobs, Choix du Gruselle, Count Denker, Baroness Luste . . . Also mentioned are: Carte Saint-Chanoix, "an idiot of the purest grade, impotent since the age of sixteen," and the aunt of Count Denker, the sadist and lesbian Stella Boix-Cossu. The crux of the story is that the aforementioned Choix du Gruselle, an aristocrat and an unusually powerful hypnotist, happened to look in the mirror at a moment when his "gaze was filled with desire, supplication, tender and imperious bidding, and a plea for obedience and love." And because "not even Choix de Gruselle himself could withstand the will of Choix de Gruselle," the poor thing fell insanely in love with himself, like Narcissus. It's a devilishly elegant and aristocratic story. It also contains the following passage: "It was his good fortune that, besides Narcissus, there had also existed a shepherd named Onan. So today the count lives with himself, takes himself out into society, and flirts with the ladies, which no doubt produces in him the arousing thrill of jealousy—toward himself, of course."

My goodness gracious! What pretentious, raunchy, fussy, lurid claptrap! And to think, it sprouted in the same corner of my soul as my *Modern Tales*, which I wrote fifteen years later, the very same corner of my soul where my Blue Folder grows today . . .

No, they won't get my "Narcissus," either. For one thing, I only have the one copy. And what's more, absolutely no one needs to know that Felix Alexandrovich Sorokin, author of the novel *Comrade Officers*, not to mention screenplays and military stories, is apparently also capable of writing all sorts of pornographic phantasmagoria.

Why don't I just give them my *Koryagins* instead? It's a play in three acts, dating to '58. Dramatis personae: Sergei Ivanovich Koryagin, scientist, approximately sixty years old; his wife, Irina Petrovna, forty-five years old; his son by his first wife, demobilized officer Nikolai Sergeyevich Koryagin, some thirty years old. And seven more characters—students, artists, cadets from the military academy . . . The setting: Moscow, present day.

> ANYA: Listen, can I ask you a question?
> NIKOLAI: You can try.
> ANYA: You won't get mad?
> NIKOLAI: It depends . . . No, I won't get mad. Is it about my wife?
> ANYA: Yes. Why did you divorce her?

Wonderful. Chekhov. Stanislavsky. Nemirovich-Danchenko. Above all, it's unfinished and always will be. And it's exactly what I'll give them.

I placed the manuscript down on the floor behind me and set to stuffing and cramming everything else back into the cabinet. Suddenly, my fingers closed around a school notebook with a sticky brown cover, swollen with extra papers. I laughed aloud with joy and said, "There you are, my dear!" For this was a cherished and precious item: my work diary, which I'd lost the last time I tried to tidy up my papers, a year ago.

The notebook fell open automatically in my lap, revealing a much-loved mechanical pencil from Czechoslovakia. This was not just any pencil: it was lucky. This pencil and no other was to be used to write down story ideas—although, admittedly, it wasn't the most comfortable writing implement: the outside had broken in two places, so if you pressed too hard, the lead retracted into the barrel.

As it happened, I'd completely forgotten that I'd started this notebook on March 30 almost exactly eleven years ago. At the time,

I was working on *Iron Family*, a novella about tank crewmen in peacetime. It was very difficult to write and sapped my very blood and ichor. I took research trips out to military units, nearly froze off my right ear, but in the end I had nothing to show for it. I'm lucky they didn't make me return my advance . . .

I leafed through page after page of monotonous entries:

04/02. Compl. 5 pp. 2 pp. in evening. Total 135.
04/03. Compl. 4 pp. 1 p. in evening. Total 140.

For me, this is a sure sign: if all I've recorded is statistics, then either work is going very well or it's not going, full stop. Actually, though, there was a strange entry on 04/07: "Wrote a letter of complaint to the Governing Senate." And also: "04/19. As vile as a cigarette butt in a urinal." And on 05/03: "Nothing like betrayal to make you feel more grown-up."

Ah, and here was the day I began devising my *Modern Tales*.

May 21, 1972. A story about a worker who just moved to a new apartment. He's got a carpenter doing his floors, a mover, and a plumber, all PhDs. And they all get stuck in the apartment. The carpenter pinches his finger between two floorboards, the mover ends up trapped behind a wardrobe, and the plumber takes a sip of vodka that's actually an elixir, and it turns him invisible. Also, there's a house elf. And a builder immured in a heat vent. And then Katya shows up.

It's not *Modern Tales* yet, far from it. I didn't manage to pull that story together in the end, and now I can't even remember: What worker? Why a house elf? What sort of elixir was it?

Or here's another idea from the same period: "10/28/72. A man (a magician) that everyone thinks is a space alien." That was when everyone was going crazy for UFOs. It's all people talked about: "kindred spirits," the stones at Baalbek, the rock art at Tassili n'Ajjer. Which is why that story occurred to me: it's about a man just living his life, a magician by trade, and quite a good one, too.

And all of a sudden he realizes that he's become the object of some troubling attention. His neighbors start odd conversations with him; the beat cop shows up, suddenly interested in his stage props, and makes nebulous statements about conservation of energy. "This disappearing egg, citizen," he says, "doesn't match our modern understanding of energy's conservation." Finally, he gets called into the personnel department at his job, where he sees someone who possibly looks familiar, except that he has one eye rather than two. And the personnel guy starts asking our hero how many churches are in his native Shitsville, and who the statue on the main square is of, and can he recall how many windows are in the facade of city hall. Our hero, naturally, can't answer any of these questions, and the atmosphere of suspicion intensifies, and now there's talk of a compulsory psychiatric examination . . . I never did figure out how this story should end—I lost interest. And now I'm very sorry I did.

On the second of November, it says, "Didn't work, tummy ache," and on the third there's a brief note: "Half-assed."

Feeling a sort of warm sadness, I turned page after page in my work diary.

"Man is but a poor soul laden with a lifeless body. Epictetus."

"Sweet flower of the prairie, ah! / Lavrenty Pavlych Beria"

"Who are you friends against?"

"Rectal literature."

"Only those sciences spread the light that promote the instructions of the authorities. Saltykov-Shchedrin."

"He distilled booze from the fingernails of alcoholics."

And then, something else for *Modern Tales*:

> A cat named Elegant. A dog named Faithful, a.k.a. Fifi. A boy wunderkind, regularly reads Yu. Manin's *Cubic Forms*; a four-eyes; loves to sing Vladimir Vysotsky songs while washing dishes. He's twelve years old in a base-eight number system. He regularly quotes Illich-Svitych, the founding father of comparative Nostratic linguistics. Every morning, the cat returns from voice lessons and hand-washes his gloves. They try to teach the dog not to snort or

> slurp at the dinner table, and also to use a knife and fork. The dog responds by demonstratively leaving the table, then loudly and indignantly gnawing a bone under the porch. The cat, Elegant, says of some guest of theirs, "Petrovsky-Zelikovich looks just like that bulldog Ramses, the one whose mug I clawed to ribbons this past spring as retribution for his boorish pestering."

More phrases:

"He had a habit of confusing sentimentalism with Simmental cattle."

"After Ostrovsky, Maria Pavlovna wore the fur coat for sixteen years, I bought it off her, started cleaning it—found three lice, one old, still speaks English . . ."

I stuffed the remaining folders and papers into the cabinet and repaired to my desk. This kind of thing comes over me sometimes: I pick up my old manuscripts or diaries and start to feel like they're my real life—all those scribble-filled papers, those diagrams I'd use to block out how my characters were standing or where they were facing, fragmentary phrases, applications for screenwriting jobs, drafts of various official letters, extremely detailed outlines of works that won't ever be written, and the drily monotonous: "5 pp. complete. In evening compl. 3 pp." Whereas wives, children, committees, seminars, work trips, Moscow-style sturgeon, chatterbox friends and taciturn ones—those are the dreams, the phantasms, the mirages in a dusty desert. I can't tell if any of it really happened.

Oh, here's another great story idea. There's no exact date, for some reason, but I know it's early '73. A little resort town in the mountains. Outside the city is a cave. And inside that cave—*drip, drip, drip*—the Water of Life trickles into a depression in the rock. It takes a whole year to accumulate a test tube's worth. Only five people in the world know about it. As long as they drink that water (one thimbleful per year), they remain immortal. But then, by chance, a sixth person finds out about it. Meanwhile, there's only enough Water of Life for five. But number six is the brother of number five, and the school friend of number four. And number three is a woman, Katya, who's deeply in love with number four, but hates number two because he's a backstabber. Conundrum! Also, number six is a great altruist and doesn't think either himself or the other five worthy of immortality . . .

As I recall, I never ended up writing this story because it got too confusing. The network of relationships turned out to be too complicated and eventually outgrew the capacities of my imagination. But it could have been quite thrilling: spying on the sixth guy, threats, attempts on people's lives, and all of it concocted on a spicy psychologico-philosophical base. And by the end, my altruistic pacifist has transformed into the most savage beast—really a sight to behold. And all because of his principles, his high-minded intentions . . .

I was rereading my notes on this story when the doorbell rang. At first I shuddered, then felt a joyful premonition. I dashed to the entryway, my feet losing and finding my slippers as I went, and opened the door. Just as I'd thought, it was finally her, my long-awaited good witch, cheeks rosy from the blizzard, body powdered with snow. Klavochka. She walked in, pearly whites aglitter, greeted me, and went straight to the kitchen, while I ran, losing my slippers again, to retrieve my passport, and then she delivered unto me 196 rubles (written out in letters) and 11 kopecks (written out in numbers). It was from the publisher, for reviews I'd written of whatever talentless crap they'd most recently released. As always, I gave Klavochka a ruble for her troubles, and as always, she refused at first, and then, as always, gratefully accepted, and, as always, I saw her to the door and said, "Stop by more often, Klavochka," and she responded, "You keep on writing, and I just might!"

In addition to the money, Klavochka had left on the kitchen table a long envelope covered in colorful labels and stamps, with the red, white, and blue airmail border all along the edge. It was from Japan, addressed to "Mr. Ferix Arexandrovich Sorokin." I took a pair of scissors, cut the edge off the envelope, and extracted two sheets of thin rice paper. It was from a Riu Takami, in Russian.

> Tokyo, December 25, 1981. Most esteemed F. A. Sorokin! We met on spring 1975 in Moscow. Do you remember me? I was in the delegation of Japanese writers, you sat next to me and kindly gave me your book *Modern Tales*. Much times I appeal to publisher Hayakawa and journal *S-F Magazin*, but editors are so conservative. However now thanks to the fact that your book has succeeded in USA, finally our publisher begins pay attention to your book and apparently want to publish your book. This means that our publishing culture is under great influence from American publishing culture and that is our reality. Regardless however this new direction in our publishing world is so joyful to you and to me. According to my work plan I finish translating your book on February of next year. But unfortunately I do not understand certain words and expressions (You will find them in attachment). I would like to ask your help. At the beginnings of every story is cited passages from works of other authors. If you are not prevented from doing this, would you please inform me, what are the names of them and what are the places in them where I could find these passages. I would like to introduce you and your writing to our readers as much detail as I can but unfortunately I do not have any detail about your latest work. I would be very glad if you would inform me of the present state of your work and send me your photographs. I also like to read articles and reviews of your literature. Could you please teach me what journals, newspapers, and books I could find them? I would like to ask you to do me much help that I asked earlier. Thank you very much for taking care of my request. With sincere respect.

His signature followed, in Japanese characters.

I read the letter over twice and soon found myself smiling benevolently while twirling my mustache with both hands. Truth be told, I remembered this man not at all, but in that moment I was overcome with warm feelings toward him, possibly even gratitude. It was finally happening: my stories had made it to Japan. *Boku no otogibanashi wa Nippon made mo yatto itadakimashita*, so to speak . . .

Various feelings washed over me—up to and including self-admiration. And as I swam in these feelings, I could easily discern an icy stream of schadenfreude. I recalled once again the sarcastic smirks, the perplexed rhetorical questions in reviews, the drunken gibes, the friendly harassment: "What's going on, old man? You've really gone and done it this time, eh?" All water under the bridge, of course, but as it happens I haven't forgotten any of it. Or any of them. And then I remembered that nowadays, whenever I speak at Houses of Culture or other organizations, people in the audience recognize me, if at all, not as the author of *Comrade Officers*, and still less for my numerous military stories, but as the creator of *Modern Tales*. On more than one occasion I've received notes asking, "Any relation to the Sorokin who wrote *Modern Tales*?"

Then I remembered that there had been a second sheet in the envelope. I took it out, unfolded it, and gave it a quick read. At first, I found Riu Takami's confusion amusing, only to realize a few minutes later that the task awaiting me would be anything but.

The task awaiting me was to explain, in writing, to a Japanese person, the meaning of the following expressions: "squeeze blood from a turnip," "look like a million bucks," "look super cheesy," "like a dog with two tails," "clean someone's clock," "be three sheets to the wind . . ." But that was only half the trouble—it's not that hard to explain to someone from Japan that when kids say they "aced" a test, they mean they got a good grade, or that calling something "gravy" marks it as very, very good (though unrelated to meats or their juices). But what do you do, say, with the expression "chip on your shoulder"? First of all, that kind of chip needed to be definitively bounded away from the sort of chip one eats, so that Takami wouldn't think that if someone has a "chip on his shoulder," you could fix things by simply walking up and brushing it away. And second, all the cultural codes in Japan are different—maybe people don't really have "chips on their shoulders," or if they do, it's for a totally different reason . . .

I didn't even notice how absorbed I'd gotten in this work.

I have to say that, in general, I don't like writing letters; my rule is to only answer the ones containing questions. As for the letter from Riu Takami, it was chock full of questions that were not only not random but of professional interest to me personally. And so I remained in my seat until I'd drafted my answer, typing it out (having first pulled out from the typewriter the unfinished screenplay page from earlier) and placing it in an envelope, which I then sealed and addressed.

Now I had at least two reasons to leave the house.

I got dressed, creakily, pulled on some zipper boots, and stuck fifty rubles in my breast pocket. At that moment, the telephone rang.

How many times have I told myself, don't pick up the phone when you're leaving the house and already have your coat on? But it could have been Rita, back from her trip, so how could I not pick up? And so I did, and immediately regretted it, because the caller wasn't Rita at all but instead Lyonya Barinov, otherwise known as "Schizo."

I have a couple of friends who specialize in these sorts of ill-timed phone calls. For example, Slava Krutoyarsky calls me exclusively when I am in the middle of eating chicken soup—though it doesn't have to be chicken soup per se. It could be borscht, or, say, solyanka. What really matters is that I be halfway through the bowl, so that the second half has time to get good and cold while I'm on the phone. Garik Aganyan always chooses moments when I'm sitting on the can waiting for an important phone call. As for Lyonya Barinov, he specializes in calling either when I'm about to leave and have already put on my coat, or when I'm about to shower and have already undressed, or, best of all, at the crack of 7 AM. He'll call me up and ask abruptly in a low, conspiratorial tone, "What's doing?"

So now, Lyonya Barinov, otherwise known as "Schizo," asked me in a low, conspiratorial tone, "What's doing?"

"I'm on my way out," I said curtly. That was the wrong move.

"Where to?" Lenya immediately inquired.

"Lyonya," I said beseechingly. "Could we talk later? Or is this about business?"

Yes, Lyonya was calling about business. And his business was as follows. Lyonya had heard a rumor (he's always hearing rumors) that writers who hadn't published in the last two years would be expelled from the Union. Had I heard anything about that? Was I sure? Maybe I'd heard but hadn't paid attention? Because I never pay attention and am always out of the loop . . . Or maybe they wouldn't expel us but only take away our Club pass? What did I think?

I said what I thought.

"All right, all right, no need to be rude," said Lyonya, peaceably. "OK. So where are you off to?"

I told him I was off to send a letter registered mail, and then to Bannaya. None of that held any interest for Lyonya.

"Where are you going after?" he asked.

I said that after I'd probably stop by the Club.

"Why do you need to go to the Club today?"

I said, my blood beginning to boil, that I had stuff to do there, like chopping some wood and checking the heating.

"You're being rude again," said Lyonya sadly. "Why are you all so rude? Everyone you call, they just bite your head off. So you don't want to talk about it on the phone. No worries—you can tell me all about it at the Club. You should know, though, that I don't have any money . . ."

I hung up the phone and looked out the window. It was really getting dark now; it was time to turn on some lights. I sat at the table in my coat and hat and my heavy, hot boots. By now I had no desire to go anywhere at all. When all was said and done, there was no need to send my letter to Japan registered mail; it'll be fine if I just stick a bunch of stamps on it and throw it in the mailbox. And Bannaya can wait, it'll still be there tomorrow . . . Would you look at that, quite a storm out there, you can't see anything at all. Not even the house across the way—all I could make out were some small, hazy yellow lights. But even if I didn't leave, it was stupid to just sit here, subsisting on dry rations, given the two hundred rubles in my possession—not only stupid, wasteful even. Why don't I run downstairs, since I'm already bundled up?

Which is exactly what I did—ran down to the bakery on the corner, our strange bakery, where frosting roses bloom on the counter to the left, and to the right, rows of bottles with strong drinks glint provocatively. Where little old ladies and women with children mill around on the left-hand side, and on the right-hand side, imposing leather-bag bearers and briefcase owners queue up in civilized fashion alongside brutish Kindred Spirits, anticipating, with excited chattiness, the pleasant sensations to come. Where on the left I needed literally nothing at all, but where, from the right, I got a bottle of cognac and a bottle of Salute brand wine spritzer.

And, as I rode the elevator back up to the sixteenth floor, wedging the bottles under my armpit and wiping melted snow from my face with my free hand, I already knew how I would spend the evening. Whether it was because of the blizzard I had just escaped—the blind, blinding blizzard, which had devoured the remains of the day—or because I, like all my Kindred Spirits, was anticipating many pleasant sensations . . . regardless, now I knew for sure: since I was fated to spend the rest of the day at home, and since my Rita still hadn't returned, I would call neither Goga Chachua nor Slava Krutoyarsky but instead spend the hours in a special way, one on one with myself—but not the self people know from all those committees and seminars, from the publishing houses or the Club restaurant. No, I'd spend it with a self unknown in any of those places.

He and I will clear off the kitchen table, set out the bottles and the tins of jellied meat (courtesy of Hotel Progress) onto woven placemats. We'll turn on every light in the house—let there be light!—and drag the floor lamp over from the study. He and I will open the only desk drawer I keep locked, take out the Blue Folder, and, when the moment comes, untie the green strings.

As I shook off snow, changed into house clothes, and checked off the items on my uncomplicated to-do list, my mind kept returning to the problem of the phone. It suddenly dawned on me that it was precisely tonight that people could and even must call me—including people I actually might want to talk to. But on the other hand, it's not like this thought had occurred to me even half an hour ago, when I'd been planning to spend my evening at the Club. And even if it had, I wouldn't have deemed those calls indispensable. And right at the height of this internal battle, my hand reached out of its own volition and unplugged the phone.

And instantly, the house became extremely quiet and cozy, though I could still hear the incompetent pianist from next door and the tape-recorded bard quacking and mumbling through a ceiling vent.

The moment had arrived, but I was in no hurry. For a little while longer, I watched the utterly unfettered blizzard beating at the windowpane with a sound like dry rustling. It's really a shame that there aren't any blizzards Over There. In fact, Over There is missing quite a few things. But on the other hand, Over There possesses much that our own world lacks.

I slowly undid the strings and opened the cover. In passing I thought, full of both joy and sorrow, that I don't often let myself do this, and probably wouldn't have today, either, if it hadn't been for . . . what? The blizzard? Lyonya the Schizo?

There was no title on the first page, only an epigraph:

I am in the third circle, filled with cold,
unending, heavy, and accursèd rain;
its measure and its kind are never changed.
. . . .
Though these accursed sinners never shall
attain the true perfection, yet they can
expect to be more perfect then than now.

The first page also bore a crappy reproduction of a painting: night clouds loom over a horror-frozen city on a hill. And winding around the city and the hill is a gargantuan sleeping serpent with smooth, wetly reflective skin.

But it was not this picture, familiar to so many, that I now saw before my eyes, but only that which no one in the entire world, in the entire universe, could see—except for me. Leaning back in my seat, hands clutching the table's edge, I gazed at the streets, wet, gray, and empty, into front-yard gardens, where apple trees were perishing quietly from the damp . . . fences sagged, mold splattered the sides of houses, every color looked faded, and rain reigned undivided over all. Rain falls just because, cascades down rooftops in a fine mist, accumulates inside gusts of wind, twisting into foggy, whirling columns that trail from one wall to the next; growling, it shoots from rusty drainpipes . . . Grayish-black clouds creep slowly along, hanging so low they almost touch the rooftops. There are no people out in the street; out here, man is an unbidden guest, and the rain makes sure he knows it.

Ten thousand people live in this city of mine—idiots, enthusiasts, and fanatics, the disenchanted and the indifferent, along with numerous officials, soldiers, respectable bourgeois, policemen, and gumshoes. Children. And it filled me with indescribable pleasure to direct their fates, to force them to confront each other and the somber magic I'd gotten them into . . .

It wasn't long ago that I'd thought I was done with them. Everyone had gotten their due; I had told each one exactly what I thought of him. And, most likely, it was precisely this sense of certainty that made my gorge rise, plunging me into stifling fretfulness and displeasure. I needed something more. One more picture, a final one, still needed painting. But what this picture should be I had no idea, and sometimes I felt anguished and frightened at the thought that I'd never find out. So be it. I might never finish this work of mine, but I'd keep thinking about it until I fell into dementia, and perhaps even after that.

Do you swear to keep thinking about your city, to never stop inventing it until you become completely demented, and perhaps even after that?

What else could I do? Of course I swear, I said, and opened the manuscript.

2. VICTOR BANEV

AMONG FAMILY AND FRIENDS

After Irma left, shutting the door carefully behind her—long-legged, smiling as politely as any grown-up with her large mouth, her lips bright like her mother's—Victor began painstakingly lighting a cigarette. That's no child, he thought in astonishment. Children don't talk like that. It's not even rudeness; it's cruelty. Not even cruelty; it's just that she doesn't care. It's like she just proved a theorem for us, calculated everything, did a full analysis, informed us of the results, all businesslike, and then took her leave, braids swinging, completely serene. Battling embarrassment, Victor glanced over at Lola. Her face had turned blotchy red, bright lips quivering like she was about to start crying—except, of course, she had no intention of crying. She was furious.

"You see?" she said, her voice high. "That brat, that snotty little . . . that little shit! Nothing's sacred, every word an insult, like I'm not her mother, like I'm a rag to wipe her feet on. I'm ashamed in front of the neighbor! Nasty little witch . . ."

Yup, thought Victor, that's the woman I used to live with. I wandered the mountains with her, I read Baudelaire out loud to her, I trembled when I touched her, her smell stayed with me for days . . . I think I even fought over her. I still can't figure out, though: What would go through her head when I read her the Baudelaire? I mean, it's amazing that I managed to get away from her. The mind boggles. How did she ever let me go? True, I was no angel. I'm probably no angel now, either, but back then I drank even more heavily. Plus, I thought myself a great poet.

"It's all the same to you, isn't it?" Lola was saying. "You live in the capital, around all those ballerinas and actresses . . . I know everything. Don't think we don't know anything around here. And money, too, the big bucks, and all your lovers, and scandal after scandal . . . If you really want to know, it's all the same to me, I never stood in your way, you always did whatever you wanted . . ."

Her problem is that she talks too much. As a young girl she'd been quiet, taciturn even, mysterious. There are girls like that, who are born knowing how to behave. She knew. Even now she's not so bad when she's sitting there quietly. For example, when she's smoking on the couch, bare knees out . . . Or when she suddenly draws her arm behind her head and stretches. That must impress the hell out of some backwoods lawyer . . .

Victor pictured a cozy little evening: this table here moved up next to that sofa over there, a bottle, champagne fizzing in two flutes, a ribbon-wrapped box of chocolates—and the lawyer himself, imprisoned in starched linen, bow tie knotted perfectly. Everything in its place . . . and then in comes Irma. What a nightmare, thought Victor. The poor woman!

"You have to understand," Lola was saying. "It's not about the money, money's not the deciding factor here." She'd calmed down; the red blotches were fading. "I know you're an honest person in your own way. You're not unstable. You're undisciplined, but you're not mean. You've always helped us, and I have no problem with you where that's concerned. But now I need a different kind of help . . . I can't say that I'm happy, but you haven't been able to make me unhappy, either. You have your life and I have mine. I'm not an old lady yet, by the way, I've still got a lot to look forward to . . ."

I'm going to have to take the girl, thought Victor. Seems like she's already decided that much. If I leave Irma here, it'll be pure hell in this house . . . OK, but where do I put her? Let's be honest, he said to himself. Actually honest. You have to be honest here, this isn't a game . . . He thought about his life in the capital, very honestly. No good, he thought. Sure, I can get a housekeeper. But that means renting an apartment full time . . . And that's not even the problem: the girl should live with me, not with a housekeeper . . . They say kids raised by their fathers turn out the best. And I do like her, even though she is a very strange girl. Moreover, it's my duty. As an honorable man and as a father. And I've wronged her.

But that's all very literary, whereas if I'm completely honest . . . if I'm completely honest, I'm afraid. Next thing I know, she'll be standing in front of me, smiling in that grown-up way with her big mouth, and what will I have to say to her? Read more, keep reading, read every day, there's nothing else you need to do, just read. She doesn't need me to tell her that, but I don't have anything else to offer. That's why I'm afraid . . .

But even that's not the whole truth. I just don't want to, that's the thing. I'm used to being alone. I like being alone. I don't want it any other way. That's about the size of it . . . Looks pretty awful, like any other truth: cynical, selfish, a little vile. Honest.

"Why don't you say something?" asked Lola. "Is that your whole plan, to say nothing?"

"No, no, I'm listening to you," Victor said hastily.

"Listening to what? I've been waiting for half an hour for you to deign to react. She's not just *my* child, after all . . ."

Do I have to be honest with her, too? Victor thought. I'd really prefer not to. She seems to be laboring under the illusion that I can decide something like this right here, right now, between the first cigarette and the second.

"Look," said Lola, "I'm not saying you have to take full custody. Believe me, I know you're not up to it, and thank God for that. You're no good at this kind of thing. But you have connections, you know people . . . Everyone knows your name, after all—so help me set her up somewhere! You people have all kinds of privileged institutions, specialized places, boarding schools. She's a smart girl, she's gifted at languages, and at math, and at music . . ."

"A boarding school," said Victor. "Of course. A boarding school. An orphanage . . . no, I'm joking. It's worth considering."

"What's there to consider? Most people would love to set their child up at a good boarding school, or a specialized one. My boss's wife—"

"Listen, Lola," said Victor. "It's a good thought, I'll work on it. But it's not so simple—it takes time. Of course, I'll write to—"

"You'll write! That's just like you. Writing won't cut it! You have to go there personally, beat down some doors! Not like you're real busy here. All you do is get drunk and sleep around. How hard can it be, for your own daughter's sake . . ."

Goddammit, thought Victor, there's no explaining things to her. He lit another cigarette, stood up, and walked across the room. It was getting dark out there, and still pouring rain—a heavy, deliberate rain, coming down in large drops. There was a lot of it and it was obviously in no hurry.

"God, I'm so sick of you!" said Lola with unexpected anger. "If you only knew how sick of you I was . . ."

Time to go, thought Victor. The holy maternal wrath beginneth, the fury of the woman scorned and so on, and in any case, I'm not giving her an answer today. And I'm not making any promises, either.

"I can't rely on you for anything," she continued. "You're a worthless husband, an incompetent father . . . Oh, look at the fashionable writer! Couldn't raise his own daughter . . . Any peasant knows more about people than you do! What are you even doing right now? You're totally useless. I run myself ragged all alone, but I can't do anything. I'm nothing to her, any clammy means a hundred times more to her than I do. Well, don't worry, you'll live to regret it! If you don't teach her, the clammies will! She'll end up spitting in your face same as she spits in mine."

"Stop it, Lola," said Victor, grimacing. "You know, you're getting kind of. . . I'm the father, that's true enough, but you're the mother. You blame everyone but yourself."

"Get out!" she said.

"All right, look," said Victor, "I have no intention of fighting with you. I also have no intention of making a snap decision. I need to think about this. And you . . ."

She had gotten up now and was standing very straight, nearly shaking, anticipating his rebuke, ready for the pleasure of rushing into battle.

"And you," he said calmly, "try not to get worked up. We'll think of something. I'll call you."

He walked out into the foyer and pulled on his raincoat. It was still wet. Victor peeked into Irma's room to say good-bye, but she wasn't there. The window was open wide, rain lashing the windowsill. On the wall was a banner inscribed with large, attractive letters: PLEASE LEAVE WINDOW OPEN ALWAYS. The banner was wrinkled, torn, and covered in dark stains, as though it had been repeatedly ripped down and trampled. Victor pulled the door closed.

"Good-bye, Lola," he said. Lola didn't answer.

It was already dark outside. The rain battered his shoulders and his hooded head. Victor hunched over, hiding his hands in his pockets. There's the square where we had our first kiss, he thought. That building wasn't there then; it was just an empty lot, and behind the lot was the trash heap where we hunted cats with slingshots . . . but I haven't seen any cats here in a good while . . . And we read diddlysquat back then, whereas now Irma's room is full of books.

What was a twelve-year-old girl back in my day? A giggly, freckled creature, all bows, stockings, picture books of bunnies or Snow White; always in pairs or triples, *whisper-whisper*, little sacks of candy, rotting teeth. Goody two-shoes, tattletales, and the best ones were just like us: scabby knees, wild lynx eyes, and a passion for tripping people. Have times changed, is that it? No, he thought. It's not the times. I mean, it's the times, too . . . Or maybe my little girl's a prodigy? There *are* prodigies out there, after all. I'm the father of a prodigy. It's an honor but a lot of fuss—much more fuss than honor, in fact. And in the end, it's not even that big an honor . . . Oh, I used to love this little street, because it's so narrow. Ah, and what do we have here—a fight? Righto, that's the one thing we just can't do without. That's the story of this town since time immemorial. And two on one, it looks like . . .

Under the streetlamp on the corner, a convertible, canvas top up, was getting drenched. Just outside the illuminated area, two men in shiny cloaks were trying to knock down a third, soaking wet and dressed all in black. All three stumbled around awkwardly on the cobblestones. Victor paused, then approached the group. It was unclear what, exactly, was going on. It didn't look very much like a fight, since no one was hitting anyone else. Still less did it look like a friendly tussle born of an excess of youthful energy—there were no avid whoops or roars of laughter . . .

The black-clad man suddenly broke free and fell over onto his back, whereupon the cloaks jumped on top of him. At that moment, Victor noticed that the car doors were wide open. It occurred to him that they had either just pulled the man in black out or were trying to stuff him back in. He walked up to the group and barked, "Stand down!"

The two cloaks turned around immediately, staring at Victor for a few seconds from underneath their hoods. Victor had just enough time to notice that they were young and that their mouths were gaping with effort—a moment later, they had already leaped into the convertible with improbable speed, slamming the doors. The car roared away into the night.

The man in black picked himself up, slowly. As soon as Victor got a good look at him, he took a step back. It was a patient from the leprosarium—a "clammy," or "four-eyes" as they were called due to the yellow rings around their eyes. A thick black neckerchief concealed the lower half of his face. His breathing was excruciatingly labored, his patchy eyebrows rising in a pained grimace. Water streamed down his bald head.

"What happened?" asked Victor.

The four-eyes stared past him, eyes bulging. Victor wanted to turn around, but something hit the back of his head with a crunch, and when he came to, he found himself lying faceup under a drainpipe. Water was pouring into his mouth; it was yellowish and rusty-tasting. Spluttering and coughing, he moved away from the pipe and sat up, resting his back against a brick wall. The water that had collected in his collar now coursed down his back. His head was filled with the buzzing and clanging of bells, the sound of trumpets, and the beating of many drums.

Through all the noise Victor discerned a gaunt, dark face hovering in front of him. The face of a boy. A familiar face. I've seen it somewhere before. Even before my jaws slammed shut . . . He wiggled his tongue and moved his jaw. His teeth were unharmed. The boy stuck his hands under the pipe, scooped up a handful of water, and splashed it in Victor's eyes.

"Whoa, little man," said Victor. "Enough."

"I had the impression," the boy said seriously, "that you hadn't yet regained consciousness."

Victor reached a hand gingerly into his hood and touched the back of his head. He felt a bump—no fractured bones, not even any blood.

"Who did this to me?" he asked in a thoughtful tone. "Not you, I hope?"

"Can you walk, Mr. Banev?" said the boy. "Or should I call someone? You see, sir, you're too heavy for me to lift."

Victor suddenly remembered who the boy was. "I know you," he said. "You're Bol-Kunatz. You're friends with my daughter."

"Yes," said the boy.

"So much the better. Let's not call anyone, or tell anyone about this . . . let's just sit here for a second and collect ourselves."

Now he could see that Bol-Kunatz was not exactly shipshape, either. A fresh abrasion was darkening on his cheek, and his upper lip was swollen and bleeding.

"Why don't I just call someone?" said Bol-Kunatz.

"Why bother?"

"You see, Mr. Banev, sir, your face seems to be twitching."

"Is it?" Victor felt his face. It wasn't twitching. "You're imagining things . . . All right, up we go. What do we need to do to get there? We need to bend our legs . . ." He bent his legs, which felt like they didn't belong to him. "Next step: push off the wall and shift your center of gravity so that—" He kept failing to shift his center of gravity—something was in the way.

What did they hit me with? he thought to himself. Did a good job, too.

"You're stepping on your raincoat," the boy informed him, but Victor had already mastered his various limbs, his coat, and even the orchestra inside his skull. He stood up. At first, he had to hold on to the wall, but then it got easier.

"Aha," he said. "So you were the one who dragged me to the pipe. Thanks."

The streetlamp was still there, but the car and the four-eyes weren't. The street was empty except for Bol-Kunatz, who was delicately stroking his scratched-up cheek with a wet palm.

"Where'd they all go?" asked Victor.

The boy didn't answer.

"Was I lying here alone?" asked Victor. "No one else around?"

"Allow me to accompany you," said Bol-Kunatz. "Which way are you going? Home?"

"Hold on," said Victor. "Did you see them trying to grab the four-eyes?"

"I saw you get knocked down," said Bol-Kunatz.

"Who by?"

"I couldn't tell. He had his back to me."

"And where were you?"

"Well, sir, I was lying just around the corner . . ."

"I don't get it," said Victor. "Or else something's up with my head . . . Why, exactly, were you lying just around the corner? Is that where you live?"

"You see, sir, I was lying there because I'd been knocked down just before. Not by whoever hit you, by someone else."

"The four-eyes?"

They were walking slowly, keeping to the middle of the road to avoid the torrents pouring down from the rooftops.

"N-No," answered Bol-Kunatz after a moment. "I don't think any of them had glasses."

"Oh, Jesus," said Victor. He reached back into his hood and touched the bump on the back of his head. "I'm talking about the leper, you know, they call them four-eyes. You know, the ones from the leprosarium? The clammies?"

"I don't know, they all looked pretty healthy to me," said Bol-Kunatz coolly.

"Come on now!" said Victor. He stopped short, starting to feel worried. "Are you trying to tell me the one guy wasn't a leper? His face covered in black cloth, dressed all in black . . ."

"He's no leper!" said Bol-Kunatz with sudden irritation. "He's healthier than you." It was the first time this boy had displayed any hint of boyishness—and then it was gone.

After a beat, he added, "I'm not entirely clear on where we're going." He had resumed his earlier tone, serious to the point of impassivity. "At first I thought you were going home, but now I see that we're walking in the opposite direction."

Victor was still standing there, looking down at the boy. Two peas in a pod, he thought. He's calculated everything, done a full analysis, and then, all businesslike, decided not to inform me of the result. He's never going to tell me what happened back there. Maybe they were criminals? Times have changed, after all . . . No, that's nonsense, I know what criminals are like.

"That's right," he said, and started walking again. "We're going to the hotel. That's where I live."

The boy, straight-backed, stern, and wet, was walking beside him. After a moment's hesitation, Victor placed a hand on his shoulder. Nothing special happened—the boy let him do it. Of course, he probably thought his shoulder was needed for utilitarian purposes, as support for an injured man.

"You know," said Victor in his most confidential tone, "you and Irma have a very funny way of talking. We didn't talk like that when I was a kid."

"You don't say?" said Bol-Kunatz politely. "And how did you talk?"

"Well, for example, the question you just asked would have sounded more like 'Huh?'"

Bol-Kunatz shrugged his shoulders. "Are you saying that would have been better?"

"God forbid. All I meant is that it would be more natural."

"It is precisely that which is most natural that least of all befits a man," Bol-Kunatz noted.

Victor felt a sort of coldness inside. It was worry, or maybe even fear. It was like a cat had just burst out laughing in his face.

"The natural is always primitive," Bol-Kunatz continued. "Man is a complex creature, and naturalness is not his element. Do you follow, Mr. Banev?"

"Sure," said Victor. "Of course."

There was something incredibly artificial about the fact that he was resting a paternal hand on the shoulder of this boy who was not a boy. His elbow even started to ache. He moved his hand away, carefully, and stuck it in his pocket.

"How old are you?" he asked.

"Fourteen," Bol-Kunatz answered absent-mindedly.

"Uh-huh . . ."

Any other boy but Bol-Kunatz would have immediately taken an interest in this irritatingly ambivalent "uh-huh," but Bol-Kunatz wasn't any other boy. He said nothing. Intriguing interjections held no special interest for him. He was pondering the relationship of the natural to the primitive. He was sorry his interlocutor was turning out to be so unintelligent, and with a head injury to boot.

They turned onto the Prospekt of the President. Here were many streetlights and the occasional passerby, harried men and women slumping under the weight of days of rain. Shop windows glowed with light. The neon-bathed entryway to the movie theater swarmed with nearly identical young people of indeterminate gender, all wearing shiny ankle-length cloaks. And up above it all, through the rain, letters of blue and gold blazed their incantations: THE PRESIDENT IS THE FATHER OF THE PEOPLE; THE LEGIONNAIRE OF FREEDOM: FAITHFUL SON OF THE PRESIDENT; THE ARMY: OUR MIGHTY FORCE.

They kept walking in the middle of the road until a passing car chased them onto the sidewalk, horn bellowing, spraying them from head to toe with dirty water.

"I would have thought you were about eighty years old," said Victor.

"*Huuuuh?*" asked Bol-Kunatz in a grating voice, and Victor laughed with relief. So he *was* a boy after all, an ordinary, normal prodigy who's read a bunch of Gabor, Zurzmansor, Fromm, and maybe even plowed his way through some Spengler.

"I had this friend when I was a kid," said Victor, "who wanted to read Hegel in the original. He did it, eventually, but along the way he became a schizophrenic. You're old enough to know what schizophrenia is, aren't you?"

"I am," said Bol-Kunatz.

"And you're not worried?"

"No."

When they reached the hotel, Victor asked, "Maybe you want to come up and dry off?"

"Many thanks. I was just going to ask for permission to come up. For one thing, I have something to tell you, and for another, I need to make a phone call. Is that all right with you?"

It was all right with Victor. They walked through the revolving door and continued past the doorman, who doffed his cap; past the lavish statues with their electric candles; and into the lobby, totally empty and saturated with restaurant smells. Victor felt a familiar rush, anticipating an evening of drinking and irresponsible prattle, an evening that would let him shove aside all that weighed on him so annoyingly today until tomorrow, an evening featuring Yul Golem and Dr. Quadriga, and maybe I'll meet someone, and maybe something will happen, a fistfight or some other story. Yes, a story—and what's more, I'm going to order lampreys tonight, and everything will be fine, and then I'll catch the last bus over to Diana's.

While Victor was retrieving the keys from the front desk, a conversation took place behind him. Bol-Kunatz was talking to the doorman. "What are you doing barging in here?" the doorman was hissing.

"I need to speak with Mr. Banev."

"Oh, I bet you do," the doorman hissed. "Loitering around restaurants . . ."

"I need to speak with Mr. Banev," repeated Bol-Kunatz. "The restaurant is of no interest to me."

"Yeah, I bet it's of no interest to you, you little punk. Let's go, get out of here . . ."

Victor picked up the key and turned around. "Um . . ." he said. He had forgotten the doorman's name again. "The kid's with me, it's all right." The doorman said nothing but looked displeased.

They went up to Victor's room. He threw off his raincoat with delight and bent down to unlace his damp boots. The blood rushed to his head and he felt a dull, painful poking sensation in the area around the bump, which was as heavy and round as a leaden pancake. He stood straight up again and leaned on the door frame, pressing the toe of one shoe into the heel of the other to help pull it off his foot. Bol-Kunatz stood nearby, dripping.

"Get undressed," said Victor. "Hang everything on the radiators, I'll get you a towel."

"May I make a phone call?" asked Bol-Kunatz, staying where he was.

"Go for it."

Victor tore off his other shoe and headed to the bathroom in his wet socks. While undressing, he could hear the boy speaking quietly, calmly, and unintelligibly. Just once he said, loudly and clearly, "I don't know."

Victor toweled off, slipped on his robe, grabbed a clean bath towel, and exited the bathroom. "Here you go," he said, and immediately saw that there was no point. As before, Bol-Kunatz was standing by the door, still dripping.

"Many thanks," he said. "You see, sir, I have to go. I'd just like to—"

"You'll catch cold," said Victor.

"No need to worry, thank you. I won't catch cold. I just wanted to ask you one question . . . Irma didn't say anything to you, did she?"

Victor threw the towel onto the sofa and squatted in front of the bar, pulling out a bottle and a glass. "Irma said a lot of things," he said, rather gloomily. He poured a finger of gin into the glass and added a little water.

"Did she pass along our invitation?"

"Nope, no invitation. Here, drink this."

"Many thanks, there's no need. Since she didn't pass it along, I will. We'd like to meet with you, Mr. Banev."

"Who's 'we'?"

"The gymnasium students. You see, sir, we've read your books and have a few questions."

"Hmm," Victor said doubtfully. "Are you sure that would be interesting to everyone?"

"I think so, yes."

"I don't exactly write with gymnasium students in mind," Victor reminded him.

"That's not important," said Bol-Kunatz with gentle insistence. "Would you be willing to come by?"

Victor swirled the clear liquid around in the glass, lost in thought. "Why don't you drink some of this?" he asked. "It's the best remedy for colds. No? Fine then, don't mind if I do." He downed the contents of the glass. "All right, I'll do it. But no posters, no announcements, nothing of the sort. Just an intimate circle. Just you all—and me . . . When is good?"

"Whenever works for you. Next week would be best. In the morning."

"Let's go with two days from now. But not too early. Say, Friday at eleven. Does that work?"

"Yes. Friday at eleven. At the gymnasium. Will you be needing a reminder?"

"Most certainly," said Victor. "I always try to forget about galas, soirees, and banquets. Also, meetings, appointments, and conferences."

"OK, I'll remind you," said Bol-Kunatz. "And now, Mr. Banev, I'm going to go, if that's all right with you. Good-bye, Mr. Banev."

"Hold on, I'll walk you out," said Victor. "I don't want that . . . doorman . . . to harass you. He's in a mood today, and you know, doormen are the sort of people who—"

"Many thanks, don't trouble yourself," Bol-Kunatz objected. "He's my father."

And with that, he was gone. Victor poured himself another finger of gin and collapsed into an armchair. I see, he thought. That poor doorman. What was his name again? I should know that. After all, we're comrades in misfortune, colleagues, in a way. I'll have to talk to him, swap stories. He's probably got more experience than I do . . . So many prodigies in my dank little hometown! Maybe it's the elevated humidity.

That bastard, what did he hit me with? He touched the bump again. Feels like a rubber truncheon. Although how do I know what a rubber truncheon does? I know what an art nouveau chair at the Fried Pegasus does. Or the butt of an assault rifle. Or, say, a handgun, or an empty champagne bottle, or a full one . . . I'll have to ask Golem . . . It's a strange business, though, it'd be good to get to the bottom of it.

And he began getting to the bottom of this strange business, to keep away the other thoughts that kept surfacing in the background, thoughts about Irma, about the necessity of denying himself things and reining himself in, writing to someone or other, asking for favors. *Sorry to bother you, old man, but it turns out I've got a daughter—about twelve years old, but her mother's an idiot and so is her father; anyway, I need to set her up somewhere far away from any stupid people* . . . I don't want to think about that today; I'll think about it tomorrow. He looked at his watch. Enough with the thinking already. Enough.

Victor stood up and began getting dressed in front of the mirror. I'm developing a gut, goddammit, what could it possibly be from? I've always been a lean, sinewy kind of guy . . . It's not even a gut, really—more of a noble working belly, born of a measured life and plenty of good food. You know, just a small, mangy belly, the tiny belly of the opposition. I bet Mr. President's belly isn't like this at all. I bet Mr. President's belly is more of a dignified, sleek, black-clad blimp.

As he knotted his tie, he put his face up to the mirror and suddenly thought about how it must have looked: his strong, confident face, so beloved by women of a certain type—not a handsome face, but manly, the face of a square-jawed warrior—how that face must have looked toward the end of his historic meeting with Mr. President. Toward the end of their historic meeting, the face of Mr. President, itself not devoid of manliness and a certain square-jawed element, resembled—let's be honest—the snout of a boar. Mr. President had wound himself up to the absolute limit, spittle spraying out of his toothy maw, and I got out a handkerchief and demonstratively wiped my cheek—which was probably the bravest deed of my whole life, if you don't count the time I had to fight off three tanks at the same time. But I don't actually remember the time with the three tanks, I only heard about it from eyewitnesses, whereas I got out that little handkerchief deliberately, I knew exactly what I was doing . . . They didn't write about *that* in the papers. The papers reported, with honesty, manliness, and unfaltering lucidity, that "fiction writer Banev sincerely thanked the President for his suggestions and clarifications over the course of their discussion." Strange how well I remember it all.

Victor noticed that his cheeks and the tip of his nose had gone pale. That's exactly how I looked back then. Only a fool doesn't go after a man who looks like that. How could the President have known, poor guy, that I wasn't turning pale with fright but with rage, like Louis XIV . . . But no use crying over spilled milk. Who cares why I did or didn't turn pale that night . . . Forget it. But just for the sake of calming down, of pulling yourself together before appearing in public, of restoring normal color to your face, which is not handsome but manly nonetheless, I must note, I must remind you, Mr. Banev, that if you hadn't flaunted your handkerchief in front of Mr. President, you would at this very moment be dwelling—most happily!—in our lovely capital, and not in this soaking-wet dump . . .

Victor drank his gin in one gulp and went down to the restaurant.

"Sure, it could be hoodlums," said Victor. "But in my time, no hoodlum would have risked hassling a four-eyes. Throw a rock at him—sure, by all means. But grab him and drag him along like that? Touch him at all? We all feared them like the plague."

"I'm telling you, it's a genetic condition," said Golem. "Absolutely noncontagious."

"Sure, noncontagious," Victor retorted. "They give you warts, same as toads! Everyone knows that."

"You can't get warts from a toad," said Golem amiably. "Or from a clammy, for that matter. Shame on you, Mr. Writer. Then again, writers *are* pretty dull folk."

"Like any other folk. Folk may be dull, but they're wise. So if they claim that toads and clammies cause warts—"

"Oh, look—here comes my inspector!" said Golem.

Pavor walked up in a wet raincoat. He'd just come in from outside.

"Good evening," he said. "I'm all wet. I'd like a drink."

"He stinks of slime again," Dr. R. Quadriga intoned indignantly, rousing himself from an alcoholic trance. "He always smells of slime. Like a pond. Pond scum."

"What are we drinking?" Pavor asked.

"Who's 'we'?" Golem inquired. "I, for instance, am drinking cognac, as always. Victor's drinking gin. And the doctor's having a little bit of everything."

"Shame!" Dr. R. Quadriga said indignantly. "Scales! And heads."

"One double cognac!" Pavor called out to the waiter. His face was wet from rain, thick hair matted. Shining rivulets coursed from his temples down his clean-shaven cheeks.

There's another tough-looking face for you—the envy of many, no doubt. Where does a health inspector get a face like that? A really tough-looking face: rain coming down, floodlights, shadows moving erratically over wet train cars, darting quickly, then fragmenting . . . everything shiny and wet, shiny and wet and nothing else, no conversation, no pointless jabbering, only commands, and everyone obeys . . . not necessarily train cars, could be airplanes, an airport. Plus, no one knows where he's been or where he came from . . . girls fall on their backs, and men feel like doing something manly, like squaring their shoulders and sucking in their gut. Take Golem: he'd do well to suck in his gut, but he can't, not really, where would it go, there's no room in there to suck anything in. Dr. R. Quadriga's a different story, but he'll never be able to square his shoulders; too much time has passed, and now the slump is permanent. In the evenings he slumps over the bar, in the mornings over a bucket, and in the daytime he's slumped 'cause his liver's sore. Meaning I'm the only one capable of sucking in my gut and squaring my shoulders at the same time. But I'll take a manly shot of gin instead.

"You nymphomaniac," said Dr. R. Quadriga to Pavor in sad tones. "Mermaidomaniac. And seaweed."

"Shut up, Doctor," said Pavor. He was wiping his face with paper napkins, crumpling them up, and throwing them on the floor. When he finished, he began drying his hands.

"Who've you been fighting with?" asked Victor.

"Raped by a clammy," said Dr. R. Quadriga, desperately forcing his eyes to look straight ahead—they kept sliding down toward the bridge of his nose.

"No one, yet," Pavor replied, and looked pointedly at the doctor. R. Quadriga failed to notice.

The waiter brought a glass of cognac. Pavor slowly decanted it into his mouth, then stood up. "Why don't I go wash up?" he said evenly. "It's muddy outside town—I'm all covered in shit." And off he went, bumping into chairs along the way.

"Something's up with my inspector," said Golem, flicking a wet napkin off the table with a fingernail. "Something of cosmic proportions. You wouldn't happen to know what, by any chance?"

"You should know," said Victor. "You're the one he's inspecting. Plus, you know everything. By the way, Golem, where do you know everything from?"

"No one knows anything," Golem objected. "Some people are starting to guess. Very few—only those who really want to. But it doesn't make sense to ask, *Where did they guess it from?* That's torturing the language. *Whereto is it raining? What does the sun rise?* You'd never forgive Shakespeare if he wrote something like that, would you? Or no, Shakespeare you'd forgive. Shakespeare gets a lot of leeway—unlike Banev . . . Listen, Mr. Belletrist, I have an idea. I'll drink this cognac, and you'll finish up that gin. Or are you good and gone already?"

"Golem," said Victor, "did you know that I'm a man of iron?"

"I'm starting to guess as much."

"And what follows from that?"

"That you should watch out for rust."

"Sure," said Victor. "But that's not what I meant. What I meant is, I can drink for a good long time without losing my moral compass."

"Oh, *that's* what you meant," said Golem, pouring himself more cognac. "Never mind, then, we'll return to this topic later."

"I can't remember," Dr. R. Quadriga said suddenly, in a clear voice. "Did I already introduce myself, gentlemen? Please, allow me: Rem Quadriga, painter, doctor *honoris causa*, honorary member . . . You I remember," he said to Victor. "You and I were in school together, and something else, too . . . But as for you, I'm afraid—"

"My name is Yul Golem," said Golem, indifferently.

"Pleased to meet you. Skoolpter?"

"No, physician."

"Sturgeon?"

"I'm chief of medicine at the leprosarium," Golem explained patiently.

"Oh, right!" said Dr. R. Quadriga, shaking his head like a horse. "Of course. Forgive me, Yul . . . But why beat around the bush? You're no doctor, you breed clammies . . . I'll introduce you around. We need people like you . . . Excuse me," he said abruptly. "Be right back."

He clambered out of his armchair and rushed to the exit, weaving between the empty tables. A waiter leaped to his side. Dr. R. Quadriga put an arm around the man's neck.

"It's the rain," said Golem. "We're breathing water. But we're not fish, so we'll either die or be forced to leave." He was gazing at Victor, his face serious and sad. "Then the rain will fall on an empty city, eroding the pavements, seeping through the roofs, the rotting roofs . . . and in the end, it will wash everything away, dissolving the city into primordial silt, but it won't stop there, it'll keep falling and falling and falling . . ."

"Apocalypse," muttered Victor, just to say something.

"Yes, apocalypse . . . It'll keep falling and falling, and then the earth will become saturated, and a new crop will grow, one never seen before, with nary any chaff among all that wheat. But nary a person, either, to enjoy this new universe."

If it weren't for those pinkish-gray bags under his eyes, if not for his saggy, gelatinous belly, if that magnificent Semitic nose looked less like a topographic map . . . Although, come to think of it, all the prophets were drunks, because it's just so depressing: you know everything, but no one believes you. If the government introduced a full-time prophet position, they'd have to give it a rank no lower than privy councillor to enhance its authority. And even that probably wouldn't help.

"For his systematic pessimism," Victor intoned, "which undermines labor discipline and faith in a reasonable future, I sentence Privy Councillor Golem to death by stoning in the execution chamber."

Golem snickered. "I'm only a collegiate councillor," he informed Victor. "And also, there aren't any prophets in our day! I don't know a single one. There are a great many false prophets, but no real ones. In our day there's no way to 'foresee the future'—that's torturing the language. What would you say if you read in Shakespeare 'to foresee the present'? Is it possible to foresee the closet in your own room? . . . Ah, here comes my inspector again. How're you feeling, inspector?"

"Fantastic," said Pavor, taking a seat. "Waiter, double cognac! Our artist is being held up by four people over in the lobby," he informed them. "They're explaining to him where the entrance to the restaurant is. I decided not to butt in. He refuses to listen to anyone and has started throwing punches . . . What closets are we talking about?" He was dry, elegant, refreshed, and smelled of cologne.

"We're talking about the future," said Golem.

"What's the point of that?" Pavor retorted. "You don't talk about the future, you make it. Here's a glass of cognac. It's full. I make it empty. Like so. A clever man once said that we cannot predict the future but only invent it."

"And another clever man said," Victor remarked, "that there's no such thing as the future—only the present."

"I dislike classical philosophy," said Pavor. "Those people knew nothing and wanted nothing. They just enjoyed abstract reasoning, the same way Golem enjoys a drink. The future is a meticulously disinfected present."

"I always get the strangest feeling," said Golem, "when I hear civilians reasoning like soldiers."

"Soldiers don't reason at all," Pavor objected. "All they have are reflexes and a few emotions."

"The same holds for most civilians," said Victor, massaging the back of his head.

"These days, no one has time for abstract reasoning," said Pavor. "Neither soldiers nor civilians. These days, you have to be able to turn on a dime. If you're interested in the future, invent it quick, on the fly, in accordance with your reflexes and emotions."

"Screw inventors," said Victor. He felt drunk and happy. Everything was in its right place. He had no desire to go anywhere. All he wanted was to stay here, in this empty, shadowy hall that was not yet dilapidated but with walls already smudged, floorboards already loose, air saturated with kitchen smells, especially given that out there, it was raining the world over. Rain over the cobblestones, rain over the sharply pitched roofs, rain flooding mountains and valleys. Someday it'll wash everything away, but not anytime soon—although, come to think of it, nowadays you can't really say that this or that "won't happen anytime soon." Yes, friends, the time is long gone when the future just repeated the past and any possible changes barely glimmered on distant horizons. Golem is right, there is no future in the world; it has merged with the present, and now you can't tell what's what.

"Raped by a clammy!" said Pavor with fiendish delight.

Dr. R. Quadriga had reappeared at the restaurant entrance. He stood there for a couple of seconds, ponderously surveying the rows of empty tables. Suddenly, his face brightened, and he lunged toward his spot, swaying mightily.

"Why do you call them *clammies*?" asked Victor. "Are they wet from all the rain that falls around here?"

"Well, why not?" said Pavor. "What would you have us call them?"

"Four-eyes," said Victor. "That good old word. We've been calling them four-eyes since time immemorial."

Dr. R. Quadriga was approaching. The front of his shirt was soaked; he'd been rinsed off over a sink, most likely. He looked weary and disenchanted.

"It's the damnedest thing," he said peevishly as he walked up. "Never happened to me before: no door! Nothing but windows, wherever I turn . . . but I'm afraid I've kept you waiting, gentlemen." He fell into his armchair and caught sight of Pavor. "Him again," he informed Golem in an intimate whisper. "I hope he's not bothering you . . . You know, the most extraordinary thing just happened to me: they drenched me, head to toe."

Golem poured him some cognac.

"Many thanks," said R. Quadriga. "But I think I'll skip a few rounds. I've got to dry out."

"In general, I'm pro everything good and old," Victor announced. "Let the four-eyes be called four-eyes. And in general, let everything remain unchanged. I'm a conservative . . . Attention!" he said loudly. "I'd like to propose a toast to conservatism. Hold on . . ." He poured himself some gin and stood, supporting his weight on the back of an armchair. "I'm a conservative," he said. "And every year I get more and more so, not because I'm getting old but because I feel it's necessary."

Sober Pavor held his glass at the ready, looking up at Victor with studious attention. Golem was slowly working his way through a plate of lampreys, while R. Quadriga appeared to be struggling vainly to understand where the voice was coming from and whom it might belong to. Everything was wonderful.

"People love to criticize conservative governments," Victor continued. "And they love to glorify progress. It's a new trend—stupid, like everything new. People should beg the Lord to grant them the most rigid, hidebound, conformist government possible."

Now Golem, too, had raised his eyes to look at him, and Teddy, standing behind the bar, stopped wiping down bottles and pricked up his ears, but the back of Victor's head suddenly began to ache, and he had to put down his glass and stroke his bump.

"In every age, gentlemen, the state apparatus has regarded maintaining the status quo as its chief objective. I don't know whether this was justified in the past, but today it's simply indispensable. I would define the corresponding governmental function as follows: to block, at every turn, the future's attempts to thrust its tentacles into our own time, to chop off those tentacles, to cauterize them with red-hot metal . . . To frustrate inventors and encourage scholastics and chatterboxes . . . To require all gymnasiums to teach only the classics. To fill all higher governmental positions with old men no younger than sixty, burdened with families and debts, who take bribes and sleep through meetings—"

"What on earth are you babbling about, Victor?" said Pavor reproachfully.

"Well, why not?" said Golem. "It's incredibly gratifying to hear such loyal and moderate discourse."

"Gentlemen, I'm not finished! . . . Appoint talented scientists to top administrative posts with large salaries. Accept all inventions without exception, but remunerate them poorly and sweep them under the rug. Introduce draconian taxes on any commercial or industrial innovation . . ." Hell, why am I standing up? thought Victor, and sat down. "Well, how do you like that?" he asked Golem.

"You're absolutely right," said Golem. "Nowadays everyone's a radical. Even the gymnasium headmaster. Conservatism will be our salvation."

Victor took a swig of gin and said sorrowfully, "There won't be any salvation. Because the idiot radicals not only believe in progress, they actually love it, they imagine that they can't go on without it. Because progress is, among other things, cheap cars, consumer electronics, and, in general, the chance to do less and get more. And that's why any government has to keep one hand . . . I mean *foot* . . . keep one foot on the brakes, and the other on the gas pedal. Like a racecar driver following a curve. You need the brakes to avoid losing direction and the gas to avoid losing speed, otherwise some demagogue, some champion of progress, will end up pushing you out of the driver's seat."

"You're a hard man to argue with," Pavor said politely.

"So don't argue," said Victor. "There's no need: in argument the truth is born, damn it to hell." He stroked the bump on his head tenderly and added, "Then again, I'm probably just an ignoramus. All scientists are champions of progress, but I'm not a scientist. Just a troubadour of modest renown."

"Why do you keep grabbing at the back of your head?" asked Pavor.

"Some bastard clobbered me," said Victor. "With brass knuckles . . . Isn't that right, Golem? With brass knuckles?"

"I think so," said Golem. "That, or a brick."

"You don't say!" said Pavor in surprise. "Brass knuckles? Here, in this podunk town?"

"You see!" said Victor didactically. "That's progress for you . . . Let's drink to conservatism again."

They called the waiter over and drank another round to conservatism. The clock struck nine, and a familiar pair appeared in the hall: a young man in powerful glasses and his beanpole companion. They sat down at their table, turned on the lamp, took a meek look around, and began perusing the menu. The young man had a briefcase, which he placed on the empty armchair next to him. He was always being very nice to his briefcase. After giving the waiter their order, they sat bolt upright and commenced staring silently into space.

A strange pair, thought Victor. Remarkably incongruous. They look like what you see through broken binoculars: one's in focus, the other's all blurry, and vice versa. Totally irreconcilable. With the young man in glasses, you could talk about progress; not so with the beanpole. The beanpole might be capable of whacking me with brass knuckles, but not the bespectacled youngster . . . Just wait, though, I'll reconcile you two, all right. But how? Try this: the vault of some government bank . . . concrete, cement, alarm system . . . the beanpole rotates the combination lock, the steel tumbler turns, the door to the treasury swings open, they both go inside, the beanpole enters the next combination, the safe door opens, and now the young man's elbow-deep in diamonds.

Dr. R. Quadriga suddenly burst into tears and grabbed Victor by the arm. "Time for bed," he said. "My place. Eh?"

Victor immediately poured him some gin. R. Quadriga drank, wiped his nose, and continued: "My place. The villa. It's got a fountain. Eh?"

"A fountain? Well done," Victor said, evasively. "What else is there?"

"Cellar," R. Quadriga said, sadly. "Footprints. Afraid. Scary. Want to buy it?"

"Sure . . . for the price of free," offered Victor.

R. Quadriga blinked rapidly. "Can't," he said.

"Tightwad," said Victor reproachfully. "You've been like that since we were kids. Look at him, can't give away his villa! Well, why don't you choke on it, then."

"You don't like me," declared R. Quadriga bitterly. "No one does."

"What about Mr. President?" Victor asked aggressively.

"'The President Is the Father of the People,'" said R. Quadriga, perking up. "A sketch in gold tones . . . 'The President in the Field.' Painting detail: 'The President Under Enemy Fire.'"

"What else?" asked Victor with interest.

"'The President in His Raincoat,'" R. Quadriga answered readily. "Panel. Panorama."

Victor, growing bored, cut himself a small piece of lamprey and turned his attention to Golem.

"Look, Pavor," Golem was saying. "Why don't you just leave me alone? What else can I do? I already gave you a full written account. I'm ready to sign your report. You want to file a complaint against the troops, go for it. You want to file a complaint against me—"

"I have no interest in filing a complaint against you," answered Pavor, pressing his hand to his chest.

"Then don't."

"Well, tell me what to do, then! Do you really have nothing to suggest?"

"Gentlemen," said Victor. "This is deadly boring. I'm off."

They ignored him. He shifted his chair, stood up, and, feeling very drunk, made his way to the bar. Bald-headed Teddy was wiping down bottles and looking at him, not incuriously. "The usual?" he asked.

"Hold on," said Victor. "What was it I wanted to ask you . . . Oh yeah! How are things, Teddy?"

"Rain," said Teddy curtly, and poured him some distilled vodka.

"The weather's gotten hideous around here," said Victor, and leaned against the bar. "What's your barometer say?"

Teddy stuck his hand under the bar and brought out the "weathervane." All three spikes were pressed tightly against the shiny, polished-looking shaft.

"Tight as a drum," said Teddy, looking closely at the "weathervane." "Diabolical invention." After a moment's thought, he added, "But on the other hand, God only knows. Maybe it's broken—it's been raining for all these years now, so how can we check?"

"We could go to the Sahara," Victor proposed.

Teddy smirked. "You're funny," he said. "Oddly enough, your friend there, Pavor, has been offering me two hundred crowns for this thing."

"A drunken whim, I bet," said Victor. "What could he possibly want with it?"

"That's what I said," Teddy gave the "weathervane" a twirl, then brought it to his right eye. "But I'm not giving it up," he declared, resolutely. "He can get his own." He stuck the "weathervane" back under the bar, watched Victor spinning his glass idly in his hands, then remarked, "Your girl Diana came by."

"When?" asked Victor nonchalantly.

"Around five, I think. I gave her a case of cognac. Rossechepert's on a bender, he can't stop himself. Keeps sending his flunkies out for more cognac, the greasy mug. MP, my foot . . . Aren't you worried about her?"

Victor shrugged. Suddenly, he saw Diana standing right next to him. She appeared at the bar in a wet mackintosh with the hood thrown back. She wasn't looking in his direction; he could see only her profile and thought that of all the women he had ever known, she was the most beautiful and that he'd never get one like her again. She stood there, leaning on the bar, and her face was very pale and very indifferent, and she was so beautiful—every part of her was beautiful. All the time, too. Laughing, crying, angry, not giving a damn, shivering from cold, and especially when she was turned on . . . Ugh, I'm so drunk, thought Victor, and I bet I reek like R. Quadriga. He stuck out his lower lip and tried to smell his own breath, but failed.

"The roads are wet and slippery," Teddy was saying. "It's foggy . . . And let me tell you, that Rossechepert is probably a lech, the old goat."

"Rossechepert's impotent," Victor objected, throwing back his vodka mechanically.

"Is that what she told you?"

"Drop it, Teddy," said Victor. "Just stop."

Teddy scrutinized him for a moment, sighed, then knelt down with a grunt. He dug around somewhere under the bar, then resurfaced, arraying before Victor a vial of ammonium hydroxide and an open packet of tea. Victor glanced at the clock, then turned his attention back to Teddy. The bartender unhurriedly drew out a clean glass, filled it with club soda, added a few drops from the vial, and, still unhurried, swirled it all together with a swizzle stick. He pushed the drink toward Victor, who drank it down and shut his eyes tight, holding his breath. Brisk and vile, vile and brisk, the briskly vile stream of ammonia went straight to his head, exploding somewhere behind his eyes. Victor sniffed the air, which was suddenly unbearably cold, and plunged his fingers into the tea leaves.

"OK, Teddy," he said. "Thanks. Put it all on my tab. They'll tell you what I had. I'm off."

He walked back over to his table, chewing the tea leaves thoroughly. The bespectacled young man and his beanpole companion were hastily consuming their dinner. A single bottle stood on the table, full of the local mineral water. Pavor and Golem had cleared a space on the tablecloth and were playing dice, while Dr. R. Quadriga, holding his unkempt head in his hands, chanted monotonously: "'The Legion of Freedom Is the President's Right Arm.' A mosaic . . . On the happy occasion of Your Excellency's birthday . . . 'The President Is the Father of the Children.' An allegorical painting . . ."

"I'm off," said Victor.

"Too bad," said Golem. "Good luck, though."

"My regards to Rossechepert," said Pavor, winking.

"'Rossechepert Nantes, Member of Parliament.'" R. Quadriga perked up. "Portrait. Inexpensive. Half-length . . ."

Victor picked up his lighter and cigarettes and made his way to the exit. Behind him, Dr. R. Quadriga said, in a clear voice, "Gentlemen, it's high time we got acquainted. I'm Rem Quadriga, doctor *honoris causa*, but I don't recall who you might be, sir . . ." In the doorway, Victor ran into the fat coach of the Kindred Spirits, the local soccer team. The coach was extremely preoccupied and extremely wet, and he stepped aside to let Victor pass.

✦✦✦

The bus stopped and the driver said, "We're here."

"The sanatorium?" asked Victor. Outside was fog, dense and milky, the light from the headlamps barely filtering through. Visibility was nil.

"Yeah, it's the sanatorium, all right," grumbled the driver, lighting a cigarette.

Victor walked up to the doors and, starting down the stairs, said, "Look at that crazy fog. I can't see a thing."

"You'll figure it out," the driver promised, indifferently. He spat out the window. "Great spot for a sanatorium. Fog all day, fog all night . . ."

"Safe travels," said Victor.

The driver didn't answer. The motor roared, and the empty bus, looking like a department store after closing time—all glass panes and indoor illumination—turned around, instantly transforming into a hazy patch of light, and started back toward town.

Victor slid his hands along the iron railing, finding the gate only with difficulty. Then he started down the path, moving by feel. Now that his eyes had adjusted to the dark, he could just make out the lighted windows of the building's right-hand wing and the even deeper darkness shrouding the left-hand one. That was where the Kindred Spirits slumbered, weary after a hectic day in the rain. Through the cottony fog, he could hear all the usual sounds: gramophone music, the clatter of plates, hoarse shrieking.

Victor kept moving, trying to stay in the path's sandy middle to avoid accidentally banging into some plaster vase. He pressed the gin bottle tenderly to his chest and was very careful, but nonetheless tripped over something soft and ended up crawling on all fours. Listless, sleepy curses sounded behind him, to the effect that it wouldn't hurt to turn on some damn lights. Victor fumbled in the dark for his fallen bottle, pressed it to his chest once more, and walked on, one arm out in front of him.

Soon he bumped into a car, felt his way around it, and promptly bumped into another one. Dammit, there was a whole bunch of cars here. Cursing, Victor wandered among them as in a labyrinth, and it was a long time before he could proceed toward the vague glow marking the lobby entrance. The cars' smooth sides were damp with condensed fog. Sounds of giggling and hands being slapped away came from somewhere nearby.

The lobby was empty tonight: no one was playing blind man's bluff or tag, fat ass jiggling as he ran, or sleeping in any of the chairs. The floor and furniture were littered with crumpled raincoats, and some clever prankster had hung his hat on a ficus. Victor went up the carpeted stairs to the second floor, where music blared. In the hallway to the right, every door to the MP's rooms stood ajar. Greasy food smells, cigarette smoke, and the stink of overheated bodies wafted through the air. Victor turned left and knocked on Diana's door. No response. The door was locked, the key sticking out of the keyhole.

Victor entered, turned on the light, and placed the bottle on the nightstand. Footsteps sounded nearby, and he looked out into the hall. A strapping man in a black dinner suit was strutting down the right-hand hallway. He paused in the stairwell to look in the mirror, threw back his head, adjusted his tie (Victor had just enough time to observe a yellowish, swarthy, hook-nosed profile and a sharp chin), but then something changed: he slouched down, twisted his body slightly to one side, and, hips waggling hideously, disappeared into one of the wide-open doors. Poseur, Victor thought, uncertainly. Off to puke, no doubt . . . He looked to the left, but saw only darkness.

Victor removed his raincoat, locked the door, and went off to search for Diana. I should stop by Rossechepert's, he thought. Where else could she be?

Rossechepert occupied three interconnected suites. The first bore signs of recent feasting. Piles of filthy plates, ashtrays, bottles, and crumpled napkins towered atop soiled tablecloths. The room was empty except for a sweaty bald guy snoring all alone in a platter of aspic.

The adjacent suite was impenetrably smoky. Scantily clad jailbait—none of it local—bucked and writhed its way across Rossechepert's gigantic bed. They were engaged in a bizarre game with the apoplectically red-faced Mr. Mayor, who buried himself in the girls' bodies like a pig in acorns, bucking and oinking with pleasure. Also present were Mr. Police Chief sans uniform jacket, His Honor the City Judge with eyes bulging out of their sockets in asthmatic agony, and a twitchy person in lavender, unknown to Victor. These three were locked in zealous combat at miniature billiards, having hoisted the table onto the nightstand. Against the wall in the corner, meanwhile, sat the gymnasium headmaster in a bespattered regimental coat, legs splayed wide and an idiotic smile playing on his lips. Victor was about to leave when he felt someone plucking at his pant leg. He looked down and recoiled. Before him, on all fours, was member of parliament, knight of various orders, author of a much-ballyhooed proposal for increasing fish populations in the Kitchigan Reservoir—Rossechepert Nantes himself.

"I wanna piggyback ride," Rossechepert bleated beseechingly. "Gimme a piggyback ride! Giddyap!" He was non compos mentis.

Victor gently freed himself and made his way into the final suite. It was there that he saw Diana. At first he didn't register that it *was* Diana; then he thought sourly, How nice! This suite was filled with men and women he barely knew standing in a circle and clapping, and in the center was Diana, dancing wildly with that yellow-faced poseur, he of the hook-nosed profile. Her eyes and cheeks were incandescent, and her hair was flying above her shoulders. She was raising hell. Hook-nose had to work hard to keep up.

Strange, thought Victor. What's the story here? Something's not right. He's a good dancer—an amazing one, in fact. Like a dancing school teacher. Not so much dancing as demonstrating how it should be done . . . Not like a teacher, even, but like a student doing his exams. He really wants that A . . . No, that's not it. Listen, buddy, that's Diana you're dancing with! Don't you get it? Victor consulted his imagination, as was his wont. An actor dances onstage, everything's good, everything's going off without a hitch, but there's trouble at home . . . Well, not necessarily trouble, it's just, they're waiting for him, when will he come back? And he's waiting, too, waiting for the curtain to fall and the lights to go out . . . No, he's not even an actor, he's just some random person pretending to be an actor playing some totally unrelated third party . . . Can't Diana feel it? It's all counterfeit. He's a dummy. Not a spark of chemistry between them, not a drop of seduction, not a shadow of desire . . . They're talking to each other, but it's hard to imagine what they could possibly have to say. Babycakes and honeybunch, together at last: *Not too hot, how about you? . . . Sure, I've read it, three times even . . .*

And now he saw Diana push her guests aside and accelerate toward him. "Let's dance!" she shouted from afar.

Someone blocked her path, someone else grabbed her arm, but she pulled away, laughing, while Victor scanned the crowd for the yellow-faced man, failed to find him, and felt a nasty jolt of worry.

She ran up to him, caught him by the sleeve, and dragged him into the center of the circle. "Come on, let's go! These're all friends, all these drunken, raggedy, shitty . . . Show 'em how it's done! That little boy didn't know what to do with me . . ."

Now they were in the circle's center, and someone in the crowd shouted, "Three cheers for Banev the Writer!"

The gramophone, which had briefly fallen silent, clanged and barked back to life. Diana pressed herself against him, then immediately leaped back. She smelled like perfume and wine, she was overheated, and now Victor had eyes only for her lovely, excited face and flying hair.

"Dance!" she shouted, and he began to dance. "So clever of you to come!"

"Yes. Yes."

"Why are you sober? You're always sober at the wrong time."

"I'll get drunk."

"Tonight I need you drunk."

"I'll do it."

"Then I can have my way with you. Not you with me, but the other way around."

"Yes."

She laughed, satisfied, and they danced in silence, seeing nothing, their minds a blank. Like in a dream. Like in battle. That's what she was like right now—like a dream, like a battle. Diana Who Is Possessed . . . Shrieks and clapping sounded all around them, and possibly someone else tried to cut in, but Victor threw him aside so he wouldn't interfere, and meanwhile Rossechepert was bellowing somewhere nearby, "Oh, my poor, drunken people!"

"Is he impotent?"

"You bet. I give him sponge baths."

"And?"

"One hundred percent."

"Oh, my poor, drunken people!" Rossechepert moaned.

"Let's get out of here," said Victor.

He caught her by the hand and led her away. The drunken and the raggedy stepped aside before them, stinking of booze and garlic. In the doorway, blocking their path, was a fat-lipped youngster with intensely rosy cheeks. He said something impudent, angling for a fight, but Victor said to him, "Later, later," and the youngster vanished.

They ran down the hall, hand in hand, and then Victor, not letting go, unlocked the door and, still not letting go, locked it from the inside . . . and it was hot, it had gotten unbearably hot and stuffy . . . and when the room, which had seemed large and spacious at first, began to feel narrow and tight, Victor got up and threw the window open, and the damp black air poured over his bare shoulders and chest. He returned to bed, fumbled in the dark for the gin bottle, took a swig, and passed it to Diana. Then he lay back down. Cool air enveloped his left side, while tender, silky heat caressed his right. Now he could hear the drunken revelers again—they were singing in unison.

"Will they be long?" he asked.

"Huh?" asked Diana sleepily.

"How long are they going to keep howling?"

"Dunno. What do we care?" She turned over and placed her cheek on his shoulder. "Cold," she complained.

They rolled around, getting under the covers.

"No sleeping," he said.

"*Mhm,*" she muttered.

"You feel good?"

"*Mhm.*"

"How about your ear?"

"*Mhm*—ow, get off!"

"Hey, can I stay here for a week or so?"

"Sure."

"But where?"

"I'm tired! Let a poor drunken woman sleep."

He stopped talking and lay still. She was already asleep. That's exactly what I'll do, then, he thought—stay here. It'll be nice, nice and quiet. Just not at night. Or maybe at night, too. Rossechepert can't drink like this every night, he's supposed to be undergoing treatment . . . I'll stay here for three or four days . . . or five or six . . . And I won't drink so much, I won't drink at all, only work . . . It's been so long since I worked . . . You have to be really bored to get going, so that all you want is to get to work . . .

He nodded off, then shuddered awake. And as for Irma . . . as for Irma, I'll write to Rotz-Tusov, that's what I'll do. So long as he doesn't chicken out—he's a chicken, Rotz-Tusov. Owes me nine hundred crowns . . . Of course, when it comes to Mr. President, we're all big chickens . . . Why, though? What are we so afraid of? We're afraid of change. We're afraid we won't be able to go to the writers' bar anymore and throw back a shot of distilled vodka . . . that the doorman will stop tipping his hat to us . . . or that there won't be any doorman at all, or that they'll make *us* into doormen. The worst thing is the mines . . . that would actually be bad. But that rarely happens, times have changed . . . practices are more liberal . . . I've thought about it a hundred times, and every time I decide there's really nothing to be afraid of, but I'm still afraid. Because it's brute force, he thought. It's terrifying when you're up against a dull, swinish, boar-bristled force, invincible, susceptible to neither logic nor feeling . . . And you can say goodbye to Diana . . .

He dozed off but was awakened by loud talking and animalistic chortling right beneath the window. There was the sound of bushes being trampled.

"Not like I can put 'em in jail," the police chief was saying drunkenly. "Ain't no law."

"There will be, soon," said Rossechepert. "Or am I not an MP?"

"Hey, is there a law says there's allowed to be a cesspit right near town?" barked the mayor.

"Soon!" Rossechepert repeated stubbornly.

"They're not contagious," bleated the gymnasium headmaster. "In the medical sense, I mean."

"Hey, nerd," said Rossechepert. "Don't piss with your fly up."

"Is there a law says honest people should go bankrupt?" barked the mayor. "Bankrupt! Is there?"

"Soon, I'm telling you!" said Rossechepert. "Or am I not an MP?"

What could I chuck at them, I wonder? thought Victor.

"Rossechepert!" said the police chief. "Are you my friend or what? I carried you, you bastard, I got you elected. And now they prance around town, the scum, and I can't do nothing. There's no laws, you understand?"

"Soon," said Rossechepert. "I'm telling you: soon. In connection with the contamination of the atmosphere—"

"Ethical contamination!" the headmaster interjected. "Ethical and moral."

"Huh? . . . In connection with, uh . . . the, uh, poisoning of the atmosphere and due to insufficient increases in the fish population in surrounding reservoirs . . . liquidate the disease and reestablish . . . uh . . . in a distant location. How's that?"

"Give us a kiss," said the chief of police.

"Good man," said the mayor. "Good head on your shoulders. Give me your cheek . . ."

"'Snothing," said Rossechepert. "Easy peasy . . . Shall we sing? No, never mind. Let's have another little nip."

"Yes, yes. Another nip, then off to bed."

More crunching branches, then Rossechepert's voice in the distance: "Hey, nerd boy, you forgot to zip your fly!" Then everything was quiet. Victor dozed off again, enjoyed some minor dream, and then the telephone rang.

"Yeah," Diana said hoarsely. "Yeah, it's me . . ." She cleared her throat. "No, it's nothing, I'm listening . . . Everything's great, I think he was very pleased . . . What?"

She kept talking, her body draped over Victor's, and suddenly he felt all her muscles tense.

"Odd," she said. "OK, I'll take a look . . . Yes . . . Good, I'll let him know." She hung up, climbed over Victor, and turned on the bedside light.

"What happened?" asked Victor sleepily.

"Nothing. Go back to sleep, I'll be right there."

Through half-closed eyes he watched her gather up her scattered undergarments, and her face was so serious it alarmed him. She dressed quickly and walked out, straightening her dress as she went. Rossechepert is ill, he thought, straining his ears. Finally drank himself silly, the old goat.

It was so quiet in the enormous building that he could clearly hear Diana's footfalls in the hallway, but instead of going right to Rossechepert's, as he expected, she turned left. A door creaked somewhere and the footfalls ceased.

He turned over and tried to go back to sleep, but in vain. He realized he was waiting for Diana and wouldn't be able to fall asleep until she returned. He sat up and lit a cigarette. The bump on the back of his head began to throb, making him wince. Diana still wasn't back. For some reason, he remembered the dancer with the hook-nosed profile. What's he got to do with anything? thought Victor. An actor playing a different actor who, in his turn, is playing yet a third actor . . . Oh, now I see: that guy came from the left, which is exactly where Diana went. Made it as far as the stairwell before turning into a poseur. First he was playing the Expert Schmoozer, then he switched to Profligate Fop . . .

Victor's ears pricked up again. It's uncommonly quiet, everyone's asleep . . . someone's snoring . . . The door creaked again, and he could hear footsteps approaching. Diana entered, her face still serious. Nothing was over; events were still underway.

Diana walked over to the telephone and dialed. "He's not there," she said. "Yes, I'm sure he left . . . Me too . . . Please, it's no bother at all. Good night."

She hung up, stood there for a moment gazing into the darkness outside the window, then sat down on the bed next to Victor. She held a small flashlight in her hands. Victor lit another cigarette and handed it to her. She inhaled silently, thinking hard, then asked, "When'd you fall asleep?"

"I don't know, hard to say."

"After me, though?"

"Yes."

She turned to look at him. "You didn't hear anything, did you? Like screaming, or a fight . . ."

"No," said Victor. "Everything seemed pretty peaceful to me. First they sang, then Rossechepert and friends were pissing right under our window, and then I fell asleep. They were all getting ready to go home at that point."

She threw her cigarette out the window and stood up. "Get dressed," she said.

Victor smirked and reached for his underpants. I hear and obey, he thought. Obedience is a great thing. Just remember not to ask any questions. He asked, "Are we walking or driving?"

"What? . . . Walking first, and then we'll see."

"Did someone disappear?"

"Seems that way."

"Rossechepert?"

He suddenly felt her eyes on him. She was looking at him doubtfully, beginning to regret including him. She was asking herself, *Who is he, exactly, that I should take him along?*

"I'm ready," he said.

She still hesitated, toying pensively with the flashlight.

"Well . . . all right. Let's go, then." She didn't move a muscle.

"Should we break off a chair leg?" Victor offered. "Or a piece of bed?"

She started. "No. A chair leg won't do it." She opened a desk drawer and took out an enormous black pistol. "Here," she said.

Victor tensed up, but it turned out to be a small-caliber sporting pistol, unloaded in the bargain. "Bullets, please," said Victor.

She looked at him uncomprehendingly, then glanced at the gun and said, "No. We won't need any. Let's go."

Victor shrugged and stuck the gun into his pocket. They went down to the lobby and out onto the porch. The fog had thinned; it was drizzling weakly. There were no cars near the porch. Diana turned off onto a little footpath between the wet bushes and switched on her flashlight. What a stupid situation, thought Victor. I desperately want to ask what's going on, but that's not allowed. It'd be great to figure out a way to ask, though. Obliquely. Not ask, but, like . . . make some casual remark where the question's implied. Will fighting be required? I really don't feel like it today.

I'll go with a good pistol-whipping, right between the eyes. How's my bump doing, by the way? The bump was exactly where he expected it to be, and it ached. Pretty strange, the job description for a nurse in this sanatorium . . . Then again, I've always thought of Diana as a woman of mystery. From the first, and then for the five days that followed. . . Ugh, it's so damp out here, I should've taken a good swig before leaving . . . Look at me, he thought with pleasure. No questions. I hear and obey.

They rounded the side of the building, made their way through the lilac, and ended up in front of the gate. Diana shined her flashlight onto it. One metal spoke was missing.

"Victor," she said quietly, "we're going to walk along the path now. Stay behind me. Watch your step and don't go off the path. Got it?"

"Got it," Victor said obediently. "A step to the left or to the right is considered an escape attempt."

Diana climbed through the hole in the gate and shined her flashlight so Victor could see. Then they started downhill, very slowly. They were on the eastern slope of the hill, where the sanatorium stood. All around them, invisible trees blustered in the rain. Once, Diana slipped, and Victor barely managed to grab her by the shoulders. She wrenched herself free impatiently and walked on, repeating, "Watch your step. Stay behind me." Victor looked down, obediently, at Diana's feet shifting in and out of the leaping disk of light. At first, he kept expecting something like another blow to the back of the head, right on top of his existing bump, but then he decided: unlikely. It wouldn't make sense. It was probably just some escaped psycho—maybe Rossechepert had finally drunk himself into delirium tremens, and now they were going to drag him back at unloaded gunpoint . . .

Suddenly, Diana stopped and said something, but her words didn't reach Victor's consciousness, because in the next second he saw, right near the path, a pair of shining eyes, immobile, enormous, scrutinizing him from under a prominent wet forehead—just eyes and a forehead, nothing more, no mouth, no nose, no body, nothing. That heavy, damp darkness, and in the circle of light, shining eyes and an unnaturally white forehead.

"Bastards," said Diana, her voice catching in her throat. "I guessed as much. Animals."

She fell onto her knees, the flashlight beam skimmed the black body, and Victor saw a shiny metal arc, a chain in the grass, and then Diana commanded, "Hurry, Victor." He crouched down beside her and only then realized it was a bear trap with a man's leg inside.

He grasped the metal mandibles with both hands and tried to separate them, but they only gave a little and then snapped shut again. "Idiot!" Diana shouted. "Use the gun!" He clenched his teeth, got a better grip, strained his shoulder muscles until they popped, and forced the jaws open. "Pull," he said hoarsely. The leg disappeared and the metal arcs closed again, catching his fingers. "Hold the flashlight," said Diana. "Can't," Victor replied sheepishly. "I got caught. Get the gun out of my pocket." Diana, cursing, reached into his pocket. He opened the trap again. She inserted the pistol grip between the jaws and he freed himself.

"Hold the flashlight," she repeated. "I need to look at his leg."

"The bone's shattered," said a tense voice in the darkness. "Take me to the sanatorium, and call a car."

"Right," said Diana. "One minute. Victor, give me the flashlight, and lift him up."

She shined the light onto the man. He hadn't moved and was sitting with his back against the trunk of a tree. The lower half of his face was wrapped in a black neckerchief. Four-eyes, thought Victor. Clammy. How'd he get all the way over here?

"Grab him," said Diana impatiently. "Put him on your back."

"One minute," he answered. He recalled the yellow rings around the eyes and felt his gorge rise. "One minute . . ." He squatted down next to the clammy and turned his back to him. "Put your arms around my neck," he said.

The clammy turned out to be skinny and light. He didn't move and or even breathe, or so it seemed to Victor. Nor did he moan when Victor stumbled, though his body convulsed each time. The path was much steeper than Victor had anticipated, and, by the time they made it to the gate, he was out of breath. The next step was shoving the clammy through the hole in the gate, but they managed it eventually.

"Where to?" asked Victor when they'd made it to the building.

"To the lobby, for now," answered Diana.

"No," said the clammy in the same tense voice. "Leave me here."

"It's raining," Victor objected.

"Quit jabbering," said the clammy. "I'm staying here."

Victor didn't answer but started up the stairs.

"Leave him," said Diana.

Victor stopped. "What the hell! It's raining out here," he said.

"Don't be an idiot," said the clammy. "Leave me . . . here . . ."

Victor, still saying nothing, bounded up the steps three at a time, opened the door, and walked into the lobby.

"Cretin," the clammy said quietly, and dropped his head onto Victor's shoulder.

"Numbskull," said Diana, catching up to Victor and grabbing his sleeve. "You'll kill him, idiot! Go back out there and lay him out in the rain! Right now, do you hear? What're you standing there for?"

"You're all insane," said Victor, irritated and confused.

He turned, kicked the door open, and walked back onto the porch. The rain had seemingly been waiting to ambush him. Just a second ago, it had been drizzling lackadaisically. Now, all at once, it came down in a real torrent. The clammy groaned softly, lifted his head, and suddenly began breathing heavily, as if he'd been run ragged. Victor still hesitated, searching instinctively for some kind of shelter.

"Put me down," said the clammy.

"Into a puddle?" asked Victor with savage bitterness.

"It's a matter of indifference . . . Put me down."

Victor lowered the clammy carefully onto the porch tiles, where he immediately opened his arms and stretched out. His right leg was unnaturally twisted, and the intense porch light gave the enormous forehead a bluish-white cast. Victor sat down on the steps nearby. All he wanted was to return to the lobby, but it was impossible—to leave a wounded man here in the pouring rain so he could go back into the warmth. How many times have I been called an idiot today? he thought, wiping his face with his palm. Too many times, methinks. But actually, there may be a grain of truth in it. After all, an idiot, also known as a numbskull, also known as a cretin, and so on, is an ignoramus who stubbornly persists in his ignorance.

But hey, look, he really seems to be doing better in the rain! He's opened his eyes, and they're not so frightening anymore . . . A clammy, he thought. Yes, he's definitely more of a *clammy* than a *four-eyes*. How on earth did he get caught in that bear trap? And where did the bear traps come from, anyway? He's my second clammy today . . . both were in trouble. They were in trouble, and now so am I, because of them . . .

Off in the lobby, Diana was on the phone. Victor listened in. "His leg! Yes. The bone's shattered . . . All right . . . OK . . . Hurry, we're waiting."

Through the glass door, Victor saw her hang up and run up the stairs. Something's gone wrong with the clammies in this town. There's some kind of fuss around them. They're in everyone's way all of a sudden, even the headmaster's. Even Lola's, he remembered suddenly. She seemed real upset about them, too . . . He looked at the clammy. The clammy looked back at him.

"How are you feeling?" asked Victor. The clammy was silent. "Can I get you anything?" asked Victor, a little louder. "A sip of gin, perhaps?"

"Stop yelling," said the clammy. "I can hear you just fine."

"Does it hurt?" asked Victor, compassionately.

"What do you think?"

What an incredibly nasty person, thought Victor. Then again, who cares—he and I won't ever see each other again. Plus, he's in pain . . . "It's OK," he said. "Just sit tight for a few more minutes. Someone's coming for you."

The clammy didn't answer; his brow furrowed and his eyes fell shut. Now he looked like a corpse lying flat and immobile beneath the pouring rain. Diana ran out onto the porch, doctor's bag in hand, knelt by the clammy, and began to manipulate the injured leg. The clammy growled quietly, but Diana uttered none of the soothing words doctors usually say in these situations. "Can I help?" asked Victor. She didn't answer. He stood up, and Diana, without turning her head, said, "Wait, don't go."

"I'm not going anywhere," said Victor. He watched her deftly apply a splint.

"You're still needed," said Diana.

"I'm not going anywhere," Victor repeated.

"Actually, though, you could run upstairs if you wanted. Go on, take a swig of something while there's still time, but then come right back here."

"Don't worry," said Victor, "I'll be fine."

Somewhere behind the veil of rain, a motor purred and headlights flashed. Victor saw what looked like a jeep carefully turning into the gate. It rolled up to the porch and out climbed Yul Golem, struggling mightily with his cumbersome raincoat. He went up the steps, bent over the clammy, and took him by the hand.

The clammy said, his voice muffled, "No shots."

"All right," said Golem, and looked at Victor. "Lift him up."

Victor picked up the clammy and carried him to the jeep. Golem got there first, opened the back door, and climbed inside.

"Give him here," he said from the darkness. "No, legs first . . . What're you waiting for . . . Hold his shoulders up . . ."

Breathing heavily, Golem squirmed inside the car. The clammy growled again, and Golem told him something Victor didn't understand, or maybe he was just swearing: "Six points on your neck . . ." Then Golem climbed back out and shut the door. As he got behind the wheel, he asked Diana, "Did you call them?"

"No," answered Diana. "Should I?"

"No point now," said Golem. "They'll just screw everything up. Good-bye." The jeep pulled away, rounding a flower bed, and sped off down the sandy path.

"Let's go," said Diana.

"Sure, let's swim away," said Victor. Now that it was all over, he felt only irritation.

Back in the lobby, Diana put her arm through his. "It's all right," she said. "You'll change into dry clothes, take a swig of vodka, and everything will feel OK again."

"I'm dripping like a wet dog," Victor complained, annoyed. "Also, maybe now you'll finally explain what just happened?"

Diana sighed wearily. "Nothing happened, really. I shouldn't have left the flashlight back there."

"Bear traps on the road—is that standard practice around here?"

"The mayor's been setting them out, the bastard."

They went up to the second floor and started down the hallway.

"Is he insane?" Victor inquired. "That's a criminal offense. Or is he actually insane?"

"No. He's just a bastard who hates clammies. Like everyone else around here."

"So I gathered. It's not like we loved them in my day, either, but bear traps . . . What did the clammies ever do to them?"

"You have to hate somebody," said Diana. "Some places they hate Jews, other places it's black people, and in our town we hate clammies."

They stopped in front of a door. Diana turned the key and entered. The lights went on.

"Hold on," said Victor, looking around. "Where have you brought me?"

"The lab," said Diana. "One second."

Victor stayed in the doorway, watching Diana make her way around the enormous space, closing all the windows. Puddles glinted darkly on the floor beneath each one.

"What was he doing over here at night?" asked Victor.

"Where?" asked Diana, not turning around.

"On the footpath . . . You knew he was here, didn't you?"

"Well," she said, "they don't really have good drugs in the leprosarium. So occasionally they come around here to ask us for some."

She closed the last window and made a final round of the lab, examining benches full of instruments and labware.

"It's all so disgusting," said Victor. "What a great government we've got. Nothing but bullshit wherever you turn . . . Let's go, I'm cold."

"One minute," said Diana.

She picked up something hanging on the back of a chair—some sort of dark clothing—and shook it out. It was a dinner suit. She hung it up carefully in the closet with the lab coats. What's a suit doing here? thought Victor. A familiar-looking suit, no less . . .

"All right," said Diana. "You can do whatever you want right now, but I'm getting into a hot bath."

"Listen, Diana," said Victor tentatively. "Who was that guy . . . with the nose . . . and the yellow skin? That man you were dancing with."

Diana took him by the hand. "Well, you see," she said after a pause, "that was my husband . . . my ex-husband."

3. FELIX SOROKIN

ADVENTURE

I'd neglected to take my nitroglycerin last night. Not because I forgot, but because it had occurred to me that nitroglycerin and alcohol don't mix. Which meant that this morning, I felt very sluggish and apathetic. I kept having to force myself to do things: wash, get dressed, tidy up, eat breakfast . . . Over half the bottle of cognac remained, and probably a glassful of the wine spritzer; I hesitated, trying to decide if some hair of the dog was in order, but then immediately remembered, quite inopportunely, that doctors today consider "hangover syndrome" the main sign of alcoholism, and abstained. Thank God there's no Clara hovering around me, I thought. Thank God I'm totally alone!

And of course, at that very moment, Katya called to ask (mostly concerned, of course, but with a touch of venom), "Have you been skipping pills again?" And of course, I once again had to lie and make excuses, especially since I had once again put no effort toward getting a fur coat made for her at the Writers' Union dressmaker. Although Katya wasn't calling about the coat after all: as it turned out, what she wanted was to stop by today or tomorrow to bring me my food order. That was all. We hung up, and, in my joy, I splashed a bit of cognac into my glass and finally felt some relief.

The weather outside was beautiful. Last night's blizzard was a distant memory; the sun, unseen since New Year's Eve, was now out, the whimsically curved snowdrift on my terrace sparkled merrily, and it was clearly freezing, billows of white steam trailing after every passing car. The barometric pressure had stabilized, and nothing on earth now prevented me from getting to work on my screenplay.

First, however, I called the dressmaker's three times in a row, striking out each and every time. I have to say, these calls were purely ritualistic: if a man really intends to have a coat made for his daughter, he has to go to the dressmaker's himself, make a vast number of allegorical movements and a vast number of allegorical statements, constantly running the risk of eliciting either open disrespect or a vile, petty evasiveness.

I then sat down at the typewriter and started right in with a sentence I'd invented but not used yesterday. I'd saved it up as fodder for today: "They aren't the ones who get hit, it's their comrades to the right . . ." At first, everything went swimmingly, zippy as a cadet at the Suvorov Military School, but in a little more than an hour I found myself sitting in a languid pose, dully reading the last paragraph I'd written, over and over again: "The Commissar can't look away from the burning tank. Tears are pouring down his cheeks behind his glasses, but he doesn't wipe them. His face is motionless and calm."

I could tell that I was stuck, hopelessly and for a good long time. The problem wasn't that I didn't know how events would unfold after this point; I'd calculated out all possible events twenty-five pages in advance. No, it was much worse than that: I was experiencing something like mental nausea.

Yes, I could clearly picture the Commissar with his half-collapsed trench and his burning Tiger tank. But it was like the whole thing was made of papier-mâché, or cardboard and painted plywood. Like it was playing out on the stage of some third-rate House of Culture.

And for the umpteenth time, I thought with glum satisfaction that you either have to write about things you know really well or about things nobody knows. Most people wouldn't agree—but so what? Like my daughter Katya always says: you always have to stay in the minority.

God damn it all, I thought, with something like despair. There do exist writers who have the gift, to whom fate has granted the ability to describe war as it really is . . . Russian Virgils capable of leading us through the bowels of that utterly unforgettable hell of fire and ice . . . We have Simonov, my dearly beloved Konstantin Mikhailovich Simonov, and Vasil Bykov, that bitter master, and the incomparable Bogomolov, and Vyacheslav Kondratiev's story *Sashka*, and Grisha Baklanov, another favorite of mine, and the early Bondarev . . . There's no way I could name them all, and I don't need to. Why bother enumerating them? I should be mourning the fact that I'll never be one of them. I didn't earn that honor by shedding my blood and sweat in the trenches, and now I never will. And so, in the end, there's no difference at all between the venerable Felix Sorokin and some kid, born in '54, who up and decides to write about the Battle of Kursk. Note that he does not decide to write about the construction of the Baikal-Amur Mainline, or about squabbles at the research institute where he works, but about something he's only seen on screen, in the war films of Yuri Ozerov. Them's the breaks, Felix Alexandrovich, if we're being honest . . .

I absolutely cannot stand spinning my wheels like this when I'm working—it makes me ill. And so I decided not to let myself sink into despair. I certainly have enough to do; there's no need to sit around and mope. They're waiting for me on Bannaya.

Hurriedly, crumpling the pages, I stuck the screenplay drafts into the plastic folder I'd reserved for them, then started getting dressed. *"The miller's joy is wandering, is wandering!"* I mumbled, pulling on my shoes (creakily). *"The water teaches us to move!"* I sang, full-throated, sticking *The Koryagins*, that brilliant play, into a separate folder. I was suppressing fear. "If worse comes to worst, I'll return the advance!" I said loudly, pulling on my coat. But the advance wasn't the problem. Lately, this wheel-spinning thing had started descending on me more and more often; and not even wheel-spinning, if we're honest—real fits of disgust, directed at the work that keeps food on my table.

As I stood waiting for the elevator, I began thinking about something that was guaranteed to distract me. It had now been three days since anything ridiculous or stupid happened to me, as though Whoever Is Supposed to Oversee My Fate had finally run out of ideas and couldn't even muster a dumb prank . . . Meanwhile, the elevators kept not coming, neither the big nor the little one, and I knocked on the doors of each in turn and strained my ears. I could make out a muffled echo of voices coming from below. Cursing, I started down the stairs.

When I got to the tenth floor, I saw that the poet Kostya Kudinov's door was open wide. A broad, white-coated back was emerging from the doorway. *Not again* flashed through my mind. I wasn't wrong: Kostya Kudinov was being carried out on a stretcher. The doors of the big elevator had been propped open to accommodate him. Kostya was pale to the point of greenness, his clouded eyes kept either rolling back or crossing at the bridge of his nose, and his bespattered, listless lips hung loosely.

I even thought, initially, that Kostya was unconscious, and I couldn't say that the sight bitterly shocked or even upset me. He and I were mere acquaintances—neighbors living in the same building and affiliates of a writers' organization whose membership numbered in the thousands. About ten years ago, during some campaign or other, he publicly denounced me in a capricious but quite caustic address. True, he later apologized, saying he'd confused me with another Sorokin, Sorokin the children's writer, and since then we'd nod to each amiably whenever we crossed paths, we'd exchange rumors, we'd lament the fact that we hadn't yet gotten together for a drink. But otherwise, he was more or less nobody to me. So now I took one look at him and figured he'd probably had a few too many again. In short, if all had been left to indifferent nature, the poet Kostya Kudinov would have been carried into the waiting elevator, the doors would have closed, concealing him from my eyes, and I would have found out the details from the doctor in the white coat and, later that night, relayed this minor event to someone or other at the Club.

But, as it turned out, Whoever Is Supposed to Oversee My Fate was still full of life.

"Felix!" said Kostya in tones of such desperation that the paramedics suddenly stopped, waiting for him to go on. "God himself must have sent you to me, Felix . . ."

Here his eyes rolled back in his head and he fell silent. But no sooner did the paramedics, confident that there was nothing further, continue on their way, than he began to speak again. He spoke haltingly, somewhat incoherently, his croak dropping down to a whisper. He kept demanding that I write something down, and I, of course, obediently opened my folder, got out a ballpoint pen, and jotted down on the inner fold: "Sokolniki Metro station, Bogorodskoye Highway, bus 239, institute, Ivan Davydovich Martinson, mafusallin." That is, I was now supposed to haul ass to the opposite end of Moscow, look for some unknown institute on Bogorodskoye Highway, and, once there, locate a certain Martinson and ask him for some of this . . . mafusallin . . . for Kostya. ("All I need is two or three drops . . . I'm not supposed to have any, but I don't care, he has to give me some . . . I'll die otherwise . . .") Then the elevator doors closed, and I was alone.

I will be perfectly frank. I felt absolutely no pity, none whatsoever; still less did I desire to perform any complex transformations in space and in my personal time. What the hell? Who was he to me? Some drunk poet I barely knew! Who, moreover, had denounced me—maybe mistakenly, but denounced nonetheless! I could always, of course, go nowhere at all, including Bannaya;

this was all just too upsetting and irritating. But just then, another man in a white coat emerged from Kostya's apartment and stood next to me, waiting for the elevator. Judging by his horn-rimmed glasses and stethoscope, he was a doctor—like the kindly Doctor Aybolit from the children's books, with an unlit Belomor in the corner of his mouth. And I asked him what was wrong with Kostya, and he said it could very well be botulism, a severe case. I felt afraid. I'd once experienced tainted canned goods in Kamchatka and nearly given up the ghost.

The elevator doors opened, the doctor and I walked in, and I asked, glancing down at the notes on my folder, whether this "mafusallin" would be of any help to Kostya. The doctor looked at me uncomprehendingly, so I repeated it again, slowly: *ma-fu-sal-lin*. But the doctor knew nothing at all about mafusallin, and I concluded that this must be a new medication, a cutting-edge one, even.

We parted ways at the ambulance. Poor Kostya was carted away to the new hospital in Biryulyovo, while I headed to the Metro.

I still had no desire to go anywhere. I confessed honestly to myself—it was like a revelation—that I'd never liked Kostya: he was an alien presence, a thoroughly stupid and talentless person. His botulism did arouse a certain amount of pity, but also irritation, and with each passing minute the irritation increasingly outweighed the pity. Why the hell should I, an ill and elderly man, schlep all the way across the city to some mysterious institute, dwelling-place of some mysterious Martinson, holder of the mysterious mafusallin, which even a doctor has no idea about? Wandering, asking directions, searching, and finally begging like a supplicant—since Kostya himself had admitted that he wasn't supposed to get any. It was bound to turn out that there was no such institute, and even if there was, that no one by the name of Martinson worked there . . . that this whole thing was a delusion, product of Kostya's semiconscious fever dreams—after all, the man's been poisoned, and quite severely, too . . .

I made my way to the Metro, sinking in snow that building caretakers had failed to clear away, slipping repeatedly on unseen icy furrows, thinking up more and more excuses, even though I was becoming increasingly certain that the more excuses I invented, the likelier it became that my path would take me all the way across Moscow, past Sokolniki, to see Ivan Davydovich Martinson. And then, three drops of precious mafusallin in hand, I'd travel back across Moscow and thence to Biryulyovo—all to rescue the poet Kostya Kudinov, whom I didn't like and certainly didn't need.

It's a straight shot from my place to Sokolniki, thank God, and at this time of day (around two), the Metro wasn't terribly crowded. I sat in a corner and closed my eyes. My thoughts took on a somewhat different, more professional character.

For the umpteenth time now I thought about how literature, even the most realistic kind, only vaguely approximates the reality of people's interior worlds. I tried in vain to recall even one piece of literature in which the hero, finding himself in a position like my own, allows himself to express the wish not to go, clearly and unequivocally. The reader would never forgive him! Even if the hero ended up going, overcoming thousands of obstacles and performing untold feats of heroism, his image would remain forever besmirched—in the eyes of the reader, and especially in the eyes of the publisher.

It's true that, in our liberal times, a positive hero can have a lot of faults. He can get drunk on a regular basis or even pilfer a few items no one would miss (for selfless reasons, of course). He can be a bad husband and father, an incompetent slob, a totally careless and superficial person. But one thing is forbidden to the positive hero: practical misanthropy. It is easier for a camel to pass through the eye of a needle than for a hero to earn the designation of "positive" if he, the hero, even once permits himself to ignore a bird with an injured wing. And therefore, domestic and international standards dictate that I, Felix Alexandrovich Sorokin, am at best a moral cripple.

This conclusion made me laugh and put me in a good mood. For one thing, now I once again had an excuse to avoid going to Bannaya—an excuse that was not only utterly legitimate but extremely humane. And for another thing . . . for another thing, one reason is quite enough. On the way back I'll take a taxi, I've got enough cash for that, thank God. I'll make a quick stop in Biryulyovo, drop off the mafusallin, then take the same taxi straight to the Club . . .

I started to doze off, thinking sleepily about the odd name of this cutting-edge medication. Mafusallin. It produces certain associations. Turkey. The Near East, for some reasons. Methuselah. The Bible? . . .

I had no trouble finding the institute. The bus stopped directly across from a security checkpoint flanked by a towering fence that stretched endlessly along the deserted road. The checkpoint's door was unmarked; near the threshold stood a man with his hands in his pockets, wearing no coat but only an ushanka with the earflaps sticking up. He looked askance at me but said nothing. I stepped into the sweltering building.

I should probably have zipped through the passageway and into the institute without a second thought, but I never get away with that sort of thing. I brought my face right up to the tiny security window and asked, imploringly, "Where can I find Ivan Davydovich Martinson?"

Behind the window sat a wizened old geezer in a greasy military tunic. He was drinking tea from a saucer, alternating sips with nibbles from a sugar cube. He placed the steaming saucer on the table, taking his time, drew out a greasy uniform cap, and carefully pulled it over his bald pate. "Permit," he said.

I said I had no permit. This confession confirmed his worst suspicions, as though they'd warned him this very morning that someone would try to weasel his way in without a permit and instructed him that this exact person should not, under any circumstances, be allowed inside. He climbed out from behind his table, pushed himself out into the passageway, and blocked the turnstile.

I began to whine and beg, but the more piteously I whined, the more intractable the cruel old man became. This went on until the moment I realized I had stumbled onto an insurmountable obstacle and could now speed away with a clear conscience—first to Bannaya, and then to the Club. Delighted, I called the old fogy an "ancient louse" and walked away, extremely pleased with myself.

But alas, it was not to be!

"So he won't let you through," affirmed the man in the hat with the cocked earflaps.

"He's an ancient shitlouse," I explained.

And then the man, entirely unprompted, told me at great length that nowadays no one goes through the checkpoint, no one's allowed through, you know, nowadays everyone goes through the fence, not a hundred steps from here is a hole in the fence, which is how everyone gets through nowadays, 'cause who wants to do a two-mile detour along the fence on Bogorodskoye Highway when you can just go *through*, straight across the compound, then through the fence on the other side, and *bam*, there are you are, right in front of the liquor store.

What choice did I have? I thanked the nice man and followed his instructions to the letter. From the breach in the fence, a well-trodden path wound through the enormous, snow-covered compound. On the right-hand side was a massive construction site, frozen in time. On the left towered a five-story white brick building with large windows of the type found in schools. This was, apparently, the institute itself. Leading to it was a second path, also well-trodden, which forked away from the first.

At the institute entrance (a low, wide portico with a wide glass door under a wide concrete overhang), three men, all coatless but wearing ushankas with the earflaps sticking up, were unsealing a crate spangled with foreign labels. I walked past them, up the steps, and into the vestibule.

This was a capacious room flooded with mercury-vapor lamplight and filled with people who looked to me like they were doing nothing at all, just standing around in little groups and smoking.

Bitter experience had taught me not to ask anyone for anything but to proceed straight to the cloakroom, where I removed my coat, holding a glumly preoccupied expression on my face and trying to keep my folder in full view.

Then I found a mirror, combed my hair, and went up the stairs to the second floor. I'm not sure I could explain why I chose the second floor, not that anyone was demanding an explanation. Here were also tile floors, mercury-vapor lamps, and groups of people smoking cigarettes. I noticed a young man standing apart from the crowd. He also had a glum, preoccupied expression, and I immediately pegged him as someone who wouldn't question who I was, what I was doing here, or if I had the right.

I wasn't wrong. Absentmindedly, without even looking in my direction, he explained that Martinson was most likely up in his "outhouse," which was located on the third floor, turn right at the skeletons, outhouse number 37.

There weren't any skeletons when I got to the third floor—I still have no idea what the imaginative young man was talking about. "Outhouse number 37" turned out to be a large, light-filled room. It contained a great deal of glassware and many blinking lights; green curves snaked across tiny screens, exactly as one might expect; it smelled like artificial life and intelligent machines, and in the middle of the room, with his back to me, was a man speaking loudly on the telephone.

"Come off it!" he boomed. "What law? Keep going! Oh please! What does Lomonosov-Lavoisier have to do with it? Keep going, that's the main thing!"

Then he threw down the receiver, turned to me, and barked, "You want the local trade union committee!"

I said I was looking for Ivan Davydovich. Blood rushed to the man's face. He was enormously tall, broad-shouldered, with a powerful neck and a mop of disheveled, piebald hair.

"I said, what you want is the local trade union committee!" he yelled. "From three to five! You and I have nothing to talk about, got it?"

"Kostya Kudinov sent me," I said.

It was as though he'd lost his balance. "Kostya sent you! What's wrong?"

I explained. While I was explaining, he stood up, walked past me, and shut the door tight. "And who, exactly, are you?" he asked. The color had drained from his face, leaving him rather pale. He avoided meeting my gaze.

"I'm his neighbor."

"Yes, I got that," he said impatiently. "Who *are* you, that's what I want to know."

I introduced myself.

"That name means nothing to me," he announced, and stared at the bridge of my nose. His eyes were black and close set—it was like looking down the barrel of a gun.

I felt enraged. Goddammit! Yet again, I was being forced to make excuses! "Your name doesn't mean anything to me either, by the way," I said. "And yet, I schlepped all the way across Moscow to see you—"

"Do you have any kind of ID?" he interrupted. "Anything at all."

I had no ID. I never do.

He thought for a moment. "All right, I'll take care of it myself. What hospital did you say he was in?"

I repeated the name.

"Oh Christ . . ." he mumbled. "It really is all the way across town . . . All right, you can go. I'll take care of it."

Seething, I turned around to leave. My hand was already on the doorknob when it hit him.

"Hey, excuse me!" he rumbled. "How did you get in here? You don't have a permit! You don't even have ID!"

"Why, through the hole!" I said, venomously.

"What hole?"

"In the fence," I said spitefully, and walked out. It was like that old joke: *So they're all sitting there covered in shit when out I come, dressed all in white!*

I was halfway down the stairs when an awful thought struck me: What if that ferocious Martinson was at this very moment making a phone call to make sure that, seconds from now, every hole in the fence is beset by carpenters and guards, and I'll be surrounded like Paulus at Stalingrad . . . I couldn't stop myself from breaking into a run, mentally cursing Kostya Kudinov, his botulism, and my own lame fate. Only after I noticed people turning around to stare did I manage to pull myself together, and by the time I reached the cloakroom, I had once again assumed the guise of a glumly preoccupied, businesslike person whose pockets teemed with permits and IDs.

When I reached the bottom of the building steps, I decided to turn around—why, I'll never know. And this is what I saw. Behind the door, pressing his enormous palms into the glass and displaying his pale face, was Ivan Davydovich Martinson himself, staring at my back as I walked away, like a vampire surveying a would-be victim.

I'm ashamed to admit that, once again, I broke into a run. In spite of my veins. In spite of my intermittent limp. Only after I'd dived through the hole in the fence and resurfaced on Bogorodskoye Highway did my dignity cry out for succor. I slowed to a walk, buttoning my coat and straightening my hat. I very much disliked this whole adventure, and I especially disliked Ivan Davydovich Martinson. I cursed Kostya and his botulism over and over again, swearing to myself that henceforth I would never, ever, for nothing and no one . . .

After all these hijinks, Bannaya was out of the question. To the Club—straight to the Club! To our union restaurant, paneled in brown wood! To that atmosphere of tantalizing smells! To my very own table with its starched tablecloth! Under Sashenka's wing . . . except no, today was an odd-numbered day . . . So the wing will be Alyonushka's. First thing I'd do is pay my tab, and order some herring, shiny with oil, so fatty it melts in your mouth, cut into little chunks, sprinkled with finely sliced scallion . . . and three or four hot, crumbly potatoes with a cube of butter straight from the ice bath, and a little potbellied carafe of vodka (no, I wouldn't forgo that today, I had earned it) . . . and also marinated milk mushrooms, all slimy, swimming in their own juices, mixed with little slices of onion, and as much mineral water as I could drink . . . or beer? No, mineral water . . . And after I'd quelled my first hunger and worked up a real appetite, we would apply ourselves to meat solyanka, which, luckily, they still know how to cook at the Club. We would receive it in a faintly glinting metal pot, amber-colored, steamy, concealing beneath its surface various meaty delicacies and black, glistening olives . . . Goodness gracious, I'd almost forgotten the most important thing! The crescent roll! Our famous Club rolls with their convenient handles, puffy, soft, brown, and crusty . . . with a couple on the side to take home. Yessiree, and for the second course—

But I never got to savor the second course, because I suddenly felt a vague discomfort, an awkwardness of some kind, and, returning to reality, found myself speeding along in the Metro, with two beanpoles holding Adidas bags looming over me. Through the gap between their bodies, a pair of pale, bespectacled eyes were staring at me intently. I glimpsed these eyes only for a second, along with a red Norwegian goatee and a white muffler peeking out from between the lapels of a checked coat. Then the train began to slow, the beanpoles stepped closer together, and the person observing me disappeared from view.

I felt he was examining me with unseemly attentiveness, as though my face were dirty or something were wrong with my clothes. Just in case, I made sure I hadn't put my hat on backward in my haste. But a minute later, the beanpoles separated once more, reforming the gap, and I saw that my observer was dozing peacefully, hands folded on his belly. He was a middle-aged man in wire-rimmed glasses and a checked coat of a type that had been in fashion several years ago. Back then, those coats had greatly impressed me by being reversible: one side would be, say, black checks on a gray background, while the other would be gray on black.

This brief episode finally distracted me from my gastronomic visions. For some reason, I now recalled a hospital stay where, for a whole month, I was fed monstrously bland, extravagantly overcooked food, which depressed me so intensely that the doctors ultimately relented and allowed Katya to bring me some cold chicken tabaka. I shuddered to think what awaited the poisoned Kostya in this regard. But I didn't have the time to think any of this through, because the train stopped at Kropotkinskaya and I hurried toward the exit.

The dim-sighted woman on duty at the Club entrance demanded to see my Writers' Union card, and for the umpteenth time I tried to explain to her that I'd been a writer for the last quarter century and walked past her ancient person into the Club for at least the last five years. She did not believe a single word I said, but then good old Uncle Kolya blared from the bowels of the cloakroom: "He's one of us, Marya Trofimovna!" And she let me through.

As I talked with Uncle Kolya about the weather, I disrobed with ostentatious languor, grabbed a copy of the Club newspaper, leaving a coin in its place, combed my hair and mustache, bowing to my reflected acquaintances as they surfaced in the depths of the mirror, and then, still bowing, filling up gradually with warm and cozy feelings, I walled myself off from all that was uncomfortable and alarming, and cheerfully walked out into the restaurant.

From that point forward, everything went according to plan, the only deviation being that they were out of marinated milk mushrooms. As I was finishing my solyanka, the usual crowd started appearing at my table. The first was Garik Aganyan, who was due at his seminar in an hour. He therefore declined to drink and ordered something small. We barely got two words out before Zhora Naumov stood up from a table in the far corner and approached us. In one hand he held a half-empty carafe, and in the other, a bowl with some leftover chicken salad. We learned that he had just arrived in Moscow that morning, stopping by on his way from Krasnodar to Tallinn. We learned that the harvests down south promised to be good, and as for everything else, it was, as always, in God's hands.

And at that moment, Valya Demchenko appeared on our horizon, holding under his arm a new walking stick with a handle shaped like a lion's head. We considered this walking stick, discussed the winter crops and last year's phylloxera blight; Garik, sketching on the tablecloth with his fork, explained how we should understand an article that had recently appeared in the central press under the title "A Hole in the Universe." And after that, I described the troubles that had befallen Kostya Kudinov and me today.

My account met with somewhat more listlessness than I had expected. Garik mumbled dismissively, "Don't worry, he'll be back—shit always rises to the top." Valya lazily rehearsed a well-worn bit he himself had written about Kostya: "Yesterday in the White Hall Comrade Kudinov, Assistant Chairman of the Foreign Commission, mistook a group of Paraguayan writers for"—*pause*—"a group of Uruguayan writers . . ." Meanwhile, Zhora Naumov, gazing at the world through his shot glass, recounted an address Kostya Kudinov, then a student at the Literature Institute and a vivacious, rosy-cheeked teetotaler, once gave at a plenary meeting for his cohort in the memorable year 1949.

When Zhora finished, everyone was silent for a moment, and then Valya asked, with interest, "So what did you do?"

"What did *I* do?" said Zhora, aggressively. "I wanted to punch him in the face, but he was huge back then, a professional weight lifter, right, whereas I'd been shot through both legs and was swinging around between two crutches like an old man's scrotum between his legs."

"But later, I mean," said Garik. "When you could walk without crutches again . . . By the way, did he happen to apologize to you when 1959 rolled around, God bless it?"

"Oh, you bet! He even dedicated a poem to me. In the *Literary Gazette*. It was in the style of Pushkin's poems about his Lyceum friends."

"If you like, be a Tatar?" Valya suggested, venomously.

We chuckled, without any special joy, and then turned to the topic of poetry, and then, somehow, the conversation imperceptibly shifted to Bannaya. It turned out that everyone except me had already been there.

Disciplined Garik had gone immediately, back in October. It was nothing to write home about. Some shabby machine, maybe an EC-1010 or possibly one of the crappier Minsk models. Sitting there is some parasite in a black lab coat; he takes your manuscript, sheet by sheet, and feeds it into the intake slot. Numbers light up on the display, whereupon you are released and can go home.

Zhora, who'd gone in right before New Year's, objected: he said there was no machine, only a bunch of gray filing cabinets; the parasite wore not a black lab coat but a white one; and it smelled like baked potatoes. It was all nonsense, a deception of the working man. If you want to know my opinion, said Zhora Naumov, a.k.a. Hirsch Naumovich, it's all very simple: some Jew from the Academy of Sciences hoodwinked our Fyodor Mikheyevich and is, as we speak, distilling a dissertation from the sweat of our collective brow.

In response to this anti-Semitic invective, Valya Demchenko noted that, were any of this true, it would only be half the trouble. The real problem, he said mysteriously, is that a cybernetic editor had been in the works now for many years, a helpful gift from the scientists to the writers. Actually, the robotic editor himself has already been created, and now they're just using our manuscripts to train him. And when that machine becomes operational, that's when it's curtains for us, dear sirs, because it's not just going to fix grammar mistakes or improve style, it'll be able to sniff out subtext from a mile away. That machine, dear sirs, will instantly know who's who and what's what.

I gazed at Valya with growing respect, sensing within his absurd flight of fancy a noble kind of insanity—one near and dear to me. Garik giggled openly, while Zhora, ever the pragmatist, asked sternly where exactly Valya Demchenko had come by this information.

"His eyes!" said Valya with heartfelt emotion. "You have to look the man in the eyes, dear sir! Not at his coat—who cares if it's black or white!—but at his eyes! As soon as I looked him in the eyes, I understood everything!"

Garik poured him some beer, and Valya continued. We learned that the robotic editor was only the beginning of a new era. It's a cumbersome, stationary, expensive machine. But if you really want to know, dear sirs, there are special typewriters already in the works—for now, only for us prose writers. And installed in those typewriters are electronic censors. Picture this: there you sit, hunting and pecking the word "ass," but what appears on paper is "hams," or "duff," or "keister," or, worst-case scenario, an "a" followed by two dots.

Suddenly, Petenka Skorobogatov—nicknamed our "Sweet Soviet Boy"—appeared in our midst. He wasn't there just a second ago, and now there he sat, between Garik and Valya, helping himself to some vodka from my carafe. His eyes, as usual, were bloodshot and shifty, and, as usual, his skin was flaky and covered in red blotches. Also as usual, he was bursting with news and rumors, which seemed important and credible at first glance but spoiled on contact with fresh air, transforming into lies and boasts. We couldn't get a word in edgewise, and so, in our sorrow, we began to listen.

To start with, on the topic of Bannaya, he claimed to possess extremely reliable information straight from the Source. (He pointed ceilingward with a fat index finger.) Valya is absolutely right: they're turning everything over to machines now, because corruption has gotten out of hand—you can't trust anyone anymore. They've already activated the prototype; its first recommendation was to fire every publisher and editor in chief in Moscow. And so he, Petenka Skorobogatov, is going to hold off on signing two contracts he recently received. Why? Well, because there's no point. There will be new publishers and new editors soon enough, and then the contracts will need to be reviewed . . .

"No, don't interrupt me, because I'm leaving for Zambia tomorrow, and I still have to go get vaccinated, and you all keep interrupting me . . . I'm trying to explain to you about Bannaya. That machine over there is special. It measures your talent. In absolute value. Did you hear what Sashka Tolokonnikov pulled? Instead of his own gibberish, he gave them five pages from Sholokhov's Nobel-winning *And Quiet Flows the Don*! Of course the machine goes berserk—it wasn't designed with numbers like that in mind—and now Sashka's being raked over the coals. For behavior unbecoming of a Soviet writer . . . But that's nothing! Iraida herself arose from her deathbed to schlep her drafts over to Bannaya. She must have thought that the machine would affirm her and praise her to the skies, but instead it spits out zero point zero! *Bam*, just like that! So then she loses it, smacks them all upside the head with her umbrella! You guys spend all your time sitting here in total ignorance, whereas I went down to Bannaya yesterday to take a peek—and it's surrounded, there's mounted police . . . Fyodor's sweating bullets, super sorry he decided to get involved at all, not to mention that he has to go there himself at some point . . . So I say to him, I say, 'Buddy, what are you so worked up about? You can take some of *my* drafts!'"

Yeah. That's what he's like, our Petenka Skorobogatov, our Sweet Soviet Boy. I downed a shot of vodka and started thinking about how there's really nothing new under the sun. Everything has already been invented. I remembered a time, some fifteen years ago, when the late Anatoly Yefimovich opened up to me and ended up describing the plot of a new comedy he was writing. It was set in a Writers' Center. One day, this inventor drags in a fantastical contraption called . . . What was it again? I feel like it was something really clumsy . . . Right! The "Litalmeter." The writers are stupid enough to rejoice—at last, everyone will know that Ivanov is shit, whereas I'm a genius! But then, when the machine began to gift them with objective truth . . . In the end, I think they dismembered it into individual nuts and bolts and then collectively denounced the inventor, which brought about exactly the consequences you'd expect . . . How disappointed Anatoly Yefimovich was when I, full of apologies and excuses, lent him Akutagawa's "Mensura Zoili," written way back in 1916 and published in Russian by the mid-1930s! It's impossible to invent anything new. Everything has either already been done or is occurring in reality.

I banged my fist on the table, looked Petenka Skorobogatov right in his piggy little eyes, and quoted loudly enough for the whole restaurant to hear: "'Now that this thing has been invented, all those writers and artists who peddle dog meat and call it mutton—they're all finished!'"

Whereupon I stood up and headed to the bathroom. I was pretty well plastered already. I could tell because my cheeks had gone numb and I had a persistent urge to thrust out my jaw. Perhaps I'd had enough for today. It was time to return to my Penates, especially since Katya was supposed to stop by with my food, not to mention the half bottle of cognac still in the Penates' possession. And there was something else that I was supposed do for the Penates. But what was it?

I remembered on the way back to my table. It behooved me to call and ask after Kostya Kudinov, the poet: Had he croaked yet? There I was, drinking vodka with Petenka Skorobogatov, our Sweet, Sweet Soviet Boy, while Kostya was maybe shoving off. Unfair!

When I called Kostya's apartment, his wife picked up. She didn't sound bad at all—in fact, she was pretty cheerful. I introduced myself, then asked, "So, how's Kostya doing?"

"I'm so glad you called, Felix Alexandrovich! I just got back from visiting him, literally just walked through the door . . . Felix Alexandrovich, he was absolutely adamant that you should come by!"

"Of course," I said. "But how's he doing?"

"He pulled through, thank God. So you'll come by?"

"Well, actually . . ." I mumbled. "Maybe tomorrow, around this time."

"No! No, Felix Alexandrovich, he said it has to be today! Just has to be! That's what he said: if Felix Alexandrovich calls, tell him that he *must* come today! He said it's really urgent, really important . . ."

"Sure, all right . . ." I replied, and we said our good-byes.

No good deed goes unpunished, I thought as I walked back to the restaurant. You give an inch and they take a mile. And by the way, I'd like it noted that there was not one word of thanks! That malingerer sends me running up and down Moscow for an entire day, I go through all kinds of hair-raising hijinks, and at the end of it—what do you know!—it starts all over again. Time to drag myself to yet another place, like a beast of burden, and not one word of thanks . . .

Garik was no longer at the table—he'd already left for his seminar—and in his place sat Petenka's buddy. I know his face, I've been introduced to him a couple of times, but I can never remember his name or his connection to literature. Seems to me he spends entire days in our billiard room—and that's the extent of his relationship with Soviet letters.

Also, in my absence, a big bottle of wheat vodka had appeared on the table, and with it, as had often happened before, my good friend and neighbor Slava Krutoyarsky, gaunt, swarthy, long haired, clad head to toe in fake leather, and inclined to theorizing. "What is literary criticism?" he was asking Zhora Naumov, who had already removed his fuzzy blazer and hung it on the back of his chair. "And by the way, I'm not talking about what passes for literary criticism today, know what I mean?" Every other sentence or so, Slava liked to ask his interlocutors if they knew what he meant.

Zhora nodded magisterially to signal that yes, he did know; pensively, Valya Demchenko followed suit. As I sat down I did the same, just in case, while Petenka and his buddy nodded in unison so energetically that vodka splashed from their glasses.

"Criticism is a science," Slava continued, looking right at Zhora. "It deals with connecting or juxtaposing the creator's hysteria with the needs of society, know what I mean? It's about teasing out the relationship between the creator's deep suffering and the everyday life of the collective. *That* is the task of criticism. Know what I mean?"

The collective found this idea so interesting and sound that we all began asking one another for pen and paper. To write it down. But no one had either of those things, so we called over Alyonushka, begged her for a pencil stub and a sheet from her notepad, and then Petenka demanded that Slava repeat his formulation. Slava made an earnest attempt and failed. Zhora Naumov also failed, but did manage to confuse everything by weaving in the word "quintessence." And as they clamored, interrupting one another, I found myself thinking that no matter how we define criticism, it does vastly more harm than good. Soviet critics aren't in the business of considering the "quintessence of creators' hysteria"; they're in the business of bulldozing the literary landscape for the purpose of settling personal and aesthetic scores. *That's* how it is.

I drank a shot and chased it with a slice of cold steak. Meanwhile, the terminological discussion about criticism had very naturally shifted to the politics of honoraria.

My own view on this question is simple: the bigger the honorarium, the better. All that writerly chatter about "stimulation by material means" isn't worth a red cent. Take our Sweet Soviet Boy: he's always shouting that if they paid him like Alexei Tolstoy, he'd write like Leo. But he's full of it, the hack. However much you pay him, what he writes will still be shit. You could pay him five hundred rubles a page, or seven hundred, and he'd keep droning on: stay in school, kids, stay in school, getting bad grades is bad, you big sillies, and also, it's wrong to pick on the weak. And they'll keep right on publishing him, because in any children's publishing house they allot 30 percent of the plan to literature about schoolchildren. Whether there are enough good writers to fill that 30 percent is another story; the assumption is that there are. Whereas Valya Demchenko could be paid two hundred rubles, or one, and he'd still write well; he wouldn't start writing worse just because they paid him worse, even though they allot exactly 0 percent of the plan to his critical urbanism, and the critics attack him like dogs—

At that moment, someone touched my shoulder. Turning around, I saw Lidiya Nikolayevna, the administrator. She drily informed me that she'd been waiting for me for a whole hour, that Konstantin Ilyich Kudinov had called from the hospital and asked me to come immediately. I don't know what lies that malingerer fed her, but her manner was cold as hell. I think she got it into her head that I'd promised to attend the bedside of my suffering friend but had instead gone on a bender, betraying all and sundry. Once again, I was to blame. For what, I ask you?

I gave Slava some money to cover my share and, my gait firm and sober, started down the carpeted path to the vestibule.

The Club restaurant was brightly lit and already full, not an empty chair in sight. Here and there tables had been pushed together to accommodate large groups; tobacco smoke settled overhead in multiple layers; transparent moisture gleamed in chalices uplifted; a chorus of metal implements clinked on ceramic and glass. The air was filled with assurances of friendship, and already, in the far corner, next to the artificially white-hot fireplace, a certain gray-haired someone in a plush turtleneck was declaiming poetry with the barking voice of a deacon, while in another corner, a group of hussars stood at attention, raising full glasses to chest level as they listened to a toast suffused with the most ambitious expectations, regretting only, no doubt, that they were no longer permitted—as had been the custom in the era of the previous Club director—to hurl their glasses to the ground after emptying them and stomp the shards underfoot; and Shura Peklevany, who was not terribly well known to readers but almost universally beloved at the Club, was already working the room, laughing in friendly greeting, clapping people on the back, kissing the hands of the ladies, and refusing again and again invitations to sit, because his destination was one very specific table (Shura always knew exactly which table it behooved him to join on a given day). A maniple of critics and literary scholars, just out of a plenary meeting, talked loudly among themselves as they descended the wooden stairs connecting the mezzanine to the restaurant, and then, arriving, split up and flowed among the tables, saying words of greeting, joining in, then taking their leave; and in the middle of this gyre, at the very center of the of the room, a clutch of young men were aggressively offering drinks to the editor of some peripheral journal—a square, even cube-shaped Asian man in a skullcap and a standard-issue suit jacket, its lapels studded with unfamiliar pins and medals . . . The beautiful life was in full swing, and meanwhile I had to drag myself to hell and back. I wondered glumly what else Whoever Is Supposed to Oversee My Fate had up his sleeve . . .

Luckily, I caught a taxi right away, and half an hour later the driver and I had found the hospital in Biryulyovo. When I entered his room, Kostya was sitting cross-legged on the bed, scraping out a bowl of cream of wheat with his spoon in disgust. He was dressed head to toe in hospital clothes but otherwise looked pretty good. Of course, I wouldn't call him rosy cheeked or robust; his face was far too pallid. But there was little of the dying man about him now, either, though his chin was still dirty—this time, it was cream of wheat.

The room turned out to have six beds in it. Someone on an IV drip lay on the one closest to the window, but otherwise the place was empty: everyone had gone to watch the hockey game.

When he caught sight of me, Kostya instantly leaped up and ran at me with such eagerness that I froze in fear: What if he intended to hug me? Luckily, he limited himself to squeezing and heartily shaking my hand. He squeezed, and shook, and chattered incessantly, for some reason constantly looking back at the body with the drip. He wouldn't let me say a single word. He told me all about how he vomited and then had diarrhea; how they first pumped only his stomach but then decided to pump his intestines, too; how they gave him shots, massaged him, and put him on oxygen. And all the while he kept glancing at his neighbor and, stepping on my toes, crowding me toward the doorway.

"What the hell are you shoving me for?" I finally asked. We were already in the hall.

"Let's have a seat," he said invitingly. "Look, there's a bench over there, near that plant."

We sat down. The hallway was completely empty; somewhere off in the distance, the duty nurse clinked and clattered her flasks. Kostya was still talking, though much less excitedly. I chalked up his frenzied joy at seeing me to a euphoria produced by frenetic gratitude, and even thought, as I recall, What do you know, the beast has feelings! And so, muscling my way into the first available pause, I benevolently inquired, "So, I gather it helped?"

"What, exactly?" he asked quickly.

"You know, your thingy . . . the Methuselah . . ."

"Yes!" he said in a voice husky with ecstasy, grabbing me by the arm again. "Yes! If not for that . . . But then they immediately started pumping my stomach, under pressure, can you imagine? They gave me *such* an enema, the wreckers! You know, I only understood today how terrible it must have been when the Spanish Inquisition tortured people that way . . . you know, by pumping water up their . . . If you can believe it, my eyes popped right out of my head—time to see an ophthalmologist, I guess!"

And off he went for round two: how he vomited and had diarrhea, and so on. He kept joking around the entire time—sometimes the jokes were even funny—and in general tried to portray everything in a humorous light, but the humor masked an unhealthy strain, and very soon it occurred to me that this was no euphoria of gratitude, that what was bubbling up and over the edge was probably the recently experienced horror of death, and I was just about to pat him soothingly on the knee when he suddenly cut himself off and asked, nearly whispering, "Why are you looking at me that way?"

"What way?" I was perplexed. "How am I looking at you?"

His gaze darted rapidly over my face, then vanished into the darkness behind the plant.

"You're not, never mind," he said evasively, then trained his eyes back on me. "I see you've been hitting the sauce, eh? Had a few, eh?"

"Perhaps," I said, and, unable to restrain myself, added, "If it weren't for you, I'd still be there now, enjoying myself."

"Don't you worry!" he said with a carefree gesture. "They'll boot me out of here tomorrow or the day after, and then you and I will have a drink. I'm going to treat you to some incredible cognac; I just had it shipped from the Caucasus . . ."

And he started telling me about the cognac he'd just had shipped from the Caucasus. Telling someone about cognac is as pointless and unnatural as describing the beauty of music in words. I stopped listening. All of a sudden, I began to feel ill. Those white walls, that smell of carbolic acid or maybe of death, the nurse's white coat bobbing around in the distance, the empty IV bags arrayed in front of every room . . . the hospital, zone of anguish and alienation . . . What the hell was I doing here? I wasn't the one who'd gotten poisoned, after all!

"Listen," I said resolutely. "You'll have to excuse me, my daughter's supposed to stop by today—"

"Of course, of course!" he exclaimed. "Go! Thanks so much for visiting."

He stood up. I followed suit, though I was now completely at sea. For a short while we gazed into each other's eyes in silence. I was perplexed and struggled to make sense of it all. Had he really demanded my presence so persistently—through his wife, through the Club administrator—just so he could tell me in exhaustive detail, twice, about getting his stomach and intestines pumped? It seemed to me that Kostya, for whatever reason, was also in turmoil. I could see it in his eyes.

And suddenly he asked—again, in a near whisper, "What?"

This question, too, was completely opaque. So I said, cautiously, "Nothing, nothing at all. I'll just be going, then."

"Yes, why don't you," mumbled Kostya. "Thanks, buddy . . ." He mumbled these words with something like caution or uncertainty, as if waiting for my cue.

"Is there anything else you want to tell me?" I asked.

"What about?" asked Kostya, now almost inaudibly.

"Jesus, I don't know!" I said, unable to contain my irritation any longer. "I have no idea why you made me leave the Club. Urgent business, they said, it's crucial that I come today, immediately . . . What business? What's the big rush?"

"Who said?" asked Kostya, and his eyes began to shift around nervously.

"Your wife . . . and Lidiya Nikolayevna . . ."

And now it came out that they'd misunderstood him. His wife had misunderstood him, and Lidiya Nikolayevna had *really* misunderstood him. He hadn't at all demanded that I come today, immediately, nor had he mentioned any urgent business to anyone . . . He was clearly lying; that much was obvious to the naked eye. But why he was lying, and where the truth actually lay, continued to elude my understanding.

"All right," I said with a wave of my hand. "So they misunderstood you. I'm glad you're feeling better. I'll be on my way now, I think."

I turned and started walking toward the exit. Kostya scurried beside me, alternately grabbing at my hand and squeezing my shoulder. He thanked me and apologized, apologized and thanked me, and then, near the telephone in the stairwell, something truly preposterous happened. Suddenly cutting off the stream of incoherent jabber, he seized me convulsively by my sweater front, pressed me into the wall, and hissed into my face, spraying me with spittle: "Don't forget, Sorokin! Nothing happened! Got it?"

This was so unexpected and even frightening that I was overcome with the same panic I'd felt as I fled that vampire, Ivan Davydovich Martinson.

"Wait, what are you doing?" I mumbled, trying to tear his unexpectedly tenacious and seemingly ossified hands from my person. "What the hell, have you gone completely out of your mind?" I shouted, filling my lungs with air and finally detaching that pale spider. Holding him with difficulty at arm's length, I said, "Pull yourself together, idiot! What the hell is wrong with you?"

I was much stronger, and soon realized I could hold him off and even immobilize him if I had to. The first wave of panic rolled away, leaving in its wake only a squeamish fear, not for my own hide, but fear of awkwardness, fear of this ridiculous situation—God forbid anyone should see us prancing around on the tile floor, breathing heavily into each other's faces.

He trembled and sprayed for a little while longer, repeating all the while "Nothing happened, got it? Nothing happened!" Then he went limp and began tearfully explaining that he'd made a mistake, that the institute was top secret, that neither I nor even he was supposed to know about it, that it was way above our pay grade, that we could get in big trouble, that they'd already warned him once, that if I breathed even one word, even one hint of it to anyone . . .

I let him go. Cringing, he rubbed at his red wrists and continued his tearful droning, saying the same thing over and over again, even verbatim. It was obvious that he was extremely demoralized and that every word he said was lies, from the first to the last. Once again, I couldn't understand why he was lying or what the truth might be. All I could gather was that a mistake had indeed been made: back when he was being carried out of his apartment, Kostya, fearing for his life, had in fact blabbed something even he wasn't supposed to know . . . But where could the wordsmith Kudinov, specialist in verses for holidays and jubilees, have possibly learned something like that? Unless the terrifying Martinson was cooking drugs in his "outhouse" near the skeletons and using Kostya to secretly sell them. At any rate, I now felt nothing toward him at all, other than squeamishness and an acute desire to get as far away from him as possible.

"All right, fine," I said, as calmly as I could. "What are you freaking out about? Use your head: What do I care about any of this? You say nothing happened—so nothing happened. Do you see me arguing?"

He launched into his explanation for a third time, but I moved him out of the way without a shred of pity and began descending the stairs at the fastest possible speed. My legs were shaking, pain shot through my right knee, and I had a strong urge to spit on the ground. But I didn't look back, not even when a hissing shriek reached me from the top of the stairs: "Sorokin! Watch yourself! I'm serious!" It was great advice, if you could look past the tone. And to think, if that bastard Lyonya the Schizo hadn't called me, none of this would have happened . . . Whoever Was in Charge of My Fate had been working overtime, that's for sure . . . Homeward, my friends, homeward, to the Penates, to my cognac and my Blue Folder!

Zipping up my coat in the cloakroom, I noticed something familiar in the mirror. On a bench directly behind me sat the black-and-gray checked coat. I turned around, continuing to pull at my zipper, and examined him. It was indeed the man from the Metro—red goatee, shiny metal frames, reversible checked coat—sitting there alone on a long white bench in the nearly empty lobby of a hospital in Biryulyovo, reading a book.

4. VICTOR BANEV

PRODIGIES

"It's been a while since I've seen you around town," said Pavor, sounding congested.

"Not that long," Victor countered. "Just two days."

"May I join you two, or do you want some privacy?" asked Pavor.

"Have a seat," Diana said politely.

Pavor sat down across from her and shouted, "Waiter, a double cognac!" Night was falling; the doorman was drawing the curtains. Victor turned on a lamp.

"I admire you," said Pavor to Diana. "To live in this climate and still have such amazing skin . . ." He sneezed. "Excuse me. This rain will be the death of me . . . How's work going?" he asked Victor.

"Not so good. I can't get anything done when it's overcast like this—all I want is a drink."

"What's this about you making a scene at the police chief's?" asked Pavor.

"Eh, it's nothing," said Victor. "Just looking for a little justice."

"But what happened?"

"The mayor, that ass, has been hunting clammies—with bear traps. One got caught and injured his leg. So I took the trap to the police and demanded they open an investigation."

"OK," said Pavor, "Then what?"

"Strange laws this town has. Since the victim never filed a report, officially there's been no crime, only an accident—for which no one but the victim is to blame. I told the police chief that I'd take that under advisement, which he said sounded like a threat. Then we parted ways."

"Where did all this happen?" asked Pavor.

"Near the sanatorium."

"The sanatorium? What was a clammy doing all the way over there?"

"I don't see how that's anybody's business," Diana said sharply.

"Of course," said Pavor. "It's just surprising . . ." He wrinkled his nose, shut his eyes tight, and sneezed noisily. "Ugh, dammit," he said. "Sorry about that."

He reached into his pocket and brought out a large handkerchief. Something fell to the floor with a clatter, and Victor bent down to retrieve it. It was a set of brass knuckles.

Victor picked it up and handed it back to Pavor. "What're you dragging that around for?" he asked.

Pavor, his face buried in his handkerchief, was looking at the brass knuckles with reddened eyes. "It's all your fault," he said in a muffled voice, then blew his nose. "You scared me with your stories . . . You know, apparently some local gang's been operating around here. Criminals, or hooligans maybe. For your information, I don't really enjoy getting hit."

"Do you get hit a lot?" asked Diana.

Victor looked at her. She sat in her chair, one leg crossed over the other, smoking with downcast eyes. Poor Pavor, thought Victor. You'll never know what hit you . . . He reached out and straightened her skirt.

"Me?" asked Pavor. "Do I look like someone who gets hit a lot? Better fix that. Hey, waiter, another double cognac! . . . Anyway, the day after our conversation I went to see some metalworkers—they made this little guy for me lickety-split." He examined the brass knuckles with a pleased expression. "It's a great little item, even Golem liked it."

"They never did let you into the leprosarium, did they?" asked Victor.

"No. They did not and will not let me in, I have to assume. I've lost all hope. I submitted complaints to three different departments, and now I'm sitting around drafting a report on the total cost of underwear requested by the leprosarium over the past fiscal year. Men's *and* women's. Riveting stuff."

"Don't forget to write that they're short on drugs," Victor advised him. Pavor raised his eyebrows in surprise.

Diana chimed in lazily, "Or you could ditch your scribbles, knock back a glass of mulled wine, and go to bed."

"I can take a hint," said Pavor with a sigh. "Off I go, then . . . You know my room number, right?" he asked Victor. "Come visit me sometime."

"Two-twenty-three," said Victor. "Will do."

"Good-bye," said Pavor, standing up. "Have a pleasant evening."

They watched him approach the bar, order a bottle of red wine, and make his way to the exit.

"You've got a big mouth," said Diana.

"Yeah," Victor agreed. "Guilty as charged. But see, there's something I like about him."

"Not me," said Diana.

"Not Dr. R. Quadriga, either. I wonder why?"

"He has a filthy mug," said Diana. "The blond beast. I know that breed. Real men. No honor, no conscience. He's a lord of fools."

"How about that!" said Victor with surprise. "And here I was, thinking he'd be just your type."

"There are no men today," Diana objected. "They're all either fascists or sissies."

"What about me?" Victor inquired with interest.

"You? You love pickled lampreys too much. And justice, at one and the same time."

"Correct. But that's a good thing, I think."

"It's not bad. The problem is, if you had to choose, you'd pick the lampreys. You're lucky you're talented."

"Why are you so mean today?" asked Victor.

"I'm always mean. You have your talent, and I have my meanness. If you took away your talent and my meanness, you'd be left with two copulating zeroes."

"Zeroes aren't all created equal," Victor remarked. "You yourself would make a pretty good zero—tall and well built. But also, if someone took away your meanness, you'd become kind, which wouldn't be the worst thing in the world."

"If you took away my meanness I'd be a jellyfish. To make me kind, you'd have to replace the meanness with kindness."

"It's funny," said Victor. "Usually women don't like to philosophize. But once they get going, they're surprisingly categorical. What on earth makes you say that you're all meanness and no kindness? It doesn't work that way. There's kindness in you too, it's just invisible behind all the meanness. Every human being is a little bit of everything, all mixed together. It's just that life tends to pick just one thing to squeeze out onto the surface."

A group of young men burst into the restaurant, and suddenly it was very noisy. They didn't stand on ceremony but cursed the waiter and sent him running for beer. Then they clustered around a table in the far corner, talking loudly and laughing at the top of their lungs. The enormous, thick-lipped, rosy-cheeked goon from before made his way to the bar, snapping his fingers and clicking his heels as he went. Teddy served him. The goon grabbed the glass with two fingers, sticking out his pinky, then turned his back to the bar and, leaning against it while crossing his legs, scanned the empty hall with an air of triumph. "Greetings to Diana!" he bellowed. "How's life?" Diana cast an indifferent smile his way.

"What on earth is *that*?" asked Victor.

"*That* is Flamen Juventa," said Diana. "Dear nephew to our police chief."

"I've seen him somewhere before," said Victor.

"Ah, screw him," said Diana impatiently. "All people are jellyfish with nothing extra mixed in. Very occasionally, you encounter someone real, who has something special—kindness, talent, meanness . . . take that away, and there'll be nothing left, they'll just be jellyfish like everyone else. You seem to think I like you because of your penchant for lampreys and justice. Bullshit! You have talent, you have books, you have fame, but otherwise you're just a brainless waste of space, same as everyone else."

"What you're saying is so deeply wrong it fails even to offend me," announced Victor. "But go on, your face changes in the most captivating way when you talk." He lit a cigarette and passed it to her. "Go on."

"Jellyfish," she said bitterly. "Slippery, stupid jellyfish. They hustle, slither around, shoot their guns—they don't know what they want or what they're doing, they don't love anyone or anything, not really . . . like worms in an outhouse . . ."

"How unseemly!" said Victor. "The image is certainly graphic, but quite unappetizing. And what's more, this is all banal. Diana, my dear, you're no thinker. This stuff might have played a century ago, in the provinces . . . Society, at any rate, would be pleasurably shocked, and pale youths with smoldering eyes would trail after you wherever you went. But nowadays, it's all self-evident. Nowadays, everyone already knows what people are—the question is what to do with them. And even that question, if we're honest, has gotten pretty old."

"Well, what do you do with jellyfish?"

"You mean, what do jellyfish do with jellyfish?"

"No. Us."

"As far as I know, nothing. Or maybe we can them."

"Whatever," said Diana. "Have you gotten anything done these past few days?"

"And how! I wrote a dreadfully touching letter to my friend Rotz-Tusov. If it doesn't compel him to find Irma a spot in a boarding school at once, you can put me out to pasture."

"Is that all?"

"Yes," said Victor. "Everything else I threw away."

"Jesus!" said Diana. "And here I was taking care of you, trying not to disturb you, shooing away Rossechepert . . ."

"Washing me in the tub," Victor reminded her.

"Washing you in the tub, making you coffee—"

"Hold on," said Victor. "To be fair, I washed you in the tub, too."

"Who cares?"

"What do you mean, who cares? You think it's easy to work after washing you in the tub? I wrote six possible descriptions of the process, none of them any good."

"Let me read them."

"Oh, no, that's for men only," said Victor. "And plus, I threw it all out, didn't I say that already? Anyway, it had so little patriotism and national identity that it wouldn't be fit for public consumption in any case."

"Tell me, how do you do it—do you first write the thing, then go back and put the national identity in afterward?"

"No," said Victor. "First, I saturate myself with national identity, to the depths of my soul. I read the speeches of Mr. President, brush up on the old heroic sagas, attend patriotic meetings. Then, when I start to puke—not when I feel nauseous, mind you, but when I actually start to puke—I get to work . . . Can we talk about something else? For example, what're we doing tomorrow?"

"Tomorrow you're meeting the gymnasium students."

"That'll be quick. What about after?"

Diana didn't answer. She was looking past him. Victor turned around. A clammy was approaching them in all his glory: black-clad, wet, a black neckerchief covering his face.

"Hello," he said to Diana. "Golem isn't back yet, is he?"

Victor was shocked at the transformation in Diana's face: it now looked like an ancient portrait. Not even a portrait, an icon—with strangely fixed features that leave you wondering: Is the effect due to the deliberate intention of a master, or to a mere craftsman's ineptitude? She didn't answer. She was silent, and so was the clammy who gazed at her, but there was no awkwardness in their silence—they were together, and Victor and everyone else were apart.

Victor disliked the feeling intensely. "Golem's probably on his way," he said in a loud voice.

"Yes," said Diana. "Please take a seat, he'll be along in a minute."

Her voice was normal, and she was smiling at the clammy with her indifferent smile. And now everything else returned to normal, too. It was Victor who was with Diana, while the clammy and everyone else were apart.

"Please!" said Victor gaily, pointing to Dr. R. Quadriga's armchair.

The clammy sat down and rested his black-gloved hands on his knees. Victor poured him some cognac. With a careless gesture, the clammy mechanically picked up the glass, rocked it back and forth, as though weighing it, then returned it to the table. "You haven't forgotten, I hope?" he said to Diana.

"Yes," said Diana. "Yes. I'll bring it right away. Victor, give me the room key, I'll be right back."

She took the key and walked quickly to the exit. Victor lit a cigarette. What's going on with you, friend? he said to himself. You've gotten a little up in your own head, gone soft or something, sensitive . . . jealous. Unnecessarily so. None of this concerns you in the slightest—all these ex-husbands, these strange friendships . . . Diana is Diana, and you're you. Rossechepert is impotent, right? Right. Let that be enough . . . He knew that it wasn't that simple, that he had already swallowed some sort of poison, but he said to himself: enough. And today—for now, at least—he managed to convince himself that it really was enough.

The clammy was sitting across from him, motionless and menacing as a scarecrow. He smelled of damp and of something else, too, something medical. Could I ever have imagined that someday I'd be sitting across a restaurant table from a clammy? Progress, my friends! It's moving along, however slowly. Or is it us, have we gotten so omnivorous—have we finally figured out that all men are brothers? Humanity, my friend, I'm proud of you . . . And you, sir, would you let your daughter marry a clammy?

"The name's Banev," he said, then asked, "How's the, uh, victim? The one who got caught in the trap?"

The clammy turned abruptly to face him. It's like he's looking at me from inside a trench, Victor thought. "Satisfactory," the clammy answered coldly.

"If I were him, I'd file a report with the police."

"No point," said the clammy.

"Why not?" said Victor. "It doesn't have to be the local police—you could file a report with the region."

"We don't want that."

Victor shrugged. "Every unpunished crime begets a new one."

"Yes. But that does not interest us."

They were silent for a moment. Then the clammy said, "My name is Zurzmansor."

"Famous name, that," said Victor politely. "Any relation to Pavel Zurzmansor, the sociologist?"

The clammy narrowed his eyes. "Not even a little," he said. "I've heard, Banev, that you're speaking at the gymnasium tomorrow—"

Victor didn't have time to answer. Someone shoved the back of his chair and said in a vigorous baritone, "Get the hell out of here, you dirty rat!"

Victor turned around. Towering over him was thick-lipped Flamen Juventa, or whatever his name was—dear nephew, in short. Victor had been looking at him for less than a second but already felt extremely irritated. "Who are you talking to, young man?" he queried.

"Your friend there," Flamen Juventa informed him genteelly, then barked out, "That means you, you soggy bastard!"

"One second," said Victor, and stood up. Flamen Juventa, smirking, looked down at him from his superior height, like a youthful Goliath, wearing a sport coat glittering with numerous logos, our rustic down-home Sturmführer, faithful support of the nation . . . rubber truncheon in his back pocket, scourge of the Left, the Right, and everything in between. Victor pointed at Juventa's tie and said, feigning concern and curiosity, "Hey, you've got a little something . . ." And when the youthful Goliath automatically bent his head to see the little something, Victor seized his nose firmly between thumb and forefinger.

"Hey!" cried the youthful Goliath, trying to free himself.

But Victor wouldn't let go. He took his time, feeling icy pleasure, thoroughly wrenching and twisting that strong, impudent nose, repeating, "Behave yourself, twerp, dear nephew, you shitty little storm trooper, you son of a bitch, you lout . . ." His position was exceptionally convenient: the youthful Goliath kicked his feet desperately, but the armchair stood between them; the youthful Goliath kneaded the air with his fists, but Victor's arms were longer, and so Victor kept on twisting, rotating, tearing, and wrenching right up until a bottle sailed over his head.

He looked up and saw the entire group blustering toward him, shoving aside tables and flipping armchairs—there were five of them, and two were very strapping indeed. For a moment everything stood still, like a snapshot: black-clad Zurzmansor, sitting back tranquilly in his armchair; Teddy, suspended over the bar in mid-leap; Diana, standing in the center of the hall with a white-wrapped parcel in her hands; and in the background, near the doors, the fierce, mustachioed face of the doorman—but closest of all were the vicious mugs with their gaping maws. Then the age of photography ended, and the era of film began.

Victor knocked the first thug down quite effectively with a punch to the cheekbone; he vanished and did not reappear for some time. But the next thug clipped Victor's ear. Someone else karate-chopped him in the face, having apparently just missed his throat. Yet a third someone—Goliath, free at last?—jumped on him from behind. They were all brutish street toughs, the support of the nation. Only one of them knew how to box. The others yearned not so much to fight as to mutilate: to put out an eye, tear apart a lip, injure a groin. Had Victor been alone, they would have maimed him, but then Teddy came up from the rear—Teddy, faithful believer in the Bouncer's Golden Rule that every bar fight must be nipped in the bud. From the left flank came Diana, Mad-Dog Diana, her teeth bared in hatred, looking nothing like herself, bearing not the white parcel but a heavy straw-wrapped bottle. Even the doorman made it into the fray—he was an older man, but, judging by his movements, a former soldier. He worked a set of keys like a sheathed bayonet. By the time two waiters came running from the kitchen, there was nothing left for them to do.

Dear nephew had fled, leaving his tape player behind. Another youngster lolled under a table—that was the one Diana felled with her bottle. As for the others, Victor and Teddy literally bore them away on their fists, cheering each other on with sporting shouts. Then they propelled them through the lobby and kicked them into the revolving door. Sheer momentum shot the defenders themselves out onto the street; it was only there, in the rain, that they became conscious of the totality of their triumph and calmed down some.

"Those shitty punks," said Teddy, lighting up two cigarettes at once—one for himself and one for Victor. "They've made a habit of it, brawling every Thursday. Last time they broke two armchairs when I wasn't looking. Who's going to pay for that? Me?"

Victor massaged his swollen ear. "Dear nephew's gone," he said with regret. "I never got the chance to work him over properly."

"So much the better," said Teddy pragmatically. "Best not to get involved with that fat-lipped bastard. His dear uncle's you-know-who, and he himself is the support of Order and the Fatherland, or whatever they call themselves . . . Hey, you've developed a taste for fighting, Mr. Writer. You used to be such a flimsy little runt—one punch would send you under the table. Good work."

"Such is my profession," sighed Victor. "I'm a product of the struggle for survival. You know how it is with us: all on one. And Mr. President for all."

"You don't mean to say that things get violent, do you?" asked Teddy with innocent surprise.

"What do you think! First they write an article about you, all full of praise, saying you're imbued with national identity and whatnot, and you go to find the critic, but he's got his friends with him already—all young, feisty scrappers, Sons of the President . . ."

"No kidding," said Teddy sympathetically. "And then what?"

"Depends. It can go either way."

A jeep rolled up to the building. The door opened, and out came the bespectacled young man with the briefcase and his beanpole companion, covering themselves with a single raincoat. The driver was Golem, who now also got out of the car. The beanpole watched with keen, somehow professional interest as the doorman smacked a straggling, still-disoriented brawler through the revolving door. "Too bad that guy wasn't with us," whispered Teddy, indicating the beanpole with his eyes. "There's an expert for ya! Not like you. He's a professional, got it?"

"Got it," Victor replied, also in a whisper. The young man with the briefcase and the beanpole trotted past them and dashed into the vestibule. Golem started in the same direction, unhurried, already smiling at Victor from afar, but Mr. Zurzmansor, white parcel in hand, blocked his way. He said something sotto voce, whereupon Golem immediately ceased smiling and returned to the car. Zurzmansor climbed into the back and the jeep zoomed away.

"Oh man," said Teddy. "Looks like we beat up the wrong guy, Mr. Banev. People bleed for him, and he gets into some random car and drives off."

"Don't start," said Victor. "He's a sick, miserable man. There but for the grace of God go you. Just think: we're about to knock a couple back, whereas he's off to the leprosarium."

"Leprosarium my foot!" said Teddy implacably. "You just don't get it, do you, writer?"

"Out of touch with the nation, am I?"

"Nation shmation—it's our life you don't get. Try living like we do: rain year after year, crops rotting in the fields, kids all out of control . . . Look around—not a single cat left in town, mice taking over . . . Bah!" he said, with a dismissive wave. "Let's go already."

They returned to the lobby, and Teddy asked the doorman, who was already back at his post, "So, what's the damage?"

"Not bad," said the doorman. "We got lucky this time. One floor lamp broken, filth on the wall, but I got some cash off of that last guy . . . Here, take it."

Counting the money as he walked, Teddy made his way to the restaurant, with Victor close behind. Order had been restored. The young man in glasses and the beanpole were already sitting, full of ennui, over a bottle of mineral water, melancholically fletcherizing their rote supper. Diana was sitting in her old spot, looking very pretty and lively. She was even smiling at Dr. R. Quadriga, now in his regular seat—usually she did not care for him.

A bottle of rum stood in front of R. Quadriga, but he was still sober and thus looked somewhat strange. "Congratulations on your victory," he said, greeting Victor glumly. "I regret that I could not be present at the event itself, if only to assist."

Victor collapsed into an armchair.

"Nice ear," said R. Quadriga. "Where'd you get it? Looks like a rooster's comb."

"Cognac!" demanded Victor. Diana poured him some cognac. "It is to her and only to her that I owe my victory," he said, gesturing toward Diana. "You pay for that bottle?"

"It didn't break," said Diana. "Who do you take me for? But did you see him fall? How beautifully he toppled, my God! If only they'd all follow suit . . ."

"Let us begin," said R. Quadriga glumly, pouring himself a full glass of rum.

"Rolled away like a mannequin," said Diana. "Like a bowling pin . . . Victor, are you OK? I saw them kicking you."

"I'm OK where it counts," said Victor. "I took special care to protect myself down there."

Burbling, Dr. R. Quadriga sucked the last drops of rum out of his glass, the same way a kitchen sink sucks in leftover water after the dishes are done. His eyes immediately clouded.

"We're already acquainted," Victor said hastily. "You are Dr. Rem Quadriga, and I am the writer Banev—"

"Please," said R. Quadriga. "I'm completely sober. But I'll drink myself to death yet. That's the only thing I still know for sure. You might not believe it, but half a year ago I arrived here a complete teetotaler. I have liver problems, enteritis, and other stomach issues. I am absolutely forbidden to drink, and now I'm drunk day and night . . . No one needs me, absolutely no one. It's never happened to me before in my life. I don't even get letters, because my old friends are away without right of correspondence, and my new ones are illiterate—"

"No state secrets, please," said Victor. "I'm unreliable."

R. Quadriga refilled his glass and began sipping at his rum as though it were cold tea. "It works better if you do it this way," he informed them. "Try it out, Banev. It'll come in handy. Don't look at me like that!" he said suddenly to Diana, enraged. "Take the trouble to conceal your feelings! And if you don't like it—"

"Hush now!" said Victor, and R. Quadriga wilted.

"They don't understand me," he said piteously. "Not a one. Only you, a little. You always got me. Except you're so rough, Banev—you always wound me. I'm all covered in wounds . . . They're afraid to scold me now, they only praise. Some bastard praises me—a wound. Another bastard praises me—another wound. But that's all behind me now. They don't know it yet . . . Listen, Banev! You've got such a lovely woman here . . . I'm begging you . . . Ask her if she'll come to my studio, please . . . Not like that, you idiot! As a model! You don't get it at all, I've been looking for a model like her for a decade already."

"Allegorical painting," Victor explained to Diana. "'The President with the Eternally Youthful Nation.'"

"Idiot," said Dr. R. Quadriga sadly. "You all think I sold out . . . And you're right, I did! But I don't paint presidents anymore . . . Self-portrait! Get it?"

"No," Victor admitted. "I don't. You want to paint your own portrait using Diana as a model?"

"Idiot," said R. Quadriga. "It will be the face of the artist . . ."

"He means my ass," Diana explained to Victor.

"The face of the artist!" repeated R. Quadriga. "You're an artist too, after all. As are those away without right of correspondence . . . and those in the ground without right of correspondence . . . and those who live in my house . . . or don't live there, rather . . . I'm telling you, Banev, I'm scared. Remember how I asked you to come live with me, at least for a little while? I have a villa, with a fountain . . . The gardener ran away, the coward . . . I can't live there on my own, the hotel's better . . . You think I drink because I sold out? Bullshit, this isn't some trendy novel . . . You'll understand once you've spent some time at my place . . . Maybe you'll even recognize them. Maybe they're not my friends at all, but yours. Then I'd understand why they don't recognize me . . . Walk around barefoot . . . laughing . . ." His eyes suddenly filled with tears. "Gentleman and lady!" he said. "How fortunate we are that Pavor is absent tonight! Your health."

"To your health," said Victor, exchanging glances with Diana. Diana was looking at R. Quadriga with squeamish worry. "No one here likes Pavor," he said. "Except me, the lone freak."

"A still pond," said Dr. R. Quadriga. "A frog jumps out. Chatterbox. Never says a word."

"Don't worry about him, he's just loaded," said Victor to Diana. "No big deal . . ."

"Gentlemen!" said Dr. R. Quadriga. "Madam! I consider it my duty to introduce myself! Rem Quadriga, doctor *honoris causa* . . ."

✦✦✦

Victor arrived at the gymnasium half an hour before the appointed time and found Bol-Kunatz already waiting for him. But he was a tactful boy and merely informed Victor that the meeting would take place in the assembly hall, then left immediately, citing urgent business. Left to his own devices, Victor wandered through the halls, looking into empty classrooms, inhaling the forgotten smells of ink, chalk, never-settling dust, the smells of fighting "till first blood," exhausting interrogations at the blackboard, smells of prison, disempowerment, of lies amplified into principles. He kept hoping for some sweet memory of childhood and youth, of chivalry, of friendship, of first pure love, but nothing came to mind, though he tried mightily and was ready to feel moved at the slightest opportunity. Nothing here had changed—the light-filled, stuffy classrooms, the scratched-up blackboards, the desks carved with initials and apocryphal jokes about right hands and wives, the barracks-like walls painted halfway up in cheery green, and the scuffed-up plaster on the corners—it was all as hateful as ever, filling the soul with rage and hopelessness.

He found his old classroom, though it took him a minute, found his old spot near the window, but the desk was different—only the windowsill still bore the deeply carved emblem of the Legion of Freedom. He could still vividly remember the heady enthusiasm of those days, the red-and-white armbands, the tin Legion Fund piggy banks, the furious bloody fistfights with the Reds and the portraits filling every newspaper and textbook, covering every wall—the face that seemed so significant and handsome at the time but was now flabby and stupid, with its boar-like snout and enormous, toothy, spittle-spraying mouth. We were all so young, so mediocre, so identical . . . And stupid, but you can't feel good about that stupidity now, even though you've wised up since. All you feel is burning shame for yourself at that age, a mediocre, pseudopragmatic pissant who imagined himself bright, irreplaceable, first-class . . . And even more shameful were the childish longings, the agonizing fear of the girl you'd been bragging about for so long that you couldn't possibly give up now, and then the morning after—your father's deafening wrath and your own burning ears, and those were your proverbial salad days: all that mediocrity, longing, enthusiasm . . . It's a bad scene, he thought. What if, fifteen years from now, it turns out that my current self is just as mediocre and unfree as my childhood one? But it'll be even worse than before, because today I consider myself a grown-up. I think I'm knowledgeable and experienced enough that I can afford to sit in judgment, be complacent . . .

Humility and humility alone, to the point of mortification . . . And always tell the truth, never lie—to yourself at least. Though it's horrible to mortify yourself when there are so many idiots around, so many philanderers, liars for profit, when even the best among us are mottled with stains like lepers . . . Would you want to be young again? No. Would you want to live fifteen more years? Yes. Because living is good. Even if you do get hit sometimes. As long as you manage to hit back . . . All right, enough. Let's leave it at this: real living is that type of existence that allows one to hit back. And now, let's go see what they're like these days . . .

The assembly hall was filled with a number of kids making their usual racket, which quieted down when Bol-Kunatz led Victor onto the stage and sat him down under an enormous portrait of the president—a gift from Dr. R. Quadriga—at a table covered with a red-and-white tablecloth. Then Bol-Kunatz walked to the edge of the stage and said, "Today we'll be hearing from well-known writer Victor Banev, a native son of our town." He turned to Victor. "Which do you prefer, Mr. Banev: Questions out loud or in writing?"

"I don't care," said Victor, without thinking. "The more, the better."

"In that case, the floor is yours."

Bol-Kunatz jumped down from the stage and sat in the front row. Victor scratched his eyebrow, scanning the hall. There were about fifty of them—boys and girls ages ten to fourteen—all gazing at him with composed anticipation. Nothing but prodigies around here, he thought in passing. He noticed Irma sitting in the second row on the right, and smiled at her. She smiled back.

"I studied in this very gymnasium," Victor began, "and once had the privilege of playing Osric on this very stage. I didn't know my lines and had to invent them on the fly. It was the first thing I'd ever invented without the threat of a C-minus hanging over my head. They say school's much harder now than it was in my day. They say you have new subjects to study, and what we took three years to learn you're now expected to master in one. But you probably don't notice that it's gotten harder. Scientists believe that the human brain is capable of accommodating much more information than you might initially think. It's just a question of shoving it all in there . . ." Aha, he thought, now I'll tell them about hypnopedia. But then Bol-Kunatz passed him a note: "Stop discussing scientific advancements. Talk to us like equals. —Valerians, 6th gr."

"All right," said Victor. "A certain Valerians from the sixth grade suggests I talk to you like equals and warns me not to explicate scientific advancements . . . Cards on the table, Valerians, I was actually about to start telling you about advancements in the field of hypnopedia. But I'm happy to renounce that intention, though I consider it my duty to inform you that most adults I consider my equals have only the foggiest notion of hypnopedia." He felt uncomfortable speaking while seated, so he stood up and walked across the stage. "I must confess, guys, I'm not a big fan of meeting my readers. You never know ahead of time what sort of reader you're dealing with, what he wants from you, and what exactly he's interested in. Which is why I try to turn all my talks into Q&A sessions. It can be pretty fun sometimes. Why don't I start? All right. Has everyone here read my works?"

"Yes," said several children's voices. "We have." "All of us."

"Fantastic," said Victor, perplexed. "I'm flattered, if surprised. All right, let's move on . . . Does the assembled body wish me to share the story of how one or another of my novels came into being?"

There was a brief silence, and then a skinny, pimply boy erected himself in the middle of the room to say "No." He sat back down.

"Fantastic," said Victor. "So much the better, since, contrary to popular opinion, there's never anything interesting about those kinds of stories. Let's move on . . . Do my esteemed listeners wish to learn about my plans for future novels?"

Bol-Kunatz rose and said politely, "You see, Mr. Banev, it would be better to leave questions directly related to your artistic technique to the end of the discussion, after the general picture is already clear."

He sat down. Victor stuck his hands in his pockets and crossed the stage again. This was getting interesting. Or unusual, at any rate. "Might you be interested in literary anecdotes?" he asked in confidential tones. "How I went hunting with Hemingway. How Ilya Ehrenburg gave me a Russian samovar. Or what Zurzmansor said to me when we happened to meet in a tram . . ."

"Have you really met Zurzmansor?" someone asked.

"No, that was a joke," said Victor. "So what's the decision on literary anecdotes?"

"Can I ask a question?" asked the pimply boy, erecting himself once more.

"Of course."

"What would you want us to be like in the future?"

Pimple-free, said a voice in Victor's mind, but he swept it away, because he realized this was getting serious. The question was a powerful one. I'd be grateful if someone could tell *me* what I want myself to be like in the present, he thought. But the time had come to answer.

"Smart," he said at random. "Honest. Kind . . . I'd want you to love your job . . . and work only for the good of humankind." (I'm bullshitting, he thought. What else can I do?) "Something like that."

His audience tittered quietly for a moment, and then someone asked, without standing up, "Do you really think that soldiers are better than physicists?"

"Me?!" said Victor, outraged.

"That's what I gathered from your novella *Disaster Strikes at Night*."

This from a flaxen-haired pipsqueak of ten. Victor grunted. *Disaster* might be a bad book or it might be a good book, but under no circumstances was it a children's book—to the point that not a single critic had managed to understand it. They all deemed it pornographic pulp that undermined public morality and national identity. The worst part was that the flaxen-haired pipsqueak had plenty of evidence for the idea that the author of *Disaster* thought soldiers "better" than physicists—in a certain sense, at least.

"The thing is," said Victor, with real emotion, "things can be . . . well . . . they can be a lot of ways."

"I'm not referring to the physiological aspects," countered the flaxen-haired pipsqueak. "I'm talking about the book's overall concept. Maybe 'better' isn't the right word . . ."

"I'm not referring to the physiological aspects either," said Victor. "What I mean is, there are situations where a person's level of education doesn't end up mattering."

Bol-Kunatz passed along two more notes from the audience: "Can a person be considered honest and kind if he works for the cause of war?" and "What is a smart person?" Victor started with the second question—it was simpler.

"A smart person," he said, "is someone who's aware of the imperfection and incompleteness of his knowledge, someone who strives to augment it and succeeds in doing so . . . Do you agree?"

A pretty girl stood up. "No," she said.

"What's the problem?"

"Your definition is nonfunctional. Any idiot can use it to determine himself 'smart.' Especially if other people support him in that view."

Wow, thought Victor. Mild panic gripped him. This was not at all like talking to one's writerly brethren. "Sure, in some sense, you're right," he said, surprising himself by switching to the formal *you*. "But the thing is, concepts like 'smart' and 'stupid' are historically contingent—subjective, really."

"Are you saying you yourself can't tell a smart person from a stupid one?" That question came from the last row, uttered by a dark-skinned, shaven-headed creature with lovely biblical eyes.

"Wait, why?" said Victor. "I can tell the difference. It's just, I'm not sure that my assessment would always agree with yours. There's an old aphorism: an idiot is anyone who doesn't think like you . . ." Usually, this bon mot made audiences laugh, but today the room just waited silently for what came next. "Or doesn't feel the way you do," Victor added.

He felt their disappointment acutely but didn't know what else to say. He couldn't establish a rapport with them. As a rule, audiences are quick to take the speaker's position, to agree with his judgments; soon enough, everyone understands who the idiots are—the implication being, of course, that this particular group is idiot-free. At worst, people disagree and get hostile, but even that's easy, because you can always needle and mock them. It's not hard for one person to argue with many, since one's opponents always contradict themselves. And there will always be someone who's louder and stupider than his peers—and that's the head you can dance on to the satisfaction of all.

"I'm not sure I understand," said the pretty girl. "You want us to be smart—meaning, according to your own aphorism, that you want us to think and feel as you do. But I've read all your books and found no positive program in them, just pure negation. On the other hand, you want us to work for the good of humankind. That is, in practice, you want us to work for the good of those filthy and unpleasant types that populate your books. But your books reflect reality, don't they?"

Victor finally felt like he was finding his footing. "You see," he said, "when I talk about working for the good of humankind, what I mean is precisely the transformation from filthy and unpleasant to clean and nice. But that desire of mine has nothing to do with my art. In my books, I try to depict everything as it is. I don't instruct anyone or say what needs to be done. At best, I depict the object to which force must be applied and call attention to things worth fighting against. I don't know how to make people change—if I did, I wouldn't be a trendy writer. I'd be a great pedagogue or a famous psychosociologist. Fiction should absolutely not, in general, either preach or lead. It should not offer specific scripts or create specific methodologies. This becomes clear if we examine our greatest writers. I worship Lev Tolstoy, but only as long as he retains his particularity, his unique talent for mirroring reality. But as soon as he starts exhorting me to walk around barefoot or turn the other cheek, I'm overwhelmed with pity and boredom . . . Writers are societal litmus tests; they can't actually produce change, except to a negligible degree. History teaches us that what changes society isn't literature—it's reforms or machine guns . . . or science, in our own day. At best, literature tells us who to shoot at, or what needs changing . . ."

He paused, remembering the existence of Dostoyevsky and Faulkner. But just as he was working out a way to mention the role of literature in investigating the seamy underbelly of the individual, someone in the audience announced, "Sorry, but this is all pretty trivial. And beside the point. The issue is that the 'objects' you depict have no desire to be changed. And what's more, they're so unpleasant, so neglected, so hopeless, that one doesn't really want to change them. They're not worth the effort, you see. Better to let them rot in peace—after all, they have no role to play. So for whose good, exactly, are you saying we should work?"

"Oh . . . now I get it!" said Victor slowly. It suddenly dawned on him: my God, these little twerps seriously think I only write about bastards, that I think everyone is a bastard, but in fact they've understood nothing, and why would they—they're children, after all. Strange children, pathologically clever ones, even—but they're still just children, with childish experiences and a childish grasp of human nature (plus the many books they've read), with childish idealism and a childish desire to pigeonhole everything as either "good" or "bad." Just like my writerly brethren . . .

"You really had me going there," he said. "Your grown-up talk made me forget that you actually aren't grown up at all, at least not yet. I know this is antipedagogical, but I do have to say it, because otherwise we'll never get out of this mess. What you just don't get, apparently, is how an unshaven, hysterical, inveterate drunk can still be a great person, a person you can't help loving, a person you worship, whose hand it's an honor to shake, because he made it through a hell it's terrifying even to imagine and managed to stay human nonetheless. You think all my heroes are filthy bastards, but that's not the bad part. You think I see them the same way you do. And that *is* the bad part. It's bad because if that's what you think, we'll never understand each other."

Who the hell knows what reaction he expected to his amiable little sermon. Did he think they would look at each other, embarrassed, or that their faces would be bathed in the light of understanding, or that the entire room would sigh with relief to signify that the confusion had been successfully resolved, and that now they could start all over again on a new and more realistic basis?

Regardless, none of those things happened. The boy with the biblical eyes in the back row stood up again and asked, "Could you please tell us what progress is?"

Victor felt insulted. Oh, sure, he thought. Next they'll ask if machines can think or if there's life on Mars. Everything's falling into place.

"Progress," he said, "is the movement of society toward a state where people don't kill, or trample, or torment one another."

"But what do they do instead?" asked a pudgy boy on the right.

"They drink and eat *quantum satis*," mumbled someone on the left.

"Well, why not?" said Victor. "There haven't been all that many times in human history where people could drink and eat *quantum satis*. To my mind, progress is movement toward a state of no trampling or killing. What people do at that point is, for me, sort of immaterial. I'll put it this way: it's the *necessary* conditions for progress that matter to me above all. As for sufficient conditions, those are a no-brainer."

"May I?" said Bol-Kunatz. "Let's consider the following scheme. Suppose automation continues at a roughly constant rate. Then, in a couple of decades, the vast majority of Earth's active population will exit both the production and service sectors, which will become obsolete. It'll be great: everyone's got enough to eat, there's no need for any kind of trampling, no one gets in anyone's way . . . but no one needs anyone else, either. Of course, some several hundred thousand people will be necessary to ensure that the old machines continue working without interruption and that new ones are constantly created. But most of the billions of people on Earth won't have any use for one another. Is that what we call 'good'?"

"I don't know," said Victor. "I mean, it's not the greatest. It's even sad, in a way . . . But it's still better than what we have today. So some kind of progress will definitely have been achieved."

"But would *you* want to live in that world?"

Victor thought about it. "You know," he said, "I'm having trouble imagining it, for some reason. But to be honest, I'd kind of like to try."

"But can you imagine a person who definitely *wouldn't* want to live in that world?"

"Of course I can. There are people, and I even know a few, who would get bored. In that world, there's no power to be seized, no one to order around, no one to trample. Of course, there'd probably be some who'd still try—because what an amazing chance to turn paradise into a pigpen! These people I'm thinking of would be all too happy to destroy your future world . . . So I guess what I'm saying is, I can't actually imagine people like that."

"What about your beloved heroes—would they be satisfied with such a future?"

"Of course, because they'd finally get some well-deserved peace."

Bol-Kunatz sat back down, but the pimply youngster stood up in his place and, with a series of sorrowful nods, began to speak: "But that's exactly it . . . The issue isn't whether we understand reality or not, but that for you and your heroes that kind of future is basically acceptable, whereas we see it as a tomb. The death of hope. The end of humanity. The final cul-de-sac. That's why we're saying we don't want to bother working for the benefit of your utterly ruined peace-loving types. No amount of energy would suffice to breathe new life into them—not at this stage. And no matter what you say, Mr. Banev, your books—and they're interesting books, no question!—never reveal the object to which force must be applied. They tell us that, in fact, there *are* no such objects, at least, not for our generation. I'm sorry, but you cannibalized yourselves, you wasted your lives fighting with each other, wasted them on lies and a war against lies that you wage by inventing still more lies. It's like that song you all like so much: '*Truth and lies, you're not so different, yesterday's truth becomes lies, yesterday's lies are today's truth, perfect and familiar . . .*' You rush from one lie to the next, you simply can't bring yourselves to believe that you're already dead, that you created—with your own hands—a world that has now become your tomb. You rotted in the trenches, crushed yourselves to pieces beneath the treads of tanks, and for what? You condemn governments and entire ways of life, as if you didn't know that your generation just simply doesn't deserve any better. It pains me to say this, but even as you were being slapped in the face, you kept on stubbornly insisting that people are inherently good. Or, worse still . . . 'Man—how proud that sounds!' as Maxim Gorky put it. You're awfully free with that distinction, aren't you?"

The pimply orator threw up his hands and sat down. Silence was restored, but then he stood up once more and remarked, "When I said 'you,' I didn't mean you personally, Mr. Banev."

"Great, thanks," said Victor with irritation. He felt angry. That pimply little punk had no right to talk with such finality . . . the gall, the nerve of it! Smack him upside the head and drag him out of here by his ear. This was awkward—much of what had been said was true, and he even thought the same thing, but now he felt forced to defend what he hated. He was at a loss, unsure what to do next, how to continue the conversation, or if it was worth continuing at all . . .

He scanned the room and saw that they were waiting for his answer, that Irma was waiting, that all of these rosy-cheeked and freckled monsters were of one mind, that the pimply smart aleck was only expressing the general consensus—earnestly, with deep conviction, and not because he'd just finished reading some radical pamphlet. He saw that they didn't have one iota of gratitude or even the most basic respect for him, Banev, that they couldn't care less that he'd volunteered for the hussar regiment, that he'd gone up against Rheinmetall tanks on horseback, that he'd nearly expired from dysentery during a siege, that he'd stabbed some sentries with a handmade knife, and that later, after returning to civilian life, he'd punched a special agent right in the kisser when he suggested Victor sign a denunciation letter, that he'd moped around with a hole in his lung and no job, that he'd peddled fruit without a permit despite being offered some very lucrative opportunities . . .

But why, in the end, do they owe me respect for any of that? Just because I advanced on tanks with sword unsheathed? But you have to be an idiot to tolerate a government that would expose its army to something like that . . . Here he shuddered, imagining the enormous thought labor these little chickens must have done to arrive, totally independently, at conclusions that adults attain only after tearing their hides to shreds, turning their souls into a shambles, ruining their own lives and numerous adjacent ones . . . and not all of them get there, even. Only a few do, while the rest think to this day that it was all for a good cause and very reasonable, and if they had to, they'd do it all over again . . . Could it really be that a new age had dawned? He looked out at the audience with something like fear. It seemed like the future had managed, after all, to thrust its tentacles into the very heart of the present, and that future was cold, and merciless, and it couldn't care less about all the achievements of the past, real or putative.

"Guys," said Victor, "you're probably not aware of this, but you're cruel. You're cruel with the best of intentions, but cruelty is always cruelty. And all it can bring is new sorrow, new tears, and new depravity. That's what you should keep in mind. And don't think that you're saying anything especially new. To destroy the old world and build a new one on its bones is a very old idea indeed. And never once has it produced the desired outcome. The very thing that calls forth merciless destruction in the old world adapts to that destruction with the greatest of ease, adapts to cruelty and mercilessness, becoming an essential part of the destructive process. Inevitably, it survives to become the master of the new world and, in the end, kills the courageous destroyers themselves. Two wrongs don't make a right, and you'll never eliminate cruelty with cruelty. Irony and pity, my young friends! Irony and pity!"

Suddenly, the whole room was on its feet. This was completely unexpected, and Victor had the crazy thought that he'd finally managed to say something that thrilled their imagination. But he could already see the clammy walking toward them, gaunt, light, almost immaterial, like a shade. Victor watched the children gazing at him—more than gazing, they seemed to stretch toward him, and the clammy gave Victor a restrained bow, mumbled his excuses and sat down at the end of a row, next to Irma, and all the children sat down, too, and Victor looked at Irma and saw she was ecstatic and trying not to show it, fairly beaming with pleasure and joy. And before he could get his bearings, Bol-Kunatz spoke.

"I'm afraid you've misunderstood us, Mr. Banev," he said. "We're not cruel at all, or if we are, from your perspective, then only in theory. After all, we're not going to destroy your old world. We're going to build a new one. You're the cruel ones: you can't imagine building the new without first destroying the old. But we can, and quite well, too. We'll even help your generation create your version of paradise, so you can drink and eat to your heart's content. All that matters is building, only building. We're not destroying anything. We're only building."

Victor finally managed to tear his eyes away from Irma and collect his thoughts. "Yes," he said, "of course. Go for it, build your new world. I'm completely on your side. You took me by surprise today, but I'm still with you. And if need be, I'll even renounce my share of the food and drink . . . Only, don't forget that the old worlds always had to be destroyed because they always got in the way . . . They got in the way of building the new; they disliked and oppressed it."

"Today's old world won't get in our way," said Bol-Kunatz, enigmatically. "It'll even come to our aid. History has ceased its flow; no need to refer to it any longer."

"Even better," said Victor wearily. "So glad it's all working out for you."

They're nice, these boys and girls, he thought. Strange, but nice. I feel bad for them, though . . . they'll get older, jump each other's bones, reproduce, and start toiling for their daily bread . . . No, he thought, despairing. Maybe it'll all work out. After all, they're nothing like us. Maybe it'll all work out . . . He scooped their notes from the table—there were quite a few: "How do you define 'facts'?" "Can a person be considered honest and kind if he works for the cause of war?" "Why do you drink so much?" "What are your thoughts on Spengler?"

"I've got a couple of your questions here," he said. "I don't know if you still want me to—"

The pimply nihilist stood up and said, "Well, Mr. Banev, I don't know what questions you've got there, but really, it doesn't matter. We just wanted to make the acquaintance of a well-known contemporary writer. Every well-known writer expresses the ideology of his society, or some part of society, and we need to familiarize ourselves with today's ideologues. Now we know more than before we met you. Thank you."

The children began to shift in their seats, calling out, "Thank you," "Thank you, Mr. Banev." Then they got to their feet and began clearing out, while Victor stood there, clutching their notes in his fist, feeling stupid. He knew he'd gone red in the face, that he looked lost and small, but he composed himself, stuck the notes into his pocket, and got off the stage.

The worst part was that he still had no idea how to relate to these children. What they said was unreal, impossible. The way they treated his writing and his statements was utterly at odds with their protruding pigtails, their scruffy cowlicks, their grimy necks, their chapped, skinny hands, and with the high-pitched noise now surrounding him. It was as if some force were amusing itself by colliding a day care with a scientific colloquium, combining two mutually exclusive entities. This must be what it feels like to be a cat in a lab that gets a piece of fish and a scratch behind the ear, followed by an electric shock, an exploding firecracker, and a blinding spotlight. I know just how you feel, said Victor to the cat, whose state of mind he could well imagine. Our brains weren't wired for this sort of thing, kitty; we might well drop dead from the shock . . .

He suddenly became aware that he was stuck. They'd surrounded him, blocking his way. For a moment he was seized with panic. He wouldn't have been surprised if they knocked him down, silently and methodically, and started vivisecting him for purposes of ideological investigation. But they had no desire to vivisect him. Their outstretched arms held open books, cheap notepads, sheets of loose-leaf. They babbled, "Your autograph, please!" They squealed, "Right here, please!" They croaked, their voices breaking, "Please, Mr. Banev!"

So he got out a pen and began unscrewing the cap, noting his own sensations with the detached interest of an outside observer. He was not surprised to discover a feeling of pride. These were the specters of the future, and, when all was said and done, it felt wonderful to have their acclaim.

✦✦✦

Back in his hotel room, he immediately ransacked the minibar. He poured himself some gin and drank it down in a single gulp, like medicine. His wet hair sent streams of water down his back; as it turned out, he'd forgotten to put up his hood. His pants were wet to the knee and stuck to his legs. He'd apparently walked along without caring where he was going, stepping into every available puddle. He craved a cigarette with animalistic fervor; evidently, he'd failed to light up even once during those two plus hours . . .

Acceleration, he said to himself, and kept on saying it as he threw his wet raincoat right onto the floor, changed, and rubbed his head with a towel. It's just a little acceleration, he soothed himself, lighting a cigarette and taking his first greedy puffs. Acceleration in action, he thought with horror, recalling the confident childish voices proclaiming impossible things. Dear Lord, save the grown-ups. Save their parents, Lord, show them the way, make them smarter, it's now or never . . . For your own good, I'm begging you, Lord, or they'll build you a Tower of Babel, a gravestone for all the idiots you unleashed on this earth to be fruitful and multiply, without thinking through the consequences of acceleration . . . You're a sucker, God . . .

Victor spat his cigarette butt onto the floor and lit another. Why am I getting so bent out of shape? he thought. My imagination's running away with me. All right, so they're children, so they're accelerating, so they're wise beyond their years. Nothing new there! Where did I get the idea that they came up with all of it on their own? They've seen all kinds of filth in town, read a bunch of books, reduced everything to its lowest common denominator, and concluded, quite naturally, that it's high time for a new world. And plus, they're not all the same. They have their loudmouth agitators—like Bol-Kunatz . . . or that pimply kid . . . or that cute little girl. Ringleaders. But the rest of them are just regular kids—sitting and listening, feeling bored . . .

He knew that last part wasn't true. Fine, so they weren't bored, they were interested. They live in the sticks, after all, and I'm a famous writer. But come on! No way in hell I would have read my books when I was their age. No way in hell I'd show up for anything other than a movie with shooting in it, or a passing circus—to admire the tightrope walker's thighs . . . I couldn't have cared less about the old world, or the new one—I had no concept of either thing. All I wanted was to play soccer till I dropped, or unscrew some light bulb somewhere and shatter it against a wall, or whale on some mama's boy I'd ambushed . . .

Victor leaned back in his chair, stretching out his legs. We all have fond memories of our own happy childhoods. And we're all sure that things haven't changed since the days of Tom Sawyer, and never will. We just know that's how it has to be. And if it's not, then the kid's abnormal and evokes slight pity in theory and pedagogical outrage in practice. And as the kid looks at you, all docile, what he's thinking is: *You may be big, and grown-up, and capable of kicking my ass. But you're a fool, you've been that way since* ***you*** *were a kid, and that's how you'll always be. You'll die a fool, but that's not enough for you—you want to make a fool out of me, too . . .*

He poured some more gin and allowed himself to remember how it all went down, which forced him to make a hasty swallow to avoid howling with shame. He'd showed up all arrogant and cocksure, trendy and supercilious, he'd started right in with the clichés and platitudes, talking down to them in pseudo-manly tones, and then they shut him down, but he wouldn't let it go and kept right on demonstrating his acute intellectual deficiency, and then they tried to set him straight—what's more, they warned him!—but he just kept showering them with banalities and trivial bullshit, thinking that he'd make it work, it's all fine, it's all whatever. And then, when they finally lost their patience and went for the jugular, he dissolved into cowardly tears and started complaining that they weren't treating him right . . . and *then,* when they took pity on him and asked for a couple of autographs, he had the shamelessness to rejoice!

Victor gnashed his teeth as he realized that, for all his performative honesty, he would never dare tell anyone what happened today. Within the next half hour or so, for reasons of self-preservation, he was going to cleverly flip it around, recoding today's shellacking as his greatest triumph—or at worst a rather ordinary, not especially interesting meeting with some marginal wunderkinder, who are only children, after all (what can you do!), and as such don't have a super sophisticated understanding of life or literature . . . I'd be perfect for the Ministry of Enlightenment, he thought bitterly. People who think like that are always in demand there . . .

The only consolation, he thought, is that there aren't so many of these kids for now, and if acceleration continues at the present rate, then by the time there are lots of them, I myself, God willing, will be good and dead. It's a great thing—to die at the right time!

There was a knock at the door. Victor shouted: "Yes!"

In walked a disheveled, swollen-nosed Pavor, wearing a faux-Oriental caftan. "It's about time," he croaked. He sat down across from Victor, extracted a large, wet handkerchief from his breast pocket, and commenced blowing his nose and sneezing. It was a sad sight—nothing remained of the old Pavor.

"What do you mean—about time?" asked Victor. "Want some gin?"

"Ugh, I don't know . . ." Pavor replied, sniffling and snorting. "This town'll be the death of me . . . *Ah-ah-ah-pshew!* Ugh . . ."

"Gesundheit," said Victor.

Pavor stared at him fixedly with watering eyes. "Where have you been?" he asked petulantly. "I've been knocking down your door. I wanted to borrow some reading material. I'm dying here, there's nothing to do except sneeze and blow your nose . . . Not a soul in the hotel, and when I asked the doorman for something, the ancient fool offered me a telephone book and some old brochures . . . 'Visit our sunny city.' Got anything to read?"

"Doubtful," said Victor.

"What the hell, what kind of writer are you! OK, I get it, you don't read other people, but surely you peruse your own books now and again . . . It's all people talk about: 'Banev this, Banev that . . .' What's that one thing of yours called? *Death in the Afternoon*? *Midnight After Death*? I forget . . ."

"*Disaster Strikes at Night*," said Victor.

"Exactly. Hand it over."

"No. I don't have a copy," Victor said firmly. "And even if I did, I wouldn't give it to you. You'd cover it with snot. And you wouldn't understand a single word."

"Now why would that be?" inquired Pavor querulously. "They say it's about the life of homosexuals—what's not to get?"

"You're the—" said Victor. "Let's drink some gin instead. Splash of water?"

Pavor sneezed, grumbled, looked around the room in despair, threw his head back, and sneezed again. "My head hurts," he complained. "Right here . . . But where have you been? They say you met with some of your readers—local homosexuals?"

"Worse," said Victor. "Local prodigies. Do you know what acceleration is?"

"Acceleration? Does it have something to do with early puberty? I heard some noises about that a while back, but then they created a committee in our ministry, which proved that all that stuff resulted from Mr. President's deep personal concern for the rising generation of lions and dreamers, and after that everything fell into place. But I know exactly what you mean—I've seen these local prodigies. God save us from lions like that; they belong in a cabinet of curiosities."

"Did you ever think that we're the ones who belong in a cabinet of curiosities?" Victor retorted.

"Could be," agreed Pavor. "Only acceleration has nothing to do with it. Acceleration is a biological or physiological thing. It starts with increased birth weight, and then they shoot up to six foot five, like giraffes, and by twelve, they're ready to reproduce. Whereas this is about the education system. The kids themselves are perfectly ordinary—it's their teachers."

"What about their teachers?"

Pavor sneezed. "It's their teachers who are extraordinary," he said nasally.

Victor recalled the gymnasium headmaster. "What's so extraordinary about the teachers here?" he asked. "That they forget to unzip their fly in time?"

"What fly?" asked Pavor, gazing at Victor in puzzlement. "They don't have any flies at all, as it happens."

"What else?" asked Victor.

"What do you mean?"

"What else is extraordinary about them?"

Pavor spent a long time blowing his nose, while Victor sucked at his gin and looked on with pity.

"You're out of the loop, I see," said Pavor, examining his snot-filled handkerchief. "As Mr. President has correctly observed, 'The main attribute of our writers is their chronic estrangement from real life and the interests of the nation.' Look, you've been here for over a week. Have you been anywhere besides the bar and the sanatorium? Have you spoken to anyone other than that drunken goat Quadriga? What the hell are they paying you for?"

"All right, that's enough," said Victor. "I get my fill of that stuff from the papers. Keep it to yourself, you snot-covered critic . . . you flyless teacher . . ."

"Not your thing, eh?" said Pavor with satisfaction. "No worries . . . Why don't you tell me about your wunderkind meeting."

"Eh, what's to tell?" said Victor. "Just some regular old prodigies."

"Details, please."

"All right, so I went there. They asked me a couple of questions. Interesting questions, quite grown-up ones . . ." Victor paused for a moment. "Frankly, they scored more than a few points."

"What kind of questions?" asked Pavor. He was looking at Victor with sincere interest, and possibly also pity.

"The questions were not the issue," sighed Victor. "To be honest, what shocked me most is that they were like grown-ups, and not just any grown-ups but really high-quality ones . . . It was this . . . hellish, sickening incongruity." Pavor was nodding with compassion. "In a word, it was horrible," said Victor. "I don't even want to talk about it."

"Gotcha," said Pavor. "You're not the first, and you won't be the last. The thing is, the parents of a twelve-year-old child are always rather pitiful creatures, saddled with numerous problems. But the parents around here are something else. They call to mind the rear lines of an occupying army in areas of intense partisan activity . . . Come on, what exactly did they ask you?"

"Well, for instance, they asked me what progress is."

"All right. So what's their take on progress?"

"Their take on progress is very simple. Corral us all into reservations so we don't get in the way, and then use their newfound freedom to study Zurzmansor and Spengler. That's the impression I got, at any rate."

"Yeah, that sounds about right," said Pavor. "The apple doesn't fall far from the tree. Here you sit, talking 'acceleration' and 'Zurzmansor.' But do you know what the nation has to say about it?"

"Uh . . . who?"

"The *nation*! The nation feels that clammies are the root of the problem. The kids've gone off the deep end because of the clammies."

"That's because there are no Jews in this town," Victor noted. Then he remembered the clammy who entered the assembly hall. How the children all stood up. The expression on Irma's face. "Wait, are you serious?" he asked.

"It's not me," said Pavor. "It's the voice of the nation. Vox populi. All the cats have run away, and the children adore the clammies, spend day and night at the leprosarium. Now they're out of control and won't listen to anyone. They steal money from their parents and spend it on books . . . They say that at first parents were only too happy that their children weren't tearing their pants to shreds climbing fences but instead sitting quietly at home reading books. Especially since the weather's so bad. But by now everyone can see where it's led, and who started it. No one's smiling anymore. But they're used to being scared of the clammies; all they can ever do is growl at their backs."

The voice of the nation, thought Victor. The voice of Lola and Mr. Mayor. We've heard that voice before . . . Cats, endless rain, televisions. The blood of Christian babies. "I don't get it," he said. "Are you being serious, or are you just bored?"

"It's not me!" Pavor repeated with heartfelt sincerity. "That's what they're saying in town."

"Yeah, I get that," said Victor. "But what do you think about it personally?"

Pavor shrugged. "That's just how it goes," he said vaguely. "Equal parts idle talk and gospel truth." He glanced at Victor over the handkerchief covering his face. "Don't take me for an idiot," he said. "Consider the children: Where else have you seen children like that? Or, at any rate, *so many* children like that?"

Yeah, thought Victor, children like that . . . The cats are one thing, but that clammy in the assembly hall is more than just cats plus rain . . . There's an expression: *a face lit from within*. That's exactly what Irma's face was like, whereas when she talks to me, her face is lit only from the outside. And as for her mother, Irma doesn't talk to her at all—just sneers something disgusted or condescending through clenched teeth . . . But if that's really how it is—if it's all true and not just a bunch of filthy twaddle—it really doesn't look good at all. What do they want with the children? They're sick, doomed people.

And plus, where do they get off, turning kids against their parents, even if those parents are like me and Lola? Don't we get enough of that from Mr. President? The nation is higher than filial ties, the Legion of Freedom is your father and your mother, and then you get a kid showing up at the nearest police station, saying that his father said Mr. President was a "strange person," while his mother called the Legion's campaigns "ruinous." And now on top of that we get some soggy, black-clad guy saying, *Guess what, kid, your dad's a drunken pig and your mom's a dumb whore*. Be that as it may—but still, where do they get off? It's just not done, and plus, it's none of their goddamn business, they're not the responsible party, no one asked them to do the work of enlightenment . . . Pathological, is what it is.

And that's if we assume what they're after is, in fact, enlightenment. But what if it's something worse? Out of the mouths of babes we get this talk of progress, all these terrifying, cruel things . . .

they don't know whereof they speak, but from a tender age they develop a taste for intellectual cruelty, the worst kind of cruelty anyone could think of. Meanwhile, behind the scenes are clammies, peeling faces all wrapped up in black cloth, and they're the ones pulling the strings . . . Which means there's no rising generation at all—just the same old crooked puppet show. I truly made an ass of myself back there, dying of embarrassment on their stage . . . What a nasty idea our civilization has turned out to be . . .

"He who hath eyes to see," Pavor was saying, "let him see: We're not allowed into the leprosarium. Barbed wire, soldiers . . . whatever. But certain things we can see from here, in town. I see clammies talking to boys, and I see how those boys respond—like little angels. But just try asking directions to the factory and they'll drench you in contempt!"

We're not allowed into the leprosarium, thought Victor. It's behind barbed wire, while the clammies get to move about freely. It's not Golem who invented this arrangement . . . That bastard, he thought, "Father of the Nation" my ass. That scumbag. So this, too, is his handiwork. Best friend of children . . . Could very well be, this is him all over. But you know, Mr. President, if I were you I'd change my moves up now and then. Your snout stands out too much from all the other snouts. Barbed wire, soldiers, IDs—that spells "Mr. President," meaning something nasty is afoot . . .

"What the hell is the barbed wire for?" Victor said.

"You're asking me?" said Pavor. "There never used to be any barbed wire."

"So you've been inside before?"

"What? No. But it's not like I'm the first health inspector to examine the place . . . the barbed wire's not the point, there's barbed wire everywhere. The kiddies can come and go as they please, the clammies can come and go as they please, it's you and me who can't get in—that's the funny part."

No, it's not the President, it can't be, Victor was thinking. The President, plus kids reading Zurzmansor, and Banev to boot? That doesn't compute somehow. And their destructive ideology . . . If I wrote something in that vein, I'd be crucified. It's all a big mystery. But something's up, no doubt about it. Why don't I ask Irma? he thought. I'll just ask her and see how she reacts . . . And by the way, Diana must know something, too.

"Are you listening?" asked Pavor.

"Sorry, I spaced out."

"I was saying that I wouldn't be surprised if the city took some sort of action. Cruel action, as befits a city."

"Me neither," mumbled Victor. "I wouldn't be surprised if I myself felt compelled to take some sort of action."

Pavor stood and walked over to the window. "Some weather we're having," he said despondently. "I can't wait to get out of here . . . Are you going to give me a book or not?"

"I don't have any books," said Victor. "Everything I brought with me is at the sanatorium. Listen, what do the clammies want with our kids?"

Pavor shrugged. "They're sick people," he answered. "How could we possibly guess? You and I are healthy, after all."

There was a knock at the door. In came Golem, heavy-footed and soaking wet.

"Let's ask Golem," said Pavor. "Golem, what do the clammies want with our kids?"

"Your kids?" said Golem, carefully examining the label on the gin bottle. "You have kids, Pavor?"

"Pavor claims those clammies of yours are turning local kids against their parents," Victor said. "You wouldn't know anything about that, would you, Golem?"

"Hmm," said Golem. "Where do you keep clean glasses? Ah, here we go! The clammies—turning kids? Heh. Wouldn't be the first time, or the last." Still in his raincoat, he toppled over onto the bed and sniffed at the gin in his glass. "And why shouldn't someone out there turn kids against their parents? If the whites are being turned against the blacks, and the yellows are being turned against the whites, and the idiots are being turned against the clever . . . What are you so surprised about, anyway?"

"Pavor claims," Victor repeated, "that your patients are gallivanting around town and teaching the kids all sorts of odd things. I've noticed something going on, too, though I'm not ready to make any claims. Anyway, I'm not saying I'm surprised, I'm just asking: Is it true or not?"

"As far as I know," said Golem, taking a sip, "clammies have had free access to the city since time immemorial. I don't know what you mean by 'teaching odd things,' but allow me to ask you, as a native of these parts: Are you familiar with a toy called 'angry top'?"

"Of course," said Victor.

"Did you have a toy like that growing up?"

"Well, no, of course not . . . but some of my friends did." Victor fell silent. "That's right," he said. "And my friends said they got it from a clammy. Is that what you're referring to?"

"Yes, exactly that. Along with the 'weathervane' and the 'wooden hand.'"

"*Excusez-moi*," said Pavor. "Might I, a transplant from the capital, learn what the natives are talking about?"

"No," said Golem. "It's above your pay grade."

"How would you know what is and isn't above my pay grade?" asked Pavor, looking insulted.

"Oh, I know," said Golem. "I have my guesses. That's just how I play the game. . . And stop lying, you've been trying to get Teddy to sell you his 'weathervane,' you know exactly what it is."

"Go to hell," said Pavor petulantly. "I'm not talking about the 'weathervane.'"

"Hold on, Pavor," said Victor impatiently. "Golem, you didn't answer my question."

"Didn't I? I thought I had . . . You see, Victor, clammies are profoundly, hopelessly ill people. Genetic conditions are no joke. But through it all they retain their kindness and their wit, so don't harass them."

"Who's harassing them?"

"Aren't you?"

"Not yet. Just the opposite, so far."

"Well, in that case, it's all fine," said Golem and stood up. "In that case, let's go."

Victor goggled at him. "Go where?"

"To the sanatorium. I'm on my way there, and I can see that you are, too, and as for you, Pavor, get to bed and quit spreading your flu around."

Victor looked at his watch. "It's not too early?" he said.

"Whatever you say. But keep in mind that as of today, they've canceled the bus line. It's unprofitable."

"Maybe we should have some dinner first."

"Whatever you say," Golem repeated. "Personally, I never eat dinner. And I'd recommend the same to you."

Victor patted his belly. "Yeah," he said, then looked over at Pavor. "I'll come along, I guess."

"What do I care?" said Pavor. He was offended. "Just bring me some books."

"For sure," promised Victor, and started getting dressed.

When they climbed into the car, with its damp canvas top and damp interior reeking of tobacco, gasoline, and medical supplies, Golem said, "Can you take a hint?"

"Sometimes," said Victor. "If I can tell that's what it is. Why?"

"Listen closely—a hint is coming. Keep your mouth shut."

"Hmm," mumbled Victor. "And how am I supposed to take that?"

"As a hint. Quit blabbing."

"With pleasure," said Victor, and fell silent, thinking.

They drove across the city, past the cannery and the deserted city park—wilted, gone to seed, half rotted from the damp—sped by the stadium, where the mud-streaked Kindred Spirits were stubbornly smashing waterlogged cleats into waterlogged balls, and finally exited onto the road to the sanatorium. All around them, shrouded in rain, lay wet, table-flat steppe—once arid, sun-scorched, and prickly, it was now slowly transforming into a sodden swamp.

"Your hint," said Victor, "reminds me of a conversation I once had with His Excellency, Mr. President's Adviser on State Ideology.

His Excellency called me into his modest office—a mere sixty-five hundred square feet—and inquired, 'Victoire, do you still like to eat your bread buttered?' Naturally, I answered in the affirmative. 'Then stop that racket!' bellowed His Excellency, and dismissed me with a wave of his hand."

Golem smirked. "What racket were you making?"

"His Excellency was hinting at my banjo stylings in the local youth clubs."

Golem gave him a squinting, sidelong look. "And what makes you so sure I'm not a narc?"

"I'm not sure about that at all," Victor retorted. "I just couldn't care less. Also, no one says 'narc' anymore. It's archaic. Nowadays all the cool kids say 'snitch.'"

"I can't tell the difference," said Golem.

"I can't either, honestly," said Victor. "All right, enough yakking. Is your patient better now?"

"My patients never get better."

"But you have such a great reputation! I'm talking about the poor guy who got caught in the bear trap. How's his leg?"

Golem was silent for a moment, then said, "Whom do you mean?"

"I'm confused," said Victor. "Obviously, I mean the one who got caught in the trap."

"There were four of them," said Golem, gazing intently at the rain-soaked road. "The first got caught in the trap, the second you carried on your back, the third I drove away in my car, and as for the fourth, you got into a hideous brawl on his behalf at the restaurant the other night."

Victor sat in bewildered silence. Golem, too, said nothing. He drove with great skill, avoiding numerous potholes in the old asphalt.

"It's all right, you can relax," he finally said. "I was joking. There was only one of him. And his leg healed that same night."

"Another joke?" Victor inquired. "Ha, ha, ha. Now I understand why your patients never get better."

"My patients never get better for two reasons," said Golem. "First, like any honest doctor, I don't try to cure genetic conditions. And second, they don't want to get better."

"Funny," mumbled Victor. "I've heard so much about these clammies of yours that by now I'm ready to believe in anything: rain . . . cats . . . the idea that a shattered bone can heal in a single night."

"Cats?" said Golem.

"Well, yeah," said Victor. "Why aren't there any cats left in the city? It's the clammies' fault. Teddy's going under because of the mice . . . Maybe you can advise them to lead the mice away, too."

"À la the Pied Piper of Hamelin?" asked Golem.

"Sure," Victor confirmed flippantly. "À la indeed." Then he remembered the ending to the Pied Piper story. "You know, there's nothing funny about it," he said. "Today I spoke at the gymnasium. I watched the kids, I saw how they responded to some clammy. So I wouldn't be at all surprised if one fine day a clammy shows up in the town square, accordion in hand, and leads the children straight to hell."

"You wouldn't be surprised," said Golem. "Gotcha. And what else would you do?"

"I don't know . . . Maybe I'd take away his accordion."

"And start playing it yourself?"

"Fair enough," sighed Victor. "You're right. I've got nothing to offer them, that's obvious. But I wonder, what are *they* offering those kids? You know, don't you, Golem?"

"Victoire, stop that racket," said Golem.

"Whatever you say," said Victor. "You're avoiding my questions very thoroughly, and more or less nimbly, I've noticed. Which is stupid—I'll find out anyway, and you'll lose the chance to give the information the emotional overtones most favorable to you."

"I'm observing medical confidentiality!" Golem affirmed. "And plus, I don't know anything. I can only guess."

He slowed down. Up ahead, beyond the veil of rain, several figures appeared in the road. Three gray figures, alongside a gray signpost with arrows reading LEPROSARIUM—4 MILES and WARM SPRINGS SAN.—1.6 MILES. The figures—an adult man and two children—stepped onto the shoulder.

"Stop the car," said Victor, his voice suddenly hoarse.

"What's wrong?" Golem asked, braking.

Victor didn't reply. He was looking at the people standing next to the signpost, at the strapping clammy with his waterlogged black tracksuit, at the similarly raincoat-less boy in flimsy, soaking-wet suit and sandals; and at the barefoot girl, her sodden dress sticking to her skin. Then he jerked the car door open and rushed into the road. The wind and rain hit him full in the face, choking him, but he didn't notice. He was in the throes of an unbearable rage, the kind where you want to break things, where you're aware enough to know you're about to do something stupid but the thought only makes you happy. He walked right up to the clammy on unbending legs.

"What's going on here?" He expelled the words through clenched teeth. Then, to the girl, who was gazing at him in surprise, "Irma, get in the car this second!" Then, to the clammy, "God damn you to hell, what are you doing?" Then again to Irma, "Are you deaf? Get in the car!"

Irma didn't move. All three of them stood as before; above his black face cover, the clammy's eyes blinked tranquilly. Then Irma said, in a tone Victor couldn't parse, "That's my father," and he suddenly realized, deep in his lizard brain, that this was not the place to yell or raise a fist, to make threats or grab people by the scruff of the neck and drag them along . . . this was not the place for any form of rage.

He said, very calmly, "Irma, get in the car, you're all wet. Bol-Kunatz, if I were you, I'd do the same."

He was certain that Irma would obey him, and she did. Not exactly as he'd want her to. She didn't ask the clammy permission to leave, not even with a glance, but Victor had just the barest impression that something had, in fact, occurred, that there'd been some exchange of opinion, some brief conference, as a result of which the matter was decided in his favor. Irma stuck her nose in the air and made her way to the car.

Bol-Kunatz said politely, "Many thanks, Mr. Banev, but, really, I'd rather stay."

"Your call," said Victor. Bol-Kunatz wasn't really his concern. He now needed to say something to the clammy, by way of goodbye. Victor knew in advance that it would be something rather stupid, but—what could he do?—he couldn't just walk away, purely for reasons of ego. And so he spoke. "And you, my good sir," he said haughtily, "are not invited. You seem to be very much in your element."

He turned on his heel, flung down an imaginary glove, and walked away. *Having uttered these words*, he thought with disgust, *the count took a dignified leave.*

Irma had folded herself into the front seat, feet and all, and was now wringing the water from her braids. Victor climbed into the back, grunting with shame, and when Golem started the car said, "'Having uttered these words, the count took his leave.' Irma, give me your feet, I'll rub them dry."

"Why?" Irma asked with evident curiosity.

"You want to get pneumonia? Feet! Now!"

"Whatever," said Irma and, rotating in her seat, stuck out a single foot.

Looking forward to finally doing something natural and useful, Victor grabbed her touchingly wet, skinny, girlish foot, fully intending to rub the filthy, bony, ice-cold thing red, beet-red, even, with his loving, strict, fatherly hands, bulwarks against all kinds of colds, viruses, respiratory infections and double pneumonias. Then he discovered that his palms were colder than her feet. Reflexively, he gave the foot one or two strokes, then carefully released it.

I knew it all along, he thought suddenly, I knew it when I was still standing there in front of them, I knew there was a catch, that the kids weren't in any danger of colds or infection, but that's not what I wanted, I wanted to rescue them, to tear them from someone's claws, to feel self-righteous anger, to fulfill my duty, and once again I've been outplayed, made to look stupid—for the second time today . . .

"Move your foot," he told Irma.

Irma moved her foot and asked, "Where are we going? To the sanatorium?"

"Yes," said Victor, and looked over at Golem, trying to figure out if he'd noticed the shameful incident. Golem, unfazed, kept his eyes on the road, his heavyset body spreading in the driver's seat, gray-haired, unkempt, stoop-shouldered, and omniscient.

"Why, though?" asked Irma.

"You'll change into dry clothes and go to bed."

"Oh please!" said Irma. "What'll you think of next?"

"All right, all right," mumbled Victor. "I'll give you some books, you can read."

She's right, why the hell am I taking her there? he thought. Diana . . . Well, we'll see about that. No drinking, nothing like that, but how will I get her home? What the hell, I'll just take someone's car and drive back . . . I could really use a swig of something right now.

"Golem—" he began, but stopped himself. Dammit, I can't, it'd be inappropriate.

"Yes?" said Golem, still staring straight ahead.

"No, nothing," sighed Victor, staring at the bottle sticking out of Golem's raincoat pocket. "Irma," he said wearily. "What were you all doing at that crossroads?"

"We were thinking the fog," answered Irma.

"What?"

"Thinking the fog," Irma repeated.

"*About* the fog," Victor corrected. "Or *of* the fog."

"Why would we think about fog?" said Irma.

"*To think* is an intransitive verb," Victor explained. "It doesn't allow a direct object. Have you covered intransitive verbs in school already?"

"It depends," said Irma. "*Thinking fog* is one thing, but *thinking about fog* is something else entirely . . . I have no idea why anyone would ever want to think *about* fog."

Victor took out a cigarette and lit it. "Hold on," he said. "You can't say 'thinking fog'—it's grammatically incorrect. There are certain verbs we call 'intransitive': *to think, to run, to walk* . . . They never take a direct object. To walk down the street. To think about . . . something or other . . ."

"To think nonsense," said Golem.

"Fine, but that's an exception," said Victor, a little confused.

"To walk quickly," said Golem.

"*Quickly* isn't a noun," said Victor testily. "Don't confuse the girl, Golem."

"Dad, can you please not smoke?" asked Irma.

Golem seemed to make some sort of sound, or perhaps it was the motor sneezing as they drove uphill. Victor crumpled the cigarette and stamped it out with his heel. They were driving up the hill to the sanatorium, while somewhere off to the side, a solid whitish wall moved toward the rain from the direction of the steppe.

"There you go: fog," said Victor. "Feel free to think it. That and dream it, run it, and walk it."

Irma wanted to say something, but Golem interrupted. "By the way," he said. "The verb *to think* can also be transitive in complex sentences. For instance: *I think that* . . . etc."

"No, that's something else altogether," objected Victor. He was sick of this. He very much wanted a drink and a smoke. He gazed longingly at the bottle. "Aren't you cold, Irma?" he asked, vaguely hopeful.

"No. Are you?"

"I've been warmer," Victor admitted.

"You should drink some gin," Golem remarked.

"Yeah, not a bad idea . . . You got any?"

"I do," said Golem. "But we're almost there now."

The jeep rolled through the gate, and now something started that Victor hadn't really considered. The first streams of fog were just beginning to filter through the fence. Visibility was still fantastic. On the driveway lay a body in soaking-wet pajamas; it looked like it had been lying there for many days and nights. Golem carefully drove around it, past the plaster vase embellished with artless sketches and correspondingly artless inscriptions, and joined the herd of cars clustered around the right-hand building's vestibule. Irma swung the door open, and immediately an alcohol-wasted mug stuck itself through the nearest car window to bleat, "Hey baby, do ya want me?" Victor, faint with shame, began climbing out of the car.

Irma looked around, curious, but Victor took her firmly by the hand and led her to the vestibule. On the steps two underwear-clad wenches sat in each other's arms, yowling out a song about a cruel pharmacist who don't give out no smack. Catching sight of Victor, they fell silent, but as he was passing by, one of them tried to grab him by the pants. Victor nudged Irma inside. Here it was dark, the windows all curtained. It stank of tobacco smoke and something sour; a projector clattered, sending pornographic images leaping on the white wall. Victor, clenching his teeth, dragged along a stumbling Irma, stepping on someone's toes as he went. Unprintable words sounded angrily behind him. When they finally made it out of the vestibule, Victor shot up the carpeted stairway three steps at a time. Irma said nothing; he didn't dare look her way.

Waiting for him in the stairwell, with open embrace, was puffy and blue-faced Member of Parliament Rossechepert Nantes. "Victoire!" he wheezed. "F-F-Friend!" Then he noticed Irma and flushed with glee. "Victoire! Not you, too? The jailbaitiest of jailbaits!" Victor squeezed his eyes shut, stomped hard on Rossechepert's foot, and shoved him in the chest. Rossechepert toppled backward, knocking over an urn. Sweat pouring down his back, Victor proceeded down the hall. Irma sped silently along by his side. He pushed at Diana's door, which was locked, the key gone. He began knocking furiously, and Diana immediately responded. "Go to hell, you son of a bitch!" she screamed, enraged. "Filthy impotent bastard! You utter piece of dog shit!"

"Diana!" Victor roared. "Open up!"

Diana stopped shouting. The door swung open. She was standing on the threshold holding a pointy imported umbrella at the ready. Victor shoved her aside, pushed Irma into the room, and slammed the door shut behind him.

"Oh, it's you," said Diana. "I thought it was Rossechepert again." She smelled of booze. "Jesus," she said. "Who'd you bring?"

"This is my daughter," said Victor with an effort. "Her name is Irma. Irma, meet Diana."

He looked hard at Diana, full of desperation and hope. Thank God—she didn't seem drunk. That, or she'd sobered up quick.

"You're insane," she said quietly.

"She's soaked through," he said. "Can you change her into dry clothes and put her to bed? And also—"

"I'm not going to bed," Irma declared.

"Irma," said Victor. "You'd better listen, or someone's going to get their ass kicked."

"Yeah, a certain someone could *definitely* use an ass-kicking," said Diana, hopelessly.

"Diana," said Victor. "Please."

"Fine," said Diana. "Go to your room. We'll figure things out."

Victor left, enormously relieved. He went straight to his room, but there was no peace to be had there, either. First, he forcibly ejected a couple of complete strangers, all relaxed and blissful, along with their soiled bedclothes. Then he locked the door, tumbled down onto the bare mattress, lit up a dank cigarette, and commenced thinking about what the hell he'd just done.

5. FELIX SOROKIN

"AND ANIMAL HUSBANDRY!"

I slept poorly, drowning in viscous nightmares. I dreamed I was reading a Japanese text, and though all the words seemed familiar, they refused to come together into anything meaningful, which was agonizing, because it was urgent, incredibly urgent to prove that I hadn't forgotten my professional specialty, and occasionally I would half wake up and realize with relief that it was only a dream, and then I'd try to decipher the text anyway, and once again fall into the despair and anguish of powerlessness.

I felt no relief even after I managed to wake up completely. Lying there in my dark bedroom, I gazed at the square patch of light on the ceiling, formed by floodlights in the parking lot next to our building. I listened to the early-morning car noise and thought glumly that these long, cheerless nightmares were quite a recent thing with me. They'd started no more than two or three years ago. Before that I'd mostly dreamed about women. This, evidently, represented the final advance of real old age; these were no temporary collapses into apathy but a new and permanent condition from which there could be no return.

My right knee ached, as did the pit of my stomach and my left forearm. My whole body ached, and it made me feel even sorrier for myself. During these predawn energy lows, which were beginning to be a regular occurrence in my life, I would inevitably begin to think about how futile it all was. There was nothing at all to look forward to anymore; none of my remaining years held anything worth forcing myself out of bed for, dragging myself to the bathroom to battle the malfunctioning toilet, shoving myself into the shower without any hope of attaining even a pale imitation of my old vigor, and then, finally, getting on with breakfast. And it wasn't just that the thought of food disgusted me: in the past, there had always been a cigarette waiting for me at the end of the meal, and I'd start thinking about it before I was fully awake, but now I don't even have that anymore.

I don't have anything anymore. Even if I finish this screenplay, and even if it's accepted, so what? At that point, some young, energetic, and inevitably stupid movie director will come barging into my life and begin respectfully—yet still presumptuously—schooling me, telling me that film has its own language, that the most important thing in film is the image, not the word, and then he'll inevitably start throwing around homegrown aphorisms like "Not a shot on native soil" or "That'll do for a Weltanschauung." How could I possibly care about him or his petty career troubles when I know in advance that the film will turn out shitty, and that during the studio previews I'll be fighting the urge to stand up and demand they take me out of the credits . . .

It was stupid of me to get involved in this at all. I've known for a long time now that I shouldn't get involved, but apparently once a dog-meat-monger, always a dog-meat-monger, and now I can never be anyone else, even if I write a hundred more *Modern Tales*, because how could I know: What if my Blue Folder, my secret pride, my strange hope against hope is no mutton at all but the same old dog meat, just from a different slaughterhouse . . .

And even assuming that it's fresh, first-rate mutton . . . so what? Never in all my days will it be published, because there's not a single publisher I know of that could be convinced of the value of my visions, even for ten people in the world besides myself. And after I die . . .

Of course, after an author dies, they often publish even his most outlandish works, as if death purged them of unstable ambiguities, inconvenient allusions, and treacherous subtexts. As if uncontrollable associations died along with the author himself. Perhaps, perhaps. But what good does it do me? I'm no longer a passionate youth, and gone are the days when I wrote each new work in hopes of bringing humanity joy or, at the very least, enlightening it.

I've long since ceased to understand why I write. I'm happy with my level of fame, such as it is . . . however dubious it might be, this fame of mine. Hackwork is easy money, easier than honest writerly labor. And as for the so-called joys of creation, they've never once deigned to grace me with their presence. So what's left? The reader? But I don't know anything about my readers. They're just a large number of unknown and totally alien people. And why should I care how unknown and totally alien people feel about me? After all, I know perfectly well that if I disappeared right now, not a single one of them would notice. And if I hadn't existed at all, or if I'd stayed an army translator, nothing, but nothing, in their lives would have changed, for better or worse.

But forget Sorokin, F. A.! For instance, right now it's morning. Who among the ten million inhabitants of Moscow woke up and thought of Tolstoy, L. N.? Other than possibly schoolkids who didn't do their homework on *War and Peace* . . . Agitator of souls. Ruler of minds. Mirror of the Russian Revolution. Maybe that's why he ended up fleeing Yasnaya Polyana—because, toward the end, he was struck by this utterly simple, utterly deadening idea.

And he'd been a believer, too, I suddenly thought. It was so much easier for him. Whereas we know for certain: there's nothing BEFORE and there's nothing AFTER. A familiar anguish swept over me. A faint spark leaping between two NOTHINGS—that's our whole existence for you. And there's no reward, no compensation in the NOTHING to come, no hope of that spark ever recurring—not anywhere, not ever. And in our despair we attribute meaning to this spark, we convince ourselves and others that each spark is unique, and that, while some of them really do vanish without a trace, others ignite gigantic fires of ideas and deeds, so that the former deserve only contemptuous pity, whereas the latter are to be emulated if you want your life to have any meaning.

So vast and powerful is the euphoria of youth that every single youngster takes this simple bait—if he stops to think about that sort of thing at all. It's only after we reach a certain peak and begin to roll inexorably downhill that we start to understand: it's all just words, the same idle words of support and consolation we use to comfort hard-up neighbors. Whereas in reality it doesn't matter if you erected an entire kingdom or merely built a dacha out of stolen construction materials, for there is only the NOTHING BEFORE and the NOTHING AFTER, and your life only has meaning until the moment you realize this fact.

My penchant for gloomy logical constructions of this type is also recent. It is, I think, a portent—if not of senility itself, then at least of age-related impotence. In the broadest sense of the word, of course. At first I was even frightened of these fits, and would hastily apply the tried-and-true remedy for all sorrows, be they physical or spiritual. I'd down a glass of booze, and within minutes, the familiar image of spark igniting flame—even if that flame was small and held only local significance—would once again acquire the persuasiveness of an unshakeable societal axiom. Later, when these plunges into the abyss of Weltschmerz became commonplace, I no longer felt afraid—and a good thing that was, too, because it turned out that the abyss of Weltschmerz had a bottom. And if I pushed off from that bottom, I could rise back up to the surface.

The thing here was that the gloomy logic of the abyss worked only in the abstract world of general human deeds, whereas every particular life consists not of "deeds," which are the only thing to which the concept of "meaning" might be applied, but of sorrows and joys—large or small, momentary or lasting, purely personal or related to world-historical cataclysms. And no matter how many sorrows rain down on a person at once, he will always keep something in reserve to warm his soul.

For example, he still has his grandsons, the small, filthy-faced twin bandits Petka and Sashka, along with the incomparably heart-melting pleasure of making them happy. He still has his daughter, Katya the Unlucky, who always evokes feelings of guilt, though I can never understand why; probably because she is yours, flesh of your flesh, and shares both your personality and your fate. And vodka chased with marinated milk mushrooms at the Club . . . It's banal, I realize, vodka—but all joys are banal! What about the irresponsible, half-drunk, meaningless conversations we have at the Club—are they not banal? What about that gratuitous delight you feel when you step out onto the terrace early on a summer morning? Blue sky, still-deserted roadway, pink buildings across the way, and long, bluish shadows already beginning to stretch across the empty lot as sparrows clamor in its lush green thickets . . . That's just as banal, and yet I never tire of it.

Of course, there are people who find joy and sorrow exclusively in deeds. They like nothing better than discovering gunpowder, mounting a forced campaign in the Valdai Hills, or commiting some other type of bloodshed. Well, good for them. But mine are the little people. For us, the morning sparrows are more than enough. And by the way, I need to get at least a box of chocolates for the twins today. Or toys . . .

I felt myself surfacing. Without getting up, I flexed my muscles a bit (mostly pro forma). Then I sat up (creakily!) and stuck my feet into my slippers. The following program now awaited me: make the bed, open the terrace door, and motivate myself to perform my morning ablutions. But this course of events was disrupted almost immediately. No sooner had I thrown my pillow onto the armchair than the phone began to jangle. I glanced at the clock to determine who was calling. It was 7:34, which meant it could only be Lyonya the Schizo.

"Hey," he said in a low, underground, conspiratorial tone. "What's doing?"

"*Ohayō*," I responded. "*Botsubotsu sa. Arigatō.*"

"Any chance you could say that in human words?"

"Sure thing," I said readily. "*Everything is OK*," I added in English.

"That's what I like to hear," he said, and paused. "So where did you leave it yesterday?"

"What do you mean?" I asked warily, suddenly remembering yesterday's man in the reversible checked coat.

"You know, whatever you were up to yesterday . . . Where did you go again?"

I finally figured out that he was just asking about my trip to Bannaya.

"Dammit!" I said. "I left my folder somewhere again!"

As I racked my brains, frantically trying to remember where I could have left the folder containing the immortal play about the Koryagins, Lyonya kept droning on. He said there was a rumor that writers who'd been married more than three times would lose their place in line for the new writers' apartment block, and thus remain eligible only for newly vacated premises. This troubled Lyonya the Schizo because he was now on marriage number four.

"The restaurant! That's where I left it!" I said with relief.

"What?" he asked, interrupting himself readily.

"My folder!"

"What folder?"

"Just a regular folder. With strings."

"What's in it?" pressed Schizo.

"Listen," I said. "Lay off, OK? I just woke up, I haven't even made my bed . . ."

"Me neither . . . So did you end up going to Bannaya yesterday?"

"No! God!"

"So where *did* you go?"

The thought of telling Schizo about yesterday's exploits horrified me. And not just because Ivan Davydovich's shotgun-like eyes stared out at me from the past, or because poet Kostya Kudinov's venomous hisses of warning rang in my ears—and not even because I felt like all of this was somehow vile and underhanded. It was so much simpler! The thing was, Schizo was a man interested not in the *what* but in the *why*. He wouldn't rest until he had separated my soul from my body with his demands for explanation, and afterward he'd shove it back in willy-nilly, expounding his own leaden theories, each of which managed to explain one single fact while contradicting all the others . . .

"Lyonya," I said resolutely, "I'm sorry, but someone's at the door. Probably the plumber." And then, ignoring his protests, I hung up the phone.

Overall, I like Lyonya Barinov. Moreover, I respect him. And that nickname I gave him—it's not for his essence but for his outward form. He's a schizo, all right—a tiny, swarthy little schizo, always running scared. Writing is torture for him; he squeezes out literally a couple of words per day, because he's always second-guessing himself. He zealously believes in that insane theory from canonical literary criticism, according to which there exists one specific word that expresses a given idea more precisely than any other, and what you need to do is really try, go the extra mile, exert yourself a little, not be so lazy, and find that one specific word. And only in this manner will you ever produce anything of value.

But I have to say, he has splendid literary taste and can instantly sniff out the weaknesses in any text. He has a rare talent for literary analysis—many of our professional critics don't hold a candle to his skill in that area. But it's precisely this talent for analysis that renders him fatally unable to perform synthesis, because in my opinion what makes or breaks a writer is not his ability to find that one right word but his ability to cast aside all the wrong ones. Whereas Lyonya, poor thing, sits there day after day, torturing himself by weighing "she touched his hand" against "she took his hand" on his internal scale until he's blue in the face . . . And in despair, he calls up Valya for advice, and cruel Valya Demchenko, not wasting a single second, answers him after the famous manner of satirist Arkady Averchenko: "She grabs him hand and ask repeatedly where you did the money." And then he calls me in despair, but I'm no picnic, either, and all he can do is brokenly admonish me for rudeness.

And yet! There's a certain kinship between us. I am certain that if I read him an excerpt from my Blue Folder, he'd understand me like no one else in the world. Except reading to him from the Blue Folder is strictly forbidden. Because he's a blabbermouth, like a bucket with a hole in the bottom—nothing stays inside him for long. That's his number-one favorite activity: first he likes to gather information, and then he likes to spread it indiscriminately all around, alongside his own proprietary commentary. Plus, with his splendid memory and dark imagination . . . No, forget it—the Blue Folder is not for him.

Whereas Lyonya has read to me from his short novel, the one he's been working on for two years straight. It's about a sprinter who's a whiz at sports but desperately unhappy in life. This hero of Lyonya's beats every short-distance record and is envied and admired by all, though no one knows how he does it. His secret is that as soon as he gets on the track, the blind, primeval fear of the hunted animal awakens in his soul. In every race, he tears his way to the finish line, forgetting all that is reasonable and human within him. He has but one goal: to save his own life at any cost, to evade the pack of carnivores pursuing him, carnivores who desire only to catch him, knock him down, and eat him alive. And so he wins prizes, world fame, accolades—all rewarding his pathological, atavistic fear. But he's an honest man, loved by a wonderful young woman . . .

I like twists like that. Publishers don't, but I do. This isn't some stormy little romance between the married head of some central directorate and a similarly married production technician unfurling against the background of boiling metal and underfulfilled pouring quotas.

Still thinking about literature, about stories and Schizo Barinov, I sat down to breakfast. The mean-spirited example I myself had invented—about the stormy little romance—suddenly seized my imagination. Decades pass, thousands and thousands of pages are written, but that type of literature still exemplifies little more than obvious hackery or, at best, poignant feebleness.

But the crazy thing is that those kinds of stories really do happen! It is indeed the case that somewhere, metal is poured, quotas go underfulfilled, and against that background—or even because of it—the married head of the central directorate meets an also-married technician, and they have a conflict that evolves into a stormy little romance, and terrible situations arise, and nightmarish moral and organizational boils come to a head and burst, up to and including criminal charges . . . All of this does in fact occur in real life, pretty often even, and it's no less worthy of representation than the stormy little romance between a playboy nobleman and a provincial maiden, up to and including a duel. But what you end up with in the former case is crap.

And so it always was—and by the way, I'm not just talking about my fellow Soviet writers. Hemingway, for example, mocks the poor hack who writes a novel about a strike at a textile factory, vainly striving to combine the problems of union work with a character's passion toward a beautiful Jewish agitator. Married technician, Jewish agitator . . . Human language rebels against formulations of this sort when what we're really talking about is a relationship between a man and a woman.

Similarly, the love story in my *Comrade Officers* occurs in the context of political education among the officers of the Nth Self-Propelled Artillery Regiment. And it's terrible. It's the reason I'm afraid to reread my own book. You need a special kind of reader for that sort of thing! And that's exactly what we have here in the Soviet Union. I don't know if we forged them ourselves through exposure to our earlier works, or if they're somehow naturally occurring. Whatever the case may be, that kind of book just flies off the shelves.

I stood at the window, drinking my kefir. A freezing day was dawning. Trees and bushes had turned completely white. One by one, the lights across the way were turning off; in the street below, dark homunculi hurried down uncleared paths past snowdrifts toward the bus stop. Cars rushed along, some of them with sidelights already off.

It's because there is no love in our day, I thought suddenly. Little romances, yes; love, no. There's no time for love nowadays—buses are overcrowded, lines snake through all the stores, the day care is on the other side of town. You have to be very young and very carefree to be capable of love. The only people who love today are older couples who managed to stay together for a quarter century, didn't succumb to the perennial "apartment problem" or devolve into beasts due to myriad other corrosive little inconveniences, and managed to split up both power and responsibility in a peaceful way. Like Valya Demchenko and his wife Sonechka. But that's not the sort of love we're told to praise. And thank God for that. Let Kostya Kudinov sing praises. Or our Sweet Soviet Boy . . .

"But that's all philosophy—isn't it high time to get to work?" I said aloud.

And so I began to wash the dishes. I can't stand it when there's even a single dirty plate in my sink. A clean and empty sink is a sine qua non for high-quality work. Especially when the work we're talking about is screenplays or articles. I like writing screenplays. Of all the ways to turn the literary crank, I most enjoy translations and screenplays. Maybe because, in both cases, the responsibility is shared.

It's nice to feel, after all, that it's the director who will answer for the eventual film—a person who, as a rule, is young, energetic, and fully conscious of the fact that film has its own language and that the most important thing about it is not the words I write but the images he invents. And if something goes wrong, he'll wave it off and say without a care, "Eh, that'll do for a Weltanschauung!" And as for his other aphorism—"Not a shot on native soil!"—just let him try filming my tank attack scenes somewhere on the Champs-Élysées! And in the end, the movie will get made. It won't be Eisenstein and it won't be Tarkovsky, of course, but people will go see it. I'll watch it too, and not without interest, because I really am curious to see how he filmed my tank attack.

(I'm a simple man. I like it when movies—and movies only!—contain one or two SS Sturmbannführers, artillery fire from every type of weapon, and a rippin' good tank attack, preferably a massed one . . . My taste in film is quite primitive; Valya Demchenko likes to call it "infantile militarism.")

I sat down at the typewriter and wrote without stopping for over two hours, until the phone rang once again.

The sun had been streaming into the room for a while now, and I was hot and in the zone, so when I picked up I didn't so much speak as bark into the receiver. But it turned out to be our dear Fyodor Mikheyevich, and I, as an expert in Japanese culture and a faithful devotee of the *kō* principle, immediately had to lower my tone.

Thankfully, the conversation didn't turn to Bannaya. Fyodor Mikheyevich asked whether I was aware of the conflict between Oleg Oreshin and Semyon Kolesnichenko. It took me several seconds to switch gears, and then I said that yes, I was aware of such a conflict; there'd been a squabble in the selection committee last month. Fyodor Mikheyevich informed me that Oreshin had filed a complaint against Kolesnichenko with the secretariat and that he, Fyodor Mikheyevich, would like to know my personal opinion on this conflict.

"He's an idiot and a troublemaker, that Oreshin," I blurted before I could stop myself, once again forgetting my firm decision never to interfere, interlope, or intercede.

Fyodor Mikheyevich pointed out sternly that this wasn't a real answer, that what the situation required was not random insults but an objective opinion on a specific matter.

But what objective opinion could I possibly offer here? At the selection committee's last meeting, this Oleg Oreshin, a sleek and polished man in a well-tailored suit, with glittering cufflinks, a thick ring, and a gold tooth, raised his hand and proclaimed his complaint against prose writer Semyon Kolesnichenko, accusing him of malicious plagiarism. Whom did Kolesnichenko plagiarize? Why, none other than poet and fable writer Oleg Oreshin himself, member of the selection committee and winner of *Machine Tool Builder* magazine's Special Prize. Two years ago he, Oleg Oreshin, published the satirical fable "Bear Troubles" in the aforementioned magazine. Imagine his amazement when literally a few days ago, in the December issue of *Sovetish heymland*, he read the novella *Train of Hope*, translated from the Hebrew, which replicated the entire story and all the characters of his "Bear Troubles"!

Astounded, Oleg Oreshin undertook an independent investigation and determined that the aforementioned S. Kolesnichenko, having plagiarized Oreshin's work, snuck his novella to the editors of *Sovetish heymland* under the guise of a translation from the Hebrew. S. Kolesnichenko further deceived the editors by claiming that the translation of this novella, allegedly written by progressive Hebrew writer so-and-so, was produced by Kolesnichenko's own bedridden friend, and so on and so forth. And so he, Oleg Oreshin, demands that his comrades on the selection committee assist him in . . . and so on, and so forth, and so on.

The most fantastical element in this delirious tale was that at least a third of the selection committee took O. Oreshin's complaint very much to heart and immediately began making recommendations, each more monstrous than the last. But the forces of reason prevailed. Our chairman, instantly realizing that responsibility for this squabble would fall squarely on his shoulders, made the following stern pronouncement: although on a personal level he certainly understands Comrade Oreshin's indignation, this matter is entirely outside the purview of the selection committee, which therefore cannot afford to dedicate time to it.

At the time, I had foolishly thought that that would be the end of it. But human stupidity is apparently limitless. That had *not* been the end of it. On the other hand, though, Fyodor Mikheyevich was right: random insults and pointless statements on the limitlessness of human stupidity wouldn't cut it here. I composed myself and, weighing my words carefully, said something to the effect that Oleg Oreshin's arguments had failed to convince me. The transformation of a fable into a novella, even if such a thing had taken place, precludes the possibility of plagiarism. As a seasoned translator, however, I would be very interested to learn how Kolesnichenko had managed to pass off his own work as a translation. In my view, such a thing would be completely impossible to accomplish.

This, finally, was "the speech not of a boy, but of a man," to borrow Pushkin's phrase. Mikheyevich heard me out without interrupting, thanked me, and hung up. Bannaya never came up.

I emerged from behind my desk, opened the terrace door, and stood awhile in the sunlight on the threshold. I felt drained, tired, and most satisfied. One way or another, I had fulfilled the day's duties, and then some. Now I could stick the screenplay in a drawer, cover the typewriter, and run downstairs for the paper. Which is what I did.

Besides the paper, I'd received two letters: one was an official invitation from the Club to a concert by some unknown bard, which I decided to give away to Katya—this could be up her alley. The second envelope had been hand-fashioned from thick brown paper, with Scotch-taped flaps. Someone had written above my address in black ink, "For Sorokin's eyes only!" But they'd omitted a return address.

I can't stand letters with no return address. They don't come often, but they always contain something nasty, or some problem, or some additional source of troubles and worries. Annoyed, I began fumbling around inside my desk for scissors, but then the phone rang again.

This time it was Zinaida Filippovna, who meekly reminded me that, though the next selection committee meeting was only ten days away, I had not yet picked up the books I was supposed to be considering. I asked how many people were up for discussion. The answer was two prose writers, two playwrights, three critics-slash-journalists, and one short-form poet. That made eight. I asked what a "short-form poet" was. She answered that no one really knew, but that this was the person everyone was expecting to cause an uproar. I promised to stop by soon.

Great, another uproar. There's a good topic for a story, I thought. A typical meeting of the selection committee. First, to get it off our plates, we discuss the matter of some poor sap writing popular science literature. A referee gives a furious speech against, in which he constantly confuses "bathysphere" with "stratosphere" and "bathyscaphe" with "pyroscaphe." The committee hearkens unto him with silent terror; some people cross themselves on the sly, while others mutter protection charms. The gist of the referee's objections: "But where's the literature here, I ask you?" The second referee is brief and honest: he was unable to finish even one book by the author in question, failed to understand anything, all those infusoriums, leprosariums . . . the author is a PhD, what the hell does he need a Writers' Union membership for? Then it's the chairman's turn: space race, the age of STS (by which he means STR, scientific-technical revolution) . . . let's not forget that the authority of our organization . . . high literature . . . Anton Pavlovich Chekhov . . . Lev Tolstoy . . . Alexander Sergeyevich Pushkin, even . . . Crap Crapovich. . . Then comes the secret ballot, and the author's bid for union membership is almost unanimously denied—though there is a lone dissenter.

The second applicant is a doctor, a colorectal surgeon, but his true love is the Russian village. A referee with hungover eyes expresses vociferous admiration for this love and describes two of the author's works. A peasant is driving his cart through the forest when, all of a sudden, a tiger. (The story is set in the region of Ryazan, in a village called Myasnoy—as in *myaso*, "meat.") The peasant takes off running. The tiger follows. The peasant plunges neck-deep into an ice-hole. The tiger sits all night at the edge of the ice, snorting. Later it turns out that it escaped from the zoo and missed being around people, which is why it wouldn't leave the peasant alone . . . General delight, amiable laughter, the hussars clamor approvingly. Now comes the second work. A peasant goes to the doctor, complaining of internal pains. The doctor asks him to bring by some "test results." The peasant decides he's being asked for a bribe and writes to the local prosecutor. Meanwhile, his pains turn out to be cancer, the doctor performs a successful operation, the peasant is saved, but then the doctor, still in the OR, receives a summons from the prosecutor . . . More delight and approving clamor; one of the hussars laughs so hard he cries, burying his nose in my shoulder. The second referee reads aloud from the author's descriptions of rural life: the general delight and approbation transform into thunderous simpering and waterfalls of tears and sobs, after which this applicant is also denied, but this time with three dissenting votes. Everyone is embarrassed. One of the hussars turns to me and says, "I just don't get it. Personally, I was in favor, and that's how I voted!"

Then it's the turn of the former public utilities minister of a southern Soviet republic, recent author of a luxuriously appointed volume, released in a deluxe edition. The title is something like *A History of Laundry and Laundering from Queen Tamar to Modern Times*.

My ruminations were interrupted by yet another phone call. Fyodor Mikheyevich said, sounding concerned, "Sorry to bother you again, Felix Alexandrovich . . . Did you end up going to Banaya yesterday?"

"Yes," I said. "Of course! Brought them my stuff, everything's A-OK."

"Oh, thank you. That's all I wanted to ask."

Fyodor Mikheyevich hung up, whereupon I arose from my chair and went straight to the entryway to put on my shoes. And only when I had already bundled up, wrapped myself in a scarf, stuck a hat on my head, pulled on my gloves, and even grabbed on to the door bolt to turn it did I remember that I'd left my guinea pig manuscript in the Club yesterday . . . and that if I stopped at the Club to get it now . . .

I returned to my living room and (creakily!) pulled a random folder, preferably on the thinner side, out of the smaller archive I keep under my desk (draft translations, copies of annotations to Japanese patent applications, draft reviews, and other wastepaper). I tied my prize with string just to be safe, stuffed the brown envelope with no return address into my coat pocket (to read on the way), and left the house.

The building on Bannaya turned out to be five-storied, gray, and made of concrete. Its left side was shrouded in scaffolding, which was deserted and clogged with snow. The middle part of the facade looked fairly fresh, while the building's right side was ready for another remodel. There was only one central entryway. The doorway was wide; its architect had evidently intended it to admit six streams of entrants simultaneously—however, as is customary, only one of the six doors was functional. The other five were tightly locked, and one was even boarded up, the boards playfully decorated to look like the palette of a messy painter. As is also customary, the walls to the right and left of the single opening were festooned with variegated glass plaques bearing the names of assorted organizations, so that it took me a while to locate the modest sign, with its silver lettering, of the INSTITUTE FOR LINGUISTIC RESEARCH, SOVIET ACADEMY OF SCIENCES.

After squeezing my way, not without difficulty, through the door's lone functional portion, I spent some time roaming in a forest of dark curtains amid a crowd of fellow unfortunates. It was a dark and disturbing place; the floor was such a hash of melted snow that we all clung to one another, fearing a fall.

When I finally broke free of the curtains, I found myself standing in front of a capacious staircase leading to an enormous round hall extending five stories high. The hall's middle section was partitioned into numerous wooden cubicles. Grayish daylight filtered through a latticed glass roof; on my left was a glass kiosk selling art supplies, and on my right was a stand with fried hand pies and jam-filled cakes.

I could not begin to imagine where I was supposed to go from here, and when I tried to find this out from those who, like me, had been tearing their way through the curtains, I found out they were all here for cakes—except one little old man, who'd been sent to buy hand pies.

The old woman at the kiosk told me this was her second day at work. Finally, a coatless, heavily made-up lady with a delivery book under her arm told me to turn right and go up one floor. It was only in the second-floor stairwell that I finally saw a relevant-looking sign, which pointed me to the third floor.

I began my ascent along a metal spiral staircase that was as dark and disturbing as the curtain forest. My feet slipped on the uneven steps. Someone going the opposite way huffed and puffed alarmingly, seemingly trying to push me down. Later, I heard a muffled female scream accompanied by the clatter of heels—someone must have slipped. A separate someone was prodding me in the back with something hard, inanimate, and wooden (based on the sensations it produced), mumbling muffled curses all the while.

But nothing lasts forever. I was standing in the third-floor stairwell puffing and panting, wondering if I should take some nitroglycerin, when I got one last blow to the small of the back and a muffled voice inquired, "Why don't you move your ass?" A wooden stepladder was then carried past me—it was so long that I could scarcely believe my eyes: How could anyone drag something like that up a spiral staircase?

Placing a crumb of nitroglycerin under my tongue, I looked around. In front of me were three doors, like in a fairytale: one to my left, another to my right, and a third straight ahead. According to the wall placard, I was meant to turn right. Behind the right-hand door was a small table, and on the table a lamp, and next to the lamp a little old lady with knitting in her lap. She gave me a friendly, questioning look, and we had a chat.

The little old lady was fully up to speed. Writers were supposed to go to room number such and such, through the auditorium, which could be reached via that hallway there, just go straight through and don't make any turns, not that there are a lot of turns you *could* make, maybe the cafeteria, although they're not open yet. I thanked her and set off, and as I walked away the little old lady said, "Except, they're having a meeting . . ." And although I didn't understand what she meant, I turned around and nodded gratefully, just in case.

The hallway. It's not often you encounter hallways like this one nowadays. It was narrow, windowless, with mysterious grated vents just under the ceiling and thick metal doors appearing now on the left, now on the right. The floor was hardwood, with creaky, uneven boards that receded dangerously under one's feet. It wasn't straight, either, this hallway, but proceeded along a classical fortress-style zigzag, with no leg exceeding twenty yards in length. It was all designed for the situation where the enemy's armored infantry finally breaks through the defenses on the spiral staircase, knocks over the little old lady and her table, and bursts into the hallway, not yet knowing what terrible trap awaits it: Will boiling oil pour down from the vents beneath the ceiling? Will the metal doors fall open, revealing bristling spears with serrated points as wide as your palm? Will the floorboards crumble underfoot? Will merciless arrows strike point-blank from behind the next zigzag? In short, by the time I reached the end of the hallway, I was drenched in sweat.

As the honest old lady had foretold, the hallway gave way to an auditorium. But only now did I grasp the meaning of her final words. There was indeed some sort of meeting going on, most likely a plenary one, since the room was packed to the gills with sitting and standing people. There was no way forward from here.

At first I did not perceive this meeting as an obstacle to my intentions. It looked fairly ordinary: a table with a green cloth, a carafe of water, someone speaking at a podium, at least three hundred male and female youths in attendance. (When they could have been advancing scientific and technical progress!) Standing on tiptoe, I examined my surroundings over the sea of heads until I located an inconspicuous door in the farthest corner. Hanging above the door frame was a white banner with black lettering reading WRITERS—IN HERE. It was only at that moment that I began to understand the awfulness of my predicament.

There was no question of elbowing my way through the meeting to get to the door. I'm no Benkei capable of stepping on people's heads and shoulders in a crowded temple—I couldn't get away with it, and plus, it's not my style. Similarly, there could be no question of proudly turning on my heel and leaving. I had come too far already. Logically, there was only one other option: to wait, secure in the knowledge that no meeting lasts forever.

Having come to this conclusion, I immediately thought of the cafeteria. Somewhere back there, behind one of the terrifying metal doors, there were cheese Danishes, salami sandwiches, Pepsi-Cola, and possibly even beer. I looked at my watch. It was ten till three; if the cafeteria was fated to open at all today, it would most likely do so ten minutes from now. And I could endure anything for ten minutes. I shifted my weight to one foot, leaned my back against the wall, and began to listen.

Very quickly I understood that I was witnessing a so-called comrades' court. The accused, a certain Zhukovitsky, had made a habit of breaking the hearts of young women in his department. He'd gotten away with it at first, but after the third or fourth case, his comrades lost patience. His crimes cried out for justice, while his victims cried out to the local trade union committee. The accused, an insolently handsome man in a gleaming patent leather jacket, sat sulking on a separate chair to the left of the presidium. He appeared stubborn and unrepentant, though obedient to fate.

In short, the case was open and shut—or so I thought. It seemed obvious that once the local committee member ceased his babbling, it would be the turn of the department head, who would crucify the defendant on the cross of public opprobrium, and then immediately, in the same breath, beg the court for leniency, because his department is all damsels and every male is worth his weight in gold; then, the chairman would sum things up in a brief but energetic speech, after which everyone would run for the cafeteria.

As I awaited this inevitable (to my mind) denouement, I began studying people's faces—my favorite activity at all meetings, assemblies, and seminars. Mere seconds later, I noted with amazement the flaky-skinned mug of our Dear, Sweet Soviet Boy, Petenka Skorobogatov, and the sad-sack profile of his friend the billiards player. Both looked like they'd been sitting there from the very beginning, immovably and by rights. The billiards player was sitting motionless, his eyes glued to the presidium, its green baize tablecloth apparently arousing pleasant associations. By contrast, our Sweet Soviet Boy was a whirlwind of activity. Every other minute, he would turn to his right-hand neighbor and attempt to convince her of something, shaking a fat index finger, then he'd lunge forward with his entire torso, thrusting his head into the next row in order to convince his neighbors there of something as well. His fat, upraised buttocks would, meanwhile, perform complicated gyrations. Finally, as though entirely satisfied with the sagacity of his interlocutors, he would lean back in his chair, cross his arms on his chest, and, cocking his head slightly, listen benevolently to whispers in the row behind.

The speaker at the podium continued: ". . . And in times like these, when we must channel all our energy into the development of specific linguistic studies, to the development and enhancement of our ties with adjacent scientific fields—in times like these, it is especially important to strengthen and heighten the labor discipline of every individual, the moral and ethical level of all and each in turn, spiritual purity, personal honesty . . ."

"And animal husbandry!" Petenka Skorobogatov cried out suddenly and demandingly, thrusting his arm, complete with outstretched index finger, upward and out.

A muffled titter swept the room.

At the podium, the speaker paused in confusion. "Absolutely . . . that is inarguable . . . and animal husbandry, too . . . But as for Comrade Zhukovitsky, we should not forget that he is our comrade . . ."

Well done, Sweet Soviet Boy! Say what you will, but there is something human with a capital *H* about him, no doubt about it. Despite his piggish, eternally hungover little eyes. Despite the alcoholic fumes that form a kind of personal atmosphere around him. Despite his exemplary lack of talent and his hacky children's stories. Despite his habit of joining groups without being invited and pouring himself drinks without asking . . . (No, I take that back. True, our Sweet Soviet Boy rarely has money on him because he's always drinking it away. But when he *does* have money, he welcomes all comers to eat and drink their fill, and then some.) He's inventive —that's his saving grace. He brings to life all kinds of impossible fantasies of the type you'd normally only encounter in fiction.

Once, at the Writers' Guest House in Murashi, that idiot Rogozhin publicly scolded our Sweet Soviet Boy for showing up intoxicated at the dining hall, lecturing him on the importance of moral character to the Soviet writer. Skorobogatov heard him out with suspicious humility, but by the next morning, a message had appeared in the vast snowdrift directly in front of the house: ROGOZHIN, I LOVE YOU! The words had been spelled out in a stream of splashy yellow liquid, which, judging by the depth of its penetration into the snow, had been quite hot.

And now, picture this: the male half of Murashi is splitting its sides with laughter. Our Sweet Soviet Boy walks around, stone-faced, repeating, "You know, this is utterly immoral. A writer would never do such a thing . . ." The female half of Murashi wrinkles its collective nose in disgust and demands that the offending substance be immediately buried in the snow. Meanwhile, Rogozhin runs back and forth in front of the snowdrift like a caged beast of prey, allowing no one near it until the appropriate authorities have had a look. The appropriate authorities, however, aren't really in a hurry, though someone does Rogozhin (and themselves, of course) the favor of taking a few photographs: the message, Rogozhin with the message in the background, Rogozhin alone, and the message again. Rogozhin wrestles the roll of film away from the photographer and rushes to Moscow; forty-five minutes on the train—no biggie.

With the film roll in one pocket and a lengthy denunciation of Petenka in the other, Rogozhin dashes to our secretariat to file a defamation complaint. The photo lab at the Club produces a dozen prints, lickety-split, which he indignantly throws onto Fyodor Mikheyevich's desk. As it happens, Fyodor Mikheyevich's office is chock full of board members, who have gathered to celebrate someone's jubilee. Many of them have already heard about the goings-on at Murashi; the room is abuzz. The photos are passed around and mostly disappear. Polina Zlatopolskikh (with a wistful roll of the eyes): "What an amazingly powerful stream he has!"

Stone-faced Fyodor Mikheyevich states that the message doesn't constitute defamation. Rogozhin is thrown off, but only for a moment. The defamation consists in the method of delivery, he declares. Stone-faced Fyodor Mikheyevich states that he sees no reason to accuse Pyotr Skorobogatov specifically. In response, Rogozhin demands that a handwriting expert be brought in. Everyone falls over themselves laughing. Stone-faced Fyodor Mikheyevich expresses doubt that a handwriting expert would be useful in this particular case. Rogozhin, losing his cool, points to certain criminological studies, which allegedly assert that the properties of ideomotorics are such that an individual's handwriting remains constant regardless of the writing implement. He attempts to corroborate this fact by placing a ballpoint pen between his teeth and straining to sign some papers on Fyodor Mikheyevich's desk. He threatens to take the matter all the way to the Soviet Central Committee and, in short, behaves very badly.

In the end, Fyodor Mikheyevich is forced to give in, and a commission sets out to survey the scene of the crime. Petenka Skorobogatov, now feeling cornered and rather frightened by the magnitude of the events he's unleashed, confesses that he is the source of the message. "But not the way you think, you perverts! How would that even be humanly possible?" It's late in the evening. The comission, fully assembled, stands on the porch. The snowdrift was freshly turned that very morning and is virginally pure. Petenka Skorobogatov walks next to the snow and, deftly manipulating a small, round teapot, writes out: ROGOZHIN, I AM INDIFFERENT TOWARD YOU! The commission leaves, satisfied. The message remains.

That's Skorobogatov, our Sweet Soviet Boy!

His thunderous exclamation of "And animal husbandry!" returned me to the present. The trial continued. A cry erupted from the breast of the billiards player, now roused to action. Something had changed during my stroll down memory lane. Now the topic at the podium was, for some reason, a fur coat. An expensive fur coat. An imported fur coat. The fur coat had been stolen. It had been stolen brazenly and provocatively. It seemed the audience was being exhorted not to steal fur coats. The victims of dissipation and voluptuousness had now been forgotten; in fact, the story of the stolen fur coat had, in some mysterious way, rehabilitated the accused. He was no longer sitting there with a look of obedience to fate; he'd straightened up and, pressing the palms of his hands into his spread knees, cast accusatory, defiant glances in the presidium's direction. The members of the presidium refused to meet his eye, and one of them was significantly redder in the face than the others.

I glanced at my watch. It was now past three, and high time to seek out the cafeteria. Just then, two pale youths with smoldering eyes, as the poet Valery Bryusov might have put it, slipped past me into the hallway and lit up cigarettes, inhaling greedily. What immediately struck me was their unnatural excitement, their strange alertness and zeal. They evinced no fatigue, no boredom—on the contrary, they clearly desired to consume their dose of nicotine as quickly as possible and return to the auditorium. I'd never seen people so captivated by a meeting in my entire life.

I asked them how long they thought this bloviation would continue. I saw that my choice of words dismayed them. Very curtly, they explained to me that the meeting was currently in full swing and unlikely to conclude before the end of the day. Then one of them figured it out: "You must be a writer!"

"Alas," I confessed.

"What's your last name?" asked the other with youthful spontaneity.

"Yesenin," said I, and started for home.

Cursing all meetings with the most terrible curse I could think of, I stopped by a toy shop on Petrovka and bought the twin bandits each a toy car. By the time I returned to my apartment, my good humor was restored. Katya was puttering around in the kitchen. My famished nose was delighted and immediately transmitted that delight to my entire body: I smelled simmering beef bourguignon.

As I was taking off my coat, Katya flew out of the kitchen, presented her hot cheek for a kiss, and, holding her greasy hands outstretched like a surgeon preparing for an operation, launched into an excited story about her work life.

At first I listened only halfheartedly, because I was once again struck dumb with amazement: such a pretty, spirited, fashionable young woman—and yet, it's like she's been jinxed! How can that be? It's utterly absurd. I always thought that a woman with flair is doomed to good luck, but there you are . . . Thirty years old. Two children. A first husband who melted into thin air. A crappy second husband belonging to some species of slug that never dries out. Problems at work. A dissertation that's been finished for three years but for some reason can't be defended. It's all so bizarre, so inexplicable . . .

Still on autopilot, I followed Katya to the kitchen, where I suddenly realized that she was talking about something very strange indeed—something directly involving me.

Apparently, shortly after lunch, she'd been called into the personnel department and formally interrogated. The inquiries were mostly the usual questionnaire kind, but occasionally, as if by accident, a different, quite incongruous sort of question would slip through. Clever Katya immediately spotted them and, without batting an eye, made a mental note. And now she was scrupulously repeating these questions to me, one by one . . . What was her earliest memory of her father, i.e., me? Had she ever visited his hometown, i.e., Leningrad? Did she know any of her father's friends from before the war? Had she ever seen her father with any of those friends? Had her father told her the fate of the house in Leningrad where he'd grown up and where he'd lived before the war?

After rattling all this off, she fell silent and looked at me expectantly. I was also silent, sensing, with horror, the blood rushing to my face and my gaze sliding suspiciously down into the corner. I felt like a complete idiot.

"Dad, what did you do this time?" she asked, lowering her voice.

She was frightened, and my reaction to her story frightened her even more. I could only huff and puff in response. Thousands of words roiled at the tip of my tongue, but all of them, unfortunately, were melodramatic, false, and would have involved gestures like the Outstretched Hand, the Upward-Turn'd Gaze, and other Schiller-esque antics. Then a terrible thought hit me: What if they'd published me somewhere abroad again without consulting the All-Union Copyright Agency? Those bastards, what the hell was wrong with them?

And I could keep silent no longer. "It's all nonsense, dammit!" I barked. "I didn't do anything! Why are you looking at me like that? So some bastard denounced me . . . Why did they have to call you in? Did they tell you?"

"For a chat," said Katya. "I might go to Ganda . . ."

"Ganda? What the hell? To Africa? What about our bandits?"

But it turned out she'd thought it all through. Clara would take the bandits, the Shchukins would sublet her apartment, and I would buy up the collected works. I hated the whole idea. If the bandits lived at Clara's, how would I see them? I have zero interest in seeing Clara or her general, no desire to buy up the collected works . . . But also—what about Albert? Will Clara take him, too? Oh, so the husband is being transferred to Syzran anyway? Fantastic! Congratulations! Same old story, right in her mother's footsteps. Of course, it's your life. But you should know they're shooting people in Ganda right now!

She knew exactly what to do with me. While I was hissing and spitting, she deftly filled my plate with meat and mushrooms braised in red wine, poured me two fingers of cognac, and sat me down at the table. I grunted, downed the drink, softened up, cast a final look full of parental reproach her way, and grabbed a fork.

"What about you?" I asked belatedly as usual, my mouth already full.

"I had some already," she answered as usual. Standing on her knees in the chair, she pooched out her round tush, rested her elbows on the table, and set to watching me eat, visibly pleased.

"If you're traveling to Ganda," I said, smacking my lips, "then don't worry about it. Personnel has just run out of things to ask you, that's all. Did they ask about your mother?"

"They did."

"You see! Cut me a piece of that roll, will you?"

"What they asked about my mother is why she divorced you," said Katya, slicing the bread.

I could barely stop myself from smashing my utensils down on the table. What the hell, that's none of their damn business! But then I thought, They can all go straight to hell, what do I care? And if they find some reason to keep Katya from going to Ganda, so much the better. Katya in Ganda is the last thing I need—Ganda, where there's shooting going on as enormous crowds of natives pour napalm all over each other . . .

"They really were very odd questions," said Katya quietly. "Unusual ones. Dad, is everything all right with you? You're not hiding anything, are you?"

And that's why I can never let my own beloved daughter, my one and only child, ever read a single page from my Blue Folder. She's been burned before, after Bryzheikin published his little piece about my *Modern Tales* and I was carted off with my first real episode of angina. She's never been the same since. Like right now—she's smiling, joking around, putting on a brave face, but in her eyes is that same fear. I can still see those eyes at my bedside in the hospital . . .

I calmed her down as best I could, and we started on our tea. Katya told me about the twin bandits, I told her about Petenka Skorobogatov and the meeting I'd witnessed. It all felt very cozy, and I hated to think that in fifteen minutes Katya would gather her things and leave. At the last minute, I gave her the toy cars for the bandits and the concert ticket. The latter she accepted with delight, telling me all about this bard and how famous he'd gotten, while I listened and racked my brain for a delicate way to convey that I hadn't forgotten about the dressmaker or the fur coat (another fur coat!), not at all, that I was keeping it in mind even though she, Katya, would never dream of reminding me about it, it's just that I have to muster the energy . . . I felt a faint hope that the coat question would die on the vine given her trip to Ganda. After all, what does she need furs for down there?

She was already putting on her coat when the phone rang, and we had to say good-bye in a hurry. I picked up. Kyrie eleison! Merciful Lord, preserve us! It was O. Oreshin.

He was calling to demand that I immediately, right away, clearly and unequivocally pledge my positive support for his just struggle against Semyon Kolesnichenko, that shameless plagiarist. Having enlisted my positive support—without concealing that I was not the first to whom he turned for same—he could tell me that several authoritative members of the secretariat had promised him their full cooperation in his merciless struggle against plagiarism, without which support, naturally, there could be no real hope of succeeding in unmasking the plagiarist mafia . . .

I wondered, with morbid curiosity, how he would disentangle himself from this bit of syntactic concertina wire. I was willing to bet that he'd already forgotten where this unimaginable morass had begun, but I'd underestimated him.

So anyway, having enlisted my positive support, he, Oreshin, would be able to raise the issue of the plagiarist mafia at the upcoming meeting of the secretariat with a specificity and urgency that is usually in woefully short supply when it is a question of those who are nominally our colleagues, but who in fact, morally and ethically . . .

I carefully placed the receiver on the table, poured myself a glass of water, and took some nitroglycerin. Oleg Oreshin was still droning on. I struggled to comprehend his psychology. To be frank, when the conflagration first began a month ago, I took him for an ordinary, zoological anti-Semite—of the same breed as the hussars. But now I could see I was mistaken. He wasn't an anti-Semite. Moreover, he wasn't even a demagogue. Apparently, he was sincerely shocked that he, suffering agony or perhaps a fit of frantic inspiration, had crafted an ethico-moral dilemma, cleverly skewering the coarse and avaricious bears as well as the sly and nimble hares, when all of a sudden—*bam!*—that artful dodger, that Kolesnichenko, comes out of nowhere like some sort of flitting moth; a literary parasite by vocation, he certainly doesn't suffer either creative agony or inspiration, all he has are sharp eyes and clever, grabby paws—and off he goes, grabbing whatever he can, altering one or two details, and presto! And then, to cover the last of his tracks, he passes his concoction off as a translation from some exotic language, on the assumption that no one can read it in the original anyway . . .

He's an idiot, our friend O. Oreshin, that's what's going on here. Not in the colloquial, mild sense of the term; he's an idiot as a representative of a special psychological type. He walks among us like some sort of extraterrestrial with a completely different system of values, a strange and alien psychology, totally foreign existential aims, so that everything that we condescendingly regard as a run-of-the-mill inferiority complex or a morbid deviation from the psychological norm is in fact the healthy heart of his worldview.

". . . But otherwise none of us honest writers—and we're the majority! . . . the Kolesnichenkos among us stick out like sore thumbs, whereas the majority is composed of people like you and me, whose priorities are honest labor, careful study of the material at hand, a level of party-minded creativity . . ."

"And animal husbandry!" I barked on a whim.

For an entire second, or maybe even two, the receiver was silent. Then Oreshin said hesitantly, "Animal husbandry? Well . . . yes . . . animal husbandry, no doubt about it . . . But do you see, Felix Alexandrovich, what I find most important in all this?"

And it was back to square one.

In the end, he and I came to the following agreement: I said I would study the issue, reading the fable and the novella and speaking with Kolesnichenko, and then we'd talk on the phone again and continue this interesting and useful discussion.

Blergh! I threw down the phone, and, like Kingsley Amis's Lucky Jim, jumped up onto the sofa and began furiously scratching my armpits while pulling hideous faces. None escape, I thought over and over. None of them escape, I repeated, leaping around and grimacing. There is no escape for them, there can't be, now and forever, and unto ages of ages, amen! Then I ran out of breath, fell backward onto the sofa, and flung my arms out beside me.

Only then did I notice that it was now completely dark. It was evening—early evening, but evening nonetheless, and I thought, not without sadness, that even just a couple of years ago this was a time when I could still sit down at the typewriter and rattle off two or three good-quality pages. Not anymore, Comrade Sorokin, no chance of rattling off anything good at this hour now, all you'll accomplish is to ruin your mood . . .

And then the phone rang again. I got up from the sofa —creakily!—and picked up.

The secret hope that the caller was Rita had not yet reached my consciousness when a man's voice said quietly, "May I please speak to Felix Alexandrovich?"

"Speaking."

After a tiny pause, the voice asked, "Excuse me, Felix Alexandrovich, but did you get our letter?"

"What letter?"

"Hm . . . It must not have arrived yet. Sorry to bother you, Felix Alexandrovich . . . We'll call in two days, then . . . Sorry . . . Goodbye . . ."

And then I was listening to the dial tone.

What the hell . . . I quickly counted all the letters I'd received over the last few days and suddenly remembered the brown envelope with no return address. Where had I put it? Aha! I'd stuck it in my coat pocket and forgotten all about it . . . The vague, unpleasant premonition I'd felt upon discovering the lack of a return address gripped me once again.

I turned on the light, retrieved the envelope from my coat in the entryway, and, sitting down at the table, began examining its postmarks. They betrayed nothing out of the ordinary. Moscow, G-69—where was that? . . . The paper was very thick, I couldn't see through it, but the envelope didn't feel like it contained anything besides the letter. I took some scissors and opened the missive very carefully, cutting just along the edge. Inside was a second envelope, also taped tightly shut. This one was a very standard mailing envelope with a picture on it. It bore no address but said only "To Felix Alexandrovich Sorokin! Personal and confidential!"

I found myself sitting there, sticking out my lower lip, utterly ambivalent. That phone call . . . *WE will call you* . . . Katya's workplace questions . . . The prospect of taking that envelope to the authorities and explaining this and that about it, especially in writing, weighed heavily on my soul. Although . . .

Sure, I got a letter. It was nonsense. I don't recall. You know, I get a lot of letters, it's not like I personally answer each and every one . . .

I resolutely unsealed the second envelope.

Inside was a piece of postage paper with blue edges. It said the following, in black ink, the penmanship clear and beautiful. No salutation.

We figured out what you are a long time ago. But don't worry. We cherish and understand your fate so well that we would never, ever threaten to unmask you. On the contrary, we are prepared to help in any way we can to extinguish the rumors that are already circulating about you and the reasons for your presence among us. If you cannot leave our planet (or our time) for technical reasons, please know: though our technological capabilities may be small, they are entirely at your disposal. We will be calling you on the phone. Nothing will disturb your work.

Damn them all to hell, the brainless bastards.

6. VICTOR BANEV

CALL TO ACTION

The next day Victor woke up late, getting on to dinnertime. His head was bothering him, but his mood was surprisingly good.

The night before, he'd polished off a pack of cigarettes, then gone downstairs, picked someone's car lock with a bobby pin, led Irma out through the service entrance, and driven her to her mother's. While he writhed in terrible angst, Irma sat next to him, neat and squeaky clean, hair styled according to the latest fashion—no pigtails in sight. It was possible she was even wearing lipstick. He had very much wanted to start a conversation, but that would have required confessing his own unfathomable stupidity, which would have been antipedagogical. In the end, Irma unexpectedly told him he could smoke (provided he rolled down all the windows) and started explaining how interesting it all was, how it was just like what she'd read about recently but hadn't quite believed, and how great of him it was to set up this unforeseen and extremely educational adventure. He was pretty OK in general, actually, he didn't make your eyes glaze over with boredom or talk nonsense, and as for that Diana, well, she's almost one of us, she hates everyone. It's a shame, though, that she's so undereducated, and she's a little too into boozing, but at the end of the day that's not so terrible, you're also into booze, but the kids at school liked you because you were honest, you didn't pretend to be some gatekeeper of higher knowledge, which is cool because you're really not one, and even Bol-Kunatz said that you're the only worthwhile person in town, besides Dr. Golem, of course, but then again, Golem has nothing to do with the city, and plus he's not a writer and doesn't express any ideology, and hey, do you think ideology is necessary, or are things better without it, lots of people today think that the future is all about de-ideologization . . .

It turned into a great conversation, both interlocutors brimming with mutual respect. By the time he returned to the hotel (having ditched the car in some junk-strewn alley), Victor was already feeling like fatherhood wasn't such an ungrateful job, especially if you knew a thing or two about life and could use even its darker sides to pedagogical ends. To celebrate, he had a drink with Teddy, who was also a father and similarly interested in child-rearing, for his firstborn was fourteen years old—a tough age, a critical one, you'll see when your kid gets there, Victor . . . Well, actually, it was his first grandchild who was fourteen; Teddy hadn't really participated in bringing up his son, who had spent his childhood in a German concentration camp. You can't hit your kids, Teddy insisted. People are going to pummel them left and right their whole lives, so if you want to pop him, best to punch yourself in the face—do a lot more good.

After a number of shots, however, Victor remembered that Irma hadn't said a single word about his bizarre behavior at the crossroads, and came to the conclusion that she was a tricky little thing and that, moreover, hitting up your lover for help every time you can't get out of a pickle you got yourself into in the first place—well, that's dishonest at best. Thinking this way made him sad, but then Dr. R. Quadriga showed up and ordered a special bottle of rum, and they drank it down together, and after that Victor once again saw everything in a rosy light, because it became obvious that Irma simply didn't want to make him feel bad, which meant she respected her father and maybe even loved him.

Then someone else showed up and ordered something else . . . After that, Victor probably went off to bed . . . Presumably . . . One must assume he went off to bed . . . His mind did preserve a solitary memory of a water-drenched tile floor, though he was totally unable to recall *what* floor and *what* water. Probably for the best.

Victor pulled himself together and went downstairs. He got some fresh newspapers from the concierge and chatted with him about the goddamn weather. "How was I yesterday?" he asked nonchalantly. "OK?"

"Yes, on the whole," the concierge said politely. "Teddy will get you the bill."

"I see," said Victor, and, deciding not to ask for specifics, made his way to the restaurant.

The number of floor lamps in the main hall seemed to have decreased. Oh, no, he thought, feeling apprehensive. Teddy wasn't there yet. Victor bowed to the bespectacled young man and his companion, sat down at his usual table, and opened the paper. Around the world it was business as usual. One country was embargoing the trade ships of another, which was expressing its vigorous protest. Countries that Mr. President liked were conducting just wars in the name of their respective nations, and also democracy. Countries Mr. President disliked for whatever reason were conducting annexationist wars—or not wars so much as thuggish, rapacious attacks. As for Mr. President himself, he'd recently given a two-hour address on the necessity of ending corruption once and for all, and undergone a successful operation to remove his tonsils. A critic Victor knew—a rank bastard—heaped praise on a new book by Rotz-Tusov, which was mystifying, since the book happened to be a good one.

A waiter approached—a new one, unknown to Victor—and affably recommended the oysters. After taking Victor's order, he gave the table a quick swipe with a cloth and went off. Victor put the newspapers aside, lit a cigarette, and, making himself comfortable, began thinking about work. It was always pleasant to think about work after a good drink.

It would be nice to write a cheerful, optimistic story . . . About how once there was a man—no dummy, loves his work, loves his friends, and his friends value him, too. About how good his life is. A great guy, you know, a little quirky, good sense of humor . . . Eh, but there's no plot. And with no plot it's boring. And plus, if you're going to write a story like that, you have to sort out why exactly this good guy's life is so good, and inevitably you'll come to the conclusion that it's because he loves his work but couldn't care less about anything else. But what kind of a good guy is he if he couldn't care less about anything besides his best-beloved work?

Of course, he could write about a man who derives meaning from loving his neighbor—a man whose life is good precisely because he loves his neighbor and his work. Except that man had already been described a couple thousand years ago by Messrs. Matthew, Luke, and John, plus one other guy—four in all. Actually, there were many more like them, but only these four authors managed to do the topic justice; everyone else was deprived of national consciousness, or of the right of correspondence . . . and the man they wrote about was, unfortunately, a halfwit . . . But actually it would be interesting to write about Christ coming to earth in our own day—not the way Dostoyevsky did it, more like Luke and friends . . . Christ shows up at HQ and goes, hey, love thy neighbor. But there in HQ, of course, sits some anti-Semite . . .

"Permit me, Mr. Banev," a pleasant masculine voice rumbled overhead.

It was Mr. Mayor, in the flesh. Not the apoplectically scarlet pig grunting with unwholesome pleasure on Mr. Rossechepert's capacious bed, but an elegantly rotund, perfectly shaven, impeccably dressed, imposing man with a modest governmental ribbon in his buttonhole and a Legion of Freedom medal on his left shoulder.

"Be my guest," said Victor joylessly.

Mr. Mayor sat, looked over his shoulder, and folded his hands on the table. "I will try not to burden you with my presence for too long, Mr. Banev," he said, "and do my best not to spoil your meal. However, the question I intend to put to you has now grown sufficiently urgent that all of us who value the honor and prosperity of our city, irrespective of station, must lay aside our personal business and resolve it as quickly and efficiently as possible."

"I'm listening," said Victor.

"I chose to meet with you here, Mr. Banev, under these rather informal circumstances, because, knowing how busy you are, I did not wish to risk disturbing you during your work hours, especially given that work's particularity. Notwithstanding, I now address you in a quite official capacity—both on my own behalf, and in the name of the municipality as a whole."

The waiter brought the oysters and a bottle of white wine. The mayor arrested his egress with a single raised finger. "My friend," he said, "half a serving of Kitchigan sturgeon and a shot of mint vodka. No sauce on the sturgeon.

"Where were we?" he continued, turning back to Victor. "Ah, yes. I fear it will be difficult to classify our conversation as table talk, for we must speak of matters and circumstances that are not only unfortunate but, I daresay, rather unappetizing. I mean to discuss with you the so-called clammies, that malignant tumor that has been consuming our ill-fated district for lo these many years."

"Go on," said Victor, suddenly interested.

The mayor gave a muted, well-thought-out, and stylistically immaculate speech. He told of a time twenty years ago when, immediately following the occupation, a leprosarium was established in Horse Hollow—a quarantine for persons suffering from so-called yellow leprosy, or "spectacle disease." In point of fact, and as Mr. Banev well knows, this disease had been known in our country since the dawn of time. Moreover, various studies have shown that, for some reason, people from our district are especially susceptible to it. However, it was only thanks to the efforts of Mr. President that this disease received serious attention; only through his personal intervention did the unfortunates previously deprived of medical attention, scattered across the land, and frequently subject to unjust persecution from the more backward segments of society (not to mention the extermination they suffered at the hands of the occupiers!) . . . yes, these very unfortunates were finally collected in a single place, thus acquiring a chance at a tolerable life, one befitting their condition. All of this is perfectly unobjectionable; the aforementioned measures can only be praised, and yet our best and noblest intentions have now been turned against us. Let us not, at this time, scrutinize the actions of Mr. Golem—actions that, though possibly selfless, are nonetheless fraught with unpleasant ramifications. Let us not, furthermore, engage in premature criticism, however bizarre we may personally find the constant refusal of certain quite highly placed authorities to heed our protests.

Let us move straight to the facts—here the mayor downed a shot of mint vodka and chased it with a bite of tasty sturgeon, which made his voice even more velvety (it was completely impossible to imagine him hunting people with bear traps). He spoke verbosely of his desire not to draw Banev's attention to the rumors engulfing the city in undue manner; these rumors, Mr. Mayor felt compelled to admit, resulted from an insufficiently precise and unanimous implementation, at all administrative levels, of Mr. President's explicit decrees. He was referring to the rather widespread view that the so-called clammies played a crucial role in the abrupt change in climate, that they were responsible for rising rates of miscarriage and infertility, for the wholesale exodus of house pets, and for the advent of a particular type of bedbug—*id est* the flying bedbug . . .

"Mr. Mayor," said Victor with a sigh, "I must admit, I'm finding it difficult to follow your various circumlocutions. Let's speak plainly, like worthy sons of our nation. Let's not talk about what we won't talk about but stick to what we will."

The mayor gave him a quick once-over and made some calculation, juxtaposing this with that. Devil only knows what he was juxtaposing, but he probably took everything into account: that Victor regularly tied one on with Rossechepert; that he enjoyed tying one on full stop, making noise enough for the whole country to hear; that Irma was a prodigy; that there existed a certain Diana; and probably much more—at any rate, some of the shine visibly went out of the mayor's eyes, and he called for a glass of cognac. Victor, too, called for a glass of cognac.

The mayor giggled, looked around the nearly empty restaurant, banged his fist lightly on the table, and said, "All right! Why not. Let's not mince words. Life in the city has become unbearable. You have your Golem to thank for that—by the way, did you know that Golem is a secret communist? Oh yes, I assure you, we have proof . . . he's hanging by a thread, your Golem . . . Anyway: they're corrupting our own children right under our noses. These vermin have infiltrated the schools and utterly ruined our kids . . . The voters are unhappy, many are leaving the city. Something's brewing, and vigilante justice may be right around the corner. The district authorities are asleep at the wheel. That's the situation."

He emptied his glass. "I should tell you, I hate that scum so much I'd tear them apart with my own teeth if the thought alone didn't turn my stomach. You may not believe this, Mr. Banev, but they've driven me to setting bear traps . . . All right, so they're corrupting the children, fine. Children are children—you can corrupt them till your face turns blue and it'll be too little for them. But put yourself in my position. This incessant rain is absolutely their doing. I don't know how they manage it, but it's definitely them. We built a sanatorium: healing waters plus luxurious climate equals pure profit—or used to. People once flocked here from the capital! And now? Rain, fog, clients with colds, everything going from bad to worse.

"A famous physicist came here recently . . . I forget his name, but you know it, I'm sure . . . stayed here two weeks, and *bam!* Spectacle disease, acute case, and off he goes to the leprosarium. That sure made the sanatorium look good! Next thing we know, there's another case, then another, and that was it—all the clients cut and run. This restaurant's bleeding cash, so's the hotel, the sanatorium's barely breathing—we're lucky that idiot coach showed up, the one training his team for games in rainy countries . . . And of course, Mr. Rossechepert has been somewhat helpful . . . Know what I mean?

"I tried to make a deal with that Golem, but it was like talking to a wall: a spade's a spade, end of story. Wrote to the higher-ups—nothing doing. Wrote even higher up than that—nothing. Even higher—they acknowledged my statement and promised to send a signal down the chain of command . . . I hate them, but I knuckled under and went to the leprosarium myself. They let me in. I begged and pleaded . . . They're so utterly disgusting! Blinking at you with their mangy eyes like you're some sparrow, like you aren't even there . . ." He leaned in and whispered: "I'm afraid of riots. Of bloodshed. Know what I mean?"

"Sure," said Victor. "Where do I come in?"

The mayor leaned back in his seat, took a half-smoked cigar from an aluminum case, and lit up. "In my position," he said, "I'm left with only one option: all systems go. What we need is publicity. The municipality has composed a petition to the Health Department, Mr. Rossechepert will sign it . . . so will you, I hope, but that's small potatoes. We need real publicity: a solid article, in a capital-city newspaper, with a famous byline. Your byline, Mr. Banev! You couldn't ask for more timely material—it's perfect for an orator like yourself. I'm asking you personally, but also on behalf of the municipality and the poor parents . . . Let's force them to move the leprosarium the hell out of here! I don't care where to, so long as I don't see hide nor hair of those filthy diseased clammies. That's what I wanted to tell you."

"Sure, I understand," said Victor slowly. "I understand quite well."

You may be a scoundrel and a pig, he thought, but it's hard to blame you. And what's going on with the clammies? They used to be so quiet and stooped, always creeping around, no one saying anything about them except that they stink, they're contagious, great at making toys and lots of other small wooden things . . . Fred's mother used to say, as I recall, that they have an evil eye, that they curdle milk and bring war, disease, and famine . . . And now here they are, sitting behind barbed wire, doing what? Quite a lot, actually. The weather, for one thing, plus luring our kids to their side (why?), plus getting rid of all the cats (again, why?). They even made the bedbugs fly . . .

"You probably think," said the mayor, "that we're just sitting here twiddling our thumbs. That's absolutely false. But what can we do? I'm preparing a trial against Golem. Mr. Health Inspector, Pavor Summan, has agreed to consult on the case. We're planning to argue that the question of the disease's infectious potential is far from decided, a fact that Golem, as a secret communist, has been exploiting. That's one thing. On top of that, we're trying to fight fire with fire. The City Legion, our pride and joy, our best and brightest . . . but something's not right. No instructions from the higher-ups . . . The police are in an awkward position . . . and so on . . . So we resist as best we can. We try to hold up any shipments headed in their direction . . . Selectively, of course, not food or, say, bed linens, but books—they sure do order a lot of books. Just today we detained a truck, and that already feels good, of course. But those are all small, desperate moves, not the radical ones we need."

"I see," said Victor. "Pride and joy, you say? What's that one guy's name . . . Flamenda? You know the one, the nephew."

"Flamen Juventa," said the mayor. "He's my deputy in the Legion, a real straight shooter! You met him already?"

"Once, yeah," said Victor. "But why detain books?"

"What do you mean, why? This is going to sound stupid, but we're only human—our patience has its limits. And plus . . ." The mayor smiled sheepishly. "It's nonsense, of course, but people do say that the clammies can't live without books . . . you know, the way normal people can't live without food and other things."

There was a pause. Victor picked listlessly at his steak with a fork, thinking. I don't know much about the clammies, and what I do know doesn't exactly dispose me in their favor. Maybe because I've never liked them, since I was a kid. But the mayor and his gang—them I do know. The greasy lard of the nation, presidential lackeys, pogromists . . . If you people are up in arms against the clammies, they can't be all bad . . . On the other hand, nothing wrong with writing an article, the more hysterical the better; no one would risk publishing it anyway, but I'd make the mayor happy, I'd get my pound of flesh out of him, enough to live happily ever after . . . What real writer can say he's living happily ever after? I could settle down in some sinecure . . . I could become some kind of municipal beach inspector and then write to my heart's content, about the good life of the good man who's devoted to his craft. I could give lectures to the prodigies on that topic . . . The only trick, though, would be to figure out how to wipe. Someone spits in your face and you wipe it away. At first you're ashamed, then confused, but sooner or later you start wiping with dignity, maybe even enjoying yourself in the process . . .

"Of course, we have no intention of rushing you," said the mayor. "You're a busy man and so forth. But inside a week, eh? We'll get you all the materials—we could even provide a little outline or something, for reference . . . and then you'll give it the magic touch and it'll shine. The article will be signed by three prominent native sons: Member of Parliament Rosseche-pert Nantes, famous writer Banev, and State Laureate Dr. Rem Quadriga . . ."

He's a quick study, thought Victor. We leftists could never in a million years be this tenacious. We'd go on endlessly, beating around the bush, worrying about offending the person, about applying undue pressure, God forbid he suspect any selfish motives . . . "Prominent native sons!" Look at him, the animal, he's totally convinced that I'll write and sign the thing for him, that I've got no choice, disgraced writer Banev's going to tuck his tail between his legs and, by the sweat of his soul, sing for his carefree down-home supper . . . The slippery bastard, he even managed to work in a hint about a "little outline." Not hard to guess what's in that "little outline" if it's capable of making anyone print Banev, still dripping with presidential spittle as he is. Well, well, well, Mr. Banev . . . if you like your cognac, and your women, and your pickled lampreys with onions—then eventually you have to pay the piper.

"I'll consider your offer," he said, smiling. "The concept is interesting enough in theory, but actually realizing it will somewhat strain my conscience. You know, surely, that we writers are a principled lot and act exclusively according to the exhortations of our conscience." He gave the mayor a grotesque, lascivious wink.

The mayor guffawed. "But of course! 'The nation's conscience, a scrupulous mirror' and so on . . . Sure, I remember . . ." He leaned in close again, looking conspiratorial. "There's a little shindig at my place tomorrow," he burbled. "Just a few close friends. Only no wives, deal? What do you say?"

"Now that," said Victor, standing up, "is an offer I must directly and decisively decline. Excuse me, I must away"—he winked again—"to the sanatorium."

They parted almost as friends. The writer Banev had now been added to the list of city elites—an honor so nerve-janglingly great it could only be mitigated with an entire snifter of cognac, which Victor lapped up as soon as Mr. Mayor's back disappeared behind the door. He could, of course, get the hell out of town. They won't let me out of the country, though, and anyway, I don't want to go abroad—what's the point, it's the same everywhere. But even within our borders I'd be able to find ten or so places to hide out until this blows over. He pictured a sunny locale, beech groves, intoxicating air, taciturn farmers, the scent of milk and honey . . . and manure, and mosquitos . . . and the stink of the outhouse, and night after night of god-awful boredom . . . and ancient televisions, and the local intelligentsia: the frisky, womanizing priest and the moonshine-swilling schoolteacher . . . But honestly, why pretend—of course, of *course* there were places he could go. Except that's exactly what they want, for me to leave, out of sight, out of mind, to bury myself in some hole—on my own steam, without being forced to, because it'd take effort to exile me, there'd be noise, chatter . . . That's the real problem: they'd be all too happy if I left, shut up, were forgotten, stopped making that racket . . .

Victor settled up, ran to his room, put on his raincoat, and went out into the downpour. He suddenly felt a strong desire to see Irma again, to discuss progress with her, to explain why he drank so much (and really, why *do* I drink so much?), and maybe Bol-Kunatz would be there too, whereas Lola would almost certainly not be . . . The streets were wet, gray, and empty. In front-yard gardens, apple trees were quietly perishing from the damp. For the first time, Victor noticed how many houses were boarded up. It was true that the city had changed quite a bit—fences sagged, mold splattered the sides of houses, every color looked faded, and rain reigned undivided over all. Rain fell as simple drops, cascaded down roofs in a fine mist, accumulated inside gusts of wind, twisting into foggy, whirling columns that trailed from one wall to the next; it shot out of rusty drainpipes with a growl and poured out onto the street, running through grooves it had worn in the cobblestones. Grayish-black clouds crept slowly along, hanging so low they almost touched the rooftops. Out here, man was an unbidden guest, and the rain made sure he knew it.

Walking into the town square, Victor finally saw people. A small group stood under the police station awning: two policemen in standard-issue raincoats and a short, grimy kid in greasy coveralls. In front of the porch, its left-side wheels on the curb, loomed a cumbersome canvas-top truck. One of the policemen was the chief himself. He was looking off to one side, thrusting his mighty jaw forward as the whiny-voiced kid, gesticulating frantically, tried to convince him of something. The other policeman stood by silently, sucking on a cigarette and looking displeased.

Victor walked toward them; about ten steps from the scene, he could already make out the kid's words. He was shouting, "Well, what about me? What do I have to do with it? Didn't I follow all the rules? Aren't all my papers in order? Nothing wrong with the load, here's the invoice. What the hell, I've done this route a million times!"

The police chief noticed Victor, and his face assumed an extremely hostile expression. Turning away, he said to the policeman as if the kid weren't even there, "All right, you stay here. Make sure it's all OK. And don't get into the truck, or the stuff'll all get stolen. Don't let anyone near it. Got it?"

"Got it," said the policeman. He was very displeased. The police chief stepped off the porch, got into his own car, and drove away.

The grimy little driver spat angrily and appealed to Victor, "What about you, can you tell me where I went wrong?" Victor stopped walking, which gave the kid confidence. "My driving's fine. I'm taking books to the special zone, like a thousand times before. And today they stop me and make me drive to the station. Why? Didn't I follow all the rules? Aren't my papers in order? Here's the invoice. They took away my license so I couldn't leave. But where would I go?"

"Shut the hell up," said the policeman.

The kid turned around in a flash. "So what did I do? Tell me, was I speeding? I was not. I'm going to get charged for the delay. And you took away my papers."

"It'll work itself out," said the policeman. "What are you getting so upset about, anyway? Go sit in that bar over there, this here's none of your business."

"You petty-ass bastards!" the kid exclaimed, slamming his hat down on his disheveled head. "There's no justice anywhere! Drive left, get pulled over. Drive right, get pulled over again." He started down the porch steps, then stopped and said to the policeman appeasingly, "Can't we work it out, man? Like with a fine?"

"Keep walking," said the policeman.

"This was a rush job! They promised me overtime! I drove all night—"

"Keep walking, I said!"

The kid spat again, went up to his truck, gave the front axle a couple of kicks, then suddenly slouched down and, sticking his hands in his pockets, booked it across the square.

The policeman looked at Victor, then at the truck, then at the sky. His cigarette went out. He spat out the butt and, pulling down his hood as he went, disappeared into the station.

Victor stood around for a little while, then began making his way slowly around the truck. It was enormous and powerful, the kind used back in the day for motorized infantry transport. Victor looked around. A few yards beyond the truck, a police Harley with a turned-in front wheel was getting soaked in the rain. Otherwise the street was empty. They might catch up to me, thought Victor, but damned if they'll be able to stop me. He felt a sudden burst of joy. What the hell, he thought. *The famous writer Banev, drunk again, stole a stranger's car for a joyride; luckily, there were no victims* . . . He knew it wouldn't be so simple, that it wouldn't be the first time an inconvenient person gave the authorities a reasonable excuse to shove him in the clink. But he didn't want to think it through—he wanted to follow the impulse. If worse comes to worst, I'll write that bastard his article, he thought in passing.

He quickly opened the driver's-side door and got behind the wheel. There was no key, so he had to cut the starter wires and jump the engine. When the motor came to life, Victor looked back at the police station porch. The policeman from earlier was standing there, cigarette hanging from his lip, face bearing the same displeased expression as before. It was obvious that he could see everything that was happening but didn't yet understand it.

Victor shut the door, drove carefully off the curb, switched gears, and shot down the nearest alleyway.

It felt amazing to speed down empty streets, streets he knew in advance would be empty, his tires raising cascades of water as he drove through deep puddles. It felt amazing to turn the heavy wheel, putting his whole body into the motion, to pass the canning factory, the park, the stadium—where the Kindred Spirits were still kicking and kicking their ball like wet automatons—and then drive on, over the highway with its potholes, bouncing in his seat and hearing the poorly secured load slamming around the truck bed. The rearview mirror showed no one in pursuit, though of course anything like that would be hard to make out at first, because of the rain. Victor felt very young, very needed, and even somewhat drunk. Magazine cutouts of naked beauties winked at him from the ceiling. He found a pack of cigarettes in the glove compartment and felt so good he nearly missed the crossroads, but slowed down just in time to turn at LEPROSARIUM—4 MILES, feeling like a pioneer. He'd never once been down this road, either driving or on foot. The road turned out to be a good one, not like the municipal highway, very even and well-maintained pavement at first, then concrete. When he saw the concrete, he immediately remembered the barbed wire and the soldiers, and then five minutes later there it all was, right before his eyes.

The single-layer barbed-wire fence extended along both sides of the road, vanishing into the rain. Directly in front of him was a high gate with a guardhouse, the door already open. A soldier in helmet and combat boots stood on the threshold, machine gun poking out from underneath his poncho. Another soldier, bareheaded, looked out of the little guardhouse window. *"I've never seen the inside of a camp,"* sang Victor. *"But don't you thank the Lord just yet . . ."* He slowed to a crawl, braking when he reached the gate.

The soldier stepped down from the guardhouse doorway and walked up to the truck. He was just a kid, a freckled little soldier of no more than eighteen. "Hello," he said. "What took you so long?"

"You know, circumstances," said Victor, bemused at such liberalism.

The little soldier looked him up and down and suddenly took an official tone. "Papers, please," he said curtly.

"What papers?" said Victor cheerfully. "I told you, there were circumstances."

The soldier's mouth was a hard line. "What's in the truck?" he asked.

"Books," said Victor.

"Got a permit?"

"Of course not."

"Oh, I see," said the soldier, and his face brightened. "No wonder . . . In that case, please wait. You're going to have to wait."

"Keep in mind," said Victor, raising his index finger, "they're probably gaining on me."

"No worries, I'll be quick," said the soldier, and, holding his gun to his chest, padded heavily toward the guardhouse.

Victor got out of the cab and, standing on the running board, looked back. He could see nothing beyond the rain. He returned to the driver's seat and lit a cigarette. This was all very amusing.

Rain was also whirling behind the gate and the barbed wire. Up ahead, he could just make out shadowy buildings of some sort—houses, or possibly towers; it was impossible to tell what, exactly. Will he really not invite me in to take a look? thought Victor. It'd be rude of him not to. He could, of course, try appealing to Golem, who was probably around here somewhere . . . That's what I'll do, he thought. Otherwise, why did I bother being all heroic?

The little soldier stepped back out of the guardhouse. Dashing after him came Victor's old friend the pimply boy nihilist, wearing only shorts. This time, he looked happy, without a trace of world-weariness. Passing the soldier, he leaped up onto the running board, glanced into the cab, and, recognizing Victor, gasped in surprise and burst out laughing. "Well, hello there, Mr. Banev! Is it really you? This is great . . . You brought the books, right? We've been waiting and waiting for them . . ."

"Everything in order?" asked the little soldier, walking up.

"Yeah, this is our truck."

"All right, in she goes," said the little soldier. "As for you, sir, you're going to have to exit the vehicle and wait outside."

"I'd like to speak to Dr. Golem," said Victor.

"We can call him out here," offered the little soldier.

"Hmm," said Victor, and looked pointedly at the boy. The boy gave a shamefaced shrug. "You don't have a permit," he explained. "They won't let anyone in without a permit. If it were up to me . . ."

There was nothing left to do but climb out of the truck into the rain. Victor jumped down onto the road, raised his hood, and watched as the gate opened. The truck jolted into motion and rolled jerkily inside. Then the gate closed. For a while, through the noise of rain, Victor could still hear the howling of the engine and the hissing of the brakes. Then all was silent, except for some rustling and splashing.

And that's that, thought Victor. But what about me? He felt disappointed. Only now did he realize that his heroic feats had not been selfless, that he had hoped to see and understand a great deal . . . to penetrate the epicenter, so to speak. Well, screw you, he thought. He looked down the road. Four miles to the crossroads, and from there to the city, about another twelve. Of course, the sanatorium was another option—that was about a mile and a half. Ungrateful pigs . . . he'd have to walk in the rain . . . Suddenly he noticed that the rain had lessened. Thanks for that, at least, he thought.

"So, should I get Mr. Golem for you?" asked the soldier.

"Golem?" Victor perked up. It wouldn't be such a bad thing to make the old geezer run out to meet him in the rain, and plus, he had a car. And a flask. "Well, sure, why not."

"Will do," said the little soldier. "I'll call him right now. It's unlikely he'll come out, though—he'll say he's busy."

"Never you mind," said Victor. "Tell him Banev's asking for him."

"Banev? All right. He still won't come out, though. It's no skin off my nose, anyway. Banev . . ." And the little soldier went off. A nice kid, that soldier, a sweetheart, nothing but freckles under his helmet.

Victor lit a cigarette. Suddenly, there was the sound of a motorcycle motor. A Harley with a sidecar zoomed out from behind the foggy veil and, moving with insane speed, flew right up to the gate, where it stopped. It was the policeman with the displeased expression, plus another one in the sidecar, wrapped head to toe in canvas. Here we go, thought Victor, yanking his hood lower over his face.

It didn't help. The policeman with the displeased expression got off his motorcycle, walked up to Victor, and barked, "Where's the truck?"

"What truck?" said Victor, looking all around in amazement. He was stalling.

"Don't you bullshit me!" the policeman bawled. "I saw you! You're going to jail for hijacking an impounded vehicle!"

"Don't you raise your voice to me," Victor objected with dignity. "Who do you think you are? I'm going to file a complaint."

The second policeman, unwrapping his canvas coverings as he went, walked up and asked, "He the one?"

"You bet he is!" said the policeman with the displeased expression, extracting handcuffs from his pocket.

"Excuse me," said Victor, stepping back. "You can't do that! How dare you?"

"Don't compound your guilt by resisting arrest," the second policeman advised.

"I'm guilty of precisely nothing," Victor declared impudently, sticking his hands in his pockets. "You've got me confused with someone else, boys."

"You stole the truck," said the second policeman.

"What truck?" Victor shouted. "What does a truck have to do with anything? I came to visit Mr. Golem, the head doctor. Ask the guards. What truck are you talking about?"

"Maybe we got the wrong guy," the second policeman said doubtfully.

"Oh, he's the right guy, all right!" retorted the policeman with the displeased expression. Holding his cuffs at the ready, he moved on Victor. "Now let's have those wrists," he said, all business.

At that moment the guardhouse door slammed and a high, piercing voice shouted, "Dis*perse*!"

Victor and the policemen shuddered. In the guardhouse doorway stood the freckled little soldier, pointing his machine gun through his poncho. "Move away from the gate!" he shouted piercingly.

"Hey, you, simmer down!" said the policeman with the displeased expression. "We're police."

"Assembly of more than one unauthorized person near the special zone gate is strictly prohibited! Three warnings, then I shoot. Move away from the gate!"

"Come on, come on, move away," Victor said anxiously, gently nudging both policemen in the chest. The policeman with the displeased expression gave him a distracted look, pushed his hand away, and stepped toward the soldier.

"Listen, kid, are you out of your mind?" he said. "This guy here hijacked a truck."

"No trucks!" the nice kid roared, loud and shrill. "Final! Warning! You two, a hundred yards away from the gate, now!"

"Listen, Rokh," said the second policeman. "Why don't we just move aside? Screw 'em. Anyway, this guy won't get far."

The policeman with the displeased expression, beet red with fury, was just about to open his mouth, but then a fat sergeant, half-eaten sandwich in one hand, glass in the other, appeared in the guardhouse doorway.

"Private Jura," he said, chewing, "why haven't you opened fire?"

The freckled face beneath the helmet assumed a brutal expression. The policemen dashed to their motorcycle, got on, did a loop around Victor, who had adopted the pose of a traffic controller, and peeled out. The beet-red policeman was shouting something, but it was lost in the rattle of the motor. They rode for about fifty steps, then stopped.

"Too close," said the sergeant disapprovingly. "What are you waiting for? They're too close!"

"Farther!" the little soldier hollered shrilly, swinging his gun. The policemen rode farther away and soon disappeared from view.

"Lately, unauthorized persons are constantly crowding around the gate," the sergeant informed the little soldier, looking at Victor out of the corner of his eye. "All right, resume watch." He returned to the guardhouse, while the freckled little soldier, gradually cooling off, strolled back and forth in front of the gate.

After waiting a couple of minutes, Victor inquired cautiously, "Excuse me, please, how's it going with Dr. Golem?"

"He's not here," the little soldier growled.

"What a pity," said Victor. "I'll be on my way, then, I guess . . ." He looked at the rain and fog where the policemen were lurking.

"What do you mean, on your way?" asked the little soldier in alarm.

"Wait, can't I go?" asked Victor, also in alarm.

"Sure," said the little soldier. "I'm just thinking of the truck. You'll leave, but what about the truck? The rule is to move any trucks away from the gate."

"What's that got to do with me?" asked Victor, his alarm growing.

"What do you mean? You brought it here, so you, uh . . . those are the rules, you know?"

Dammit, thought Victor. What am I going to do with it? . . . He could hear the rattle of the idling motorcycle motor a few hundred feet away.

"Did you really hijack it?" asked the little soldier curiously.

"Well, yeah! The police detained the driver, and I decided to help, like an idiot."

"Oh, I see," the little soldier drawled sympathetically. "I'm afraid I don't know what to advise."

"Well, what if I just . . . took off?" asked Victor in confidential tones. "You won't shoot, will you?"

"I don't know," the little soldier confessed earnestly. "I don't think it's required. Should I ask?"

"Yes, why don't you," said Victor, trying to figure out if he'd have time to escape beyond the limits of visibility.

At that moment, a car honked beyond the fence. The gate opened, and the ill-fated truck slowly rolled out. It stopped next to Victor, the door swung open, and Victor saw that behind the wheel was not the boy he'd been expecting but a bald, stoop-shouldered clammy, who looked at him expectantly. Victor didn't move a muscle. The clammy took a black-gloved hand off the wheel and patted the seat next to him invitingly. Ah, so they deigned to condescend, thought Victor bitterly.

The little soldier spoke, his voice joyful, "Well, great! It all worked out. Go on now—Godspeed."

The thought flashed through Victor's mind that if the clammy really intended to return the truck to the city (or wherever) himself—provided he was intending to face the police alone—it would be great for him, Victor, to say his good-byes on the spot and then book it straight across the field to the sanatorium, circumventing the ambush entirely.

"There's police up ahead," he said to the clammy.

"No worries, get in," said the clammy.

"Thing is, I stole the truck. It was impounded."

"I know," said the clammy patiently. "Please get in."

The moment was lost. Victor said a heartfelt and courteous good-bye to the little soldier, got into the passenger side, and slammed the door. The truck was off, and in a minute they caught up to the Harley. The police had parked the motorcycle perpendicular to the road and now stood beside it, gesturing at them to pull over. The clammy slowed down, turned off the engine, and, leaning out of the cab, said, "Move the motorcycle. You're blocking the road."

"Pull over, now!" commanded the policeman with the displeased expression. "And let's see some ID."

"I'm on my way to the police station," said the clammy. "Maybe we could talk there?"

The policeman, somewhat at a loss, grumbled something like "Yeah, right." The clammy waited patiently.

"All right," said the policeman at last. "Except I'll drive the truck, and this one'll take the motorcycle."

"Sure," the clammy agreed. "But if possible, I'd prefer to take the motorcycle myself."

"Even better," growled the policeman with the displeased expression. His face even brightened. "Get out."

They switched places.

The policeman gave Victor a dirty look, then started squirming and writhing around in the seat, straightening his raincoat, while Victor, keeping the policeman in his peripheral vision, watched the clammy, pigeon-toed and increasingly stoop-shouldered, walking away and getting into the sidecar. From behind he looked like an enormous, gaunt monkey. The rain resumed pouring in buckets, and the policeman turned on the windshield wipers. The cortege moved out.

I'd love to know how all this ends, thought Victor, rather languidly. True, the clammy's seeming willingness to go to the police station seemed like a good sign. They've gotten so cocky now, these clammies, absolutely shameless! Anyway, they'll definitely stick me with a fine, no avoiding that. The police never miss a chance to stick someone with a fine . . . Eh, I couldn't care less, I'm going to have to get the hell out of here as it is. It's all fine. At least I got it out of my system.

He took out a pack of cigarettes and proffered it to the policeman. The policeman grunted with indignation—but took one. His lighter wasn't working, and he was forced to grunt again when Victor offered him his. Hard to blame the guy, really . . . no longer young, probably forty-five or so, and still just a beat cop, evidently a former collaborationist. Put the wrong people away, kissed the wrong asses—after all, how could he tell the right ass from the wrong one? The policeman was smoking and already seemed less displeased; his day was looking up. Man, too bad I don't have a bottle with me, thought Victor. I'd give him a swig, tell him a couple of Irish jokes, rag on bosses and their favoritism, talk some shit about students—and before you know it, he'd be putty. "Look at that crazy rain," said Victor.

The policeman grunted rather neutrally, without anger.

"Not like the climate we used to have," Victor continued. Then inspiration struck. "Did you notice that there's not a drop down there by the leprosarium? Yet as soon as you drive up to the city, it starts to pour."

"You said it," replied the policeman. "They sure have got it good up there in the leprosarium."

A rapport was developing. They discussed the weather—how it used to be and how it was now, goddammit. Talked about mutual acquaintances in the city. Spoke about city life, miniskirts, about the scourge of homosexuality, about imported brandy and contraband drugs. Naturally, they noted that people had lost all respect—not like before the war or, say, right after. That policing was a dog's life, no matter what the papers might say—"kind but stern guardians of order, indispensable cogs in the machinery of government," sure. Meanwhile they keep raising the age of retirement and lowering pensions, and now they've even taken away our weapons—who's going to bust his ass under these conditions? In short, the situation was shaping up such that, a couple of good swigs later, the policeman might have said, *You know what, kid, don't worry about it. I didn't see nothin', you didn't see nothin'.* But there were no swigs, nor was the time yet ripe for the gifting of cash, and so by the time the truck rolled up to the police station, the policeman had once again grown surly. He curtly invited Victor to follow him, and to hurry it up.

The clammy declined to explain anything to the policeman on duty, and demanded an audience with the chief of police. The duty cop answered, sure, the chief will see you, personally, but as for this gentleman here, he's accused of car hijacking. There's no need for him to see the chief; instead, he needs to be interrogated and write a statement. No, said the clammy quietly but firmly, that's not how this is going to go. Mr. Banev will not answer any questions or sign any statements, for reasons that concern only Mr. Police Chief. The cop, who didn't care, shrugged his shoulders and went off to report to the chief. While he was away, the little driver in the greasy coveralls turned up; he was three sheets to the wind and none the wiser, and immediately started shouting about justice, innocence, and other similarly frightening things. He was waving around his invoice, which the clammy gently took from him. Then he perched on a railing and signed it with a flourish. The driver went silent with amazement, and at that moment the clammy and Victor were taken back to see the boss.

The chief of police greeted them severely. He regarded the clammy with displeasure, and as for Victor, the chief avoided looking at him altogether. "What can I do for you?" he asked.

"May we sit?" inquired the clammy.

"Please do," the chief said begrudgingly, after a slight pause.

They all sat.

"Sir," said the clammy, "I am authorized to express our formal protest against this second unlawful impounding of goods addressed to the leprosarium."

"Yes, I heard all about it," said the chief. "The driver was drunk, so we were forced to detain him. I believe the matter will be cleared up in a matter of days."

"You detained not the driver but the load," the clammy retorted. "But that's immaterial. Thanks to Mr. Banev's kindness, the load was delivered with only a slight delay. You should really thank Mr. Banev, since a significant delay due to your actions, sir, could have produced major difficulties."

"How amusing," said the chief. "I cannot and will not understand what you mean, since as a government official I do not tolerate threats. As far as Mr. Banev is concerned, his situation is entirely provided for under criminal law." He continued to avoid looking at Victor.

"I see you really fail to understand your position," said the clammy. "But I am authorized to inform you that should any goods addressed to us be impounded again, you will have to deal directly with General Pferd."

No one spoke. Victor had no idea who General Pferd was, but it was obvious that the chief knew him very well. "That sounds like a threat," he said uncertainly.

"So it is," the clammy agreed. "What's more, a very real one."

The chief stood up abruptly. Victor and the clammy followed suit.

"I will take into consideration everything I have heard here today," announced the chief. "Your tone, sir, leaves much to be desired, but I promise to those who have authorized your complaints that I will investigate and, should guilty parties be found, punish them. Which, incidentally, also applies to Mr. Banev."

"Mr. Banev," said the clammy, "if you have any trouble with the police in connection with this incident, please inform Mr. Golem at once. Good day," he said to the chief.

"All the best," the chief replied.

At eight in the evening, Victor went down to the restaurant and was about to go to his usual table, where the usual crowd had already gathered, when Teddy called him over.

"Hiya, Teddy," said Victor, leaning up against the bar. "How are things?" Then he remembered. "Oh, right! The bill. Was I pretty gone last night?"

"The bill's no big deal," growled Teddy. "Not too much damage—you broke a mirror and tore a washbasin off the wall. But do you remember the chief of police?"

"Wait, why?" asked Victor in surprise.

"I knew you wouldn't remember. Your eyes were like a boiled pig's. You were wasted . . . You, my friend," Teddy said, pointing his finger at Victor's chest, "locked the poor guy in a toilet stall, stuck a broom handle in the door, and wouldn't let him out. At all. And none of us knew who was in there—he'd just arrived, we thought it was Quadriga. Well, OK, we thought, let him sit there for a while . . . And then you extracted him and started shouting 'You poor thing, you're all filthy!' and sticking his head in the washbasin. Knocked it clear off the wall! We barely managed to drag you away, man."

"Seriously?" said Victor, astounded. "No kidding. No wonder he's been glowering at me all day."

Teddy nodded sympathetically.

"It's awkward, dammit," said Victor. "I should apologize . . . But why did he let me do it? He's still strong . . ."

"I worry they're going to try to pin something on you," said Teddy. "The fuzz was around here this morning taking statements . . . You're guaranteed Article 66, aggravated assault. But it could be worse than that. Terrorism, for example. You got that? If I was you, I'd—" Teddy shook his head vigorously.

"You'd what?" asked Victor.

"They say the mayor came to see you today," said Teddy.

"Yeah."

"What about?"

"Eh, nothing much. He wants me to write an article condemning the clammies."

"Oho!" said Teddy, perking up. "Well, then it really is nothing much. Write up that article for him and everything's fine. If the mayor's happy, the chief of police will keep his mouth shut. At that point you could stick 'im in the toilet every day if you wanted to. The mayor's had it up to here with him . . ." Teddy showed Victor an enormous, bony fist. "So everything's fine. Why don't I pour you one on the house to celebrate? Vodka?"

"Sure, why not," said Victor pensively.

Now he saw the mayor's visit in an entirely new light. So that's how they're doing me, thought Victor. Yup . . . Either get out or do as you're told—if not, we'll reel you in. And by the way, it won't be so easy to get out. If the charge is terrorism, they'll find me. You stupid alcoholic, you . . . It just had to be the chief of police, didn't it? Though, to be honest, the planning and execution weren't bad, not at all . . . He still remembered nothing except a completely flooded tile floor, though he could pretty much reconstruct the scene in his imagination. Alrighty then, Victor Banev, my dear man, you boiled pig you, you armchair revolutionary (toilet revolutionary, more like), Mr. President's favorite . . . looks like the time has come for you to sell yourself, so to speak . . .

As Rotz-Tusov, who's experienced in these matters, always says: be sure to sell yourself quickly and expensively—the more honest your pen, the more it should cost the powers that be. That way, you harm your ideological opponent even as you sell yourself, and it's worth trying hard to maximize that harm . . . Victor downed his first shot, feeling not a whiff of pleasure. "All right, Teddy," he said. "Thanks. Now let's see that bill—is it a big one?"

"You'll live," Teddy smirked, drawing a piece of paper from the cash register. "Here's the inventory: one bathroom mirror, seventy-seven; one bathroom sink, porcelain, large, sixty-four, which makes, as you well know, one hundred forty-one. As for the floor lamp, we chalked it up to the previous fight . . . What I can't figure out," he continued, watching Victor count out the money, "Is what you used to trash the mirror. It's a huge-ass mirror, two fingers thick. You ram a head into it or something?"

"Whose?" asked Victor gloomily.

"Hey, don't sweat it," said Teddy, taking the money. "You'll write your little article, rehabilitate yourself some, get a little dough—that'll make up for it, for sure. Another?"

"No, later . . . I'll stop by again after dinner," said Victor, and went to his table.

It was business as usual in the restaurant—the semidarkness, the smells, the clatter of dishes in the kitchen; the bespectacled young man with the briefcase, the companion, and the bottle of mineral water; bent-backed Dr. R. Quadriga; Pavor, straight-backed and fit in spite of his cold; Golem, melting into his chair, with the nose of a prophet on a bender; the waiter.

"Lampreys," said Victor. "A bottle of beer. And something with meat in it."

"So you've finally gone and done it," said Pavor reproachfully. "I told you, dry out."

"When did you say that to me? I can't remember."

"What did you do?" inquired Dr. R. Quadriga. "Did you finally kill someone?"

"Do you not remember anything either?" Victor asked him.

"Are you talking about yesterday?"

"Yes, I'm talking about yesterday . . . My alcoholic ass," said Victor to Golem, "got completely smashed, chased Mr. Police Chief into the bathroom—"

"Oh, that!" said R. Quadriga. "That's all lies. I said as much to the detective—a detective came to see me this morning. You know how it is: terrible heartburn, splitting headache, I'm just sitting there looking out the window, when in comes that blockhead and starts trying to frame me."

"What did you say?" asked Golem. "Frame?"

"Yeah, frame," said R. Quadriga, making a square with his thumbs and index fingers. "Not a picture, though . . . me. I told him straight out: it's all lies, I spent the whole evening in the restaurant, everything nice and quiet, like always, no brawling—deathly boring, in fact . . . So don't worry about it," he said to Victor encouragingly. "No biggie . . . But why did you do it? Do you not like him?"

"Let's not talk about it," offered Victor.

"Well, what *should* we talk about?" asked R. Quadriga, sounding offended. "All these two do is argue about which of them isn't letting the other one into the leprosarium. Once in a blue moon something interesting happens, and suddenly it's 'Oh, let's not talk about it.'"

Victor bit off half a lamprey, chewed, took a sip of beer, and asked, "Who's General Pferd?"

"Horse," said R. Quadriga. "Stallion. *Der Pferd*. Or *das*."

"No, seriously," said Victor. "Does anyone know a general by that name?"

"When I was in the army," said Dr. R. Quadriga, "our division was commanded by His Excellency, Infantry General Arschmann."

"So?" said Victor.

"*Arsch* means 'ass' in German," Golem, previously silent, informed them. "The doctor is making a joke."

"Where did you hear about General Pferd?" asked Pavor.

"In the police chief's office," answered Victor.

"And?"

"And that's it. So no one knows? That's fine, I was just asking."

"And the sergeant major was named Nalgas," R. Quadriga announced. "Sergeant Major Nalgas."

"Oh, so you speak Spanish, too?" asked Golem.

"That much I can do," answered R. Quadriga.

"Let's drink," offered Victor. "Waiter, a bottle of cognac!"

"Why a whole bottle?" asked Pavor.

"So everyone can have some."

"You're going to cause another scene."

"Oh please, Pavor," said Victor. "Like you're so abstinent."

"I'm not," objected Pavor. "I like to drink and never miss a chance to do so, as befits a real man. But what I can't understand is getting drunk. And I especially can't understand getting drunk every single night."

"Him again!" said R. Quadriga in despair. "When did he get here?"

"We won't get drunk," said Victor, pouring cognac out for everyone. "We'll just have a drink. Like half the nation is doing at this very moment. The other half is getting drunk—and God bless 'em. *We're* just having a nice, quiet drink."

"But that's just it," said Pavor. "When drunkenness is endemic in a country—and not just in the country itself, in the whole world—then every decent person must keep his wits about him."

"Are you calling us 'decent'?" asked Golem.

"Well, cultured, in any case."

"I think," said Victor, "that cultured people have far more reason to get drunk than uncultured ones."

"Perhaps," agreed Pavor. "But a cultured person is obliged to keep himself in check. Culture obliges him to do so . . . Take us, for example: we sit here almost every night, drinking, chatting, playing dice. But has any one of us said anything intelligent this whole time? Forget intelligent, serious even! Giggling and jokes . . . nothing but giggling and jokes."

"What good would it do to be serious?" asked Golem.

"I'll tell you: everything's going to hell in a handbasket, and all we can do is giggle and joke. A Feast in Time of Plague. Shame on us, gentlemen."

"All right, Pavor," said Victor peaceably. "Why don't you say something serious? Forget intelligent! Just stick with serious."

"I don't want serious!" announced R. Quadriga. "Leeches. Tussocks. Ew!"

"Shush!" Victor said to him. "Take a nap, why don't you . . . Yes, Golem, let's talk about something serious for once. Pavor, you start: tell us about this handbasket of yours."

"Another joke?" said Pavor bitterly.

"No," said Victor. "I promise you, no. I may be ironic. But that's because I've been hearing about hell and handbaskets my whole life. Everyone keeps saying that humanity's going to hell in a handbasket, but they never have any proof. And on closer examination it always turns out that all this philosophical pessimism is because of family squabbles or insufficient funds."

"No," said Pavor. "No . . . Humanity's going to hell in a handbasket because it's bankrupt."

"Insufficient funds," mumbled Golem.

Pavor ignored him. He spoke exclusively to Victor, bowing his head and looking up at him sullenly. "Humanity is bankrupt from a biological perspective: the birthrate is falling; cancer, dementia, and neurosis are all on the rise. Everyone's a drug addict. Every day, people gulp down hundreds of tons of alcohol, nicotine, or just plain old drugs, from hash and coke to LSD. We're simply degenerating. We destroyed the first, authentic nature, and the second, false one is destroying us in turn . . . Furthermore, we are ideologically bankrupt: we've gone through every philosophical system and discredited them all; we tried out every possible moral system, but are still the same amoral beasts as the troglodytes. The worst part is that the general population today is as big a bunch of assholes as ever. It's always pining after and demanding gods and leaders, law and order, and every time it gets its gods, leaders, law, and order, it becomes dissatisfied, because it actually doesn't give a good goddamn about any of those—what it wants is chaos and anarchy, bread and circuses. Humanity is still fettered by the ironclad obligation of earning a weekly salary check, but it chafes against that obligation, escaping into drugs and alcohol on a nightly basis. Screw it, that rotting pile of shit, it's stunk to high heaven for ten thousand years and can't do anything else. The worst part is that the decay extends to you and me, to people with a capital *P*, people of value. We see that decay and imagine that it has nothing to do with us, but it still poisons us with despair, weakens our will, sucks us in . . . And on top of that we have the scourge of democratic education: *égalité, fraternité*, all men are brothers, all cut from the same cloth . . . We're constantly identifying ourselves with rabble and berating ourselves if we happen to discover that we're smarter than the mass, that we have other needs, other goals in life. It's time to figure that out and draw conclusions—it's time to save ourselves."

"It's time for a drink," said Victor. He was already sorry that he agreed to a serious conversation with the health inspector. It was unpleasant to look at Pavor. He was overexcited and had even gone cross-eyed. It was out of character, and plus, like all experts on handbaskets and hell, he was spewing hideous banalities. Victor longed to tell him, *Quit embarrassing yourself, Pavor; show us your profile, won't you, and let's see that ironic smirk.*

"Is that all you can say?" Pavor queried.

"I can also give you a piece of advice. More irony, Pavor. Don't get so excited. You can't do anything about it anyway. And even if you could, you wouldn't know what to do."

Pavor smirked ironically. "Oh, I know," he said.

"Do you?"

"There's only one way to stop the decay."

"Sure, sure!" said Victor lightly. "You dress up all the idiots in golden shirts and send them marching. All of Europe under our heel. Been there, done that."

"No," said Pavor. "That's just procrastination. There's only one solution: destroy the mass."

"Someone's in a good mood!" said Victor.

"Destroy ninety percent of the population," Pavor continued. "Maybe even ninety-five. The mass has fulfilled its purpose: it has birthed from its bowels the flower of humanity, which created civilization. But now the mass is dead, like a rotten potato that gave its life to new growth. When a corpse begins to rot, it's time to bury it."

"Jesus," said Victor. "Is this because you have a cold and no permit to the leprosarium? Or is it family squabbles?"

"Don't play dumb," said Pavor. "Why don't you want to think harder about something you know all too well? What perverts the brightest ideas? The idiocy of the gray mass. What causes wars, chaos, disorder? The idiocy of that same gray mass, which elects the only governments it deserves. Why has the golden age receded so hopelessly far away? Due to the inertia and ignorance of the gray mass. Hitler had the right idea; underneath it all, he could sense that the earth was filled with refuse. But he ruined everything, being himself the product of the gray mass. It was stupid to attempt a wholesale annihilation based on race. Besides, he didn't have the right tools for the job."

"And how will you decide whom to annihilate?" asked Victor.

"It'll be based on obscurity," answered Pavor. "If a person is mediocre and obscure, he must be destroyed."

"But who's going to decide if a person is obscure?"

"Come on, those are details. I'm talking about the principle; the what and the how are details."

"So why've you hitched your wagon to the mayor?" asked Victor, who had grown sick of Pavor.

"What do you mean?"

"What the hell do you need that trial for? It's petty, Pavor! But it's always like that with you *Übermenschen*. You start out wanting to remake the world, three billion corpses or no deal, but in the meantime you're obsessing over rank, or treating your gonorrhea, or helping sketchy people do their sketchy business—for peanuts."

"Watch it," said Pavor. It was clear he'd got his back up. "You yourself are a drunk and a slacker."

"At least I don't instigate trumped-up trials or try to reform the world."

"Oh, sure," said Pavor. "Because you couldn't even do that much, Banev. You're nothing but a bohemian—in other words, a lowlife, a shitty armchair anarchist. You have no idea what you want, so you just do as you're told. You pander to the tastes of other lowlifes and labor under the illusion that you're an iconoclast, a liberated artist. You're nothing but a fourth-rate rhymester whose best work is his bathroom graffiti."

"That's all true," agreed Victor. "I'm just sorry you didn't say it earlier. I had to insult you to get it out of you. And so it turns out that you're a vile and petty little man, Pavor. One among many. So if they start with the annihilation, you'll be first up. On the basis of obscurity. A philosophizing health inspector? To the ovens with him!"

I wonder how we'd look to an outside observer, he thought. Pavor is disgusting. That smirk! What's going on with him today? Quadriga's asleep . . . he couldn't care less about arguments, the "gray mass," and all that philosophy . . . Meanwhile, Golem's sitting back and enjoying the show, wineglass in one hand, the other dangling behind his chair . . . he's waiting to see who throws the first punch. But hey, why's Pavor so quiet? Is he gathering his wits?

"All right," said Pavor finally. "Good talk."

His smirk had disappeared, and his eyes had resumed their Sturmbannführer look. He threw some bills on the table, swallowed the last of his cognac, and left without saying good-bye. Victor felt pleasantly disappointed.

"For a writer, you're an incredibly poor judge of character," said Golem.

"That's not my job," said Victor lightly. "I leave the judging of character to psychologists and departments of public safety. My job is to pick up on trends, using an artist's heightened sensitivity . . . But what are you driving at? Is it 'Victoire, stop that racket' all over again?"

"I warned you not to mess with Pavor."

"What the hell," said Victor. "First of all, I didn't mess with him. He messed with me. And second, he's a pig. You know he's helping the mayor prepare a case against you?"

"So I gathered."

"You're not worried?"

"No. Their reach exceeds their grasp. The mayor's and the court's, to be precise."

"And what about Pavor?"

"Pavor's reach is long," said Golem. "So stop making a racket around him. Haven't you noticed that I don't?"

"I wonder who you *do* make a racket around," Victor grumbled.

"You, sometimes. I have a soft spot for you. Pour me some cognac."

"With pleasure." Victor poured him a glass. "Should we wake up Quadriga? What's wrong with him, anyway? Why didn't he defend me against Pavor?"

"Let's not wake him. Let's you and I talk. Why are you getting involved in all this? Who asked you to hijack that truck?"

"I felt like it," said Victor. "Impounding books is hitting below the belt. And plus, the mayor upset me. He was infringing on my freedom. And when someone infringes on my freedom, I get ornery . . . By the way, Golem, can General Pferd intercede with the mayor on my behalf?"

"He doesn't give two shits about you or the mayor," said Golem. "He's got enough problems of his own."

"Well, can you ask him to intercede? If you don't, I'll write a scathing article about that leprosarium of yours. I'll say you use the blood of Christian infants to treat spectacle disease. You think I don't know why the clammies are taking the children under their wing? They suck their blood, that's number one, and number two, they defile them. I'll expose you to the whole world. 'Bloodsucking Pervert Behind Doctor's Mask.'" Victor clinked glasses with Golem and drank. "I'm serious, by the way. The mayor is pressuring me to write pretty much that exact article. As I'm sure you already know."

"No," said Golem. "But that's not important."

"Seems like nothing's important to you," said Victor. "The whole city's against you—not important. You're about to be dragged into court—not important. Health inspector Pavor is irritated at your behavior—not important. Fashionable writer Banev is also irritated and prepares his poison pen—again, not important. Is General Pferd one of Mr. President's pseudonyms or something? . . . By the way, does this omnipotent general know you're a communist?"

"And why is writer Banev irritated?" Golem asked calmly. "And keep it down, Teddy's looking at us."

"Teddy's one of us," Victor retorted. "And by the way, he's irritated too: mice are eating him out of house and home." He furrowed his brow and lit a cigarette. "Hold on, what did you just ask me . . . Oh, right. I'm irritated because you wouldn't let me into the leprosarium. After all, I did a noble deed. Sure, it was stupid, but so are all noble deeds. And also, earlier I carried a clammy on my back."

"And fought for him," Golem added.

"Well, yeah! I did fight for him."

"With fascists," said Golem.

"With fascists, exactly."

"Well, do you have a permit?" asked Golem.

"A permit . . . Look, you've been keeping Pavor out, too, and he's turning into a demophobe before our very eyes."

"Yeah, poor Pavor can't catch a break," said Golem. "He's a good worker, but he isn't getting anywhere. I keep waiting for him to do something stupid. Seems like he's already started."

Dr. R. Quadriga raised his disheveled head and said, "Hard. Let me have a crack at him. Separate soul from body." His head fell back onto the table with a crash.

"So tell me, Golem," said Victor, lowering his voice. "Is it true you're a communist?"

"I seem to recall that the communist party is illegal here."

"Jesus," said Victor. "What party isn't illegal? I'm not asking about parties, I'm asking about you."

"As you can see, I am perfectly legal," said Golem.

"You do what you want," said Victor. "It's no skin off my nose. But the mayor . . . Then again, you couldn't care less about the mayor. But what if General Pferd were to find out?"

"But we won't tell him, will we?" Golem whispered confidentially. "Why should the general concern himself with such a small matter? He knows there's a leprosarium, and that at the leprosarium there's someone named Golem, and also clammies, or whatever. Let's leave it at that."

"What a strange general," said Victor pensively. "A leprosarium-specific one . . . By the way, the clammies are sure to give him trouble soon. I feel it with the heightened sensitivity of an artist. All roads in our city lead to the clammies, it seems."

"And not only in the city, alas," said Golem.

"What's the problem? They're just sick people, and not even contagious, or so I hear."

"Stop screwing around, Victor. You know very well that they're not just sick people. Even the issue of contagiousness isn't so simple."

"Meaning?"

"Meaning that, say, Teddy isn't in any danger of catching it from them. Neither is the mayor, to say nothing of the police chief. But someone else might be."

"You, for example."

Golem picked up the bottle and held it up to the light with evident enjoyment. Then he poured out two glasses. "I'm not, no. Not anymore."

"What about me?"

"I don't know. In any case, it's just a theory. Pay it no mind."

"I won't," said Victor sadly. "What else makes them special?"

"What else makes them special . . ." Golem repeated. "You may have already noticed, Victor, that there are three kinds of people in the world. Or rather, there's two big groups and one little one. There are people who can't live without the past—they exist entirely in the past, whether near or distant. Their lives are all about traditions, customs, and covenants. They draw on the past for both joy and inspiration. Take Mr. President—what would he be without Our Great Past? What would he refer to, where would he have come from in the first place? Then there are people who live in the present and want nothing to do with the future or the past. You, for example. Any ideas you might have had about the past, Mr. President has spoiled; no matter what past you contemplate, all you see is Mr. President ad infinitum. As for the future, you don't have the faintest idea about it, and might even be afraid to develop one, it seems to me. Finally, there are people who live in the future. Only recently have they accumulated in appreciable numbers. They quite reasonably expect nothing from the past and see the present as little more than a bridge to the future, raw material . . . They're pretty much living in the future already—on islands of the future that formed around them in the present." Smiling strangely, Golem looked up at the ceiling. "They're clever," he said tenderly. "Devilishly clever, unlike the majority of people. Every one of them is talented, Victor. Their desires are all strange. As for ordinary desires, they have none."

"By ordinary desires, you mean . . . women, for example?"

"In some sense, yes."

"Bread and circuses? Booze?"

"Without a doubt."

"What a terrible disease," said Victor. "I wouldn't wish it on anyone . . . but still, I don't get . . . well, any of it. Or rather, it makes sense that clever people are kept behind barbed wire. But why are they allowed out, whereas we're not allowed in?"

"Have you ever considered that maybe they're not the ones behind barbed wire?"

Victor smirked. "Hold on," he said. "That's not all I don't get. What does Pavor have to do with any of this, for example? So they won't let me in—that makes sense, I'm just some stranger. But someone has to inspect the bed linens and bathroom facilities, after all! What if you have sanitation violations?"

"What if he's not interested in sanitation violations?"

Victor looked at Golem in confusion. "Are you joking again?" he asked.

"Again, I'm not," answered Golem.

"Are you saying he's a spy?"

"'Spy' is too broad a concept," Golem retorted.

"Hold on," said Victor. "Level with me. Who put up the barbed wire and called in the soldiers?"

"That damned barbed wire," sighed Golem. "It's torn an unbelievable amount of clothing. Plus, the soldiers constantly have the runs. You know the best cure? Tobacco and port wine . . . Or rather, port wine with tobacco."

"Fine," said Victor. "So General Pferd. I see . . ." he said. "And that young man with the briefcase . . . Oh, now I get it! So you've got a top-secret military lab up there. Gotcha . . . Whereas

Pavor has nothing to do with the military. He's from a different department. Or maybe he's not a domestic spy but a foreign one?"

"God forbid!" said Golem with horror. "That's the last thing we need."

"So . . . does he know who that young man with the briefcase is?"

"I think so, yes," said Golem.

"Does the young man know who Pavor is?"

"I don't think so, no," said Golem.

"You didn't tell him anything?"

"What do I care?"

"And you didn't tell General Pferd, either?"

"Didn't even occur to me."

"That's unfair," said Victor. "You should tell him."

"Listen, Victor," said Golem. "I let you jabber on about all this in hopes of scaring you straight, so you stop sticking your nose into other people's business. You absolutely don't need this. You're already on their radar—they could snuff you out before you even made a peep."

"I'm not hard to scare," Victor said with a sigh. "I've been scared since I was a kid. But still, I can't understand: What do they all want with the clammies?"

"Who's 'they'?" said Golem with weary reproach.

"Pavor. Pferd. The young man with the briefcase. All those crocodiles."

"Good God," said Golem. "What do crocodiles ever want from intelligent and talented people? What I don't get is what *you* want with them. Why do you keep meddling in all this? Don't you have problems of your own? Isn't Mr. President enough for you?"

"More than," Victor agreed. "I've had it up to here."

"Well, splendid. So get on over to the sanatorium, grab a ream of paper . . . If you want, I can gift you a typewriter."

"I write the old-fashioned way," said Victor. "Like Hemingway."

"Splendid. Then I'll gift you a pencil stub. Work, make love to Diana. Or maybe you need something to write about, a topic? Maybe you have writer's block?"

"Topics are born of subjects," said Victor importantly. "I study life."

"By all means," said Golem. "Study life as much as you want. Just don't interfere with its processes."

"That's not possible," Victor objected. "The instrument inevitably affects the experiment. Have you forgotten your physics? After all, we don't observe the world as such but the world plus the effects of the observer."

"You already got some brass knuckles to the skull; next time you might just get shot."

"Well," said Victor. "First, maybe it wasn't brass knuckles. Maybe it was a brick. And second, anyone could hit me on the skull. I could get strung up at any moment. So what should I do, never leave my room?"

Golem bit at his lower lip, showing yellow horse teeth. "Listen, you instrument, you," he said. "That time, you interfered with the experiment purely accidentally, and immediately earned a blow to the head. If you now start to interfere deliberately—"

"I wasn't interfering with any experiment," said Victor. "I was minding my own business, walking home from Lola's, when suddenly I saw—"

"Idiot," said Golem. "He's walking home and suddenly he sees. You should have crossed the street, you brainless ass!"

"For what reason should I cross the street?"

"For the reason that a good friend of yours was dispatching his direct responsibilities—and then you show up like a bull in a china shop."

Victor sat up straight. "What good friend of mine? I didn't know a single person there."

"The good friend who came from behind, brass knuckles a-blazing. You know anyone with a set?"

Victor downed his cognac in a single gulp. With astounding clarity, he remembered Pavor, his nose red from flu, pulling a handkerchief from his pocket and sending a set of brass knuckles—heavy, dully glinting, ergonomic—tumbling to the ground.

"No," said Victor, clearing his throat. "Nonsense. There's no way Pavor—"

"I didn't name any names," Golem retorted.

Victor placed both hands on the table and examined his clenched fists. "What do his direct responsibilities have to do with anything?" he asked.

"Someone needed a live clammy, apparently. Kidnapping-style."

"And I got in the way?"

"Or tried to."

"So they got him, in the end?"

"And took him away. Be grateful they didn't bring you along, to prevent information leaks. After all, they are uninterested in the fate of literature."

"So it was Pavor . . ." said Victor slowly.

"No names," Golem reminded him sternly.

"That son of a bitch," said Victor. "Well, we'll see . . . But what did they want with a clammy?"

"What do you mean? Information . . . Where can they get it? You know the drill: barbed wire, soldiers, General Pferd . . ."

"So are they interrogating him right now?" said Victor.

Golem was silent for a long time. Then he said, "He died."

"They beat him to death?"

"No. The opposite." Golem fell silent again. "They're numbskulls. Wouldn't let him read, so he starved."

Victor gave him a quick look. Golem was smiling sadly. Or crying from grief. Victor suddenly felt horror and anguish, suffocating anguish. The light of the floor lamp had dimmed. It felt like a heart attack. Victor gasped for air and loosened his tie with difficulty. Good lord, he thought, what a piece of shit, what filth, he's a criminal, a cold-blooded killer . . . and then, an hour later, he washed his hands, sprayed himself with perfume, spent a while calculating what thanks he'd get from his bosses, and then he came and sat down next to me, and we clinked glasses, and he smiled at me and talked to me like a friend, the scum, lying the whole time, smiling and lying, lying with pleasure, enjoying himself, mocking me, laughing behind my back, winking to himself, and then asking me sympathetically what was wrong with my head.

As if through a black fog, Victor saw Dr. R. Quadriga slowly raising his head, opening his chapped lips in a silent scream, and fumbling at the tablecloth convulsively, as if blind, and his eyes were like the eyes of a blind man as he shook his head and screamed and screamed, but Victor heard nothing . . . Serves me right, I'm a piece of shit, too, no one needs me, I'm an empty space, I deserve to get hit in the face, trampled with boots, for someone to hold my arms back and prevent me from wiping away the spittle, who the hell needs me, they should have hit me harder, hard enough that I stayed down, but it felt like a dream, I was swinging with fists of cotton, dear God, why the hell am I even alive, why is anyone, it's so simple, just creep up behind me and hit me in the head with something metal, and nothing will change, nothing in the world will change, because this very second, a thousand miles from here, some other pig is being born . . .

Golem's fat face sagged even lower; it was black with new stubble, his eyes had nearly swollen shut, he was lying motionless in his chair, like a tub of rancid oil, only his fingers moving as he slowly picked up glass after glass, breaking the stem, dropping it and picking up another, breaking the stem again and dropping it . . . And I don't love anyone, I can't love Diana—so what if we're sleeping together, I sleep with lots of people . . . anyway, how can you love a woman who doesn't love you back, and a woman can't love you unless you love her, and so it goes, spinning round and round in that accursed inhuman wheel, spinning like a snake chasing its own tail, like animals, copulating and bolting, except animals don't invent words or write poetry, all they do is copulate and bolt . . .

Teddy was crying, elbows on the bar, bony chin in bony fists, bald forehead glinting saffron in the lamplight, tears running unceasingly down his sunken cheeks, and they, too, glinted in the lamplight . . . It's all because I'm shit, I'm no writer, what the hell kind of writer could I possibly be if I hate writing, if writing is torture for me, if it's shameful and unpleasant, satisfying a painful physiological need like diarrhea, like squeezing pus from a boil, I hate it, it's horrible to think I'll be forced to do it all my life, that I'm doomed now, that they'll never let me go and instead demand, *come on, come on*, and I'll do it, but right now I can't, I can't even think about it, Jesus God, let me not think about it, or I'll puke . . .

Bol-Kunatz stood behind R. Quadriga, looking at his watch, slender, drenched, his face fresh and wet, with lovely dark eyes, and the scent coming off him tore apart the dense, hot, stuffy air, a fresh scent redolent of grass and spring water, of lilies, of sun and dragonflies over a lake . . . And the world returned. All that remained was a fleeting, dim memory, or a feeling, or a memory of a feeling: a desperate, truncated shout, an odd grinding sound, a crash, the crunching of glass . . .

Victor licked his lips and reached for a bottle. Dr. R. Quadriga, his head on the tablecloth, mumbled hoarsely, "I don't need anything. Hide me away. Screw them . . ." Golem was busily sweeping shards of glass from the table.

Bol-Kunatz said, "Please excuse me, Mr. Golem. A letter came for you." He placed an envelope on the table in front of Golem and glanced at his watch again. "Good evening, Mr. Banev," he said.

"Good evening," said Victor, pouring himself some cognac.

Golem read the letter carefully. Behind the bar, Teddy was blowing his nose loudly into a checkered handkerchief.

"Listen, Bol-Kunatz," said Victor. "Did you see who hit me that time?"

"No," answered Bol-Kunatz, looking him in the eye.

"What do you mean, 'no'?" said Victor, frowning.

"His back was to me," explained Bol-Kunatz.

"You know him," said Victor. "Who was it?"

Golem made an ambiguous noise. Victor quickly looked around. Golem, paying no attention to anyone, was pensively tearing the note into tiny pieces, which he stuck in his pocket.

"You're mistaken," said Bol-Kunatz. "I don't know him."

"Banev," mumbled R. Quadriga. "I'm begging you . . . I can't live there alone. Come with me . . . It's so scary . . ."

Golem stood up, searched around inside the pocket of his vest, then shouted, "Teddy! Put it on my tab . . . make sure to include the four broken wineglasses . . . I'll be on my way now," he said to Victor. "Think things over and make the reasonable choice. It might be best if you left town."

"Good-bye, Mr. Banev," said Bol-Kunatz politely. Victor thought he saw the boy give a barely perceptible shake of the head.

"Good-bye, Bol-Kunatz," he said. "Good-bye."

They left. Victor finished his cognac, lost in thought. The waiter approached; his face was swollen and covered in red blotches. He began clearing the table, his movements strangely awkward and uncertain.

"Are you new here?" asked Victor.

"Yes, Mr. Banev. Just started his morning."

"What happened to Peter? Is he sick?"

"No, Mr. Banev. He left. Couldn't take it anymore. I'll probably leave too . . ."

Victor looked over at R. Quadriga. "Take him to his room later," he said.

"Yes, of course, Mr. Banev," the waiter answered, his voice shaking.

Victor settled up, waved good-bye to Teddy, and walked out into the lobby. He went up to the second floor, got to Pavor's door, raised his knuckles to knock, stood there motionless for a while, then returned downstairs without knocking. The concierge, sitting behind his desk, was examining his own hands in amazement. His palms were wet; clumps of hair clung to them. Hair also littered his uniform tailcoat, while fresh scratches swelled on both of his cheeks. When he looked at Victor, his eyes were crazed. But now was not the time to notice all these strange happenings, that would be tactless and cruel, still less could he speak of them, he had to pretend like nothing had happened, pushing it away until later—tomorrow, or maybe even the day after. Victor asked, "Where's the room of . . . you know, that young man with the glasses, he's always walking around with a briefcase."

The concierge squirmed. Seemingly searching for a way out, he looked over at the key rack. After a while, he replied, "Three twelve, Mr. Banev."

"Thank you," said Victor, placing a coin on the desk.

"They don't like to be disturbed, though," the concierge warned him uncertainly.

"I know," said Victor. "I have no intention of disturbing them. I was just asking . . . you know, I had a bet with myself: if the room number's even, everything will turn out all right."

The concierge smiled wanly. "What problems could you possibly have, Mr. Banev?" he said politely.

"All kinds," sighed Victor. "Big and small. Good night."

He went up to the third floor, unhurried, as though giving himself time to think it all through, to deliberate, ponder possible consequences, calculate everything for three years ahead, but all he could think about was that the stairway rug was long overdue for a change. It had worn thin, this rug—gone threadbare. Mere moments before knocking at the door of room 312 (luxury suite, two bedrooms and a living room, television, top-quality radio set, refrigerator, and bar), he nearly said aloud, "Are you the crocodiles, gentlemen? Pleased to meet you. And for my next trick, I'll make you devour each other."

He had to knock for quite a long time, delicately at first, with the backs of his knuckles, and then, when there was no answer, more resolutely, with his fist, and when even that produced no reaction (except creaking floorboards and breathing at the keyhole), he turned his back to the door and began unceremoniously bashing it with his heel.

Eventually, a voice behind the door said, "Who's there?"

"Your neighbor," said Victor. "Open the door for a minute."

"What do you want?"

"I have a few things to say."

"Come back in the morning," the voice behind the door said. "We're sleeping."

"God damn you to hell," said Victor, who had gotten angry. "You want someone to see me out here? Open up, what're you afraid of?"

A key turned inside the lock and the door opened a crack. Victor could just make out the dimly glinting eye of the beanpole professional.

He displayed his open palms. "Just for a minute," he said.

"Come in," said the beanpole. "No funny business, though."

Victor stepped into the entryway. The beanpole closed the door behind him and turned on the light. The entryway was narrow, barely fitting the two of them.

"All right, talk," said the beanpole. He was wearing pajamas with a stain down the front of the top. Victor sniffed the air, amazed—the beanpole stank of alcohol. As custom dictated, he kept his right hand in his pocket.

"Is this where you expect us to converse?" Victor inquired.

"Yes."

"No," said Victor. "That's not how I do things."

"Whatever you say," said the beanpole.

"Whatever *you* say," said Victor. "It's your funeral."

They were silent for a moment. The beanpole, dropping all pretense, scrutinized Victor openly. "Your name is Banev, yes?"

"Last I checked."

"I see," said the beanpole, scowling. "Then in what sense are you my neighbor? You live on the second floor."

"I'm your neighbor in this hotel," Victor explained.

"I see . . . So what is it you want? I couldn't begin to guess."

"I need to tell you something," said Victor. "I have some information. But I'm starting to change my mind—it might not be worth it."

"Fine," said the beanpole. "Let's go in the bathroom."

"You know what," said Victor, "I think I'll be on my way."

"Why don't you want to go in the bathroom? What's wrong with you?"

"You know what," said Victor, "I've changed my mind. I really will be on my way. This is really none of my business." He started to turn around.

The beanpole grunted, trying to wrap his mind around all these contradictions. "You're a writer, yes?" he said. "Or am I confusing you with someone?"

"I'm a writer, all right," said Victor. "Good-bye."

"No, no, hold on. Why didn't you say so? Follow me. This way."

They entered the living room, where there was a multitude of curtains—curtains on the right, curtains on the left, curtains straight ahead, covering the enormous window. An enormous color television glittered in the corner, sound off. In the other corner, the bespectacled young man, also in pajamas and bedroom slippers, sat in a soft armchair beneath a floor lamp, observing Victor over the top of his open newspaper. A tall, rectangular bottle and a soda siphon stood on the coffee table next to him. The briefcase was nowhere to be seen.

"Good evening," said Victor.

The young man gave him a silent nod.

"He's with me," said the beanpole. "Pay him no mind."

The young man nodded again and disappeared behind his paper.

"Please, follow me," said the beanpole. They walked into the right-hand bedroom, and the beanpole sat down on the bed. "There's a chair," he said. "Now sit down and talk."

Victor sat. The bedroom smelled strongly of stale tobacco smoke and officers' cologne. The beanpole, his hand still in his pocket, sat on the bed, watching Victor. Newspaper rustling could be heard from the living room.

"All right," said Victor. He had not quite gotten over his revulsion, but now that he was here, it was time to talk. "I'm pretty sure I know who the two of you are. Maybe I'm wrong, in which case everything is fine. But if I'm not wrong, then you should know you're being watched and that obstacles are being put in your way."

"Let's say I believe you," said the beanpole. "Who do you think is watching us?"

"You are of great interest to a man named Pavor Summan."

"Huh?" said the beanpole. "The health inspector?"

"He's not a health inspector. Anyway, that's really all I wanted to tell you." Victor stood up, but the beanpole didn't move.

"Let's say I believe you," he repeated. "How, exactly, did you come by this information?"

"Is that important?" asked Victor.

The beanpole thought for a while. "Let's say it's not," he said.

"Your job is to check it out," said Victor. "I don't know anything else. Good-bye."

"Where are you going, hold on," said the beanpole. He leaned over to the bedside table and took a bottle and a glass out of the drawer. "You wanted so badly to come inside, and now you're running off . . . Do you mind? I've only got one glass."

"Depends," said Victor, and sat down again.

"Scotch whisky," said the beanpole. "That work?"

"Is it really Scotch?"

"It's really whisky. Here you go." He handed the glass to Victor.

"You people sure know how to have a good time," said Victor, and drank.

"We can't compete with writers, though," said the beanpole, and also drank. "Why don't you start from the beginning . . ."

"Forget it," said Victor. "This is why they pay you the big bucks. I gave you a name, you know the address, so figure it out.

Especially since I don't know anything, really. Except . . ." Victor paused and pretended like a thought had just entered his head. The beanpole immediately took the bait.

"Yes?" he said. "Yes?"

"I know he kidnapped a clammy, and that he was working with the city legionnaires. What's his name . . . Flamenta . . . Juventa . . ."

"Flamen Juventa," the beanpole said helpfully.

"Exactly."

"About the clammy—are you sure?" asked the beanpole.

"Yes. I tried to interfere, and Mr. Health Inspector bopped me on the head with some brass knuckles. And then, while I was rolling around on the ground, they took him away in a car."

"I see, I see," said the beanpole. "So it *was* Summan. Listen, Banev, you're all right! Want more whisky?"

"Sure do," said Victor. No matter what he told himself, no matter how he wound himself up or worked himself over, he still felt disgusted. Well, good, he thought. I should be grateful, at least, that I make such a poor informer. Doesn't feel good at all, even though now they're bound to devour each other. Golem was right: interfering was a mistake . . . Or is Golem smarter than I think he is?

"Here you go," said the beanpole, handing him a full glass.

7. FELIX SOROKIN

LITALMETER

I slept well. No nightmares. I dreamed a name: Katya. Just the name and nothing else.

I woke up late and decided to have breakfast at the Pearl Oyster. That's our neighborhood watering hole, located directly across from the regional Young Pioneer Palace. From the outside, it looks pretty strange—just like that famous artillery bunker from the Winter War, the "Million," which was blown to bits by a two-thousand-pound bomb. Clumps of boring gray concrete stick out in all directions, interspersed with snarls of rusty iron rebar that the architect evidently intended to represent seaweed. Elongated, embrasure-like windows run along the facade at sidewalk level. But inside, it's an entirely decent, unpretentious establishment: an entryway with a cloakroom, and behind it a friendly, well-lighted round room. They always have beer; you can get regular cold appetizers; the hot dishes include beef stroganoff and their trademark, beef in a clay pot. One thing I've never seen there, though, is freshwater crab. I go there for breakfast sometimes when I get tired of boiled eggs and fruit-flavored kefir.

I arrived just as the place was opening, quickly got rid of my coat, and commandeered a table near the wall, next to a window. The waiter, who managed to be overfamiliar and sleepily sullen at once, brought me a mug of beer and took down my order: beef in a clay pot. All around, people talked loudly. They also smoked, probably on an empty stomach.

No one sat down at my table, though the seat across from me was empty. On the one hand, this was of course wonderful. I can't stand talking to strangers. On the other hand, it suddenly occurred to me that this sort of thing has happened to me before. Whether I'm on a trolley, on the Metro, or in some hole-in-the-wall where no one knows me, like this one, people only take the empty seat next to me when all the others are occupied. I read somewhere that there are people whose very appearance inspires timidity, or disgust, or just an instinctive wish to keep away. For some reason, this train of thought made me think of yesterday's letter. Today's episode was just another piece of evidence, however circumstantial, that proved the letter was no stupid joke, that someone out there really did find me alien in some way, which ultimately led them to their fanciful conclusions.

But of course the main cause isn't some trivial detail; it's my *Modern Tales*. God, that book truly is like a flesh-and-blood child: the troubles and sorrows associated with it far exceed any joys or pleasures. Editors cut it into ribbons, minced it fine, practically made noodles out of it. If not for Miron Mikhailovich, it would have ended up permanently disfigured.

And then, when it finally came out, the critics descended on it. In those days, science fiction was still in a formative stage—clumsy, helpless, burdened with the genetic diseases of the '40s. Critics treated it like a clay pigeon at target practice. I would read a review of *Modern Tales* and hiss in pain, my mind's eye conjuring up a pale, handsome youth in a high-necked coat of Circassian wool, with the dead-eyed gaze of an utterly depraved

White officer. He sucks his skinny cigarette down to the butt, then uses two fingers to carefully remove the slimy remnant from his lower lip. Squinting at my defenseless book, he bares his saber languidly, takes a running start, stepping lightly on tiptoe, and raises the blue steel above his head . . .

The critics said my book was a derivative imitation of mediocre American works. (Today, these same works are considered exemplary.) They wrote that my human characters were overshadowed by my machines. (The book featured no machines at all, with the possible exception of buses.) *Where did the author ever see anyone like the heroes he depicts?* they inquired rhetorically. *What can such literature possibly teach the reader?* they asked each other. *Sorokin's utterly inadequate book is a false note in this year's offerings from Such and Such Press . . .*

Then came the deluge: Gagashkin's long review plus Bryzheikin's feuilleton, both in *Voluntary Informant*. I ended up in the hospital, and only then did my big-cheese benefactors take notice, realizing that a basically good man—even if he had inadvertently gone astray—was being cut to pieces before their very eyes. They took some measures. I don't really like to remember this episode.

Back then I hadn't yet read Bradbury's *Martian Chronicles*; I'd never even heard of them. I didn't have the slightest inkling, as I was working on my *Tales*, that they were a kind of inverse *Martian Chronicles*, a cycle of sad and funny stories about extraterrestrials trying to adapt to our own planet. What I wanted most was to turn the mirror on us earthlings, to see our everyday lives, our passions and hopes, through the eyes of an outsider—an alien outsider, who isn't ill intentioned but simply indifferent, who doesn't think or feel anything like we do. The result was quite amusing, if I do say so myself, except that certain critics still consider me some sort of renegade from Great Literature, and certain readers—as it turns out!—believe I'm one of my own characters . . .

The waiter brought me my beef in a clay pot; I ordered another beer and tucked in.

"May I?" said a quiet, rather hoarse voice.

Looking up, I saw a strapping hunchback standing before me, his hand resting on the back of the empty chair. He was wearing tattered jeans and a sweater. Wavy, shoulder-length blond hair framed his pale, narrow face. I nodded, trying to look unfriendly, but he immediately sat down—sideways, his back apparently making it hard to face front. After settling into his seat, he placed a skinny black folder on the table and began drumming on it with his fingernails. The waiter brought my beer and looked at the hunchback expectantly. He mumbled, "Same for me, please."

I finished my beef, picked up my mug, and suddenly noticed that the hunchback was scrutinizing me, a smile playing on his long lips—I would have called his expression pleasant if it weren't so uncertain. I knew already that he was about to speak, which is what he did. "You see," he said, "I was told to speak to you."

"To me?"

"To you, yes. To you specifically."

"I see," I said. "And who told you to speak to me?"

"It was . . ." he promptly began looking around, craning his neck as though trying to look over people's heads. "That's odd, he was sitting right there a second ago . . . Where did he go?"

I looked at him. His whole person seemed somehow grubby. The sleeves of a grubby undershirt peeked out from the cuffs of his grubby gray sweater, and the undershirt's collar was similarly greasy and dirty. His long-fingered hands hadn't seen water for a long time, nor had his wavy golden hair or his gaunt, pale face with whitish stubble covering the cheeks and chin. He smelled, too—like a poultry yard, sour and unkempt. An odd guy: too respectable to be an alcoholic yet too dingy to be a regular person.

"He went somewhere," he informed me sheepishly. "But never mind him . . . You see, he told me that you might understand, even if you don't believe me."

"I'm listening," I said, failing to suppress a sigh.

"Well . . . here!" He pushed his folder across the table and gestured at me to open it.

"Sorry," I said resolutely. "But I don't read unsolicited manuscripts. You might try—"

"It's not a manuscript," he said hastily. "Or rather, it's not what you think."

"Still," I said.

"No, please . . . This will interest you, I promise!" And, seeing that I had no intention of touching his folder, he opened it himself.

Inside was sheet music.

"Listen," I said.

But he refused to listen. Lowering his voice and leaning across the table, he began explaining the nature of his business, making orator-like gestures with his right hand and bathing me in his complex odor, equal parts poultry yard and beer barrel.

The nature of his business was this: Would I like to purchase, for the low, low price of five rubles, exclusive rights to the musical score for the Trumpet Call at the Last Judgment? He had personally transcribed the original into modern musical notation. Where did he get the original? That was a long story, which moreover would be difficult to convey in commonly understood terms. He was . . . how could he put this . . . well, call it a fallen angel. He ended up here, down below, without any means of making a living, literally with just what he had in his pockets. It was practically impossible for him to find work, since he naturally didn't have any identification documents . . . Solitude . . . Futility . . . Hopelessness . . . Only five rubles, is that really so much? Fine, he'll give it up for three, even though he was told not to come back with less than five . . .

This was not the first time I had been forced to listen to more or less tearful tales of lost train tickets, stolen passports, apartments burned to the ground. These stories had long since ceased to elicit not only my compassion but even ordinary squeamishness. I would silently thrust a twenty-kopeck piece into the supplicant's hand and depart from the scene with all due speed. But the story offered by the golden-haired hunchback struck me as exquisite, from a purely professional point of view. This grubby fallen angel had talent! His tale would have done credit to H. G. Wells himself. The fate of the five rubles had been decided, no question about it. But I wanted to test the soundness of his story. Or really, its dimensionality.

I picked up the sheet music and looked through it. Not that I'd ever been able to make head or tails of all those sticks and dots. All right. So you claim that if, for instance, you played this melody in a cemetery . . .

Of course. But you'd better not. It would be too cruel . . .

To whom?

To the dead, of course! You'd be condemning them to thousands and thousands of years of restless wandering over the earth. And don't forget about yourself. Are you ready to behold such a sight?

I appreciated his argument, but I had to ask: In that case, what use would I have for this score?

He was very surprised. Was I really not interested in possessing such an object? Wouldn't I want to own the nail driven into the hand of the Teacher as he hung on the cross? Or, for instance, the stone slab bearing the fiery hoofprints of Satan himself, from the time he had stood on the tomb of Pope Gregory VII, born Hildebrand of Sovana?

The example of the stone slab really tickled me. It was the product of a mind unacquainted with tiny apartments. Well, all right, I said. But what if I played the melody not at a cemetery but, say, in Gorky Park?

The fallen angel shrugged his shoulders uncertainly. It was probably best not to. After all, how could we know for sure what lay three yards beneath the pavement?

I took out five rubles and placed them on the table in front of him. "That's your honorarium," I said. "Keep up the good work. You have a great imagination."

"I don't have a great anything," the hunchback retorted forlornly.

He casually stuck the money into the pocket of his jeans and walked off without saying good-bye.

"Don't forget your score!" I shouted after him, but he didn't turn around.

I sat there waiting for the check, looking through the sheet music to kill some time. It was only four pages long. On the back of the last sheet, I found a sloppy note in ballpoint pen: 19 Granovsky Prospekt, Pearl Oyster, check. coat."

I guess I'd been just a teensy bit on edge lately; events were unfolding a little too thick and fast, and Whoever Is Supposed to Oversee My Fate had been a wee bit too generous. And so, no sooner did I read the words "check. coat" than I leaped up as though pricked by an awl and glued myself to the embrasure-like window, looking left and right. I'd nearly missed him: my friend in the reversible checked coat was just disappearing from my field of vision, his hand clasping the elbow of the golden-haired hunchback, who was now clad in a filthy canvas duster.

I sank into my chair, desperate for beer.

That this amusing though not entirely pleasant story had ended in this manner oppressed me so utterly that I wanted to return home at once, and for good. Incoherent suspicions whirled through my mind, congealing into tales of a truly disgusting nature before immediately falling apart. What prevailed in the end, however, was the most reasonable and realistic of these thoughts: if I went home now, what would I tell Fyodor Mikheyevich?

The waiter showed up with the bill and I complied unquestioningly, paying for the meat and both beers—mine and the fallen angel's, which was unfinished. Then I picked up my folder, slipped the sheet music into it, left the hunchback's empty folder on the table, and went to the cloakroom to find my coat.

I kept my eye out for the man in the checked coat all the way to Bannaya, but to no avail.

This time, the auditorium was empty and half dark. I walked between the rows of chairs to the door marked WRITERS—IN HERE, and knocked. No one answered, and carefully pushing open the door, I stepped into a brightly lit space not unlike a short hallway. At the end of that hallway was yet another door. Above it hung a small object shaped like a stoplight. It looked like those doodads you see at the entrance to X-ray rooms. The top half of the stoplight was illuminated with the words Do Not Enter! The lower half was dark, but I could easily discern the words Come In. Several chairs stood against the hallway's right-hand wall, and on one of them, his long limbs folded into the seat, pressing the edge of a luxurious (if worn-out) document case into his pointy knees, sat Fulminating Pustule—in the flesh.

As soon as I caught sight of him, the usual chill ran down my spine. And as usual, I thought, What do you know, he's still alive!

I greeted him. He answered, his toothless jaws working. I sat two chairs away from him and stared straight ahead. Seeing nothing except a rather battered wall carelessly slathered with light-green oil paint, I could nonetheless feel the ancient, faded eyes palpating my person, honing in on me like gun sights. I could sense the mental gears grinding just a few steps away, doing their usual work, mechanically shuffling cards bearing every possible shred of data. Was I or wasn't I, had I been a member or not, all the facts and gossip, rumors and their possible interpretations, and annotations to the gossip. Now he was drawing conclusions, compiling certain results, formulating action items that may or may not come in handy at some future point.

Some part of me knew that this was all just my own psychosis. I doubted the old bastard even knew who I was, and even if he did, we don't do things that way anymore, times have changed, he's old now and utterly irrelevant, no danger to anyone. Not a year passes without some rumor that he's finally given up the ghost; by now he's more of a character from a historical anecdote than a living person, a rotting shadow stretching through the years into our own time. Be that as it may, I couldn't help myself. I was afraid.

Suddenly, he spoke. His voice was creaky and unintelligible, probably due to bad dentures. Nonetheless, I managed to make out that he found our current winter abnormally snowy, plus something else about climate and weather.

He was addressing me for the first time in my life. His words were banal enough—anyone could have spoken them. But I was tempted to make the sign of the cross and shriek, like Dr. Frankenstein, "It's alive!"

Many, many years ago, when I was still relatively young, inwardly honest, and impenetrably stupid, I was suddenly struck with the thought (it was like a bucket of cold water) that all those vile and macabre personages, objects of terrifying rumors, black epigrams, and bloody legends do not dwell in some abstract, anecdotal plane. You wish! There's one, sitting at the next table over: several drinks deep already, engrossed in good-natured argument with his tablemates, he's fishing an olive out of his solyanka. There's another one, walking with an arthritic limp, coming toward you down the white marble steps. And another one: a rotund, perpetually sweaty little man zealously making the rounds of the Moscow Soviet, brandishing a list of writers in need of apartments . . .

And when this thought hit me, it raised an excruciating question: How should I treat them? How should I treat people who, according to all my usual moral and ethical rules, are criminals; worse, executioners; worse, traitors! Rumor had it that people slapped them in the face, poured bowls of soup on their heads in restaurants, publicly spat in their eyes. That was the rumor. Personally, I never saw anything like that. Rumor had it that people refused to shake their hands, turned away when they crossed their path, said harsh words to them at meetings and assemblies. And sure, things like that sometimes happened, but I don't know of a single incident in which the underlying cause wasn't utterly unromantic—vacation vouchers snatched right from under one's nose, a banal case of adultery, a not-so-anonymous negative review.

They walked among us, arms bloodstained to the elbow, dripping with the pus of unimaginable details, their consciences barely breathing or choked to death, heirs to suddenly ownerless apartments, suddenly ownerless manuscripts, suddenly ownerless positions. And we had no idea how to deal with them. We were young, honest, and hot-blooded, we wanted to slap them in the face, but they were old, their bloated cheeks were furrowed with wrinkles, and it felt unseemly to kick them when they were already down; we wanted to pillory them, to brand them publicly, but they seemed to be pilloried and branded already, thrown on the rubbish heap, never to rise again. Why harass them—as a lesson to posterity? But the horrors they had perpetrated would never repeat themselves, and anyway, was this really the lesson posterity needed? And what's more, it seemed like in a year or two they would finally vanish into the abyss of history, rendering automatically moot the question of whether to shake their hands or turn away demonstratively . . .

But a year passed, then two, and suddenly everything was somehow imperceptibly different. True, some of them had receded into the shadows, but the vast majority had no intention of vanishing into any kind of abyss. They sat as if nothing had happened, engrossed in good-natured argument, fishing olives out of their solyanka, limping hurriedly down marble staircases, trying not to be late to some meeting; running, with a gambler's zeal, up and down the halls of power, brandishing lists they themselves composed and ratified. What vanished into the abyss of history were the black epigrams and bloody legends, while their heroes, who, on closer inspection, turned out to have mirror reflections after all, once again began blending in seamlessly with their surroundings, distinguished from the rest of us perhaps only by age, by the power of their connections, and by their clear-headed understanding of what was appropriate—right now, at least—and what was not.

And off we went, petitioning them for vacation vouchers or advances, writing lukewarm reviews of their work, seeking their support on various committees, and suddenly the possibility of *not* shaking hands with Comrade So-and-So began to seem outlandish. So what if, back in the day, he'd condemned Ivanov, Petrov, and two Rabinoviches to death in obscurity? Listen, forget it, they say that stuff about everyone! Half of our old folk accuse the other half of that sort of sin, and most likely, both halves are right. I'm sick of hearing about it. You think our generation's any better?

Judge not lest ye be judged. Don't knock it till you've tried it. Don't blame the mirror if you're ugly. But most important: don't bite the hand that feeds you or spit against the wind.

Because it's frightening. As it always was, right from the start.

The nasty old man sitting two chairs away could do anything he wanted to me. Write a letter. Drop a hint. Express confusion or certainty. This creature seemed to me a vestige of a completely different age, or completely different environmental conditions. You try to jaywalk and the creature bites off your legs. Your manuscript contains an inappropriate word and the creature bites off your hands. You win some money in a lottery and the creature bites off your head. You're defenseless against it because you never can or will know what laws govern its hunting behavior or the purpose of its existence. One of the science fiction writers—possibly Efremov, or maybe Belyaev—describes a monstrous beast called the *gishu*, devourer of prehistoric elephants, who has survived into the age of man. Man could not escape it, because he didn't understand its habits, which had formed back when he did not and could not yet exist. There was only one way for man to save himself from the *gishu*: band together with his fellows and kill it . . .

We discussed the weather. Then, after a brief pause, we discussed it again. Then he expressed his indignation—there's no elevator, you have to trek up three flights of spiral staircase. I kept my silence. The topic of the staircase seemed fraught to me.

Then the door under the little traffic light opened wide, and Petenka Skorobogatov burst into the hallway.

"Good God, are you all right?" I exclaimed, standing up to greet him.

Petenka's head was wrapped in a turban of white gauze. His left arm, bandaged up fat as a log, hung in a sling. His right hand leaned heavily on a stick. What the hell had they done to him? I thought, horrified.

However, I soon learned that *they* hadn't done anything to him. It was just that on the way back from yesterday's meeting, deep in argument with the chairman of the local trade union committee, Petenka Skorobogatov, our Sweet, Sweet Soviet Boy, missed a step on the spiral staircase and plummeted down from the third floor to the first. As a result, three people ended up in the hospital, where they remained to this day. Recovering from trepanation procedures. But Petenka was right as rain!

"And that's how I ended up tumbling headfirst down three flights of spiral staircase. Head over heels, over and over again. But here I am, right as rain! I got lucky, you know, landed on the chairman, and he's real big and fat, all soft, you know . . ."

He sprawled next to me, stretching out his injured leg. It was all like water off a duck's back to him. Choosing not to dwell on details like his torn earlobe, dislocated arm, or sprained ankle, he preferred to yank my chain, telling me all about how yesterday, he was called into the State Committee for Publishing and offered a contract for a two-volume deluxe edition of some of his work. It was going to be illustrated by the famous caricaturist collective known as the Kukryniksy; a press in Leipzig was ready to do the printing . . .

Hearing the word *Leipzig*, I involuntarily glanced to my right. Luckily, Fulminating Pustule was already gone.

"Hey, what's this?" Petenka suddenly shrieked, grabbing the folder out of my hands. "Oh! So you dabble in music, too?" he asked, seeing the score. "You should quit, that's my advice. It's a dead end." He stuck the folder back into my hands. "Take me for example . . . God, I'm still in shock. I got an insane index just now. Just insane. The guy wouldn't return my manuscript. 'I'm keeping it,' he says. 'It's exemplary.' I go, 'Oh please, I wrote it in my spare time, it's just some random commission.' And he goes, 'For you, it's a random commission, but for us, it's exemplary.' You can't fool a machine, Felix! Forget it!"

The door under the little traffic light swung open once more, and Fulminating Pustule returned to the hallway. He crossed the threshold, shut the door tightly behind him, and paused. For a couple of seconds he stood, clutching the wall for support with one hand as the other pressed his document case to his chest. He was as green in the face as a rotting corpse. His mouth gaped in anguish; his eyes bulged.

"How can it be?" he hissed. "How did this happen? I saw, with my own eyes . . ."

He swayed, and Petenka and I rushed to his side, intending to hold him up. But he moved us aside with one arm, the one holding the document case.

"But I personally . . ." he whisper-screamed, still hissing and staring into the gap between us. "Personally! Myself!"

"No worries," said Petenka cheerfully, grabbing him around the waist with one arm—the one that held his cane. "No big deal. You're not the first, you're not the last, Mefody Kirillovich—"

"Are you hearing yourself?" asked Mefody Kirillovich. He sounded almost despairing. "Or maybe the trumpets of the Last Judgment have sounded?"

"Oh no, no, no, no, no!" Petenka protested. "No chance of that. You have my personal guarantee. No trumpets, nothing tube-shaped at all, in fact—other than large-diameter gas pipes. Why don't you and I have a seat, Mefody Kirillovich, just to catch our breath a little . . ."

"Personally!" the old man grated, sitting down obediently. "And later on, I read it myself . . ."

"But see, Mefody Kirillovich, you were reading only the lines themselves, when you should have been reading between them," said Petenka, giving me a brazen wink. "There was probably a subtext there, and you just didn't catch it. And that's what the machine ferreted out."

"What subtext? What machine? Don't you understand what I'm saying, young man?"

I felt oppressed and disgusted; turning away, I suddenly noticed that the traffic light was now telling me to COME IN. Like a sleepwalker, I rose from my seat and did as I was told.

This wasn't my first time in a computing center, so neither the rough gray cabinets, the panels blinking with lights, nor the various other screens and dials in the large, brightly lit room captured my attention. Infinitely stranger and more fascinating to me was the man sitting at the table, which was piled high with folders and scrolls of rolled-up paper.

He looked to be about my age, on the skinny side, with fine, sandy-colored hair and features that were simultaneously quite ordinary and imbued with some subtle significance. There was something in that face to give you pause, to make you sit up inwardly straight and speak concisely, eloquently, and directly. He wore a blue lab coat over a gray suit. His shirt collar was snow white, while his tie was understated, made of old-fashioned fabric and tied in an old-fashioned knot.

"Please shut the door," he said in a soft, pleasant voice.

I looked behind me and noticed that I'd left the door ajar. I apologized and shut it, then introduced myself. Something changed in his face, and I understood that my name was familiar to him. He did not give his own name but only said, "Pleased to meet you. If you don't mind, let's have a look at what you brought today. Please come through and take a seat."

In these simple words, which could not have been more ordinary or obvious, I could hear—or thought I could hear—a sense of superiority so overwhelming that I suddenly felt compelled to explain, to make excuses, to say I hadn't meant to come so late, that I'd been unavoidably detained, that I'd actually come in yesterday and been no more than twenty steps from his door—again, for reasons entirely beyond my control.

However, this fit of guilty respectfulness—acute and almost physiological—quickly passed, and of course I didn't say a word of it to him. All I did was approach the table, place my folder down, and sit in a rather comfortable chair. The pendulum now swung in the other direction and I suddenly felt like making myself at home, crossing my legs and, dreamily examining my surroundings, emitting some frivolous banality like *Great setup—you scientists sure know how to pick 'em!*

But I didn't say anything like that to him, either, nor did I hoist up my leg. I sat there like a good boy, watching as he picked up the folder, deftly and carefully untying the strings. I thought I saw him smiling with his long, thin lips, and possibly glancing up at me through his fine hair—curiously or ironically, I couldn't tell, but in a spirit that was definitely friendly.

He opened the folder and saw the sheet music. His eyebrows rose slightly. Mumbling awkward apologies, I reached for the accursed score, but he, without shifting his eyes from the notes on the page, stopped me with a wave of his hand. It was obvious that he could sight-read music and was interested in what he was seeing, since, when he finally let me expunge the fallen angel's composition from my folder, he looked at me with mirthless gray eyes and said, "You certainly do find curious papers in writers' old folders sometimes, don't you?"

I couldn't think of anything to say, nor did he expect an answer. He was already leafing—quickly but carefully—through my reviews of mass-produced hackwork, now in advanced stages of decomposition in the archives of various presses; my annotations to Japanese patents; manuscript versions of translations I'd done from Japanese technical journals; and other junk left over from that difficult period when they'd stopped publishing me and started blackening my name . . .

He turned page after page, obviously hoping to extract something minimally useful from that pile of trash, and I suddenly felt horribly ashamed. I felt like the world's biggest pig—after all, here sits a man, stern and mirthless, neither a hack nor an opportunist, someone who'd clearly read Sorokin and was therefore expecting something serious from him, some material suitable for use in his own work; he'd expected that Sorokin would display elementary decency, but Sorokin brought over a sack of shit and dumped it out on the table: *There ya go! Enjoy.*

Such were the thoughts tormenting me when he finally closed the shameful folder, covered it with his pale, long-fingered hands, and looked up at me again. "Felix Alexandrovich," he said,

"I see that you are totally uninterested in the objective value of your work."

I don't know if he meant to reproach me, but something about his words, or perhaps his tone, made me bristle and filled my heart with a plebeian urge to contradict. "What makes you say that?"

"Well, what else am I supposed to think?" He tapped the folder with a fingernail. "Based on what you brought me, all I can say is that you have terrible handwriting and that the Japanese have spent a great deal of time working on fuel cells."

A capricious, querulous demon stirred within me, pushing cowardly and evil excuses to the surface: *I don't care, I was told I could bring in any manuscript, so that's exactly what I did—you people don't know what you want, leave me out of it* . . . But I didn't say anything like that; I just went limp, then said, "It just kind of worked out like this . . ."

And added, to my own surprise, "Please don't be angry."

"Come now," he said, and suddenly smiled—an odd, gentle, sad smile. "How could I be angry with you, Felix Alexandrovich? After all, you need this more than we do."

And at that moment, I finally registered the astonishing thing he'd just said. "Wait a second," I said, lowering my voice for some reason. "Was that a joke just now? How did you mean it—the thing about objective value?"

"Quite literally," he said, no longer smiling.

"How is that possible? Am I supposed to believe that you all invented a real-life Mensura Zoili?"

"Well, why not? And besides the Mensura, we've invented lots of other things."

"Hold on—but that's nonsense! How can a work of art have anything like an 'objective value'?"

"Well, why not?" he repeated.

"Well, for one thing . . . Excuse me, but it's banal! Let's say I like a given work, whereas to you, every word is nauseating. Today the whole world's talking about it, but tomorrow it's forgotten . . ."

"All that may be true, Felix Alexandrovich, but what does it have to do with objective value?"

"What it has to do with objective value," I said, blood rising to my face, "is that an objectively valuable piece of art should be valuable to both you and me, and if it was valuable yesterday, it should be valuable tomorrow, but that's impossible, that simply cannot be!"

He responded, however, that I was confusing objective with *eternal* value. The latter, indeed, didn't exist, because there's nothing in literature or art that could be equally valuable to everyone and for all time. But hadn't I noticed that many works, having apparently earned all possible accolades and fully lived out their lives, are suddenly reborn centuries later—and cause another furor, existing even more loudly and energetically than before? Might it make sense to consider exactly this capacity for renewal the measure of objective value? Moreover, that is only one possible approach to the problem . . . There are other, more functional approaches, ones more suitable to algorithmization . . .

As I listened to him, I felt my rising blood draining away like water into sand. I love to argue, especially on abstract, impractical topics like this one. But for me, abstract argument requires a very specific atmosphere: mild euphoria, a cozy group of friends, a little carafe, naturally, and a second one in the offing, locked and loaded. Here, by contrast, among the rough cabinets, in the deathly light of mercury tubes, among scrolls and diagrams, not with my cozy group but in the company of a man who made me feel intimidated . . . No, citizens, that's not my preferred setting for debate.

And, as if guessing my thoughts, he spoke again: "It just doesn't make any sense to argue this point, Felix Alexandrovich. The machine that measures the objective value of works of art, the Mensura Zoili, as you call it, already exists. It's actually been around for a while already. And when it was created, Felix Alexandrovich, it raised another question, a much more important one: Is this notion of 'objective value' useful to anyone? The fate of the machine's first functional iteration, and the fate of its creators, is quite instructive in this respect . . . I'm not boring you, am I?"

Dark premonitions had already gripped me. I nodded hastily, trying desperately to convey that I was not at all bored but waiting impatiently for him to continue.

My premonition turned out to be correct. Thirty years ago, he said, a young amateur inventor rode up on his motorcycle to the Writers' Guest House in Kukushkino, bringing with him the very first Litalmeter. And lo, Zakhar Kupidonovich, without asking permission, threw the manuscript of Sidor Amenpodespovich into the machine and subsequently, delighted, read the Litalmeter's verdict out loud, a verdict that, it must be noted, surprised no one; and lo, an ugly brawl broke out next to the indifferent machine between Flavius Vespasianovich and the tactless editor in chief of Moscow Litterateur Press; and lo, the jubilee birthday of Gaussiana Nikiforovna was utterly ruined following the total waste of 107 servings of sturgeon kebab and Suvorov-style fillet, specially delivered from the Club by personal limousine; and lo, Lukyan Philosophovich vainly tried to bribe the inventor to "adjust" his accursed apparatus—offering first a case of vodka, then money, and finally an apartment in one of the new highrises . . . Thus did my interlocutor sing of the circles of hell into which the Writers' Guest House in Kukushkino descended for eight full days. And lo, on the ninth day the machine was smashed to smithereens, and a day later, Mefody Kirillovich wrapped up the whole affair . . . in accordance with strategies of conflict resolution no longer in use today.

I listened eagerly, and as soon as he fell silent, asked, "So you knew Anatoly Yefimovich too?"

"But of course!" he said with some surprise. "What brought him to mind?"

"Come on! The story you just told me was part of a comedy Anatoly Yefimovich was intending to write."

"Oh, right," he said, as though just remembering. "You should know, though, that he didn't just *intend* to write it, he actually did.

Wrote himself into it, too—under another name, of course. And then, in March of '52 in Kukushkino, all of it actually occurred."

Something stabbed at me from that last sentence, but my mind had already snagged on another contradictory detail. "What do you mean, he actually wrote it? Anatoly Yefimovich told me all this literally a month before his death. He said it was an *idea* for a comedy!"

He smirked mirthlessly. "No, Felix Alexandrovich. By the time he told you that story, the play had already been in existence for a quarter century. It lay, copyedited and in triplicate, in one of his desk drawers. It just needed to be printed. You remember his desk, yes? It was enormous and ancient, with lots of drawers. The one where he kept his awkwardly titled comedy 'Litalmeter' was on the left-hand side, on the very bottom."

He said all this with such gravity, and yet so sadly, that I felt I had no choice but to observe a moment of silence. So we sat there silently while he opened my folder and leafed through my manuscripts again.

I felt mildly offended that Anatoly Yefimovich had not trusted me enough to show me this part of his life. And all this time I'd thought he liked me and set me apart. Although, on the other hand, who did I think I was that he should trust me? He thought me worthy of conversing with him over tea in his kitchen, which admitted only the elect—let that be enough.

But mixed with this feeling of mild offense was surprise. What I found surprising was not that the Mensura Zoili had long since been invented and even tested out. The surprising thing was how unsurprising I found this fact. After all, the existence of such a machine in reality overturned much of what I had believed about the possible and the impossible.

The source of my unsurprise was probably in the very personality of my interlocutor, which was so far outside the bounds of my imagination that other things could only feel strange and astonishing as corollaries of this initial strangeness. I desperately wanted to ask whether he himself was that young inventor who had first brought about the week of horrors in Kukushkino, and then become the subject of a play by Anatoly Yefimovich. I had already cleared my throat and even opened my mouth, but when he looked at me with his limpid gray eyes, I instantly understood that I would never dare ask him such a question. And so I blurted out at random, "So what are you saying? That all these cabinets contain the Litalmeter? That the rumor I've been hearing is true—that is, that your task is to measure the level of our talent?"

This time, he didn't even smile. "Of course not," he said. "Or rather, in some sense, yes. But actually, we're interested in quite different problems, very specialized ones, which are more in the area of linguistics . . . or sociolinguistics, to be more precise."

I asked if it was correct to say that these rough cabinets could in principle measure my level of talent but are currently occupied with some other problem. He said that in a certain sense that was the case. Then I inquired, not unsarcastically, what units they used to measure talent: Was it a five-point scale, like in high school, or a twelve-point one, like in seismology? He responded that it would be naive to assume that such primitive units could be used to value a sociopsychological phenomenon as complex as talent. Talent is a specialized phenomenon and must therefore be measured in specialized units.

"Actually," he said, "it would be simpler just to show you how the machine works. Its outputs relate to talent only indirectly, but still . . . Let's take, say, this page, your review of a short story titled 'The Birth of a Female Dove' . . . The title alone tells us all we need to know about its quality . . . But the machine, Felix Alexandrovich, will assess not the short story but your review."

With some effort, he detached the staple holding the sheets together in a death grip, took the top sheet, and placed it in a sort of small drawer the size of a standard piece of typewriter paper. He then pushed the drawer into a corresponding slot, casually threw a couple of switches on the control panel, and pressed a red button, which immediately lit up. Then the button went out, but numerous lights began to fuss and blink on a vertical panel flanked by two large screens, which now also came to life. Curves snaked across them; numbers leaped and jumped amid the whining and clicking of klystrons, kenotrons, and other electronic entrails. The age of scientific and technical progress was truly upon us!

All of this lasted about thirty seconds. Then the whining ceased. Peace and order were restored to the panel and the screens. Now all that glowed on their surfaces were two smooth curves and an enormous quantity of numbers.

"And that's all there is to it," he said, pulling out the little drawer and replacing my sheet in the folder.

Before I could even open my mouth, he began explaining to me that these numbers over here represented the entropy of my text, whereas those numbers over there characterized something or other. This curve was the approximate coefficient of blah-deblah (I didn't quite catch it), while that one pointed to the distribution of such and such—which I caught and even committed to memory, but then promptly forgot.

"Note this figure," he said, tapping his finger on a lonely number 4 sitting in orphaned solitude in the lower right-hand corner of one of the screens. "Your colleagues have somehow come to the conclusion that this is the true valuation, or 'genius index,' in the words of that strange bandaged-up man."

"Our Sweet Soviet Boy," I mumbled automatically.

"Yes, perhaps. Although today he said his name was Kozlukhin. He's come here many times, each time with a new manuscript and a different name. Anyway, he persists in calling that figure the 'genius index' and believes that the larger it is, the more of a genius the author in question . . ."

And he told me how, in an attempt to dissuade Petenka Skorobogatov, he had once torn a random sheet out of a newspaper feuilleton about crooks in Soviet commerce and cast that into the machine, which had produced a seven-digit number. And even though it was obvious to the naked eye that the feuilleton could never in a million years be confused with a work of genius, Petenka Skorobogatov was not, in the end, disabused. Instead, he gave a crafty wink and carefully placed the scrap of newsprint into his bloated notebook.

"So what did it mean, that seven-figure digit of yours?" I asked curiously.

"I'm sorry, Felix Alexandrovich, but 'digits' always consist of a single figure. *Numbers*—those can be seven-digit. Anyway, the number appearing on this particular line of the display," and he tapped my 4 again, "is, in layman's terms, the maximally probable number of readers of a given text."

"'Readers of a given text'. . . you mean, any old text?" I asked with timid vengefulness.

"Indeed, that phrase may seem repellent to a litterateur, but in this case the 'reader of a given text' is a specialized term. It refers to a person who has read a particular text or will read it at some future point. So this number, 4, is not some mythical index of your genius, Felix Alexandrovich. It is only the maximally probable number of people who will read your review, the so-called MPRN, or simply RN."

"What's the *MP* for?" I asked, just to say something; my head was spinning.

"*MP*, for 'maximally probable.'"

"I see," I said, and paused, but then my mind cleared for a moment, allowing me to ask indignantly, "So what does this MPRN of yours have to do with talent or ability, or with the quality of any given 'text,' as you put it?"

"I warned you, Felix Alexandrovich, that this measure has only an indirect relationship—"

"But it's not even indirect!" I interrupted, my brain accelerating. "The number of readers depends first and foremost on the print run!"

"But what do print runs depend on?"

"Come on," I said, "don't try that with me. We all know on what, or more importantly on *whom*, print runs depend! I can name any number of monstrously hacky books released in print runs of half a million."

"But of course, Felix Alexandrovich, of course! You're really starting to resemble your bandaged friend, Kozlukhin, in your stubborn and naive assumption that the size of the MPRN and the quality of the text are directly proportional."

"You're the one making the assumption! Whereas I think that there's no relationship at all, direct or otherwise."

"What do you mean, no relationship, Felix Alexandrovich? Here is a text"—and he grabbed a corner of my ill-fated review and held it up with two fingers—"with an MPRN of four, as you can see. Do you have any objections to that valuation?"

"But . . . Of course if you take a review, and an internal one at that . . . The editor will read it . . . The author, maybe, if they show it to him . . ."

"I see. So you have no objections."

And suddenly, as nimbly as any magician, he took from my folder a school notebook with a faded cover covered in yellow blotches and brought it so quickly up to my face that I shrank back. "What do we have here?" he asked.

What we had was a heartbreakingly familiar image, known to all of us from childhood: a bearded knight bidding farewell to a mighty long-maned steed. It was Pushkin's "The Song of Wise Oleg," the one that starts with the words *"Oleg, the wise prince, roused to arm . . ."*

"What's the problem?" I asked defiantly. "That happens to be wonderful, extraordinary poetry . . . Even school literature lessons couldn't kill it."

"Sure, sure," he said. "But that's not what I'm asking. What do you think would happen if we put this sheet through the machine?"

My intellect flailed and floundered. "Well, uh," I mumbled, "you'd probably get a big number . . . just schoolchildren alone . . . ten or twenty million?"

"Over a billion," he said, his voice flinty. "Over a billion, Felix Alexandrovich!"

"Sure, over a billion," I said obediently. "Like I said, a big number."

"Ergo," he said, "a trivial review produces an MPRN of four, while 'wonderful, extraordinary poetry' gives us an MPRN of over a billion. And you still insist that there's no relationship."

"But . . ." I waved my hands and snapped my fingers. "'The Song of Wise Oleg' has been published! Many, many times! It's even been set to music!"

"It sure has," he nodded. "And it will be again in the future. And they'll keep on printing it."

"Exactly! Whereas my review—"

"Will not be set to music. Or printed. Ever. Which is why its MPRN is only four. For all past eras and all future ones. It will perish, unread by anyone."

An amazing feeling swept over me. It was like he was trying to give me a hint, lead me to some conclusion. Like he was knocking on some door in my consciousness that even I couldn't access, crying, "Open up! Let me in!" Taken at face value, though, his words and thoughts seemed banal to the point of colorlessness and thus evoked no response in me. It was like hitting the steel door of a tightly locked safe with a feather pillow.

"Well, good," I said uncertainly. "That's as it should be. I never said it had any artistic value."

He was silent, massaging his forehead with his fingertips. "I was joking, Felix Alexandrovich," he said suddenly, almost with remorse. "You're absolutely correct, of course."

He fell silent again. I followed suit, trying to figure out what exactly I'd been correct about—*absolutely* correct, even. And also, what the point of the joke was. And when the silence became awkward and even impolite, I said, "All right then . . . I guess I'll head out."

"Yes, of course, thank you very much."

"And I'll take the folder with me?"

"Of course, please do."

"Maybe you—"

"No, no, thank you very much. We've squeezed everything out of it that we could."

"So I don't need to come here again?"

He raised his mirthless eyes to look at me once more. "I'll always be happy to see you, Felix Alexandrovich. Although I won't be here tomorrow. Come the day after, if you like."

I couldn't tell what he really meant. To me, his invitation sounded like an order. And again the querulous demon stirred within me—but I reined it in, confining myself to shrugging as I tied the strings of my folder.

Then he said, "Felix Alexandrovich! Don't forget your sheet music, please."

It turned out I'd nearly forgotten the stupid score on the table. He watched me stuff it into the folder and retie the strings, and after we'd already said good-bye and I was walking toward the exit, he said, "Felix Alexandrovich, I wouldn't recommend carrying that score around on the street. Who knows what could happen?"

I decided not to press him for more details. I'd had quite enough. I pretended not to hear him and silently exited into the little hallway, shutting the door behind me tightly. The waiting area was empty.

I walked all the way from Bannaya to the Metro. I trudged along, slipping repeatedly on the icy sidewalks, pushing my way through groups of provincial visitors crowding the doorways of fashionable shops, weaving through clusters of cars in the intersections, barely noticing my surroundings as I went. My thoughts circled relentlessly back to my conversation with my strange new friend. Incidentally, he never did give me his name! How on earth did he manage that? Strange, strange . . .

On the one hand, what was the big deal, anyway? Two intelligent people met for professional reasons and began getting to know each other. So what if one of them never gave his name and the other didn't realize it until after the conversation was over? That was hardly the strangest thing about their meeting. Two intelligent people, who definitely hit it off, exchanged fairly abstract opinions on a rather banal set of issues: genius, art, literature, readers, print runs, etc. But why, after that conversation, do I feel like splinters have lodged somewhere in my consciousness? Like something is buzzing in the space behind my ears? What could it be, and what's making it buzz?

It was only in the Metro, squeezed between two strollers (one contained a child, the other inner tubes for the tires of a Moskvitch), that I suddenly heard his soft voice cutting through the rumble of the train: *Anatoly Yefimovich didn't just* ***intend*** *to write that comedy, he actually did. And then, in March of '52 in Kukushkino, all of it actually occurred . . .*

Aha. So that was the first splinter. First he wrote it, and then it actually occurred. Nonsense, I'd just misheard, that's all. Or he'd misspoken. What bothered me was the nature of his relationship with Anatoly Yefimovich. When did he manage to get so close to him? Unlike the vast majority of my colleagues, Anatoly Yefimovich was an extremely private person—even reclusive, I'd say. He habitually skipped meetings, including very important ones. He never attended salons, to say nothing of hosting any of his own. His appearances at the Club were few and far between; he eschewed alcohol in favor of fine tea, brewed with his own two hands in the privacy of his own home. He had lost practically all his friends: some had died even before the war, others during, and still others "hath chosen that good part," as he once put it. When you came right down to it, he was a loner—a fact I was reminded of every time I saw, in the corner of his office, the pile of sealed packages containing numerous new editions of his prize-winning trilogy. He didn't even give out signed copies; he had no one to give them to.

He opened his home to seven others besides myself. I knew them all and am certain that none of them had even heard of the "Litalmeter." Whereas my new acquaintance had not only heard of this comedy but had obviously read it! Strange, strange . . . Maybe they'd been close at some moment long before my time, and later fell out? But *he* was approximately my age, young enough to be Anatoly Yefimovich's son, so when could he have . . .

I never did manage to figure this out; soon enough, every thought flew out of my head: right in front of my building, I slipped for real, executed a fantastic pirouette, and crashed down onto my side, knocking down a passing lady with a lapdog in the bargain.

Six or so people ran over to help us. There followed a quantity of grunting and panting, cries of encouragement and disingenuous lamentations to the effect that the Soviet right to work apparently does not include the right to sprinkle sand on icy sidewalks. The greatest victim here was the dog, I think, whose paw was crushed in the melee, but I, too, received some pretty hard knocks. I stood there, pressing my palm to my side, trying to breathe, hearing people all around me saying that this was the worst Moscow winter they'd ever seen . . . bedlam . . . end of the world . . . Last Judgment . . .

Finally catching my breath, I managed some words of thanks to my rescuers and mea culpas to the unfortunate lady and her lapdog. We said our good-byes, and I limped over to my black-tiled porch.

The eschatological reminiscences that had sounded in the indignant choir of passersby, all of them championing the right to work of building caretakers, sent my thoughts in an entirely new direction. I remembered the fallen angel and his stupid sheet music, and then, by natural association, recalled my new friend's parting words. "I wouldn't recommend carrying that score around on the street. Who knows what could happen?" But what's the big deal? What was in this sheet music that made people repeatedly advise me not to carry it around? Was it "God Save the Czar"? The official anthem of the Nazi Party? In this arena, too, my mind yielded nothing but the obviously improbable notion—unrivaled in explanatory power!—that the score in my possession really *was* the Trumpet Call at the Last Judgment.

On this matter, at least, I knew exactly whom to consult. Rather than ride up to my own sixteenth floor, I exited the elevator on the sixth, where the popular composer and songwriter Giorgi Luarsabovich Chachua—jovial host, epicurean, and insanely hard worker—lived in a four-room apartment. He and I had been close since practically the first day I moved into this building.

From behind his door, with its faux-leather upholstery, I could hear the crashing of a piano and the roulades of a beautiful female voice. Evidently Chachua was at work. I heard an explosion of laughter. Then the piano fell silent, as did the voice. Perhaps Chachua wasn't working after all. I rang the doorbell. At that moment the piano crashed back to life and several male voices launched into something Georgian-sounding. It certainly didn't seem like Chachua was working. I rang again.

The door swung open and Chachua appeared on the threshold, wearing black concert slacks with bright suspenders over a blindingly white dress shirt unbuttoned at the collar. His flushed face was preoccupied, his enormous nose covered in sweat. Dammit, so he *had* been working after all . . .

"I'm so sorry!" I said, pressing the folder to my chest.

"What's wrong?" he inquired, sounding both worried and slightly irritated.

"Nothing's wrong," I answered, violently suppressing an urge to speak with a Georgian accent. "I just had a really quick ques—"

"Listen," he said, shifting his weight impatiently. "Can you come by a little later? I've got people over, we're working. In two hours, OK?"

"Hold on, it's really quick," I said, hurriedly untying the strings on the folder. "Here's some sheet music—would you mind taking a look, whenever you have a second?"

He took the sheets from me and leafed through them, looking quizzical. I could hear male voices arguing in the depths of his apartment. The argument was about music.

"Uh . . . OK . . ." he said, drawing out the words, his eyes glued to the score. "Listen, who wrote this? Where'd you get it?"

"I'll tell you all about it later," I said, stepping away from the door.

"Right you are, my dear," Chachua agreed readily. "Later is better. I'll stop by myself. I have about an hour to go here, then there's the football game—Spartak's playing!—and then I'll come by." He waved the sheets at me and shut the door.

After getting home and taking off my coat, the first thing I did was take a shower. I was soaked in sweat, my injured side ached mercilessly, and anyway, I needed to calm down. Turning my body this way and that under the spray, I devised a program for the evening. First would be dinner, also known today as lunch. I'd have to cook. Potatoes—check. Sour cream—check. I think. There were also peas. Oh, wait! I've got some canned beef! Screw soup! I'll boil some potatoes and dump the can of beef out on top! Plus I have onion, and pickled ramps . . . And some lovely cognac. What more does a man need? I felt better already.

The reason I don't mind peeling potatoes is that it leaves your mind completely free. By the way, none of my friends can peel potatoes as clean and quick as me. It's my army training, comrades! Hundredweights, tons, whole wheelbarrows full of peeled potatoes! And what potatoes! Time was, they were rotten, frozen solid, greenish blue, with black spots running all the way through the flesh . . . Whereas these peacetime potatoes—from the open-air market no less!—were a pure pleasure to peel. And my God, how wonderful not to be on the hook with Bannaya anymore!

I gave the peeled potatoes a triple rinse, filled a pot with water, and threw them in, cutting each into two or three chunks. Then I put the pot on the stove.

Say whatever you like, but this MPRN idea of theirs is utter nonsense and a hideous waste of public funds—like most egg-headed notions about literature, or art more generally. To think, they shove a hundred thousand rubles worth of cabinets in a lab just to demonstrate that if you publish a writer, then he'll have a lot of readers (although maybe not), and if you *don't* publish him—if you keep that son of a bitch on a short leash—then he won't have any readers at all, the dirty, dirty bastard. Or even better: if you publish, say, Alexander Sergeyevich Pushkin—if only a volume of his prose—and simultaneously release a novella by Crap Crapovich Terlet about passion in a foundry bucket, then Pushkin will have dramatically more readers. That's what my new friend's arguments boiled down to in the end. That and the trivial idea that good is always good, but bad isn't always bad . . .

Or was there some mistake? Was there something I'd failed to understand back there, and still didn't understand now? Ugh, why did he have to beat around the bush? Why couldn't he just say what he meant in the moment? I'll be damned if I ever go back there again to find out. Aha—here come the potatoes!

And now everything was ready and laid out on the table: steam rose from a highly appetizing mixture of potato and rosy beef, the kitchen was redolent with smells of meat, onion, and bay leaf, and I'd poured some cognac into a snifter. Life was good. The future suddenly seemed brighter, as if illuminated by hopeful premonitions. I'd written over half my screenplay; I no longer needed to go to the dressmaker's for the fur coat; nor, for that matter, was there any earthly reason to visit Bannaya. All my debts were paid up before sundown, as Kipling's young Mr. Corkran used to say.

I downed my cognac, stuffed my mouth full of meat and potatoes, and turned on the television.

On Channel 1, someone was sawing away on a violin. For a while, I admired the sawer's tortured face, then changed the channel. Channel 2 featured an amateur dance performance that swirled its colorful skirts, banged its heels on the floor, drew its arms together and swung them apart, and now and again gave a soul-piercing squeal. I stuffed my mouth with more potato and changed the channel again. This time I saw several elderly people sitting and talking at a round table. They were discussing frontiers that had been breached, the resolve to supply something to someone or other, the great reconstruction work being done on some metal object . . .

I watched, chewing on my suddenly tasteless potato, as my heart filled with passionate curses. Ah, television! That shining twentieth-century miracle! The truly fantastical product of the effort, talent, and inventiveness of tens, hundreds, thousands of the era's—*my* era's—most splendiferous minds! All so that tens of millions of tired people, finally home from work, could frantically change channels as I was now doing, gripped by a truly unsolvable dilemma: What to choose? The inspired sawer? Or the boisterous, sweaty mob of amateur dancers? Or these sad-making, inarticulate specialists sitting at their round table?

In the end, I chose the sawer. Pouring myself a second glass, I took a drink and settled in to listen. It's like a curse, I thought suddenly. They've been shoving classical music down my throat practically since I was born. Someone, somewhere must have said at some point that if you shove classical music down a person's throat every single day, he gradually gets used to it and ultimately can't bear to live without it, not even for a moment—which is the ultimate goal. And so it began. We thirsted for jazz, we were crazy for jazz, so they choked us with symphonies. We adored heartrending romantic ballads and criminal ditties, so they banged us over the head with violin concertos. We craved the songs of bards and troubadours, so they poisoned us with oratorios. If those titanic efforts to imbue our minds with musical culture had the efficiency even of Denis Papin's seventeenth-century proto–steam engine, we would even now be living in a golden age of classical music lovers and connoisseurs, myself among them. Thousands upon thousands of radio hours, thousands upon thousands of television programs, millions of records . . . And what was the result? Garik Aganyan has an almost professional knowledge of pop music. Zhora Naumov is still building his collection of records by contemporary bards. Our Sweet Soviet Boy is much like me: the less music, the better. Lyonya the Schizo hates music. On the other hand, there is Valya Demchenko. But he's loved classical music since he was little; musical propaganda has nothing to do with it . . .

As I was pondering all this, the violinist disappeared. A group of hockey players now burst onto the screen; immediately, one of them hit the other over the head with his stick. The camera panned sheepishly away, and I turned off the television. I was full, slightly buzzed, and the only thing I still needed to do was wash the dishes.

Then I went to my study and walked slowly along the bookshelf-lined wall, tracing my finger over the glass.

War and Peace. Not today. It hadn't been six months yet.

Chekhov's Letters. Not in the mood.

Chukovsky. *From Chekhov to Our Times*. That one I'd recently reread.

OK. What about Anton Pavlovich himself, in ten volumes? Should I reread "A Boring Story"? No. Let's save it for a gloomier day.

Mikhail Afanasyevich Bulgakov. I spent some time examining the brown cover, already creased and peeling in places, with a weird hangnail at the bottom . . . That does it, I'm not letting anyone borrow that book ever again. Stupid slobs. "Great and terrible was the year of Our Lord 1918, of the Revolution the second . . ."

"No," I said aloud. "What I'm going to read right now is the *Theatrical Novel*. There's nothing better in this world than the *Theatrical Novel*, and I don't care who knows it."

And I took the small Bulgakov volume off the shelf and caressed it with my hand, smoothing my palm over its smooth binding, and thought, for the millionth time, that it was wrong—sinful, even—to treat a book like a living person.

The phone thundered behind my back and I started, because I was no longer in my study. I was already transported to a tiny, filthy garret, home to a sofa with a protruding spring, excruciating as Kafkian delirium. My injured side suddenly began to ache, and, pressing the cool volume to my ribs, I walked over to the table, collapsed into the armchair, and picked up the phone.

It was Valya Demchenko. I had completely forgotten, but Saturday was apparently Sonechka's birthday, and I was invited. This made me happy, because, first of all, Sonechka's birthday isn't celebrated every year, far from it, and if they're celebrating, it means all is well with them: they're enjoying a period of financial well-being and good health, and Lieutenant Commander Demchenko, surfacing from the salty depths, has sent a cheerful letter from the city of Murmansk on the Something Sea, and in general everything is great. And second, I felt glad because only a select few are ever invited to Sonechka's birthday parties.

We talked. I asked how things were going with Valya's latest short novel, *Old Fool*. Valya replied that since his recent troubles, the *Quarterly Warden* wouldn't even look at it—they'd recoiled from it like it was leprous. Not so the *Provincial Herald*, which gave it a read. But he hasn't heard from them yet; they're waiting for the return of their editor in chief, who's currently in Sweden, or maybe in Switzerland, or maybe in the Land of Cockaigne. Which means that no one at the *Provincial Herald* has formed an opinion on Valya's novel. Only when the editor in chief returns and reads it will the collective opinion come into being, as if by magic . . .

I asked how he was planning to fight for the title. He said he had no such plan—the novel was now called *Wise Old Man*—but he'd decided to leave in the seduction scene. What the hell! He refuses to be the one to cut the best chunks of flesh from his own bones. Let them do the cutting, that's why they pay them the big bucks.

I told him not to worry—they wouldn't flinch. He didn't argue. He knew all this as well as I did, if not better. Then he asked if Lyonya had called me yet today. Oh, he hadn't? Well, he will. He's written a new sentence but isn't quite sure how he feels about it . . .

I hung up and began mulling over what to give Sonechka. I'm no good at presents. Especially presents for women. Cognac? Nah, doesn't work, even though Sonechka enjoys good cognac. Perfume? Who the hell can tell them apart? Maybe I should just give them fifty rubles' worth of Beryozka vouchers? No, that's awkward somehow. A book, that's what I should give them. Ugh, I wish I had even one art book . . . Or some money, at least, say, 350 rubles—the local bookstore's selling a National Gallery catalog to die for!

Perhaps by association with Washington, DC, I thought of my Dashiell Hammett collection. Sonechka's had her pretty little eye on it for a very long time. His best works in a single tome, the really top-notch selections—it's the same principle as my brown Bulgakov volume. *Red Harvest* is in there, and *The Maltese Falcon*, and *The Glass Key* . . . I know the whole book almost by heart, anyway. And Sonechka is so special that she has just as much right to it as I do.

And having made this decision, I placed the Bulgakov back on the shelf, walked over to my foreign books section, and, moving aside the model *thuyền rồng*, a dragon-shaped boat the ancient Vietnamese once used to transport their kings, I retrieved *The Novels of Dashiel Hammett*. Here's what I'll do, I thought, flipping the pages with their gilt edges. I'll give it a last read today and tomorrow, then say good-bye. I reclined on the sofa—carefully, so as not to disturb my long-suffering side—and instantly, the book fell open at *The Maltese Falcon*.

I got as far as the part when Lieutenant Dundy and Tom, the detective, show up at Sam Spade's early one morning, and then I couldn't bear it any longer. I put the book aside, raised myself up (creakily!), and swung my legs down to the floor.

My side was hurting me—how many times already had my poor, unfortunate left side hurt like this! I trudged to the bathroom, hiked up my shirt, and took a look in the mirror. It was fat, my side, and flabby, but it bore no signs of grievous bodily harm. It had been that way all the previous times, too. I went to the kitchen, poured the rest of the cognac into my glass, and drank it up in tiny sips, the way the Japanese drink sake.

I'd first broken that rib in winter of '65, in Murashi, when the devil himself made me take the risk of riding down a steep slope in a Finnish sled, all the way to the bay. Everyone was doing it, and I thought, I'm just as good as they are! But I wasn't just as good, because I panicked halfway down the slope. Feeling like I was approaching cosmic speed and anxious to avoid flying off to bloody hell, I decided to catapult myself off the sled. Which I did. For twenty or so steps of rugged terrain, I skipped along on my left side. "Broken a rib, have we?" said the surgeon at our clinic when, after returning from Murashi, I came to him complaining of pain in my side. That was number one.

Two years later, I stopped by the Club for lunch. I was looking around in search of a free table when all of a sudden I was ambushed by an extremely well-lubricated Sweet Soviet Boy. Being in a state of aggressive ecstasy (having just received payment for his latest hackwork), the Boy clasped me to his bosom with his long appendages, much like Hercules once embraced Antaeus. I was lifted high above Mother Earth and squeezed so tightly that my rib gave a mournful crack. "You've got a crack there, old man," said my doctor friend when I complained to him of pain. That was number two.

Then, the year before last, I was traveling on a cargo ship from Vladivostok to Petropavlovsk as part of a writers' brigade when an eight-point storm caught us abreast of Matua Island. The other writers, all covered in puke, were safely dying in their beds, whereas the devil compelled me, a man insusceptible to seasickness, to walk the top deck. I took my hand off the railing for one single second and was immediately thrown with terrible force against the coaming—you guessed it, left side first. "I'm afraid you've got a fracture," the medic told me, and, as it later turned out, his fears were well founded. That was number three, and I thought that since God specifically loves the Trinity, my rib's misfortunes had now come to an end. But I'd forgotten that the earth has four corners . . .

Gloomily, I lifted the bottle to the light for a moment, then crammed it into the cabinet under the sink. Tea, that was the ticket now. I put the kettle on and stood by the window, leaning my forehead on the cool glass.

God, what an unholy mess. Just when it seemed like everything was finally on an even keel, like all my troubles were in the past, I got this damn rib again. Whoever Is Supposed to Oversee My Fate had utterly given up on refined inventions and turned instead to the crudest, meanest, most direct maneuvers. It's unheard of! In broad daylight, inside an enormous megalopolis, a serious older man—not some careless sportsman, not some rowdy, not an alcoholic—up and breaks his rib! It's galling, comrades. Galling and unseemly . . .

I went back to the study for my Dashiell Hammett and began settling in by the kitchen table, searching for the least painful position. As on the previous occasions, it turned out that the pose that suited me best was Katya's favorite: knees on the stool, elbows on the table, ass in the air. So that's the pose I decided to live in from now on. That's the pose in which I drank my tea and read about the weighty falcon statuette made of solid gold, which Maltese knights had once crafted as a gift for the king of Spain, and which in our day had become the object of bloody gangster strife. When I got to the part where the captain of *La Paloma*, perforated with some half-dozen bullet wounds, bursts into Sam Spade's office, the doorbell rang.

Creaking and moaning, tearing myself away from Sam Spade with extreme displeasure, I trudged to the door. By now, I'd forgotten all about the fallen angel's music score and Goga Chachua, which is why I was shocked to see him on my doorstep, especially since his face—

Well, strictly speaking, he had no face. All I could see was his enormous, light-blue nose, its dark-blue veins rising over a thick mustache parted in the middle; his pale, trembling lips; and a pair of mournful black eyes filled with melancholy and despair. Two hairy fists clutched the accursed score, now rolled into a tube that he was pressing to his chest. He was silent, and seized by a terrible premonition, I lost my breath and with it the power to say a single word. All I could do was step aside, letting him pass by me into the entryway.

He dashed inside like a blind man, running into the wall, then staggered over to my study. Once there, he threw the score onto the table with both hands, as though the rolled-up papers burned his flesh. He then fell into an armchair and pressed his palms into his eyes.

My legs buckling, I stood on the threshold, grabbing the door frame for support. He still said nothing. To me, his silence felt unimaginably long, possibly eternal. I clung to the wild hope that he would in fact be silent forever, so that I wouldn't have to hear the horrors that Chachua had doubtless brought to my door.

But finally, he spoke. "Listen," he croaked, tearing his hands from his face and plunging his fingers into the thick, woolly hair above his ears. "Spartak choked again! What're you gonna do, huh?"

8. VICTOR BANEV

UGLY SWANS

"What time is it?" Diana asked sleepily.

Victor carefully lifted a strip of foam from his left cheekbone with a razor, then looked in the mirror and said, "Sleep, baby, sleep. It's still early."

"So it is," said Diana. The bed squeaked. "Nine o'clock. What are you doing over there?"

"Shaving," Victor replied, lifting away the next strip of foam. "All of a sudden I wanted to shave. Why don't I shave? I thought."

"Psycho," said Diana, yawning. "Should've thought of that last night. You cut me to ribbons with your stubble, you cactus."

In the mirror, he could see her coming toward the armchair on unsteady legs. She sat down, tucking her feet up beneath her, then turned her gaze on him. Victor gave her a wink. She was different again today—ever so tender, ever so soft and gentle, basking like a well-fed cat, perfectly groomed, silky smooth, benevolent—quite a change from the woman who had burst into his room the night before.

"You look like a cat today," he informed her. "Not even a cat—a kitty, a tiny lady cat . . . What are you smiling about?"

"Nothing to do with you. Something I remembered, for some reason." She yawned and gave a leisurely stretch. Victor's pajamas swam on her. Only her lovely face and slender arms could be seen, bobbing in the amorphous tangle of silk as though emerging from the waves. Victor started shaving faster.

"Don't hurry," she said. "You'll cut yourself. I have to go now anyway."

"That's why I'm hurrying," Victor retorted.

"No thanks, I don't like it like that. Only cats do . . . How are my clothes?"

Victor reached out and felt her dress and stockings, which hung on the radiator. Everything was dry. "What's the hurry?" he asked.

"I told you—Rossechepert."

"I forget, for some reason. What's his deal again?"

"He injured himself, remember?" said Diana.

"Oh, right!" said Victor. "You did mention that, I remember now. He fell out of something or other. Is it bad?"

"That idiot," said Diana, "suddenly decided to end it all and flung himself out the window. Went headfirst, like a bull, and broke the window frame. Except he forgot he was on the first floor, injured his knee, and screamed bloody murder. He's been flat on his back ever since."

"Why'd he do it?" Victor asked indifferently. "Delirium tremens?"

"Something like that."

"Hold on," said Victor. "Is that why you haven't visited these last two days? Because of that meathead?"

"I mean, yeah! The chief of medicine told me to watch him, because he—Rossechepert, that is—was incapable of doing anything without me. Just incapable, full stop. Of anything. Including pissing. I had to imitate the sound of rushing water and tell him tales of urinals."

"Like you're such an expert," mumbled Victor. "And while you were regaling him with urinal stories, I was suffering here alone. I couldn't do anything either, didn't write a single line. You know, I don't enjoy writing in the first place, and lately . . . My life in general, lately . . ." He stopped. What did she care? he thought. We're done copulating—time to bolt. "Hey, listen . . . When did you say Rossechepert took his tumble?"

"Three days ago," answered Diana.

"In the evening?"

"*Mhm*," said Diana, nibbling on a biscuit.

"At ten," said Victor. "Between ten and eleven."

Diana stopped chewing. "Correct," she said. "But how did you know? Did he send you a necrobiotic telepatheme?"

"Hold on," said Victor. "I'm about to tell you something interesting. But first—what were you doing then?"

"What was I doing? . . . Oh, right. I went a little crazy that night, as I recall. I was rolling bandages when all of a sudden this wave of sadness hit me, like a headache—just suicide level. I put my head down, right on top of the bandages, and just bawled! Real waterworks—I haven't cried like that since I was a kid."

"And then, suddenly, it just stopped," said Victor.

Diana thought for a moment. "Yes . . . No . . . Right then, Rossechepert started howling. I freaked out and ran outside."

She wanted to say something else, but there was a knock at the door, someone pulled on the knob, and then Teddy's voice said hoarsely, "Victor! Victor, wake up! Open up, Victor!" Victor froze, razor in hand. "Victor!" Teddy croaked. "Open up!" The doorknob jiggled madly. Diana leaped up and turned the key. The door swung open and Teddy burst in—all wet and mangled, a sawed-off shotgun in his hand.

"Where's Victor?" he barked hoarsely.

Victor came out of the bathroom. "What's going on?" he asked. His heart began to pound. Arrest . . . war . . .

"The kids are gone," said Teddy, breathing heavily. "Get dressed, the kids are gone!"

"Hold on," said Victor. "What kids?"

Teddy threw the gun onto the pile of ink-filled, bescribbled, crumpled-up paper covering the desk. "They lured the kids away, the bastards!" he screamed. "They lured them! Well, this is it. This is the last goddamn drop. I've had it!"

Victor was still far from understanding what was happening, but he could see that Teddy was beside himself. He'd only seen Teddy like that once before, when during a row in the restaurant, someone broke into the register right under his nose. Victor was still standing there, blinking and confused, but Diana had already grabbed her clothes off the back of the chair, slipped into the bathroom, and closed the door behind her. And at that very moment, the phone rang with a nerve-racking sharpness.

Victor grabbed the receiver. It was Lola. "Victor," she moaned, "I don't get it, Irma's gone somewhere, she left a note saying she was never coming back, that all the kids have left town . . . I'm scared! Do something!" She was on the verge of tears.

"All right, all right, one sec," said Victor. "Let me just put on some pants." He threw down the phone and looked over at Teddy. The barman was sitting on the unmade bed and, mumbling terrible threats, pouring the last of any bottle he could find into a glass. "Hold on," said Victor. "Nobody panic. I'll just be a second . . ."

He returned to the bathroom and finished shaving in a hurry, shearing his foamy chin. He cut himself several times—there was no time to aim the blade—and then Diana dashed out of the shower and rustled into her clothes behind his back. Her face was harsh and resolute, like she was readying herself for a fight—and yet she was completely calm.

As for the children, they were walking in an endless gray column down a gray, muddy road, walking, stumbling, slipping and falling in the pouring rain, walking, huddled, soaked to the skin, clutching pitiful wet bindles in little blue paws; they were little themselves, helpless, understanding nothing, crying as they walked silently, looking back as they went, hand in hand or clinging to each other's coats, while gloomy, faceless black figures marched alongside, neckerchiefs covering the spaces where their faces should have been. And above the neckerchiefs, inhuman eyes looked coldly and mercilessly out at the world, while hands in skintight black gloves clasped machine guns, rain pouring onto the blued steel, drops trembling and running down the barrels . . . Nonsense, thought Victor, nonsense, it's not like that at all, not today . . . though I did see all that, a long time ago . . . but this time it's different.

Their departure was joyous, the rain was their friend, they splashed through the puddles with warm, wet feet, they chattered happily, singing, never looking back, because they'd already forgotten everything, because only the future lay ahead, because they'd banished all thought of their snoring, snuffling, predawn city, that labyrinth of bedbug burrows, that pit of petty passions and desires, that vast belly pregnant with monstrous crimes and criminal intentions, which it spewed out as incessantly as a queen ant birthing more ants. They left it all behind, chatting and tittering, and disappeared into the fog, even as we, drunk off our asses, breathed the stale air, plagued with foul nightmares they'd never known, and never would . . .

Victor was jumping around on one leg, pulling on his pants, when the windowpanes began to rattle. The roar of an engine permeated the air. Teddy sprinted to the window, Victor close behind, but saw only rain and the empty, wet street. Someone bicycled by, looking like a wet canvas bag on laboriously pedaling legs. Yet the windows continued to rattle and ring, and the low, anguished roaring continued. Moments later, they heard a series of short, sorrowful whistles.

"Let's go," said Diana. She had already put on her raincoat.

"No, wait," said Teddy. "Victor, you got any weapons? A pistol, or a machine gun?"

Victor didn't answer. He grabbed his raincoat, and the three of them ran down to the lobby, now completely empty, missing even the doorman and the concierge. The hotel looked deserted.

Only R. Quadriga still sat at his table in the restaurant, looking around in confusion—he had evidently been waiting for his breakfast for some time. They dashed into the street and climbed into Diana's truck, squeezing into the cab. Diana got behind the wheel, and soon they were speeding through the city. Diana was silent; Victor smoked, trying to collect his thoughts; and Teddy spewed unimaginable curses under his breath. Many of the words were unknown even to Victor, because only someone like Teddy could truly understand their meaning—Teddy, shelter rat, child of the dockside slums, who'd started as a drug peddler and gone on to become a whorehouse bouncer, a soldier in the funeral guard, a criminal and a marauder, and finally a barman, a barman, a barman, and once again a barman.

The streets were almost completely empty, though Diana did stop on the corner of Sunnyside to pick up a bewildered married couple. The air raid siren roared on, unceasing, accompanied by the squeaky whine of factory whistles, and there was something apocalyptic about this moan of mechanical voices in an uninhabited city. It was a stomach-churning noise, it compelled one to run somewhere and either hide or shoot, and even the Kindred Spirits chased their ball without their usual enthusiasm, while several of them, mouths agape, were looking all around, as if straining to understand something.

People began to appear in increasing numbers on the highway beyond the city limits. Some walked, nearly drowning in rain, pitiful, scared out of their wits, barely knowing what they were doing and why. Others, on bicycles, had run out of steam, forced as they were to ride against the wind. On several occasions, Diana's truck passed abandoned cars that had broken down or that the owners, in their haste, had failed to fill with gas; one car had been driven into a ditch. Diana would stop and pick up everyone they encountered, and soon the truck was filled to capacity. Victor and Teddy moved into the back, giving up their seats to a mother with a newborn and a half-crazed old woman. Later, when even the space in the back ran out, Diana drove without stopping, and the truck sped forward, spraying torrents of water over the tens and hundreds of people muscling their way to the leprosarium. They were passed several times by motorcycles and overstuffed cars, and later, another truck appeared behind them and began to follow.

Diana was used to hauling cognac for Rossechepert or taking the empty truck for joyrides, so being in the back as she drove was scary. There wasn't room for everyone to sit, so those forced to stand clung to one another and clutched at the heads of the seated, and everyone fought to get into the middle, farther away from the edges. No one talked; heavy breathing and swearing predominated, except for one woman, who wept loudly and constantly. It was raining harder than Victor had ever experienced; he could scarcely imagine rain like that anywhere on earth—a dense tropical downpour, not warm but icy, half hail, with a strong wind propelling the drops at an angle into their faces. Visibility was awful—you could only see about fifty feet ahead and fifty feet behind, and Victor was terrified that Diana, to top it all off, would hit a pedestrian or crash into a braking car. But everything turned out all right, mostly: Someone stepped hard on Victor's foot as everyone in the back fell onto each other one last time. The truck veered to a stop, braking sideways in front of an enormous cluster of cars assembled at the leprosarium gates.

It seemed like the whole city had gathered here. There was no rain, and one felt that people had fled here from a flood. On either side of the highway, a vast crowd stretched along the barbed wire as far as the eye could see; its mass swallowed up scattered, poorly parked, empty cars—luxurious long limousines, battered little sedans with canvas tops, trucks, buses, and even a crane with several people perching on the boom. A dull murmur filled the air, punctuated by the occasional piercing shout.

Everyone jumped out of the back of the truck, Victor immediately lost Diana and Teddy, he was surrounded by strange faces—gloomy, embittered, perplexed, crying, shouting faces, faces with eyes rolling back in a faint, faces with bared teeth . . . Victor tried to elbow his way to the gate, but a couple of steps in he found himself hopelessly stuck. People stood in a dense wall, no one wanted to give up his spot, even pushes, kicks, or blows could not make them so much as turn around; they just bowed their heads, struggling to push forward, forward, closer to the gates, closer to their children . . . They stood on tiptoes and craned their necks, but nothing could be seen beyond the swaying mass of hoods and hats.

"Why, God? How have we sinned against you, O Lord?"

"Bastards! We should've gotten rid of them a long time ago. We were warned!"

"Where's the mayor, eh? What the hell is he up to? Where's the police? Where are all those fat cats?"

"Sim, I'm getting trampled . . . Sim, I can't breathe! Ah, Sim . . ."

"What did we deny them? What did they want for? We were ready to give them our last piece of bread, the shirt off our backs, to make sure they were clothed and fed . . ."

"If we all lean on that damn gate together, we can knock it down . . ."

"I never laid a finger on him! I saw you going after yours with a belt, but that would never, ever happen in our house . . ."

"See those machine guns? What the hell is that for, to shoot at the people? Because we came for our own kids?"

"Munichka! Munichka! Munichka! My baby! Munichka!"

"What is this, ladies and gentlemen? It's madness! An outrage!"

"Don't worry, the legionnaires'll show 'em . . . They're coming up from the other side, right? They'll open the gates, then we'll rush in . . ."

"Yeah, but did you see the machine guns? That's right, exactly . . ."

"Let me go! Dammit, let me go! My daughter's in there!"

"This has been a long time coming, I could tell, but I was afraid to ask."

"Maybe it'll be OK . . . they're not animals, after all . . . They're not occupiers, they're not taking them to be shot, or to the ovens . . ."

"I'll tear them limb from limb! With my teeth!"

"We must have really hit bottom if our own kids left us for those lepers . . . Oh, stop, they wanted to leave, no one forced them to, come on . . ."

"Hey, anyone have a gun? Step forward! Who has a gun? Step forward, toward me, I'm right here!"

"They're my own children, dear sir—I fathered them, and I will dispose of them as I see fit!"

"Jesus, where's the police?"

"We have to send a telegram to Mr. President! Five thousand signatures is no joke!"

"A woman's been trampled! Move, you bastard! Can't you see?'

"Munichka, my little one! Munichka! Munichka!"

"A petition won't do shit. They're not crazy about petitions around here, they'll just use it to knock you down somehow . . ."

"Open the gate, you goddamn dirty bastards! You snakes, you filthy clammies!"

"The gate!"

"Open up!"

Victor began maneuvering his way backward. It was tough going—he got hit several times—but in the end he broke free, made it to the truck, and climbed into the back. Fog blanketed the leprosarium, already obscuring everything outside a thirty-foot radius of the fence. The gate remained tightly shut. Directly in front of it stood ten or so Internal Service troops, helmets pushed down low over their eyes, legs spread wide, guns pointing at the crowd. An officer stood on the guardhouse threshold, shouting strenuously, tension drawing him up on tiptoe, but his voice was inaudible. Above the guardhouse roof, a wooden tower rose into the foggy sky like an enormous bookshelf. Men in gray bustled around on its upper level. Behind the barbed wire, a faintly clanging half-track rolled by and, bouncing over clumps of grass, disappeared into the fog. Once they caught sight of the vehicle, people quieted down, briefly allowing the officer's apoplectic shouts to be heard (". . . stay calm . . . I'm under orders . . . to your homes . . ."). Then the crowd buzzed back to life, murmuring and roaring.

Suddenly, there was movement in front of the gate. Here and there among the brown, blue, and gray raincoats and ponchos, Victor could see the all-too-familiar copper-colored helmets and gold shirts. They appeared in the crowd like flashes of light, tearing their way toward the gate and coalescing into a golden-yellow mass directly in front of it. Gigantic youths in gold-colored knee-length tunics, yoked with heavy-buckled officers' belts, wearing the polished, coppery helmets that had earned the legionnaires the nickname "firemen," armed with short but weighty truncheons, and all of them, to a man, bespangled with Legion emblems that blazed on their belt buckles, their left sleeves, their chests, their truncheons, their helmets, their mugs, ugly as sin—ugly, athletic, muscular mugs with wolves' eyes . . . There were medals, too, whole constellations of medals: for Excellent Shooting, Excellent Parachuting, Excellent Submarining, and also medals with Mr. President's face on them, medals with portraits of his son-in-law, founder of the Legion, and his son, Legion commander in chief . . . Every one of them had a tear gas capsule in his pocket, and if even one of these idiots, in a paroxysm of thuggish enthusiasm, decided to throw it, well, that would be the signal for the machine gun in the tower, and the guns on the half-track, and the soldiers' guns, all of which would fire on the crowd—the crowd, not the goldshirts.

The legionnaires were lining up in front of the soldiers, and running back and forth along that line, waving his truncheon, was Flamen Juventa, dear nephew himself, and now Victor was looking around in despair, not knowing what to do, but then they brought the officer a megaphone, which cheered the man enormously, to the point that he actually smiled. The officer began to roar, at thunderous volume, but managed to get out only "Your attention please! I ask the assembled—" before the megaphone broke again, and he, growing pale, blew into it, whereupon Flamen Juventa, who had paused briefly to listen, redoubled his running and arm-waving, and suddenly the crowd raised a menacing clamor. Everyone seemed to cry out at once, those who had been shouting all along joined by those who had been silent, or simply talking among themselves, or crying, or praying, and then Victor, too, began to shout, mindless with terror at what was about to happen. "Get those idiots out of here!" he yelled. "The firemen! They'll kill us all! Stop! Diana!"

Heaven only knew what was being shouted and by whom, but now the crowd, which had so far kept still, began swaying rhythmically like a gigantic dish of aspic. The officer, his pale face blotched with red, dropped the megaphone and backed away, toward the guardhouse doors. Under their helmets, the soldiers' faces bristled and looked brutish, while up in the tower, all was still: every man stood motionless, aiming his gun. And at that moment, a Voice rang out.

It was like thunder, it came from everywhere at once, and it immediately covered all other sounds. It was calm, even melancholic, conveying a kind of boundless boredom, a boundless condescension, as though the speaker was huge, supercilious, filled with contempt, standing with his back to the tiresome crowd, speaking over his shoulder, taking time away from important business to finally deal with this irritating nonsense.

"Stop shouting already," said the Voice. "Stop shaking your fists and making threats. Is it really so hard to quit jabbering and think calmly for a minute? You know perfectly well that your children left of their own free will—no one forced them, no one pulled them by the scruff of the neck. They left because you finally made yourselves insufferable. They no longer wish to live the way you and your ancestors lived. You certainly love to imitate your ancestors—you even think it's dignified—but they do not. They don't want to grow up to be drunks and lechers, petty little men, slaves, conformists. They don't want to turn into criminals. They don't want your kind of family or your kind of government."

The Voice fell silent for a minute. And for a full minute, not a sound was heard—only a vague swishing noise, as if the fog were rustling as it crawled over the earth.

Then the Voice spoke once more: "You don't need to worry about your children. They're going to be fine—better than if they were with you, and far better than you yourselves. They can't see you today, but feel free to come by starting tomorrow. A Meetinghouse will be established in Horse Hollow; you can visit every single day if you want, after three in the afternoon. Every day at two thirty, three large buses will depart from the city square. That won't be enough—not for tomorrow, at least. Your mayor can figure out additional transportation."

The Voice was quiet again. The crowd stood there like a motionless wall, as though people were afraid to move a muscle.

"But keep in mind," the Voice continued, "whether your children will want to see you depends on you. At first, we'll still be able to make the children keep their appointments, even if they don't want to, but in the long run, it's up to you . . . And now, disperse. You're disturbing us, and the children, and yourselves. I strongly encourage you to think, really think, about what you might have to offer them. Take a look at yourselves. You created them, and now you're deforming them after your own image. Think hard. And now, disperse."

The crowd did not move. Perhaps it was trying to think. Victor was, at least. His thoughts were fragmentary, not even thoughts but snatches of memory, bits of conversation, Lola's stupid painted face . . . Should I get an abortion? Why do we need this right now . . . Her father, lips trembling with rage . . . I'll make a man of you yet, you mangy dog, I'll have your hide . . . My twelve-year-old daughter's shown up on my doorstep, would you be able to find her a spot somewhere decent? . . . Irma, looking curiously at the shit-faced Rossechepert . . . not at Rossechepert, but at me . . . and yeah, I'm ashamed, but what does she know, the little snot? Go home, this second! . . . Here's a doll, you like the doll, yes? You're too young, you'll find out when you're older . . .

"Well, what are you standing there for?" said the thunderous Voice. "Dis*perse*!"

A cold, rough wind began to blow in their faces, then ceased. "Go. Now," said the Voice.

And the wind started up again, stronger than before. It was like a heavy, wet palm pressing up against their faces and pushing them back, but then it eased off. Victor wiped his cheeks and saw the crowd beginning to back away. There was a loud cry, then a series of uncertain shouts. Small eddies began forming around the cars and buses, and people started climbing into the back of Diana's truck. Suddenly, everyone was in a hurry, pushing each other out of the way, getting into cars, hastily pulling apart bicycles with entangled handlebars, starting up sputtering motors. Many were also leaving on foot, looking back again and again, though not at the machine gunners or the tower or the armored vehicle, which had rolled up, metal gears grinding, and opened its hatches for all to see . . . Victor knew why they kept looking back and why they were all in such a hurry. His own cheeks burned, and if he feared anything at all, it was that the Voice would repeat "Go!" and that a wet, heavy palm would push him away in disgust.

A small group of idiots in gold shirts was still milling around the gate, unsure of what to do next, but their numbers were dwindling, and when the officer came to bark at them—imposing, confident, clearly pleased to do his duty—they, too, began backing away, and then they turned on their heels and plodded off, picking up discarded brown, gray, and blue raincoats as they went, and soon not a single gold-colored splotch remained, and meanwhile buses and cars kept passing Diana's truck, and everyone around Victor was asking, looking around in impatience and alarm, "But where's the driver?"

And then, out of nowhere, Diana resurfaced, Diana the Fierce. She jumped up onto the truck's running board, turned to face the people in the back, and called out sternly, "I'll take you to the crossroads, but that's it! This truck is heading to the sanatorium!" No one dared contradict her; everyone was unusually quiet and submissive. Teddy didn't come back—he must have gotten into a different car. Diana turned the truck around and they rolled out onto the familiar concrete road, leaving groups of pedestrians and bicyclists in their wake, while overloaded, heavily sagging cars passed them in turn. There was no rain, only fog and a fine drizzle. It started pouring again in earnest only when Diana approached the crossroads and everyone climbed out of the back. Victor returned to the cab.

They were silent all the way to the sanatorium.

When they arrived, Diana immediately went to see Rossechepert, or so she said. Victor threw off his raincoat, collapsed on his bed, lit a cigarette, and trained his eyes on the ceiling. He spent an hour, or maybe two, smoking cigarette after cigarette, tossing and turning, getting up, walking around the room, gazing aimlessly out the window, pulling the curtains shut and opening them again, drinking water straight from the tap, tormented by thirst, and then collapsing back into bed.

It's humiliating, he thought. Yes, of course. They slapped us in the face, called us scum, chased us away like annoying panhandlers, but in the end, those were fathers and mothers, they loved their babies; they hit them, sure, but they were ready to die for them. They corrupted them through their own corrupt example, but not on purpose—out of ignorance. Their mothers suffered giving birth to them, and their fathers fed and clothed them. They were all proud of their children and bragged to each other about them. They may have cursed them from time to time, but they couldn't imagine life without them . . . And now their lives would be truly empty; they'd been left with nothing at all. They didn't deserve to be treated so cruelly, with so much contempt, so coldly, so rationally, and then slapped in the face as a parting gift . . .

God, was it really true that everything animal in man was vile? Even motherhood, even the smiles of Madonnas, their soft, gentle hands guiding infants to the breast . . . Of course, it's just instinct, and a whole religion built up around that instinct . . . maybe the problem lies in extending that religion to child-rearing, where instinct doesn't work anymore, and if it does, it can only do harm . . . Because the she-wolf tells her babies "Bite like me," and that's enough, and the she-hare tells her babies "Flee like me," and that's also enough, but humans tell their young "Think like me," and that's already a crime . . . Well, but what about the clammies, those lepers, those parasites—call 'em what you like, just not human, they're superhuman at least—anyway, what about them? They start with "Here's how people used to think, and look where it led! That's bad because blah blah blah, whereas things *should* be like this and like that. Got it? And now, start thinking for yourself, figure out how to make it so that 'blah blah blah' goes away, leaving only 'this and that.'" Except I have no idea what the "blah blah blah" and the "this and that" are supposed to be.

And anyway, been there, done that; we've tried it all before, and the result was good individuals, while the majority of humans charged straight ahead along the old path, never turning off, doing everything the same way as before . . . And how were we supposed to parent, anyway, when our own fathers hadn't parented us at all, but only taught us to "bite like me and hide like me," which is also how our father was trained by his grandfather, and his grandfather by his great-grandfather, and so on until caveman times, the days of hairy spear-toters, devourers of mammoths. Personally, I feel sorry for all these hairless descendants, the same way I feel sorry for myself, but as for them . . . well, they couldn't care less, they don't need us at all, they have no intention of reeducating us, they're not even planning on blowing up the old world, it's of no interest to them, they have their own concerns. They ask only one thing of the old world: don't interfere. Nowadays it's finally possible to trade in ideas, there are powerful buyers of ideas who will protect you, drive the entire world behind barbed wire so it can't bother you, that bad old world . . . They'll feed you, take care of you . . . They'll do everything in their power to sharpen the axe you're using to cut the very branch on which they perch, medals and embroidery shining . . .

And dammit, it's impressive, in a way—we've tried everything except bringing children up coldly, without simpering or tears . . . although, what the hell am I saying, how do I know what they do over there! It's all cruelty and contempt, that much is clear . . . They'll accomplish nothing, because reason is one thing—go ahead, think, analyze, learn! But what about the hands of a mother, those gentle hands that take away the pain and bring warmth to the world? And the rough chin of the father, who plays at war and pretends he's a tiger, who teaches you to throw a punch, the strongest and smartest person ever? Because that was part of it too! Not just your parents' screamy (or quiet) bickering, not just the belt and drunken mumbling, not just the haphazard box on the ears that transforms, without rhyme or reason, into random gifts of candy or movie-ticket cash . . . But what do I know—maybe they've figured out some equivalent to the good parts of motherhood and fatherhood. The way Irma looked at that clammy! Who do you have to be to earn that kind of look? In any case, though, neither Bol-Kunatz, nor Irma, nor even that pimply, hypercritical nihilist would ever put on a gold shirt. And that's saying a lot. Dammit, what more could I ask?

Hold on, he said to himself. Figure out what's most important here. Are you on their side or not? There's also a third option: let it go. But I can't. Oh, how I'd love to be a cynic—it's so easy, so simple, so luxurious to live that way! Good God, my whole life they've been trying to make a cynic out of me . . . they've really worked hard, expended enormous resources, wasted bullets, paper, rhetorical masterpieces, spared neither fists nor cash nor even other people, all to make sure I become a cynic . . . and all for nothing.

All right, enough. Am I for, or am I against? *Against*, of course, because I can't stand being looked down on, I hate elites of every kind, I hate all forms of intolerance, and I especially dislike getting smacked in the face and booted from the premises . . . But also I'm *for*, because I like clever, talented people and hate fools and dullards, because I hate the goldshirts, because I hate fascists . . . Obviously, though, this isn't the way to decide, I know too little about them, and what I do know, what I've seen with my own eyes—well, there, I'm struck first of all by what's bad: their cruelty, their contempt, their inhumanity, their physical deformity, yes . . . So in the end, there's only this: on their side is Diana, whom I love, and Golem, whom I love, and Irma, whom I love, and Bol-Kunatz, and the pimply nihilist . . . And who's against them? The mayor, that old bastard, that fascist demagogue, and the police chief, that venal sleazebag, and Rossechepert Nantes, and that idiot Lola, and that horde of goldshirts, and Pavor . . . But on the other hand, their side also has the beanpole professional and a certain General Pferd (I can't stand generals), whereas the other side has Teddy and lots of others like him, probably . . . Yeah, this can't be decided by majority vote. It's a little like free democratic elections: the majority is always pro-scumbag . . .

Around two Diana showed up, Diana the Cheerfully Ordinary, wearing a tightly belted white lab coat, made up and neatly coiffed.

"How's work?" she asked.

"I'm all aflame," he answered. "I'm burning to give light to others."

"There's plenty of smoke here, that's for sure. You could open a window at least . . . Hungry?"

"Yes, dammit!" said Victor. He remembered that he'd skipped breakfast.

"Well then, let's go, dammit!"

They went down to the cafeteria. Sitting at long tables, the Kindred Spirits, faces dark with exhaustion, were gulping down dietetic soup in solemn silence. Their fat coach, wearing a tight blue sweater, walked around behind them, clapping them on the shoulders, ruffling their hair, and gazing attentively into their plates.

"I'm going to introduce you to someone," said Diana. "He's going to eat with us."

"Who's that?" Victor inquired with displeasure. He'd been hoping for a quiet meal.

"My husband," said Diana. "My former husband."

"I see," said Victor. "I see. Well . . . I'll be pleased to meet him."

What's come over her? he thought despondently. Who needs this? He turned piteous eyes on Diana, but she was already leading him quickly to the service table in the far corner. The husband stood up to meet them—yellow-faced, hook-nosed, wearing a dark suit and black gloves. He did not shake Victor's hand but simply bowed and said softly, "Hello, nice to see you."

"Banev," Victor said, with the counterfeit warmth that always beset him at the sight of husbands.

"We've actually already met," said the husband. "I'm Zurzmansor."

"Oh, right!" exclaimed Victor. "Of course! My memory, you know . . ." He fell silent. "Wait," he said. "Zurzmansor who?"

"Pavel Zurzmansor. I'm sure you've read my work, and recently you came to my defense at the restaurant—quite energetically, I might add. We've also met in one other place, under similarly unfortunate circumstances . . . Let's sit."

Victor sat. All right, he thought. Fine. So that's what they look like without the neckerchief. Who would have thought? Wait, but where are his "spectacles"? Zurzmansor, also known as the hook-nosed dancer, who was only playing a dancer, who was actually a clammy, four clammies at the same time, really, or even five, if you count the one at the restaurant—this Zurzmansor had no "spectacles" at all. It was as though they'd spread out over his whole face, giving his skin a yellowy, Latin American hue. Diana, smiling a strange, somehow maternal smile, looked at Victor, then at her husband, then back again. And this was unpleasant. Victor felt something like jealousy, which he'd never felt in his previous dealings with husbands. The waitress brought soup.

"Irma sends her regards," said Zurzmansor, breaking a piece of bread in two. "She says not to worry."

"Thank you," Victor responded mechanically. He picked up a spoon and began to eat, tasting nothing. Zurzmansor also ate, glancing up at Victor from time to time—unsmiling, but with an expression that seemed somehow humorous. He had not removed his gloves, but the elegant way he broke his bread, handled his spoon, deployed his napkin all spoke of good breeding.

"So you're really *that* Zurzmansor," said Victor. "The philosopher . . ."

"I'm afraid not," said Zurzmansor, touching the napkin to his lips. "I'm afraid that at this point, I am only very distantly related to that famous philosopher."

Victor couldn't think of anything to say, and decided to abstain from further conversation. After all, I'm not the one who initiated this meeting, my role's a minor one, *he* wanted to see *me*, let him start . . .

The second course arrived. Victor began carving the meat, paying close attention to his own movements. Over at the long tables, the Kindred Spirits were slurping in friendly, ingenuous unison, utensils clinking. Well, I'm definitely the idiot here, thought Victor. Kindred goddamn spirit. She probably still loves him. He got sick, they had to part ways, but she didn't want to, otherwise why would she waste her time in this shithole, emptying Rossechepert's chamber pot . . . And they see each other often, he sneaks into the sanatorium, removes his face covering, and dances with her. He pictured them dancing together—babycakes and honeybunch . . .

Never mind. She loves him. What do I care? But I do, that's the thing. Why pretend? Except—why? They took away my daughter, but I'm not jealous as a father. They took away my woman, but I'm not jealous as a man . . . Good God, those words! *My* woman, *my* daughter . . . The daughter who just met me for the first time in twelve years . . . or is she thirteen? A woman I've known only a few days . . . But please note, I'm jealous! Though not as a father, or a man. It would be so much easier if he'd just said, "My dear sir, I know everything, you have besmirched my honor, now how about some satisfaction?"

"How is the article coming?" asked Zurzmansor.

Victor looked at him gloomily. He didn't seem to be joking, nor was he just asking a polite question to start a conversation. This clammy, it seemed, was actually curious to know how the article was coming. "It's not," said Victor.

"I'd be curious to read it," Zurzmansor remarked.

"Do you know what kind of article it's supposed to be?"

"We've got a pretty good idea. But come, you're not going to write anything of the sort."

"What if they force me to? General Pferd's not going to protect me."

"The thing is," said Zurzmansor, "you won't be able to produce the article that Mr. Mayor is expecting anyway. Even if you try your hardest. There are people who automatically, regardless of their own wishes, transform any task they take on in their own unique way. You are one of these people."

"Is that good or bad?" asked Victor.

"From our perspective, it's good. Very little is known of human personality if we exclude the part composed of reflexes. Of course, as a rule, personality contains little else. Which is why so-called creatives are so valuable—that is, people who process information about reality in their own special way. By comparing some widely known, well-studied phenomenon with its representation in the creative output of a person of this type, we can learn a great deal about the psychic apparatus that processes information."

"And you don't think that sounds insulting?" said Victor.

Zurzmansor, his face strangely contorted, looked up at Victor. "I get it," he said. *"I'm an artist, not a guinea pig* . . . But, you see, I mentioned only one of the circumstances that make you so valuable in our eyes. The other ones are common knowledge—the accurate information you present about objective reality, the machine of your emotions, your way of exciting the imagination, your ability to meet the need for empathy . . . Actually, I was trying to flatter you."

"In that case, I'm flattered," said Victor. "But what you're talking about has nothing to do with writing slanderous articles. All I have to do is take Mr. President's most recent speech and rewrite it from top to bottom, replacing the phrase 'enemies of freedom' with 'so-called clammies,' or 'the patients of the bloodthirsty doctor,' or 'the leprosarium vampires' . . . so actually, my psychic apparatus doesn't enter into it at all."

"That's what *you* think," objected Zurzmansor. "You'll read that speech and immediately find it hideous. Stylistically hideous, I mean. You'll start fixing the style, trying to find more precise expressions, your imagination will engage, you'll start to feel sick from all that stale verbiage, you'll want to make the words feel alive again, to replace the bureaucratic lies with living, palpitating facts, and before you know it, you'll start writing the truth."

"Maybe," said Victor. "In any case, I have no desire to write that kind of article at the moment."

"And do you desire to write anything else?"

"Yes," said Victor, looking Zurzmansor in the eye, "I'd love to write about the children leaving the city. A new Pied Piper of Hamelin."

Zurzmansor gave a satisfied nod. "Excellent idea. You should go for it."

Go for it, thought Victor bitterly. Sure. But dammit, who's going to print it? You? "Diana," he said, "is there anything to drink around here?"

Diana rose wordlessly and walked away.

"Also, I'd love to write about a doomed city," said Victor. "And about all that mysterious fuss around the leprosarium. And about evil sorcerers."

"Are you out of money?" asked Zurzmansor.

"Not at the moment, no."

"You should know that you'll most likely receive this year's Leprosarium Literary Prize. You're up against Tusov in the final round, but Tusov is less likely to win, that's obvious. So you won't have to worry about money."

"No kidding," said Victor. "That'll be a first for me. Is it a lot of money?"

"Three thousand or so . . . I can't remember exactly."

Diana returned and placed a bottle and a single glass on the table, again without a word.

"One more glass," Victor requested.

"None for me," said Zurzmansor.

"Well, I . . . uh . . ."

"Or for me," said Diana.

"Is it for *Disaster*?" asked Victor, pouring himself a glass.

"Yes. And for *Lady Cat*. So you'll be set for something like three months. Or is it less?"

"More like two," said Victor. "But that's not the point . . . Listen, I'd like to visit you all in the leprosarium."

"Absolutely," said Zurzmansor. "That's where you'll be awarded the prize. But you'll be disappointed. You won't see any miracles. It'll be on the weekend. Ten or so cottages, the treatment center . . ."

"Treatment center," Victor repeated. "And who exactly are you treating there?"

"People," said Zurzmansor with a strange expression. He smirked, and suddenly something horrible happened to his face. His right eye turned glassy and slid down to his chin, while his left cheek, along with his ear, split away from his skull and hovered in place. It lasted only for a moment. Diana dropped her plate. Victor turned away automatically, and when he looked back at Zurzmansor, the man had resumed his former state—yellow and polite. *Vade retro*, said Victor in his mind. Begone, unclean spirit! Or had it been an illusion? Hastily, he pulled out a pack of cigarettes, lit one, and began staring into his glass.

The Kindred Spirits rose noisily from their places and trudged toward the exit, calling loudly to each other. Zurzmansor said, "In general, we'd prefer it if you felt at ease. You have nothing to fear. You've probably already guessed that our organization occupies a certain position and enjoys certain privileges. We do a great deal, and are therefore permitted a great deal. We are permitted to experiment with the climate, to prepare the generation that will succeed us, and so on. No need to get into it . . . Certain people imagine that we work for them, and we see no reason to disabuse them." He was silent for a moment. "Write whatever and however you want, Banev, and pay no attention to the dogs at your heels. If you meet resistance from publishers or have money troubles, we'll support you. If worse comes to worst, we'll publish you ourselves. For our internal use, of course. Not to worry: you're guaranteed your lampreys."

Victor downed his glass and shook his head. "Gotcha," he said. "I'm being bought off again."

"If you like," said Zurzmansor. "The main thing is for you to understand that there exists a subset of readers—not a very large one at the moment, to be sure—that is quite interested in your work. We need you, Banev. Moreover, we need you exactly as you are. We don't need Banev as our champion or singer of praises, so there's no need to rack your brains about whose side you're on. Be on your own side, like any creative person should be. That's all we ask."

"My goodness," said Victor. "Such preferential treatment! Carte blanche in my work and whole regiments of lampreys on the horizon . . . and on my plate, with mustard sauce. To quote Walter Scott's *Ivanhoe*, 'Where was the widow might say him nay?' Listen, Zurzmansor, you ever happen to sell your soul and your pen?"

"Yes, of course," said Zurzmansor. "And at a disgustingly low price. But that was a thousand years ago, on another planet." He was silent once more. "It's not what you think, Banev," he said. "We're not buying you off. We just want you to be yourself—and we worry you'll get crushed. It's happened to so many already . . . Moral values can't be sold, Banev. They can be destroyed, but never bought. Any given moral value is needed by one side only; it makes no sense to steal or buy it. Mr. President imagines that he's bought off the painter R. Quadriga. But he's mistaken. He bought the hack R. Quadriga, while the painter slipped through his fingers and died. Whereas we don't want the writer Banev to slip through anyone's fingers, even our own, and die. We need artists, not propagandists."

He stood up. Victor also stood, feeling awkward, and proud, and mistrustful, and humiliated, and disappointed, and burdened with a sense of obligation, and something else besides, but he couldn't quite make it out.

"It was very nice talking to you," said Zurzmansor. "Best of luck in your work."

"Good-bye," said Victor.

Zurzmansor bowed curtly and walked off, his head thrown back, his gait steady, his stride broad. Victor watched him leave.

"And that's why I love you," said Diana.

Victor collapsed onto his chair and reached for the bottle. "Why?" he asked absentmindedly.

"Because they need you. You, the horndog, the drunkard, the slob, the scandalmonger, bastard that you are, are needed by people like that."

She leaned over the table and kissed him on the cheek. Here was one more Diana: Diana in Love, with enormous, dry eyes, Maria from Magdala, Diana Who Looks Up at You in Adoration.

"Whatever," mumbled Victor. "Intellectuals . . . queens for a day."

But those were just words. The reality wasn't so simple.

The next day, after breakfast, Victor returned to the hotel. As they said their good-byes, Diana gave him a small birch-bark basket. Rossechepert had just received twenty pounds of strawberries from the hothouses in the capital, and Diana correctly judged that even Rossechepert's abnormal appetite would be no match for such a vast number of berries.

The doorman opened the door for Victor, looking gloomy. Victor offered him some strawberries. The doorman took a couple, placed them in his mouth, chewed them like they were bread, and said, "Turns out my rug rat was one of their ringleaders."

"Don't be too hard on him," said Victor. "He's a great kid. Whip-smart, and he has great manners."

"Well, those I beat into him!" said the doorman, looking more cheerful. "Worked my ass off . . ." He fell into gloom again. "The neighbors won't let it go," he reported. "But what could I do? I didn't know . . ."

"Screw the neighbors," Victor advised. "They're just jealous. You've got a wonderful son. I, for one, couldn't be more pleased that my daughter's friends with him."

"Ha!" said the doorman, perking up again. "So, should we start planning a wedding?"

"Why not," said Victor. "Anything could happen." He pictured Bol-Kunatz. "Really, why not . . ."

They spent a while laughing and joking.

"You hear any gunshots last night?" asked the doorman.

"No," said Victor, suddenly on the alert. "Why?"

"Well," said the doorman, "when we all went our separate ways back there, some people . . . didn't. Daredevils. Slashed their way through the barbed wire and climbed inside. Got machine-gunned."

"No kidding," said Victor.

"I didn't see it myself," said the doorman. "It's just what people are saying." He gave a cautious look around, beckoned Victor closer, and whispered in his ear: "Teddy was with them. He got hit, but it's going to be OK—he's at home right now, sleeping it off."

"That's too bad," Victor mumbled, feeling upset.

He offered the doorman more strawberries, grabbed his key, and went up to his room. Still in his coat, he dialed Teddy's number. Teddy's daughter-in-law reported that everything was basically OK, that it was a through-and-through, that the man was lying on his stomach, cursing and sucking down vodka. She herself was getting ready to go to the Meetinghouse to see what was up with her son. Victor asked her to convey his greetings to Teddy, promised to stop by, and hung up. He felt he should call Lola, but then he imagined how the conversation would go—the reproaches, the yelling—and decided against it. He took off his raincoat, looked at the strawberries, went down to the kitchen, and asked for some cream.

When he returned, he found Pavor sitting in his room. "Good day," he said with a blinding smile.

Victor walked up to the table, shook some strawberries into a finger bowl, covered them with cream, and poured sugar on top. Then he sat down. "Hello yourself," he said gloomily. "What's up?"

He had no desire to look at Pavor. First of all, Pavor was a bastard, and second, it turns out it's unpleasant to look at someone you informed on, even if he is a bastard, and even if you informed on him with the most unimpeachable intentions.

"Listen, Victor," said Pavor. "I'm ready to apologize. We both acted stupid, me especially. Chalk it up to work troubles. I sincerely beg your pardon. I'd be incredibly sad if you and I fell out because of something so silly."

Victor swirled his spoon around in the strawberries and cream, then took a bite.

"God, I've had the worst luck lately," Pavor continued. "I'm angry at the whole world. I get no sympathy from anyone, no support. The mayor, that animal, got me involved in this filthy business—"

"Mr. Summan," said Victor. "Quit screwing around. You're a great actor, but thankfully I've figured you out. Observing your artistic talents no longer gives me any pleasure. Quit spoiling my appetite and go home."

"Victor," said Pavor reproachfully. "Come on, we're both adults. You can't take a bunch of tableside chatter so seriously. Did you really think I believed all that nonsense I was spouting? It's all migraines, work troubles, my cold . . . What more can you ask of a man?"

"I'd ask that a man not come up from behind and crack my skull with his brass knuckles," Victor explained. "And if he does—sometimes you gotta do what you gotta do—then at least I'd ask that he not pretend to be my buddy after."

"Oh, so *that's* what you're talking about," said Pavor thoughtfully. His face looked suddenly haggard. "Victor, listen, let me explain. It was a total accident. I had no idea it was you. And plus . . . like you just said, sometimes you gotta do what you gotta do."

"Mr. Summan," said Victor, licking his spoon, "I never liked people of your profession. I even shot one once—he was very brave at HQ when he was accusing the officers of treason, but when he was sent to the front lines . . . What I mean to say is, get out."

But Pavor didn't get out. He lit a cigarette, crossed his legs, and sat back in his chair. Sure, I get it—he's a big guy, probably knows karate, plus he's got those brass knuckles . . . It'd be great to get good and mad right about now . . . I mean, he's ruining my special dessert!

"I see you know a lot," said Pavor. "That's no good. For you, I mean. Be that as it may. What you don't know is that I genuinely respect and like you. Come on, don't grimace and act nauseated. I'm being serious. I'm happy to express my regret for the incident with the brass knuckles. I'll even admit that I knew whom I was hitting, but I had no choice. One witness was already on the ground around the corner, then you come charging in . . . Anyway, the only thing I could do at that point was hit you as delicately as possible—which I did. Please, accept my sincerest apologies."

Pavor made an aristocratic gesture. Victor was looking at him with increasing curiosity. Something about this situation felt fresh, new, unimaginable.

"On the other hand," Pavor continued, "I can't apologize for working for the ministry I do—you know the one. I can't and, what's more, I don't really want to. Don't imagine that it's chock full of stranglers of free thought or scumbag careerists. Yes, I'm in counterintelligence. Yes, it's a dirty job. The thing is, all jobs are dirty—there aren't any clean ones. You pour your subconscious, your famous libido, into your novels; I do the same thing, but in my own way . . . I can't tell you any details, but I'm sure you probably have your guesses. Yes, I keep an eye on the leprosarium. I hate those damp monsters, I'm afraid of them—not only for my own sake, but for the sake of anyone who's at all worthwhile. You, for instance. Because you really don't get it. You're a free-spirited artist trafficking in emotions . . . *Ooh, ahh!*—that's your whole deal. But we're talking about the fate of the system. The fate of humankind, if you like. You're always trashing Mr. President, you say he's a dictator, a tyrant, an idiot . . . And meanwhile, a dictatorship is brewing the likes of which you free spirits can't even imagine. I said a lot of nonsense in the restaurant the other night, but my underlying message was correct: humans are anarchic creatures, and that anarchy will devour them if the system fails to be sufficiently harsh. Your beloved clammies represent a level of cruelty that precludes the existence of ordinary people. That's what you don't get. You think if someone quotes Zurzmansor or Hegel, they must be amazing. But they look at you and see a pile of shit, they don't care about you at all, because you're shit according to Hegel, and you're shit according to Zurzmansor, too. You're shit by definition. And anything outside the bounds of that definition holds no interest for them. Mr. President might chew you out due to his innate narrow-mindedness. Worst-case scenario, he orders your imprisonment, and then some holiday will roll around and he'll amnesty you, out of the fullness of his heart, and even invite you to lunch. Whereas Zurzmansor will examine you with a magnifying glass, classify you as utterly useless dog shit, and studiously, intellectually, out of the fullness of his philosophical mind, sweep you into the trash with a dirty rag, only to forget you ever existed . . ."

Victor had ceased eating in amazement. Something strange and unexpected was happening, right before his eyes. Pavor was agitated: his lips quivered, the blood had rushed away from his face, he was gasping for breath. He obviously believed in what he said, and his frozen gaze reflected the horror of a horrifying world. Hey now, Victor admonished himself. That's your enemy, a lowlife. He's an actor, remember, he's playing you like a damn fiddle . . . He suddenly realized he had to force himself to reject Pavor. Don't forget: He's a bureaucrat. He's incapable of idealism by definition. The higher-ups give the orders and he obeys them—that's what they pay him for. If they tell him to defend the clammies, that's what he'll do. I know these bastards, I've seen enough of them in my day . . .

Pavor pulled himself together and smiled. "I know what you're thinking," he said. "I can see it in your face—you're trying to guess: Why's this jerk on my case? What does he want from me? But guess what: I don't want anything from you. I am genuinely trying to warn you, I genuinely want you to figure things out, to choose the right side . . ." He bared his teeth in anguish. "I don't want you to become a traitor to humanity. You'll live to regret it, but by then it'll be too late . . . It goes without saying that you really should get out of town. That's why I came to see you, actually—to insist on it. Hard times are coming, the higher-ups are in a frenzy of bureaucratic zeal, they got the memo that they're not doing such a great job, that law and order's in trouble . . . But that's not important, we'll talk about that later. I want you to figure out what's most important. Which is not what's going to happen tomorrow. Tomorrow they'll still be behind barbed wire, guarded by those idiots . . ." He bared his teeth again. "But ten years down the line—"

Victor never learned what would happen ten years down the line. The door opened silently, admitting two men in identical gray raincoats, and Victor immediately understood who they were. By sheer force of habit, his heart skipped a beat. He stood up obediently, feeling sick and powerless. But they said to him "Sit" and to Pavor "Get up."

"Pavor Summan, you're under arrest."

Pavor, his face white—bluish-white, even, like skim milk—stood and said hoarsely, "Warrant."

They showed him a piece of paper and, as he examined it with unseeing eyes, took him by the elbows, ushered him out of the room, and closed the door. Victor was left sitting there, limp of limb, gazing into his finger bowl and repeating, *Let them all devour each other, let them all devour each other . . .*

He kept waiting for a motor to roar outside, for car doors to slam, but the noises never came. Then he lit a cigarette and, feeling like he could no longer just sit there, like he needed to talk to someone, to find some distraction or at the very least share a glass of vodka, went out into the hall. I wonder how they knew he was with me. No, never mind, I don't. Nothing wonder-worthy there . . . He found the beanpole professional hanging around in the stairwell. It was so odd to see him on his own that Victor looked closer, and indeed—there in the corner, on a sofa, sat the young man with the briefcase, just unfurling a newspaper.

"Speak of the devil," said the beanpole. The young man looked at Victor, stood up, and began refolding his paper. "I was just on my way to see you," said the beanpole. "But since you came out yourself, why don't we go to our room, where it's even quieter."

Victor didn't care where he went and obediently shuffled up to the third floor. The beanpole spent a long time unlocking the door of room 312. He had a whole bunch of keys, and it seemed like he tried them all. Meanwhile, Victor and the bespectacled young man stood side by side, and the young man had a bored expression on his face, and Victor thought about what would happen if he cracked him on the head, snatched his briefcase, and bolted.

Then they went inside, and the young man immediately repaired to the bedroom on the left, while the beanpole said to Victor "Just a minute" and disappeared into the bedroom on the right. Victor took a seat on the mahogany table and began finger-tracing the rough rings left on the polished surface by cups and glasses. There were quite a few of them; the table had been treated unceremoniously, they hadn't cared that it was mahogany: they'd put out cigarettes on it and, on at least one occasion, stained it with ink from a pen.

The young man emerged from his room sans briefcase and blazer, wearing bedroom slippers and holding his newspaper in one hand and a full glass in the other. He sat down in the chair under the floor lamp; at that very moment, the beanpole reappeared, carrying a tray that he immediately placed on the table. The tray held a half-empty bottle of scotch, a glass, and a large, square box bound in blue morocco.

"First, the formalities," said the beanpole. "Or wait, no, let's get another glass first." He looked around, grabbed a pencil cup from the desk, examined the inside, and blew into it. Then he placed the cup on the tray. "All right, formalities," he said.

He stood upright, hands at his sides, and bulged his eyes out severely. The young man put his newspaper aside and also stood up, gazing at the wall with a bored expression. Victor followed suit.

"Victor Banev!" the beanpole declared in lofty, official tones. "Dear sir! On behalf and by special order of Mr. President, I present you with the Silver Trefoil, Second Class, in recognition of services rendered to the department that it is my honor to represent here today!"

He opened the blue box, solemnly extracted a medal on a white moiré ribbon, and began pinning it to Victor's chest. The young man gave a burst of polite applause. Then the beanpole handed Victor a certificate along with the box itself, shook his hand, took a step back, admired his handiwork, and clapped his hands. Victor, feeling like an idiot, clapped too.

"This deserves a toast," said the beanpole.

They all sat. The beanpole poured out the whisky, taking the pencil cup for himself. "To the Knight of the Order of the Trefoil!" he proclaimed.

They all stood once again, smiled at each other, downed their drinks, and sat back down. The young man in glasses immediately got out his newspaper and disappeared behind it.

"You already had the Third Class, right?" said the beanpole. "Now all you need is the First, and you'll be a full knight. Ride public transportation for free and so on. What'd you get the Third Class for?"

"I forget," said Victor. "It was for something, all right . . . I killed someone, maybe? Oh, right. It was for the Kitchigan Bridgehead."

"Wow!" said the beanpole, pouring another round. "I didn't serve, you know. Before my time."

"You're lucky," said Victor. They drank. "Just between you and me, I don't really get why they gave me this thing."

"Didn't you hear? For 'services rendered.'"

"You mean Summan?" said Victor with a sorrowful little laugh.

"Don't be silly!" said the beanpole. "You're a VIP, you run in certain circles, you know . . ." And he waved his finger vaguely somewhere in the vicinity of his ear.

"What circles?" said Victor.

"Don't pretend!" the beanpole exclaimed coyly. "We know everything! General Pferd, General Pucky, Colonel Bambarja . . . You're a big deal."

"First I heard of it," said Victor nervously.

"It was the colonel's idea. As you might expect, no one was against—no big shock there! And then General Pferd was at a briefing with the President and slipped him a report on you." The beanpole laughed. "It was hilarious, apparently. The old man bellowed, 'Which Banev? The satirist? No way in hell!' But the general took a stern tone: 'Your Excellency, you must!' Anyway, it all worked out. The old man was all choked up by the end. 'All right,' he says, 'I forgive him.' What happened between you two?"

"Eh," Victor said reluctantly. "Just a friendly disagreement about literature."

"Do you really write books?" asked the beanpole.

"Yup. Like Lawrence of Arabia."

"Does it pay well?"

"Comme ci, comme ça."

"I'll have to give it a shot myself," said the beanpole. "I just can't find the time, that's the problem. It's just one thing after another."

"Yeah, time is an issue," Victor agreed. Every time he moved, the medal swung and hit him in the ribs. It was like a mustard plaster: as soon as you take it off, you feel better. "You know, I think I'll head out," he said, rising. "Time, you know."

The beanpole leaped up, hastily. "Of course," he said.

"Good-bye."

"It's been an honor," said the beanpole. The young man in glasses lowered his newspaper slightly and bowed.

Victor walked out into the hallway and immediately tore off the medal. He had a strong urge to throw it in the trash, but he restrained himself and stuck it in his pocket instead. He went down to the kitchen and grabbed a bottle of gin. As he was leaving, the concierge called out, "Mr. Banev, you got a call from Mr. Mayor. You weren't in your room, so I—"

"What did he want?" Victor asked, sullenly.

"He asked you to call back as soon as possible. Are you on your way to your room? If he calls again—"

"Send him straight to hell," said Victor. "I'm about to disconnect my phone, and if he calls you, tell him in exactly these words: *Mr. Banev, Knight of the Order of the Trefoil, Second Class, would like for you, Mr. Mayor, to go straight to hell.*"

He locked himself in his room and disconnected the phone, for some reason covering it with a pillow. Then he sat down at the table, poured himself some gin, and, without adding water, drank the whole glass in one gulp. It burned all the way down. Then he grabbed a spoon and began devouring the strawberries and cream, not registering the taste, not knowing what he was doing. Enough, I've had enough, he thought. I don't need anything, no medals, no honoraria, none of your handouts, I don't need your attention, or your rage, or your love, leave me alone, I've had it up to here with my own self, don't drag me into your affairs. He clutched his head in his hands, trying to blot out the image of Pavor's bluish-white face and those colorless, merciless thugs in their identical raincoats. General Pferd is with you, General Nalgas, General Arschmann with his medal-conferring embrace, plus Zurzmansor with his peeling-off face . . . He struggled to recall where he'd seen all this before.

He sucked down another half a glass and discovered he was crouching in a contorted pose at the bottom of a trench, and the ground underneath him was shifting; roiling tectonic plates, enormous masses of granite, basalt, and lava were buckling, groaning with tension, swelling up, bulging out, and incidentally, in passing, pushing him toward the top of the trench, higher and higher, squeezing him out entirely, forcing him to protrude beyond the trench's lip. Times are hard, the authorities are in a frenzy of bureaucratic zeal, they got the memo that they're not doing such a great job, and meanwhile, there he is outside the trench, naked, covering his eyes with his hands, totally exposed.

If only I could sink to the bottom again and lie there, he thought. Just lie there so they couldn't hear or see me. On the very bottom, like a submarine, he thought, and then something said in his mind: get off the grid. Exactly, sink like a sub to the bottom, get off the grid where I've been for so long. Never send out any signals again. Gone fishing. No more talking. Figure it all out without me. Good lord, why can't I just become a cynic, finally? . . . Sink like a sub to the bottom, get off this grid where I've been for so long. Sink like a sub to the bottom, he kept repeating, and never send out any signals again. He was already feeling the rhythm, and now it all clicked into place: Sick of it all, couldn't get any sicker . . . Don't wanna drink and I don't wanna write . . . He poured out some gin and drank it. Don't wanna sing and I don't wanna write . . . Sick of the guitar and sick of the pen . . .

Where's my banjo, he thought. Where'd I stick the banjo? He fumbled around under the bed until he found his banjo. Hey, I don't give a damn about you. You don't even know! Wish I could sink like a sub to the bottom, get off this grid where I've been for so long. He slapped the strings rhythmically, transmitting the rhythm to the table, and then the whole room, and then the whole world was tapping its feet and shaking its shoulders. All those generals and colonels, all those soaking-wet people with their peeling-off faces, departments of public safety, presidents, Pavors Summan—each of whom was having his arms twisted and his face punched . . . I've had enough, I really can't stand it, sick of the guitar and sick of the pen . . . It's not a guitar, it's a banjo, but "guitar" sounds better, so that's what it's going to be . . . Submarine boat . . . vodka gin float . . . torn-up C-note . . . gulag remote . . . That's right, that's right . . .

Someone had been knocking at the door for a long time now, louder and louder, and Victor finally heard it but had no fear, because it wasn't THAT knocking. It was the ordinary, gratifying knock of a peaceable person who is annoyed that no one is answering. Victor opened the door. It was Golem.

"Having fun?" he asked. "Pavor's been arrested."

"I know, I know," said Victor happily. "Sit down and listen."

Golem wouldn't sit, but Victor hit the strings anyway, and sang:

Sick of it all, couldn't get any sicker,
Even fed up with performing my songs.
Wish I could sink like a sub to the bottom,
Get off this grid where I've been for so long.

"That's all I've got so far," he shouted. "Next comes vodka gin float . . . torn-up C-note . . . gulag remote . . . And then—listen:

But both the drink and the girlies betrayed me:
Booze hurt my head and the girls are all gone.
Wish I could sink like a sub to the bottom,
Get off this grid where I've been for so long.

I've had enough and I really can't stand it,
Sick of the guitar and sick of the pen,
Wish I could sink like a sub to the bottom
*And never send out any signals again.**

"That's it!" he shouted, and threw the banjo on the bed. He felt enormous relief, like something had shifted, like suddenly he was desperately needed outside the trench, where everyone could see him—like he had wrenched his hands away from his screwed-shut eyes and looked around the gray, filthy field, the rusty barbed wire, the gray sacks that used to be people and the tedious, disgraceful scene once known as life, and all around him other people rose up from the trenches and looked around, too, and someone took his finger off the trigger . . .

"Good for you," said Golem. "But isn't it time to start working on that article?"

"Nothing doing," said Victor. "You don't know me, Golem, I'm done with all of them. Sit down, sit down, dammit! I'm drunk, and you should get drunk too! Take off your raincoat . . . Take it off, come on!" he yelled. "And sit! Here's a glass, drink! You just don't get it, Golem, even if you are a prophet. And I won't let you. Not getting it is my prerogative. Everyone gets it all too well in this world, they know what must be, what is, and what will come to pass, but there's a big shortage of people who *don't* get it. For instance, why am I of value? Only because I don't get it. Perspectives unfold in front of me, but I say nah, I don't get it. They try to bamboozle me with unimaginably simple theories, but I say nah! Does. Not. Compute. That's why they need me . . . Want some strawberries? Except I ate them all. So let's smoke . . ."

He stood up and walked across the room. Golem, glass in hand, watched him without turning his head.

---

* Authors' Note: Lyrics derive from Vladimir Vysotsky's "Sick of It All" (a.k.a. "Sink to the Bottom"), slightly modified and used with permission of the singer-songwriter.

"It's an amazing paradox, Golem. There was a time when I understood everything. I was sixteen years old and I was elder knight of the Legion. I was on top of absolutely everything, and no one had any use for me! Someone bashed in my skull in a brawl and I spent the next month in the hospital. And meanwhile, life went on: the Legion moved ahead triumphantly without me, Mr. President was irrevocably transforming into Mr. President—and again, I was on the sidelines. Everyone managed just fine without me. The same thing happened during the war. I officered around, snagged medal after medal, and all the while I understood everything. Got shot through the chest, wound up in the hospital again, and do you think anyone was worried, do you think anyone expressed any interest in me? Where's Banev, where did our Banev go, our brave, omniscient Banev? Not one bit! . . . And then, when I stopped understanding anything, even a little—suddenly everything changed. All the newspapers noticed me. So did a bunch of government departments. Mr. President honored me personally . . . Eh? You know how rare that is, a person who just doesn't get it? He's well known, he's of concern to generals and corpses . . . I mean *colonels* . . . the clammies desperately need him, he's considered quite a figure, it's crazy! And why? Because, ladies and gentlemen, he just doesn't get it." Victor sat down. "I'm pretty drunk, aren't I?" he asked.

"No kidding," said Golem. "But it doesn't matter, keep going."

Victor shrugged. "That's all," he said sheepishly. "I've run dry . . . Wanna hear a song?"

"Sure," said Golem.

Victor picked up his banjo and began to sing. He sang "We Brave Boys," then "Men of Uranium," then "Of the Shepherd Whose Eye was Gored by a Bull and Who Violated the National Border," then "Sick of It All," then "Indifferent City," then something about truth and lies, then "Sick of It All" again, and then he howled out the national anthem to the tune of "Ah, What Lovely Legs She Has" but forgot the words, mixed up the stanzas, and put the banjo aside.

"Run dry again," he said sadly. "So, Pavor's been arrested, you say? I knew that. He was actually in my room when it happened, right where you're sitting now . . . Would you like to know what he wanted to say but didn't have time to? That in ten years the clammies will take control of the whole world and crush us all. What do you think?"

"Unlikely," said Golem. "Why bother crushing us? We'll crush each other without outside help."

"But what about the clammies?"

"Maybe they'll stop us from crushing each other . . . Hard to say."

"Or maybe they'll help us out!" said Victor with a drunken laugh. "'Cause we can't even crush anyone properly. Ten thousand years and we haven't managed it yet . . . Listen, Golem, why did you lie to me about treating them? They're not sick at all, they're as healthy as you or me, except their skin is yellow, for some reason . . ."

"Hmm," said Golem. "Where did you come by that information? I wouldn't know anything about that."

"Right, sure. Forget it, you can't fool me anymore. I talked to Zurz- . . . Zu- . . . Zurzmansor. He told me everything: a secret institute . . . wrapped up in neckerchiefs, for protection . . . You know, Golem, your guys think they can spin General Pferd like a top, indefinitely. But the reality is they're queens for a day. He'll devour them—neckerchiefs, gloves, and all, as soon as he gets hungry . . . Ugh, dammit, I'm so drunk—the room's spinning . . ."

But he was being a little sly. He could see Golem's fat, purplish face and the unusually attentive little eyes perfectly well.

"So Zurzmansor told you he's healthy?"

"Yes," said Victor. "Or really, I can't remember . . . probably not, actually. But you can tell!"

Golem scratched at his chin with the edge of his glass. "It's too bad you're drunk," he said. "Although it may be for the best. I'm in a generous mood today. Want me to tell you everything I think, or suspect, about the clammies?"

"Go for it," Victor agreed. "Only no more lies."

"Spectacle disease," Golem began, "is a very curious thing. You know who falls victim to spectacle disease?" He fell silent. "No, forget it, I'm not telling you anything."

"Oh, come off it," said Victor. "You already started."

"That was stupid of me," Golem retorted. He looked at Victor and smirked. "Ask me questions," he said. "If they're dumb enough, I'll be happy to answer them . . . Come on now, before I change my mind again."

Someone knocked on the door. "Go to hell!" barked Victor. "I'm busy!"

"I'm sorry, Mr. Banev," said the timid voice of the concierge, "But your wife is on the line."

"Lies! I have no wife . . . Although . . . ah, *excusez-moi*. I forgot. Fine, I'll call her back now, thank you." He grabbed his glass, filled it to the top, stuck it in Golem's hand, and said, "Drink and don't think about anything. I just need a second."

He plugged the phone back in and dialed Lola's number. Lola spoke in a very dry tone: please excuse the intrusion, but I was about to go visit Irma, would you deign to join.

"No," said Victor. "I would not deign to join. I'm busy."

"She's your daughter, after all! Have you really sunk so low—"

"I'm! Busy!" barked Victor.

"You don't care what happens to your daughter?"

"Stop screwing around," said Victor. "I seem to remember you wanting to get rid of Irma. It's done now. What more do you want?"

Lola began to cry.

"Stop it," said Victor, wrinkling his nose. "Irma's happy there. Happier than in the best boarding school. Go down there and see for yourself."

"You rude, soulless, egoistic pig," Lola announced, and hung up. Victor cursed at her under his breath, unplugged the telephone, and returned to the table.

"Listen, Golem," he said. "What are you all doing over there with my children? If you're preparing your own successors, I'm against."

"What successors?"

"What successors . . . That's what I'm asking you!"

"As far as I know," said Golem, "the children are quite happy."

"Whatever . . . I don't need you to tell me that. But what are they *doing* over there?"

"Didn't they tell you?"

"Who?"

"The kids."

"How could they tell me anything at all, if I'm here and they're there?"

"They're building a new world," said Golem.

"Oh, right . . . yeah, that they did tell me. But that's just talk, philosophizing . . . You're lying to me again, Golem. What kind of new world can there be behind barbed wire? A new world under the command of General Pferd! . . . And what if they catch it?"

"Catch what?"

"Spectacle disease, obviously!"

"For the millionth time: genetic diseases aren't contagious."

"Million shmillion . . ." Victor grumbled, losing the thread. "But what is spectacle disease, really? What hurts when you have it? Or is that a secret, too?"

"No, that's public knowledge."

"So tell me about it," said Victor. "And spare me the jargon, please."

"It starts with skin changes: pimples, nodules, especially on the hands and feet . . . Boils, sometimes . . ."

"Come on, Golem, does any of that matter?"

"To what?"

"To the essence of the thing."

"Not to the essence of the thing, no," said Golem. "I thought you were interested."

"I want to understand the essence of the thing!" said Victor ardently.

"That's the one thing you won't do," said Golem, raising his voice slightly.

"Why?"

"Well, first of all, because you're drunk."

"That's not a good reason at all," said Victor.

"And second of all, because it's impossible to explain in the first place."

"No such thing," Victor declared. "You just don't want to tell me. But I won't be mad at you. Nondisclosure agreements, disclosure violations, military tribunals . . . I get it. I just don't understand why the children have to build a new world inside a leprosarium. Couldn't you find a better place for it?"

"No, we couldn't," answered Golem. "The leprosarium is where the architects are. And the contractors."

"Yeah, machine guns and all," said Victor. "I saw them too. But I just don't get it. One of you is lying. Either you or Zurzmansor."

"It's Zurzmansor, of course," said Golem coolly.

"Or maybe both of you are lying. And as for me, I believe both of you, because it all has the ring of truth to it . . . Just tell me one thing, Golem: What is it they want? Only be honest."

"Happiness," said Golem.

"Who for? Themselves?"

"Not only."

"But at whose expense?"

"That question has no meaning for them," said Golem slowly. "At the expense of the grass, the clouds, of flowing water . . . of stars."

"So they're just like us," said Victor.

"Not at all," Golem objected. "Not in the slightest."

"Why not? We're also—"

"No, because we trample the grass, scatter the clouds, dam the water . . . You understood me too literally—that was an analogy."

"I don't get it," said Victor.

"I warned you. I myself don't understand a lot of it, but I have my guesses."

"Is there anyone out there who does understand?"

"I don't know. I doubt it. Maybe the children . . . but even if they do get it, it's in their own way. Very much in their own way."

Victor picked up the banjo and touched its strings. His fingers wouldn't obey him. He placed the banjo on the table. "Golem," he said. "You're a communist. What the hell are you doing in the leprosarium? Why aren't you at a meeting? Why aren't you on the barricades? You won't get any praise from Moscow."

"I'm an architect," said Golem calmly.

"What the hell kind of architect are you if you don't understand anything? And why do you keep stringing me along? I've been sparring with you for an hour, and what have you told me? All you do is snarfle up my gin and pull the wool over my eyes. For shame, Golem. Not to mention your compulsive lying."

"Oho, compulsive!" said Golem. "You're not wrong, though. They don't get pus-filled boils."

"Give me your glass," said Victor. "I'm cutting you off." He splashed some gin into the glass and drank. "Who the hell knows with you, Golem. Why in God's name do you need all this? What game are you playing? If you can tell me, do, and if it's a secret, then you should've kept it quiet in the first place."

"There's a simple explanation here," said Golem amiably, stretching out his legs. "I'm a prophet, you said so yourself. And prophets all end up in the same position: they know a great deal, and they want to talk about it—to share their knowledge with a pleasant interlocutor, to brag a little, to puff themselves up. But as soon as they start talking, they get this feeling of unease, this awkwardness . . . And so they're forced to wiggle around, like Jesus when they asked him about the stone."

"Whatever," said Victor. "I'll go to the leprosarium and find out for myself, without you. Why don't you tell me a different story?"

He observed the increasing numbness of his limbs with interest, thinking that it would be great to drink one more glass—to complete the set—and fall into bed, and then wake up and drive over to Diana's. Everything was going to turn out all right.

Everything was already all right, actually. He pictured himself singing to Diana about the submarine and felt very good indeed. He grabbed the wet oar from the side of the boat, pushed off shore, and the boat immediately began to rock. There was no rain, not even clouds, just a red sunset, and he sailed toward it, the oars bouncing off the tops of the waves. Sink to the bottom . . . And he would have, but he felt constrained because Golem's voice was buzzing lazily right next to his ear: ". . . They're very young, they have their whole lives ahead of them, whereas all we have ahead of us is them. Of course humanity will conquer the universe, but not as red-cheeked muscly strongmen, and of course humans will figure themselves out too, except first they have to change themselves . . . Nature never lies, it always keeps its promises, just not the way we might have thought, and mostly not the way we would have wanted . . ."

Zurzmansor, who was sitting on the prow, turned to face Victor, and now he could see that Zurzmansor had no face; he was holding his face in his hands, and that face was gazing at Victor—a nice face, an honest one, but it made him want to throw up, and Golem just kept droning on . . .

"Go to sleep," Victor mumbled, stretching out in the bottom of the boat. Its ribs dug into his sides, and it was very uncomfortable, but he was very sleepy. "Go to sleep, Golem . . ."

When he woke up, he found himself lying in bed. It was dark, and rain was drumming rhythmically against the windowpanes. With difficulty, he lifted an arm and reached for the bedside lamp, but his fingers bumped up against a cold, smooth wall. Odd, he thought. Where's Diana? Or is this not the sanatorium? He tried to lick his lips, but his tongue, thick and rough, refused to obey him. He very much wanted to smoke, but that would be a huge mistake . . . Actually, what I would really like is some water. "Diana!" he called out. Oh, wait, this isn't the sanatorium. In the sanatorium, the bedside lamp is on the right-hand side, whereas here there's a wall . . . Aha, so this is my hotel room! he thought with delight. How did I get here?

He was lying under a blanket in his underwear. Except I don't remember getting undressed, he thought. Someone must have undressed me. Although who knows, maybe I took off my own clothes. If I still have my shoes on, I did it myself . . . He rubbed one foot against the other. Aha, so my feet are bare. Crap, my hands are itchy . . . what's the deal with these bumps, stupid bedbug-filled hotel . . . I'm going to move out. But when was I in the boat? . . . Oh, the bedbugs are probably Pavor's fault . . . He suddenly remembered Pavor and sat up, but felt nauseous and had to lie back down on his back. It's been a long time since I got this shit-faced . . .

Pavor . . . Silver Trefoil . . . When was all that? Yesterday? He grimaced and scratched desperately at his left hand. Is it morning or nighttime right now? Morning, probably . . . Or maybe evening. Golem! he remembered. Golem and I polished off a whole bottle. Straight. And before that, I polished off half a bottle with the beanpole. And before that there was other booze, too. Or was that yesterday? Wait, is it today or yesterday right now? I should get up and drink some water, etc. . . . No, he thought stubbornly. I have to figure things out first.

Golem was talking about something interesting, he decided I was drunk and wouldn't understand, so he could speak frankly. And I really was drunk, but if I recall correctly, I understood everything he said. But what was it I understood? . . . He rubbed the back of his hand furiously against the woolen blanket. Hard times are coming . . . No, that's the Book of Pavor . . . Aha, here's the Book of Golem: They have their whole lives ahead of them, but all we have ahead of us is them. And genetic disease . . .

Well, sure, sounds plausible. It had to happen sometime. Maybe it's been going on for a while already. A new species arises inside our own and we call it a genetic disease. The old species is adapted to the old conditions, and the new one to other ones. In the past, we needed strong muscles, fertility, resistance to cold, aggression, and something we might call "street smarts." We still need all that in the present, although it's mostly inertia. You can waste a million people using your street smarts, with little in the way of meaningful results. That's for sure—we've tried it enough times to know. Who was it that said if we removed only about a couple dozen people from history . . . all right, a couple hundred . . . that we would immediately return to the Stone Age? Even if it was a couple thousand . . . What people are those? Quite different people, my friend.

But yeah, why not: Newton, Einstein, Aristotle—all mutants. Of course, the environment wasn't always so favorable, and it's entirely possible that the vast majority of those mutants died without ever finding out who they were, like that boy from the Karel Čapek story . . . Of course, they're special: no street smarts, no normal human needs . . . Or is that just an illusion? Maybe the spiritual side is so hyperdeveloped that everything else is invisible by comparison. Eh, unlikely, Victor said to himself. Didn't Einstein always say that the best job of all is lighthouse keeper? Which already sounds . . . But it would be interesting to imagine, actually, how *Homo super* is born in our day. A great topic . . . Dammit, my arms are unbelievably itchy . . . It'd be great to write a utopia in the style of Orwell or Bernard Wolfe. Of course, it's hard to picture what a proper *Homo super* looks like: the huge, bald skull, the feeble little arms and legs, the impotence—it's all so banal. But yeah, some detail like that would need to be included. Or in any case, a displacement of normal desires. No need for vodka, for any special grub, for luxuries of any kind, and even women they'd need only for serenity and to improve concentration. He's the picture of efficiency: all he needs is a private office, a desk, some paper, a bunch of books . . . a tree-lined avenue for peripatetic pondering, and in exchange he produces ideas . . . But that's not a utopia at all—he'd be snapped up by the military, end of story. They'd create a secret institute, shove all the *supers* in there, put a guard out front, and that'd be it . . .

Groaning, Victor stood up and walked barefoot across the cold floor to the bathroom. He twisted the tap as far as it would go and slaked his thirst luxuriantly without turning on the lights. The very thought of turning on the lights frightened him. Then he returned to bed and scratched himself for a while, cursing the bedbugs. It really is great fodder for fiction: a secret institute, guards, spies . . . the patriotism of Clara, patriotic cleaning lady . . . ugh, it's all so cheap. The difficulty is to imagine their work, their ideas, their capabilities . . . that's above my pay grade . . . And impossible to do, as a rule. A chimpanzee can't write a novel about humans. How can I write a novel about a human being with no needs besides spiritual ones? Of course, I can convey something about it. The atmosphere. The state of unending creative ecstasy. The feeling of one's own omnipotence and independence . . . freedom from neuroses, total fearlessness . . . Man, to write something like that, you'd have to get absolutely twisted on acid . . . And really, from an ordinary person's point of view, the emotional sphere of a *super* looked like pathology. Illness . . . Life is the disease of matter; thought is the disease of life. Spectacle disease, he thought.

And suddenly, everything fell into place. So that's what Golem meant! thought Victor. They're all smart and exceptionally talented . . . So what can we conclude? We can conclude that they're not people at all. Zurzmansor wasn't just putting one over on me. So it's already begun . . . You really can't hide anything, he thought with satisfaction. Much less something like this. I'm going to go see Golem—enough of his prophecies. They probably told him quite a bit . . . Dammit, this is the future, that same future that thrusts its tentacles into the heart of the present! All we have ahead of us is them . . . He was seized with feverish excitement. Every second was historic; it was a shame he hadn't realized it yesterday, because yesterday, and the day before, and a week before, every single second had also been historic . . .

He leaped up, turned on the light, and, grimacing from the pain in his eyes, started fumbling around for his clothes. He failed to find them, but then his eyes got used to the light, and he grabbed his pants, which were hanging on the headboard, and suddenly caught sight of his arm. His arm was covered up to the elbow with a red rash and deathly white lumps, some of which had been scratched bloody. The other arm looked the same. What the hell, he thought, chilled to the bone, because he already knew what it was. He had already remembered: skin changes, rashes, nodules, and possibly pus-filled boils. The pus-filled boils had yet to make an appearance, but still, he dropped his pants and sat down on the bed in a cold sweat.

It can't be, he thought. Not me too. Could it really be? . . . He gingerly stroked his bumpy skin, then closed his eyes and, barely breathing, listened to his body. His heart pounded loudly and slowly, the blood rang faintly in his ears, his head felt enormous and empty. There was no pain, no cottony weight in his brain. Idiot, he thought, smiling. What am I hoping to notice? It must be like death: a second ago you were a human, and then, an atomic fraction of a second passes, and now you're a god, but you don't know it, and you never will, the same way an idiot doesn't know he's an idiot, the same way a clever man, if he's really clever, never knows it . . . It must have happened while I was asleep. In any case, before I fell asleep, the essence of the clammies was quite nebulous to me, whereas now I see it in sharp relief, and I got there with bare logic without even knowing it . . .

He laughed out loud with joy, stood up, and, stretching his muscles, walked up to the window. That's my world, he thought, looking through the soaking-wet windowpane, drenched with rain, and then the windowpane disappeared, and somewhere far below the city, frozen with horror, finally drowned in the rain, followed by the enormous, soaking-wet country, and then everything shifted and floated away, and all that remained was a little blue ball with a long blue tail, and he saw the vast porridge of the galaxy, hanging crooked and dead in the shimmering abyss, the snatches of glowing matter, tightly bound with force fields, and the bottomless, lightless pits, and he stretched out a hand and submerged it in the puffy white nucleus, and felt a light warmth, and when he closed his fist, matter passed through his fingers like soapsuds. He laughed again, gave his mirror image a flick on the nose, and tenderly stroked the bumps on his swollen skin.

"This deserves a celebratory drink!" he said out loud.

There was still a little gin left in the bottle; poor old Golem couldn't finish it, poor old pseudoprophet . . . Not because his prophesies are false, but because he's just a talking marionette. I'll always love you, Golem, thought Victor, you're a good man, a clever man, but you're still only a man . . . He poured the remaining gin into a glass and dumped it down his throat with a practiced motion—and, before he could swallow it, rushed to the bathroom. He vomited. Dammit, he thought. How vile. In the mirror, he saw his face—crumpled, a little saggy, with unnaturally large, unnaturally black eyes. Well, that's it, he thought, that's it, Victor Banev, you drunken braggart. No more drinking and belting out songs for you, no more laughing at nonsense, no more silly jabbering with a wooden tongue, no more fighting, no more hooliganism or rowdiness, no more scaring passersby, no more arguing with the cops, no more quarrels with Mr. President, no more barging into nighttime bars with a clamoring crowd of young fans . . .

He returned to bed. He had no desire to smoke. He had no desires at all, everything made him nauseous, and he felt sad. The feeling of loss, mild at first, barely noticeable, like the touch of a spider's web, grew larger; gloomy rows of barbed wire rose up between him and the whole world, which he had loved so much. Everything has its price, he thought, no one gets anything for free, and the more you got, the more you had to pay—you pay for the new life with the old one . . . He scratched his hands furiously, not noticing that he was tearing off the skin.

Diana walked in without knocking, threw off her raincoat, and stopped in front of him, smiling, seductive. She raised her arms to straighten her hair.

"I'm cold," she said. "Any chance I can warm up?"

"Yeah," he said, barely noticing what he was saying.

She turned off the light, and now he couldn't see her, just heard the key turning in the lock, the sound of buttons being undone, the rustle of her clothing, her shoes hitting the floor, and then she was next to him—warm, smooth-skinned, fragrant, and all he could think about was that this was the end of everything: endless rain, gloomy houses with sieve-like roofs, alien strangers in wet black clothes with wet neckerchiefs over their faces . . . there they are, removing their neckerchiefs, their gloves, and then their faces, placing them in special cabinets, and their hands are covered in pus-filled boils—anguish, horror, solitude . . . Diana pressed against him, and he put his arms around her, by sheer force of habit. She was the same as ever, but he had changed; he couldn't do anything anymore, because he didn't need anything.

"What's wrong, baby?" Diana asked, gently. "Had a few too many?"

He carefully removed her arms from around his neck. Fear overwhelmed him. "Wait," he said. "Wait."

He got up, felt around for the switch, turned on the light, and stood with his back to her for a couple of seconds, not daring to turn around, but then he did, finally. No, she was lovely. She was probably even more beautiful than usual—she was always more beautiful than usual, but tonight she looked like a painting. It aroused his pride in humanity, his admiration for the perfection of the human form, but nothing else. She looked at him, and then apparently took fright, because she sat up quickly, and he could see her lips moving. She was saying something, but he couldn't hear.

"Wait," he repeated. "It can't be true. Wait."

He was dressing with feverish haste and kept repeating, wait, wait, but he wasn't thinking of her anymore, she wasn't the important thing here. He dashed out of his room and tried Golem's locked door. It took him a second to think of where to go next, and then he sprinted downstairs, to the restaurant. I don't want it, he kept repeating, I don't want it, I never asked for this.

Thank God Golem was in his usual spot. He was sitting there, one arm bent at the elbow over the back of his chair, examining his glass of cognac in the light. Dr. R. Quadriga, for his part, was red faced and aggressive, and when he caught sight of Victor, he said—loud enough for the whole room to hear, "Those clammies. Bastards. Away."

Victor collapsed in his armchair, and Golem, without saying a word, poured him some cognac.

"Golem," said Victor. "Oh, Golem, I've caught the disease!"

"Douching!" proclaimed R. Quadriga. "Me too."

"Have a little cognac, Victor," said Golem. "Don't get so excited."

"Go to hell," said Victor, staring at him in horror. "I have spectacle disease. What do I do?"

"All right, all right," said Golem. "Just take a drink." He raised a finger and called out to the waiter: "Soda water! And more cognac."

"Golem," said Victor in despair. "You don't get it. I can't. I'm ill, I tell you! I caught it! It's not fair . . . I didn't want it . . . You told me it wasn't contagious . . ."

Horrified at the thought that he was being too incoherent, that Golem couldn't understand him and just thought he was drunk, Victor stuck his arms into his face, overturning the glass of cognac, which rolled off the table and fell to the ground.

Golem initially recoiled, then looked closer, bending forward, grasped Victor's hands by the fingertips, and began examining the scratched-up, lumpy skin. His fingers were cold and hard. This is how it ends, thought Victor, the first doctor's exam, followed by more exams and falsely hopeful promises, and calming potions, but in time he'd get used to it, there wouldn't any more exams, and they'd take him to the leprosarium, cover his mouth with a black rag, and it'd all be over.

"You eat any wild strawberries?" asked Golem.

"Well, yes," Victor said obediently. "Regular ones, actually."

"Like five pounds of them, I bet," said Golem.

"What do strawberries have to do with anything?" screamed Victor, tearing his hands away. "Do something! It can't be too late. It's only just started—"

"Stop screaming. Those are hives. An allergic reaction. In the future, avoid shoving quite so many strawberries down your gullet."

Victor still didn't understand. He gazed at his hands and mumbled: "But you said it yourself . . . bumps . . . rashes . . ."

"Bedbugs also cause bumps," said Golem didactically. "You have a reaction to certain foods. And more imagination than brains. As is the case with most writers. You—a clammy? Please."

Victor felt himself coming back to life. It's OK. The words drummed over and over again in his head. It's all OK, I think. If it's really OK, I don't know what I'll do. I'll quit smoking . . . "You're not lying, are you?" he said piteously.

Golem smirked. "Drink some cognac," he offered. "Usually it's contraindicated with allergic reactions, but you should have some. You really do look terrible."

Victor accepted a glass from him, shut his eyes tight, and drank. Hey, not bad! A little nausea, but that's probably the hangover. It would pass. And so it did.

"My dear writer," said Golem. "A few bumps on the skin do not an architect make."

The waiter came by with some cognac and soda water. Victor sighed, deeply and freely, inhaling the familiar ambiance of the restaurant, smelling the wonderful smells of tobacco smoke, pickled onion, slightly burned oil, and grilled meat. Life had come back to him.

"My friend," he said to the waiter. "A bottle of gin, lemon juice, ice, and four portions of lampreys to room two sixteen. And quickly! . . . You alcoholics," he said to Golem and R. Quadriga, "can go to hell, for all I care—I'm off to see Diana!" He could have kissed them.

Golem said to no one in particular, "Poor beautiful duckling!"

For a second, Victor felt regret. The memory of unbelievable missed opportunities rose rapidly to the surface, then disappeared. But then he laughed, pushed back his chair, and headed toward the exit.

9. FELIX SOROKIN

"WHY DO YOU KEEP PLAYING THE HORN, YOUNG MAN?"

And again I had a dream full of powerlessness and despair. I dreamed that, with a blast of cannon thunder, all my windows and doors suddenly flung themselves open, and a stiff breeze blew everything I'd written right out of the Blue Folder and down into a sixteen-story abyss illuminated by smoldering red light. I could see the pages whirling, flickering, and tumbling as the wind carried them away, and nothing was left in the Blue Folder, but I knew I still had time to run downstairs, to catch and gather the pages, rescuing at least some fraction of them, except my feet felt rooted to the ground and the hooks holding me over my terrace had burrowed deep into my body. "Katya!" I shouted, and burst into tears of despair, and awoke to discover that my eyes were dry, that I had cramps in both feet, and that my side hurt unbearably.

I spent some time just lying there under the lighted rectangles on my ceiling, patiently wiggling my feet to get rid of the cramp, my thoughts flowing lazily in no particular order. I was thinking that, after all, I was very unwell, and that I'd have to heed Katya's exhortations and check myself into the hospital for observation . . . Then everything will grind to a halt, everything will stop, and my Blue Folder will shut for a long time . . .

It also crossed my mind that it might be good to have it typed in duplicate, and to give Rita a copy for safekeeping . . . Although, on the other hand, she's no spring chicken, either—something's not right with either her kidneys or her liver . . . It's entirely unclear: I just can't imagine how, or where, or who I could possibly ask to hold the manuscript for me. It had to be someone who would both keep it safe and not stick their nose in it . . .

Because it's entirely possible that this dream I just had is prophetic: I won't be able to finish anything, and that stiff breeze will scatter the contents of my Blue Folder across ditches and dumps. Not a single sheet will remain to be placed inside the machine in order to determine its MPRN . . .

And no sooner had I remembered the MPRN (randomly, by association, according to the principle of irony and pity) than the solution presented itself, as clear and dry as a mathematical formula: it's not the value of the work that they're determining there; what they're doing is predicting its fate!

That's what he kept trying to tell me, my mirthless friend from yesterday! The Maximally Probable Reader Number includes everything! Print runs, quality, popularity, the writer's talent—and the reader's talent, too, by the way. You could write the most sublime work of genius and the machine will still give you bubkes, because your genius work isn't going anywhere, and the only people who will read it will be your wife, your close friends, and maybe an editor acquaintance, and that's where its road into the wider world will end: *You get it, don't you, old man . . . Only don't misunderstand me . . .*

What a clever, crafty little machine! And what a fool I'd been to bring it my reviews, the contents of my wastepaper basket. I sat up, hugging my knees. That's what he was driving at. And that's why he'd all but made a future appointment with me. What he meant was the essential, the real. He wanted to give me a chance to really understand where I stood, to figure out if I needed to keep struggling or whether, like so many before me, it made more sense to stop trying, full stop, and start trying to make a buck . . .

These thoughts chilled me, raising goosebumps on my skin, and I pulled my blanket over my shoulders, feeling a sudden and terrible urge to smoke.

What a scary little machine. Terrifying, even. What in God's name did they want it for? Of course, humankind has craved to know the future since time immemorial—it's a perennial dream, like a flying carpet or seven-league boots. Czars, kings, and emperors were willing to pay a pretty penny for foreknowledge of the future. But if you think about it, that principle held on one essential condition: that the future be pleasant. Because who wants to know about a future that's unpleasant? Like, say I go to Bannaya with my Blue Folder, and the machine says to me in a human voice, "Looks like you're in deep shit, Felix Alexandrovich. All you get is three readers, so suck it up . . ."

I threw the blanket aside and began fumbling for my slippers with my feet.

Now it's impossible for me *not* to go back to Bannaya! I had to know . . . But why? Why did I need to know that my life, my life's work, if you got right down to it, had all been in vain? But on the other hand, why did it all have to be in vain? And if it *was* in vain, what did that mean? Am I not the same person who longs to entrust the Blue Folder to someone who will prevent the sweaty, prying nose of some Bryzheikin or Gagashkin from getting anywhere near it? To be fair, though, sweaty, prying noses are in a different category: Bryzheikin is one thing, but the reader's another. After all, what I do isn't masturbation—I write for others, not to please myself. Of course, I'd been ready to accept, from the very beginning, that the Blue Folder would never be published in my lifetime. It's the same old story; I'm neither the first nor the last. But the thought of it just perishing, falling into oblivion, dissolving in time without a trace . . . No, that I could never accept. Sure, it's stupid. But I just couldn't. That's what's scary about it!

Such were the thoughts that occupied my mind as I washed up, made my bed, and cooked breakfast. It was half past six, but there was no way I could go back to sleep, or even lie down in bed. I was practically shaking with nervous tension, with the desire to do something immediately, or at least come to some sort of decision.

It's amazing how deeply convinced we've become that manuscripts don't burn. And yet they do—and how! Practically to a crunchy crisp! It's chilling even to guess at the sheer number that perished without ever coming into public view . . . I don't want that fate for my creation. Even if that's the fate in store for it, I'd rather not know . . . No wonder, no wonder my mirthless friend spoke in riddles—he could have said straight out what he meant, but he must have figured that if I didn't guess it myself, then bless my simple heart. And if I did, then I wouldn't have a choice: I'd show up, draft in hand, ready to find out . . .

And somehow, unconsciously, I ended up sitting at my desk, with the Blue Folder open wide in front of me, my fingers moving of their own volition to transfer each sheet carefully from the right side to the left, smoothing the pages out as I went, evening out the quite substantial stack. And I felt suddenly very bitter that, late last night, I'd reread the very last of the existing lines. It would have been nice if today, right now, in my moment of doubt and panic, as I inexorably approached a fork in the road—it would be nice if I could read that final, still unknown, still unwritten line, followed by the words THE END. Then I could say, with a clear conscience, "That's all philosophy, gentleman—and now, feast your eyes on this!" and wave the Blue Folder in their faces.

And so unbearable was the wish to bring that much-desired moment closer that I hurriedly unsheathed the typewriter, inserted a clean sheet of paper, and typed out:

> The clock showed quarter to three. He stood up and flung the window open. It was pitch black outside. Still standing at

the window, Victor finished his cigarette, threw the butt into the night, and rang the concierge. An unfamiliar voice answered.

I took my hands off the keys and scratched my chin. As always, when I try to take the work by storm, with sheer enthusiasm and inspiration, everything jams up.

Over the next half hour, all I did was insert the phrase "and rain glittered in the darkness" after the words "pitch black." This was no way to accomplish anything serious. The way to accomplish something serious was, for example, to book a stay at the Writers' Guest House in Murashi. Before going this route, one must screw up one's courage, completely abandon worldly vanity, and cut off all paths to retreat. One must know for damn sure that the voucher has been paid up for the full amount of time, and that there is absolutely zero chance of getting one's money back. As for inspiration—forget it! Nothing but mechanical, slave-like, exhausting daily labor. Like a machine. Like a horse. Five pages before lunch, two pages before dinner. Or four pages before lunch, but then you have to do three pages before dinner. No cognac. No chatting with friends. No appointments. No meetings. No phone calls. No scandals or birthday jubilees. Seven pages a day, and after dinner you can sit around in the billiard room, talk sluggishly with friends and semifriends among your writerly brethren. And if you stay strong, if—God forbid!—you don't fall into self-pity and exclaim, "Dammit, don't I have the right, just once a week . . ." then, in twenty-six days, you'll come home like a successful hunter, arms and legs numb from fatigue but in high spirits and with a bag stuffed full of game . . . Whereas at the moment, I hadn't yet invented the game that was supposed to go inside my bag!

At 8:30 sharp, the phone rang, but it was not Lyonya the Schizo. Actually, I couldn't tell who it was. The phone breathed at me; it listened closely to my irritated cries of "Hello?" "Who is it?" "Hang up!" And then I heard the dial tone.

I threw down the receiver, tore the page I'd been typing out of the typewriter in disgust, shoved it in the very back of the folder, and covered the typewriter back up. It was getting lighter outside, and another blizzard had started. Once again, I felt stabbing pains in my side and lay down. I'm definitely a choleric. Just a second ago I was shaking with agitation, feeling like there wasn't anything more important in the world than my Blue Folder and its fate in eternity. And now I'm lying here like a squashed frog, with no need of anything eternal, except maybe peace.

My side hurt, and an overwhelming weakness pressed down on me. I was paralyzed with self-pity, and I began to remember, gutlessly surrendering to memory, the way you surrender to a faint when you can no longer endure . . .

She occupied a tiny room in apartment 19, who knows by what rights. She was a first-year student at the Leningrad Polytechnic Institute, and she was around nineteen years old. Her name was Katya, and as for her last name, F. Sorokin didn't know it then and never will. Not in this life, anyway.

F. Sorokin had just turned fifteen; he'd started the ninth grade and was a tall and handsome young man despite his rather protuberant ears. When the boys arranged themselves by height in physical education, he was third after Volodya Pravdyuk (killed in '43) and Volodya Zinger (now a big boss in the aviation industry). When he first met Katya, they were the same height, but by the time they were separated by the Separator of All Unions, Katya was already half a head shorter.

F. Sorokin had seen her a couple of times before they got to know each other—either on the stairs or at the house of Anastasiya Andreyevna, but she failed to evoke any personal or manly feelings in him at the time. At the time, he was a pissant and a simpleton, that tall and handsome young man named F. Sorokin. The gulf between a university student and a schoolboy seemed unbreachable; the tedious and fruitless fondling in which he was then engaged with Lyusya Neverovskaya (now the widow of an admiral, a pensioner, and, I believe, already a great-grandmother) had erected an impenetrable barrier between his longing and all the other breasts and thighs out there, and plus, the going wisdom was that before draining your testicles, you first had to sneak into enemy camp and then kill or capture alive both Hitler and Mussolini (Hideki Tōjō being unknown to F. Sorokin at the time), placing their severed heads at the feet of the beloved.

That the little student Katya set her sights on a schoolboy could probably be explained by one or another psychiatric principle. It's quite normal for pubescent boys of fifteen to attract older women, but then again, what do I know about psychiatry? On the other hand, who would dare claim that the romance between Katya and F. Sorokin was unique? F. Sorokin wouldn't dare. (He is biased, however.) Only later, after two or three months, would Katya confess to F. Sorokin—simply and calmly—that she'd fallen in love with him at first sight, after their very first chance encounter on the stairs or in the vestibule. It's possible she wasn't telling the truth. But F. Sorokin was flattered.

In their case, the following factor was also at play: about a year and a half before they met, something bad had happened to Katya. At the time, she was in the tenth grade, living in some tiny town outside Leningrad (Kolpino? Pavlovsk? Tosno?). One day, she was assigned class monitor duty and stayed late to clean up. Suddenly, two of her classmates showed up, grabbed her, wrapped her head in their jackets, and shoved her down on the floor between the desks. They didn't get anywhere—maybe they were scared, or maybe just inexperienced. All they managed to do was soil her belly and legs with their copious gunk and run away. Katya was still a virgin. Physically. But what about in her mind?

To be fair, by the time she fell in love with F. Sorokin, she'd become a woman. She never said who'd been her first, and it never occurred to him to ask.

One hot day in early September, F. Sorokin came home from school and went to apartment 19 to pick up his key from Anastasiya Andreyevna. He didn't find Anastasiya Andreyevna herself, but only a note that said she'd left the key with her housemate Katya. He found Katya's door in a hallway plunged into semidarkness and crammed with all kinds of junk. He knocked, and the door immediately swung open. And he saw her. And was shaken to his core.

When all is said and done, the ends justify the means. What's more, they say that all's fair in love and war. Of course, she'd been waiting for him and was ready. But F. Sorokin was not. Later he realized that if there'd been even a little more (a little more what?), he would have either run like hell or fallen into a dead faint . . .

I stood up, whimpering and moaning, looked under the sofa, and extracted, from the furthest and darkest corner, the cigarette butt I'd been thinking about for an entire year. I took it to the kitchen and lit up, standing at the window, and felt briefly surprised at how little effect the tobacco smoke had on me, as if I were inhaling not smoke but warm, scented air . . .

Katya was a skinny little thing, narrow-shouldered and narrow-hipped, with round, protruding breasts. She was wearing a baggy gray robe of the kind you find in orphanages. She took F. Sorokin silently by the hand and led him into her garret, then went off to shut the door, quietly but firmly, and locked the bolt. Then she returned to F. Sorokin and began to gaze at him, her arms at her sides. Her robe was hanging open, and beneath it was bare skin, but all F. Sorokin noticed at first was how flushed she was from forehead to chest. The rest came later. What a sight for his pissant pubescent eyes, which had previously beheld the female nude only in prints of Rubens paintings! Well, those and the pornographic pictures displayed to him by Borya Kutuzov (blasted to bits by a shell in August of '41).

After that, they met regularly, if not quite every day. Precisely on the appointed date, at the appointed hour on the dot, F. Sorokin would bound noiselessly up the stairs to the door of apartment 19. Usually this would be in the afternoon, at 3:00 or 4:00, immediately after he returned from school. Naturally, he never rang or knocked. The door would open. Katya, wearing her orphanage robe with nothing underneath, would grab his hand, lead him into her room, and they'd shut themselves inside and drink their fill of one another, greedily and hastily, and some twenty minutes later, F. Sorokin, as noiseless and careful as a brave on the warpath, would flit out into the half-darkened hallway, automatically feeling for the bolt in the door, and find himself in the stairwell. They spoke little, and only in whispers, and for the entirety of their monotonous but unbelievably eventful love story, they never managed to spend more than a half hour in each other's presence.

Their story really was unbelievably eventful—for F. Sorokin without a doubt, and probably for Katya, too. No sooner would he start down the stairs from apartment 19 than F. Sorokin would begin to pine. Within a day or two, the pining would give way to tense impatience. The appointed hour would strike, and everything inside him would tremble with feverish joy and burgeoning fear—what if their tryst couldn't take place? (This sometimes happened.) Then came the tryst itself—and immediately afterward the pining, the impatience, the joy and the fear, followed by another tryst. And so it went, week after week, through fall, winter, spring, and finally the accursed summer of '41. And not once did F. Sorokin tire of Katya, not once before a tryst did he wish for it not to take place. In all likelihood, the same was true for her.

Interestingly, during this same ninth-grade year, F. Sorokin was successfully tackling higher mathematics and spherical trigonometry alongside Sasha Aronov (died of starvation in January of '42), constructing telescope after telescope, working his tail off in the hobby workshops at the House of Entertaining Science, and, last but not least, effortlessly handling his schoolwork. And continuing his platonic romance with Lyusya Neverovskaya, and, after the New Year, embarking on a flirtation with Nina Khalyayeva (disappeared after evacuation from Leningrad), plus all sorts of other foolishness and nonsense in the bargain. F. Sorokin lived an active life of study, of science, of public and personal relationships—but not once, under no circumstances, nowhere, and to no one did he breathe a word about Katya.

Sexual passion alone, however crazed, was not the only thing keeping them together; an affair like that could never have lasted as long as it did, or been so constantly accompanied by fits of pining, joy, and fear. By the same token, however, theirs was likely not a love of the romantic type, immortalized in verse. It was a little bit of both: equal parts the pride of a boy possessing a real woman and the grateful tenderness of a girl toward a man who doesn't hurt her or pretend. And also, there was probably a premonition.

Their final meeting occurred in late May, right at the start of exams.

Sometime in the second week of July, F. Sorokin returned from mandatory airfield construction near Kingisepp, all grown up. He'd killed his first man—an enemy, a fascist—and was very proud of that fact. He'd heard through the grapevine that a week earlier, Katya, along with her entire cohort at the university, had been sent to build anti-tank ditches somewhere in Gatchina (or was it Pskov?).

At the end of July, the building management received word that Katya had been killed in an air raid.

Weakness. This is all because of my weakness. I've gone weak today somehow. But why do I always forbid myself to remember this? The name—yes. Katya. Katya. But only the name. Probably because I never loved anyone after that. Since that time, F. Sorokin had numerous one-night stands, two or three long affairs, but not a single love.

The phone rang, and I dragged myself back into my study. It was Rita—at long last, and right on time.

She had just returned from East Nowheresville and desired the company of an intelligent man from the literary milieu. Her voice was clear, joyful, and healthy, and that was wonderful, and I wanted to see her immediately. I asked about her plans for the day, and she said she was in the office until lunch, but afterward she'd hightail it out of there. I rejoiced, and we immediately hammered out a plan: we'd meet at the Club at 1500 hours sharp and unite there in gastronomic ecstasy. That's for a start, I said, businesslike. We'll see, she said, even more businesslike.

That conversation, as one might expect, fundamentally changed my view of my surroundings and of reality in general. My surroundings, previously hostile, now became friendly, while reality ceased to be gloomy and was infused with every possible hue of pink and baby blue. The world outside seemed significantly brighter, while the evil blizzard transformed into a light, even festive flurry. And everything that had besieged me so grimly in the last few days, all those strange and unpleasant meetings, all those frightening statements and omissions, all my suddenly flesh-and-blood problems, which had seemed so abstract until recently, all of the dark hopelessness that had enclosed me like a sinister fence suddenly resolved, retreated upstage left, while the world before me was now emerald green, filled with silvery sunlight and hazy blue sky, with gaily twinkling letters running across it reading WE'LL GET BY! Even my side had almost stopped hurting . . .

As the poet Osip Mandelstam once wrote:

Why do you keep playing the horn, young man?
Why not lie for a spell in a coffin, young man . . .

First things first: I headed to the bathroom and gave myself an extremely thorough shave. Rita cannot abide even a hint of stubble. Then I took a damp cloth to every table and cabinet. Rita cannot abide dust on polished surfaces. I changed my sheets. Rita and I recognize only fresh, crisp, starchy sheets. I thoroughly wiped down all wine and shot glasses, fastidiously holding each one up to the light, and polished all the silverware with a special Lithuanian cleaning paste. I even pulled myself together and washed my tub and toilet. And finally, for an encore, I got out the vacuum cleaner and vacuumed every inch of floor.

While I was doing all this, the phone rang twice. The first time it was Lyonya the Schizo, but I wouldn't let him say even one word after his standard "What's doing?" The second time it was that shy heavy breather from before, and I, feeling frisky, told him that although I greatly appreciated the offer, his help would not be required—I had almost finished my business here and would shortly depart this planet, this time forever.

I have no idea what my shy friend thought of that, but, at any rate, he didn't call again.

I donned my best suit, the one with the pin from my one and only literary prize in the jacket lapel. At quarter to two, I left the house—the idea was to give myself the time to stop by the selection committee and pick up my share of the reading material. Lord preserve and protect me! The elevators weren't working. Like, not at all: both the large and the small one were out of commission.

And instantly my imagination supplied the hilarious image of Rita and me ascending to the sixteenth floor on foot, following a nice big lunch and a nice long walk through snow-covered Moscow. I saw my future self, heart beating furiously and irregularly, taking a break on every single landing, sitting down on benches provided for the purpose, furtively throwing some nitroglycerin down the hatch. And I saw Rita, a beautiful woman, the woman of my heart, my lover, my last woman, tactfully making light conversation, looking down on me with humiliating pity and repeating, "Take your time, take your time, there's no hurry!"

I chased the shameful vision away and started down the stairs. And who do you think I met on the landing between the eighth and seventh floor? Who was speeding upward, taking the stairs two at a time and gripping the railing only lightly with his left hand? Who is he, that rosy-cheeked man whistling a Gershwin tune, holding a heavy bag of groceries in his right hand—special-order groceries, judging by certain signs?

Naturally, it was him! Kostya Kudinov, the poet, the very same poor fellow who, pale and covered in puke, had recently needed to get his poor dying stomach pumped in the Biryulyovo hospital!

"Hiya, old man!" he shouted as soon as he saw me. He was in high spirits. "Great to see you! Are you in a hurry? You should know that I wrote you into my brigade. We'll go to the Baikal-Amur Mainline. Twenty days, fifteen public appearances, chartered flights there and back . . . What do you think of that, eh?"

Truly, today was my lucky day. This might seem strange, but I, an elderly, introverted man who generally avoids meeting new people, a conservative homebody—I enjoy public appearances.

I like standing in front of a packed room, seeing a thousand faces at once, all united in an expression of interest—avid interest, skeptical interest, mocking interest, amazed interest, but always interest. I love to shock them with proprietary secrets, reveal to them various mysteries of publishing, mercilessly disabusing them of various illusions—hoary stereotypes like "inspiration," "epiphany," or "divine spark."

I like answering questions passed up to me as notes, to mock the fools in the audience—subtly, so that not one single son of a bitch, should one happen to be present, could possibly find fault with what I say; I like to walk on the razor's edge, navigating between what I really think and what public opinion believes I *should* think.

And afterward, when it's all over, I like to come down from the stage and stand surrounded by true fans and connoisseurs, autographing copies of *Modern Tales* that have been read well-nigh to pieces, finally conversing on equal terms—no fooling—to argue hard, till we're all blue in the face, feeling fully and delightfully protected from rude outbursts and tactless remarks, no longer worried about making a false step, with people willing to let even obviously stupid remarks go, only because you're the one who made them.

But my favorite place to do all this isn't Moscow or any of the other capitals, be they administrative, scientific, or industrial. What I love most are the distant places out on the edge of civilization, where all those engineers, technicians, operators, all those recently graduated students are starving for culture, for Europe, for something as simple as intelligent conversation.

So of course I told Kostya I was in and started asking when we were flying out, who else was in the brigade, and where to go for the pretrip briefing. I had already stretched out my palm for a farewell handshake, but he suddenly grabbed my thumb, narrowed his eyes craftily, and sang out in coquettish tones, "I never thought I'd say this, but you're a ballsy guy, Felix Alexandrovich! You certainly put one over on them! But don't you think it'll come back to bite you one of these days? Down the line, eh?"

He squinted flirtatiously, holding my hand and swinging my suddenly limp arm from side to side. I could feel my innards recoiling as if from an evil premonition. Perhaps it was because none other than Kostya was speaking these words. I couldn't say. But I immediately realized that it wasn't over, that idiotic story with the . . . whatever it was called . . . that goddamn elixir I myself had invited into my stupid life. Nothing was over—so what if I'd completely forgotten the spy in the reversible black-and-white checked coat, the crucial point was that they hadn't forgotten me. The story continued, and now I'd supposedly made some clever move, put something over on someone, taken some idiotic risk, and eventually it would apparently come back to bite me! Of course it would come back to bite me . . . no doubt about it!

Jesus, Mary, and Joseph! Would that the earth would open up and swallow Kostya Kudinov forever! Him and his mysterious gestures, hints, and half hints. But in another minute, which Kostya filled with squinting, winking, and arm-swinging, it turned out that he was referring to something else entirely.

In early December, an editor friend of mine from *Playboy Moscow* asked me to review a piece by Babakhin, chairman of our housing distribution committee. He gives me the manuscript and says, "Lay into him and don't hold back, it's an internal review, plus Babakhin's about to give our editor a heart attack." The novella really was monstrous, so I laid into it. Hard. Really enjoyed myself. And then, right before New Year's Eve, the housing committee gave Babakhin the boot—and how. Not, of course, because he wrote novellas capable of causing heart attacks even in a man as battle-scarred as *Playboy Moscow*'s editor in chief. No, he got the boot because he "ate the bread of wickedness and drank the wine of theft." And now this idiot, Kostya Kudinov the poet, was imagining that I'd foreseen all this ahead of time and took the risk of denouncing Babakhin back in early December, when it was still possible that things would turn out well for him . . .

Moreover, that idiot, Kostya Kudinov, felt I had acted recklessly, if heroically, for he suspected—not groundlessly, mind you—that the Babakhins of the world never die. They always return, and they never forget.

Who among those alive today would want to be suspected of reckless heroism? But I was so grateful to Kostya for apparently forgetting my adventures with the elixir of life that I just patted him condescendingly on the shoulder and gave him to understand that it was no skin off my nose, that my connections meant I had nothing to fear from any number of Babakhins. Leaving him to ponder the benefits of close friendship with such a significant personage as myself, I resumed my unhurried and, in some sense, even majestic journey down the stairs.

But in the end, I couldn't escape the checked coat. It managed to make itself known, albeit in somewhat surprising fashion.

Exiting the Metro at Kropotkinskaya, I saw next to the tobacco kiosk that greatest of twentieth-century achievements: a red-and-yellow mobile drunk tank. Its back doors were open wide, and two policemen were thrusting a man in a reversible checked coat into its depths. The coat bucked its hind legs against the thrusting, or perhaps it was not so much bucking as seeking a firmer footing. I didn't see his face, or anything else, for that matter—with the exception of a pair of glasses in metal frames. These were carried past me by a third, businesslike policeman, who held them gingerly with two fingers and immediately vanished behind the van. Then the doors swung shut, the engine released a cubic yard of vile-smelling fumes, and the van slowly rolled away. And that was the whole adventure. There was no one around I could ask about what happened; these days, incidents like this one no longer draw a crowd. And so I went on my way.

I entered the Club at quarter till three, as planned. This time, the woman on door duty was not the half-blind Marya Trofimovna, but a youngish pensioner who'd been working there barely a week—and yet she knew everyone already. Or at least she knew who I was. We exchanged greetings, and I let her know I'd be joined by a lady. Then I hung up my coat and trudged upstairs to the office of the selection committee. Zinaida Filippovna, dark of eye and fair of face, was as usual very busy and preoccupied. She pointed me toward a cupboard where union applicants' writing samples lay on three shelves, in separate piles. And to think: only eight of them in total, and already they'd produced such an ungodly number of pages!

"I pulled some manuscripts for you, Felix Alexandrovich," said Zinaida Filippovna, smiling absentmindedly. "You prefer military and patriotic themes, correct? Look in the third pile, there's one called Khalabuyev. I've already put your name down for it."

Pitiful and forlorn was the stack of papers into which the unknown Khalabuyev had distilled his spirit and thoughts. Three skinny issues of *NCO*, neatly bookmarked with little paper tails, and one solitary, equally skinny book from the North Siberian Press: a novella called *Defenders of the Sky*.

Who could possibly have recommended you, Khalabuyev? I thought. What imprudent soul sent you to be eaten alive by us, with your three little stories and your one trifling novella? It's not even a novella, really, just a lightly fictionalized account of life among pilots or rocketeers. You'll hardly be a decent mouthful for our hussars, Khalabuyev—that is, if you haven't taken the time to ingratiate yourself in advance. But even if you have, Khalabuyev, you won't be even half a mouthful for our specialists in medieval French literature! But if, Khalabuyev, you have contrived to insinuate yourself into their good graces, then I commend you—truly, Khalabuyev, you'll go far, and it may very well be that in five years or so, all of us will be beating down your door, begging for the chance to rent a dacha near Moscow.

With a sigh, I put the Khalabuyev under my arm and, politely taking my leave of Zinaida Filippovna, headed straight to the restaurant.

As it happened, though the hour was early and the restaurant not that crowded, there was only one convenient free table, and when I sat down, I found that my neighbor was Vitya Koshelnikov, famous humorist and author of numerous sketches. He was wearing a bow tie and holding an issue of the *Morning Star*, which he perused over a cup of coffee with an unapproachable air.

At the next table over, two ladies of indeterminate age—though quite appetizing in appearance—squawked away, chewing incessantly. They were either "wrives" or "wraughters," to borrow Zhora Naumov's terminology.

As for the table right in front of me, it was occupied by Apollon Apollonovich Vladimirsky, who was treating one of his numerous grand- or even great-granddaughters to a champagne lunch. He noticed me, and we exchanged greetings. He looked exactly the same as when I'd first laid eyes on him almost a quarter century ago. His tiny head, bald as a balloon, rested atop the long, many-folded neck of an iguana; his enormous black eyes were all pupil, no iris; and his loose mouth held chaotically chattering dentures that seemed to have a life of their own. He possessed the smooth gestures of an orchestra director and the sharp, high voice of a man indifferent to the opinion of others. He wore an old-fashioned little suit with too-short sleeves—hailing from the beginning of the twentieth century, no doubt—with blindingly white shirt cuffs. To me, he seemed like an immigrant from an unimaginably faraway, almost textbook past; it was impossible to imagine that this fossil had authored the words to the energetic, zealous, uplifting songs that have been sung at demonstrations and student parties since the days of collectivization.

I sat there, keeping one eye on a random Khalabuyev page and the other on the main doors, where Rita was set to appear any minute. Meanwhile, Apollon Apollonovich, gazing patronizingly at his young relative's steady progress on a steak and driving his recalcitrant shirt cuff back into his sleeve with a series of elegant finger-snaps, declaimed yet another oral memoir to the accompaniment of chaotically chattering dentures.

I'd heard plenty of these memoirs over the last few decades, so today my well-accustomed but absentminded ear noted only the tale's highlights. First came Mayakovsky and his strange relationship with Osip Brik. Then the cameo by Pasternak, who said something comical and was instantly succeeded by A. Fadeyev —already very ill, seen a day before his death. Oh, and now it was the turn of A. N. Tolstoy to show up with his usual jokes: "His Excellency the Soviet Count is off to the Central Committee . . ." Marshak . . . Chukovsky . . . Now Veniamin Kaverin made an appearance at Maxim Gorky's, very young and very arrogant . . . And then Babel stepped onto his brief final path . . . "And when it came time to get our shots, dear heart, just picture it: all the writers scattered—into the bushes and thence into the woods—and the nurses, needles at the ready, went chasing after them, leaving only Mikhail Svetlov standing by the hospital window, saying, 'There they go, butts a-blazing'" . . . Stanislavsky to Nemirovich-Danchenko: "If you're not careful, Vladimir Ivanovich, you're going to end up in the GUM!" . . . Pushkin (that leap into the nineteenth century jolted me out of my reverie) . . . Vissarion Belinsky and his son Joseph Stalin. . .

I glanced over at Apollon Apollonovich. He was inexhaustible. His relative, however, looked rather indifferent to this unique stream of information. Of course, I couldn't exclude the possibility that, like me, she wasn't hearing it for the first time. And at that moment, Apollon Apollonovich said cheerfully, "Ah, speak of the devil—here comes Mikhail Afanasyevich himself! *Comment ça va, Michel?*"

I looked up.

One winter night in '41, I was returning home from the munitions factory during an air raid when a bomb hit a wooden building right behind me. I was lifted into the air, borne peacefully over the metal spikes of a garden fence, and carefully deposited on my back in a deep snowdrift. There I lay, gazing into to the black sky, watching with dull amazement as burning logs sailed slowly and majestically over my head like old-fashioned sailing ships.

It was with this same dull amazement that I now watched my mirthless friend from yesterday—Mikhail Afanasyevich, apparently—taking a diagonal path through the restaurant. He was without his blue lab coat but otherwise looked no different than before—he even wore the same gray suit. I saw his lips moving as he answered Apollon Apollonovich, but he did not notice—or did not recognize—me. Then he continued on toward the old countess's vestibule, where the exit was. And when he disappeared behind the door, I heard, in the deadly silence that follows a horrible explosion, Apollon Apollonovich's creaky voice saying in solemn or perhaps confidential tones, "He's off to the library. Or to the party committee."

I found myself standing up, ready to run after him. Did I have questions for him? Yes, I did. Of course. Did I want to ask his advice? Most certainly. Naturally. Everything I'd figured out this bitter morning rose up in me again like the poisonous brew at the bottom of a witch's cauldron. I felt an acute need to know if I'd understood him correctly before, and if so, what I was supposed to do with my new understanding. That alone would have made running after him worthwhile, but it wasn't even the most important thing.

I suddenly realized who my mirthless friend from Bannaya really was—*which* Mikhail Afanasyevich. It now seemed as obvious as it was unbelievable. This meeting was the perfect ending to my week of phantasmagoric idiocy, over the course of which Whoever Is Supposed to Oversee My Fate had arrayed a panoply of opportunities before me, which I had entirely failed—or simply not wanted—to exploit. And now it was all in the past, trickled away like water through sand, leaving nothing behind but the grubby foam of philistine relief. And this, right now, was my last chance. Possibly the longest shot of all. And maybe it didn't promise me anything over and above my usual bread and butter, but if I let it pass me by, if I sacrificed it for a bowl of solyanka with olives, or even for my perfumed Rita, then I'd be left with nothing, and there would be no further reason ever to open my Blue Folder.

As if in a dream, I heard an imperious, cantankerous voice bleating out, "I refuse to eat this slop, or I'm not a great Russian writer . . ."

And, as if in a dream, I turned my head and saw a long, plump face with a cantankerously curling lower lip, brooding over a steaming plate. And in the next moment it was gone, vanishing behind the bent back of a waiter.

Right then I, now completely alert, saw Rita appear in the restaurant doorway, wearing my favorite sandy-colored suit, and my sight was assailed by light reflecting off her earring as she slowly turned her head, seeking me out in the crowd. I, however, hid my eyes in cowardly fashion and, crouching slightly, ran hastily away, toward the door behind which I had seen Mikhail Afanasyevich disappear. The thought flashed sadly through my mind that I was once again committing an act for which I would later have to apologize and make excuses, but I shooed it away, because that would all come later, whereas right now I had before me a task of immeasurably greater importance.

Mikhail Afanasyevich was not in the offices of the party committee. Tatochka, however, was, banging away on her typewriter. Sprawling in the chair beside her, his perfectly spherical belly liberated from the confines of his blazer, was a red-nosed, red-lipped, and generally rosy satyr, reading dictation off a sheet as though declaiming from a podium: ". . . And we must fight abstraction in literature! It is a necessary and inevitable battle. We must fight abstraction in literature as implacably as we fought it in painting, in sculpture, in architecture . . ."

"And animal husbandry!" I shouted to shut him up.

He shut up, evidently dazzled by this thematic pivot, which gave me just enough time to ask Tatochka, "Was Mikhail Afanasyevich just here?"

"No," she answered, still banging away. "He won't be in today." Then she turned back to the satyr and said demandingly, "'In architecture and animal husbandry.' Continue!"

I found Mikhail Afanasyevich in the journal reading room, sitting in complete solitude and poring over the most recent *Quarterly Warden*. Yes, that *Quarterly Warden*. The one with Valya Demchenko's novella—mutilated, lacerated, triple-amputated, but still alive, indomitably, defiantly alive.

I walked up to him and stopped, not knowing what to say or where to begin. A feeling of overwhelming awkwardness swept over me. I felt confused and ready to leave, but then he put down the journal, looked up at me inquiringly, and immediately smiled. "Ah! Felix Alexandrovich," he said in his quiet, even voice. "Hello. Be so good as to sit down. There is an empty chair just here."

"Is that a quote from Čapek?" I asked, sitting down obediently.

"No, it's Hašek. Now, how may I be of service, Felix Alexandrovich?"

"I see you're well versed in literature."

"It's more than that. I love literature dearly. Good literature, that is."

"And if you have doubts about its quality, do you just stick it into your machine?"

"Good gracious, Felix Alexandrovich! That's somehow unbecoming to me. Although it is my own fault. I misspoke. Of course, there is no 'good' or 'bad' literature. There is only good literature, while everything else is best described as waste paper."

"Exactly!" I continued, pressing on in a kind of sorrowful despair. "As we know from *The Master and Margarita*, 'There is only one freshness—the first—and it is also the last. And if sturgeon is of the second freshness, that means it is simply rotten.'"

He closed the journal (keeping his place with his finger) and gave me a long look. And I returned his look, amazed at his resemblance to the portrait in my little brown volume, amazed that in three months not one of our vapid gasbags had recognized him, and that even I had not managed to recognize him at first sight, back on Bannaya.

"Felix Alexandrovich," he finally said, "I see that you are mistaking me for somebody else. I can even guess who."

"Excuse me, excuse me!" I exclaimed eagerly, because his attempt at evasiveness disappointed and even offended me. "You can't possibly deny—"

"Oh, but I can!" he said, leaning toward me. "It's true that my name is Mikhail Afanasyevich, and people do say I look like him, but think about it: How could I be him? The dead are gone forever, Felix Alexandrovich. And that is as true as the fact that manuscripts burn to ash. However much *he* would like us to believe otherwise."

I could feel sweat flooding my face. I hurriedly took out my handkerchief and wiped it away. My head was spinning, my ears were ringing, my blood pressure had probably climbed sky-high, and I felt like I was in a dream again.

"But let's not delay our business any longer," he continued, taking his finger out of the journal, which he placed on the sofa next to him. "As I expected, you came to the correct conclusion: that my machine determines not the absolute artistic value of a work but only its fate in the foreseeable historical future."

I nodded, wiping away the sweat that had once again poured into my eyes.

"And having figured this out, you had to confront the question of whether it was worth taking the risk and submitting your Blue Folder to be analyzed."

I nodded once more.

"So why don't you and I try to discover what it is you fear, Felix Alexandrovich, and what you might be hoping for. What you fear, of course, is that my machine will reward all your efforts with some pathetic number, as if you had just offered it not your life's work but instead some trashy review you wrote in disgust, just to get it over with, or maybe for a quick buck. And what you're hoping for, Felix Alexandrovich, is a miracle: that my machine will reward you with six or even seven figures, as though you were truly bestowing on the world a New Apocalypse that breaks down all possible barriers to reach its readers . . . But you know quite well, Felix Alexandrovich, that the only miracles that actually happen in our world are crappy ones. So, in sum, you have little to hope for. As for your fears, did you not yourself entomb your folder in the depths of your writing desk—doom it from its very inception, Felix

Alexandrovich, bury it before it had fully seen the light of day? Do you follow?"

I nodded.

"And you understand that all I've done is verbalize your own thoughts?"

I nodded again and said in a voice so hoarse it even momentarily shocked me, "You missed a third option . . ."

"No, Felix Alexandrovich! I did no such thing! I have a pretty good idea of your childish threat of immolation. And so, to punish you for it, I will tell you now of a fourth option, so shameful and ignoble that you haven't even dared to allow it into your consciousness; your terror before it sits somewhere on the very outskirts of your mind, a shriveled, denuded, foul-smelling terror . . . Want to hear it?"

A premonition of that shriveled, outskirt-sitting terror tore at me like a heart spasm until I gasped for air. Yet I was certain that there was nothing he could say that I hadn't thought about before, that I hadn't suffered thinking through thirty-three times already. I gritted my teeth and let the words percolate through the handkerchief pressed against my mouth: "I'd be curious to find out . . ."

He told me. I swear, on my honor, on the life of my daughter Katya and the lives of my grandsons, I had not known ahead of time, nor could I have imagined the things he told me about myself. And it was especially humiliating and shameful because my fourth option was so obvious, so petty, so superficial . . . any normal person would have thought of it first . . . For our Sweet Soviet Boy, for instance, that option is the only one, he knows no others . . . Only people like me, who fancy themselves above it all for no reason whatsoever, puffed up with pride to the point that they don't even sense their own puffed-up-ness, people who imagine God-knows-what about their own scribblings and the blessings they confer on the world—only people like me, in short, are capable of burying that option so deep that they themselves have no idea about it.

How in the world did I, Felix Alexandrovich Sorokin, author of the unforgettable novel *Comrade Officers*, fail to imagine the accursed machine on Bannaya displaying on its screens neither recognition of my world-historical achievements in seven figures nor a proud and lonely number less than five, which would prove that global culture had not yet progressed to the point that it could admit the Blue Folder's contents into its bosom . . . The machine, after all, could spit out a round and robust number like ninety thousand, which would mean that the Blue Folder was happily accepted, happily incorporated into the annual publication plan, and released from the presses to alight on the shelves of neighborhood libraries alongside other stacks of waste paper, leaving neither trace nor memory, buried not in the honorable sarcophagus of the desk drawer but in a crumpled bargain-bin dust jacket.

"Forgive me," he concluded, his voice full of pity. "But I could not leave this option unmentioned, even if I hadn't wanted to give you a slap on the wrist."

I nodded silently. For the umpteenth time. Verily, the celestial demon had utterly broken my pride.

"As for your threat to burn your Blue Folder and consign it to oblivion," continued Mikhail Afanasyevich, "I called it childish, I admit, only in a moment of bad temper. In reality, I find this threat serious, quite serious indeed. But, Felix Alexandrovich! There is not one case in the whole thousand-year history of literature of an author burning his *favorite* creation with his own hands. Yes, people burned their own works, but only those that caused them disgust, or irritation, or shame . . . Whereas you love your Blue Folder, Felix Alexandrovich, you live in it and for it . . . How could you let yourself burn something like that only because you don't know what awaits it in the future?"

He was right, of course. All my threats of burning and oblivion were just a bunch of petulant nonsense . . . And even if I wanted to, how would I go about burning it, given that our building is steam-heated? I gave a nervous giggle—maybe we print so much crap precisely because they stopped putting wood-burning stoves in people's homes.

Mikhail Afanasyevich also laughed, but immediately grew serious again. "Please don't misunderstand me, Felix Alexandrovich," he said. "You came to me for advice and sympathy. To me, the only person you think capable of giving you advice or expressing sincere sympathy. But what you refuse to understand, Felix Alexandrovich, is that you won't get any of that from me—neither the advice nor the sympathy. You refuse to understand that all I see in front of me right now is a sweaty and alarmingly red-faced fellow with a downturned mouth and dangerously clogged arteries, a middle-aged man who is rather worse for the wear, who is not especially clever and certainly not wise, a man burdened with shameful memories and an assiduously repressed fear of physical extinction. Such a man does not evoke sympathy, still less the desire to offer advice. And why should he? Please understand, Felix Alexandrovich, I couldn't care less about your internal struggles, or your spiritual turmoil, or—and please excuse me—your self-regard. The only thing of interest to me is your Blue Folder. I want your novel to be written and completed. But how you do it, at what cost . . . I'm not a literary scholar or your biographer, so none of that is of any interest to me at all, truly. People naturally expect their exertions and sufferings to be rewarded, which is only fair, but there are exceptions: there is and can be no reward for suffering in the service of creation. That suffering *is* its own reward. And that is why, Felix Alexandrovich, you should not expect for yourself either light or peace. You will never get either."

And then it was silent. As though I'd gone deaf. And in that deep silence, a librarian entered with soundless steps, accompanied by two old ladies, who walked up to the book cupboard, talking soundlessly among themselves, opened it, still soundlessly, and began laying out and leafing through some dust-choked bound newspapers. The strange thing was that they seemed not to notice us. They didn't look in our direction once; it was like we weren't there at all.

And in that silence, the pleasant, sonorous voice of Mikhail Afanasyevich began to sound. He was neither speaking nor narrating. No—he was reading aloud from an invisible book.

"The city gazed at them with empty windows—moldy, slimy, disintegrating, as if it had spent many years rotting at the bottom of the sea until it was finally dragged to the surface to be mocked by the sun. And now the sun, having mocked its fill, began to destroy it. Roofs were melting and evaporating; the tin and tile emitted rusty fumes and disappeared before their eyes. Streetlamps broke softly into pieces and dwindled to nothing, kiosks and billboards dissolved into thin air. Everything around was crackling, hissing faintly, and rustling, turning porous and transparent, transforming into drifts of dirt, and disappearing . . ."

Mikhail Afanasyevich fell silent, leaned back in his chair, and closed his eyes. But I had already guessed what he was reading, and why it sounded so familiar. It was not the very end, not the final lines, but now I saw that final picture, and I already knew what the last line would be, after which there would be nothing more, other than the words THE END and possibly the date.

The entire Club restaurant watched as well-known writer Felix Sorokin, author of military-patriotic works, a somewhat overweight but handsome man with silver hair and a lush black mustache, his laureate's pin glinting on his jacket lapel, passed gracefully between the tables, walked up to a lovely woman in an elegant sandy-colored suit, and kissed her hand. And the whole restaurant heard him say clearly, turning to Misha the waiter, "Bring me meat! Any kind of meat. Except dog. I've had enough dog meat, Misha!"

Half the room ignored these strange words, while the other half took them to be a failed joke, and Apollon Apollonovich, shaking his turtle-like head, mumbled, "Odd . . . When did he manage to get so plastered?"

But Felix Sorokin had no intention of joking. And as for getting plastered, he certainly hadn't done so yet—that was still to come. It was just that he was outrageously, inappropriately, and incompetently happy, though he himself couldn't have said why.

10. VICTOR BANEV

EXODUS

A month after war's end, Lieutenant B. received a medical discharge. They pinned a Victoria medal to his chest, then greased his palm with a month's pay and a cardboard box containing a gift from Mr. President: a trophy bottle of schnapps, two tins of Strasbourg-style pâté, two loops of smoked horse-meat salami, and trophy silk underwear to help him along in his family life. Now back in the capital, the lieutenant is of good cheer. He's a competent mechanic who can find work anytime at the same university shop he left to volunteer for the army, but he's in no hurry. He reestablishes old contacts, makes new ones, and in the meantime drinks away all the swag he confiscated from the enemy as reparations.

One night at a party, he meets a woman named Nora, who looks a lot like Diana. Description of the party: scratched-up prewar phonograph records, home-distilled methylated spirit, American canned meat, silk blouses on bare skin, carrots in every possible guise. The lieutenant, jangling his medals, instantly routs the various civilians tirelessly placing seconds of boiled carrot onto Nora's plate, and begins a tactically correct siege. Nora's behavior is odd. On the one hand, she's obviously interested, but on the other hand, she makes clear that he'll be in danger if he gets involved with her. But the ex-lieutenant, all hopped up on methylated spirit, won't listen to reason. They leave the party together and head to Nora's place.

Nighttime postwar cityscape: the occasional streetlamp, pothole-pitted pavements, fenced-in ruins, a half-constructed circus, home to six thousand prisoners rotting under the guard of two invalids, a mugging underway in a pitch-black alley. Nora lives in an ancient three-story house. The stairwell is filthy; the words A German Shepherd Lives Here are written in chalk on one of the doors. As they walk down a long hallway crammed with assorted junk, various squalid persons flee into the shadows. Nora, jangling numerous keys, unlocks a door upholstered with miraculously preserved shiny leather. In the entryway she gives B. one more warning, but B. assumes she's just referring to criminal activity of some sort and so tells her only that back in the day, he went up against tanks on horseback.

Nora's small apartment is anachronistically clean and cozy; there's a huge sofa. Nora looks at the lieutenant with something like pity, briefly leaves the room, and returns, looking extremely seductive, half-empty bottle of cognac in hand. It turns out that they only have half an hour. At the end of the half hour, the satisfied lieutenant leaves, looking forward to many happy returns. By the time he reaches the end of the hallway, two squalid persons from the shadows are waiting for him. Smirking unpleasantly, they block the way and invite him to chat. The lieutenant, wasting no words, begins throwing punches and attains an unexpectedly easy victory.

The squalid persons, knocked off their feet, clarify Lieutenant B.'s position to him, crying and giggling. The ex-lieutenant has just beaten up his own—they're all in it together now. Nora is not just any seductive lady, Nora is queen of the capital's bedbugs. It's curtains for you now, Mr. Officer, see you in the Atacama, that's where we meet every night. Go on home, and when you can't stand it anymore, come on down, we're open all night . . .

On the western end of the capital, in an apartment building next to the chemical plant, lives Titular Councillor B. plus numerous children. Ostentatiously detailed and boring description of the hero's life circumstances: three small rooms, kitchen, entryway, a threadbare wife, five greenish kids, and a robust old mother-in-law who's just arrived from the countryside. The chemical plant stinks, plumes of multicolored smoke hang over it day and night, and poisonous fumes kill the trees, turn the grass yellow, and cause wild and weird mutations in the local insects.

For several years now, the titular councillor has been waging a campaign to get the plant under control: furious demands to higher-ups, tearful petitions to every branch of government, scathing op-eds in all the papers, fruitless attempts to organize protests at the plant gates. The plant, however, remains unassailable. Police posted to the nearby embankment are poisoned and drop dead; pets die en masse; whole families abandon their apartments and become homeless; an obituary for the plant director, gone before his time, appears in the paper. The wife of Titular Councillor B. also dies; his children take turns suffering from bronchial asthma.

Down in the cellar in search of firewood one evening, B. discovers a trench mortar, preserved there since the days of the Resistance. That very night, he drags the thing up to the attic and opens a roof window. He sees the plant spread out before him: in the harsh floodlight, workers rush around, loaded carts roll along, poisonous yellow and green smoke billows through the air. I will kill you, whispers the titular councillor, and opens fire. He doesn't go to work the next day, or the day after. He neither sleeps nor eats; all he does is crouch beside the roof window and shoot. He takes an occasional break to give the mortar's barrel a chance to cool down. He is deafened by the noise of shots and blinded by gunpowder smoke. Sometimes he feels like the chemical stench has lessened, and then he smiles, licks his lips, and whispers, I will kill you. Then he falls down, exhausted, and when he wakes up, he sees he's out of mortar blasts. Only three remain. He uses them up, then sticks his head out the window.

The vast courtyard in front of the plant is littered with craters; broken windows gape; dark hollows pit the sides of the enormous gasholders. The ground is furrowed with a complex system of trenches, through which workers move in short bursts. Carts glide along, faster than ever, the drivers of the vehicles shielded by metal sheets. Occasionally the wind chases plumes of poisonous smoke away from the brick wall of the plant administration building, exposing freshly painted white lettering: ATTENTION! DURING SHELLING, THIS SIDE IS ESPECIALLY DANGEROUS . . .

Victor finished reading the final page, lit a cigarette, and looked at the sheet currently inside the typewriter. So far, it contained only a line and a half: "After leaving the editorial offices, journalist B. almost caught a taxi, then changed his mind and went down to the subway." Victor knew exactly what would befall journalist B. next, but he could write no longer. The clock showed quarter to three. He stood up and flung the window open. It was pitch black outside, and rain glittered in the darkness. Still standing at the window, Victor finished his cigarette, threw the butt into the damp night, and rang the concierge. An unfamiliar voice answered. Victor asked what day of the week it was. After a pause, the strange voice informed him that it was Friday night.

Victor blinked, hung up the phone, and resolutely pulled the sheet of paper out of the typewriter. Enough. It had now been two straight days—two days of bent-backed toil, of seeing and talking to no one, of disconnected phone, knocks on the door ignored, no Diana, no liquor, and possibly even no food—just climbing into bed from time to time to dream about the Queen of the Bedbugs sitting on the door frame, waggling her black antennae . . . enough. Journalist B. can wait on the platform for a train flashing a NOT IN SERVICE sign. He's not going anywhere. In the meantime, we'll have a bite to eat—we deserve it, by God.

Victor put away the typewriter and the manuscript, and felt around in the empty minibar. In the end, he chowed down on a stale jam bun, cursing himself bitterly for pouring half a bottle of brandy down the sink to avoid temptation, but happy he'd finally managed to start the cycle of stories he was going to call *Backstage in the Big City*—and the beginning wasn't bad, not bad at all, fully satisfactory, even. Although he'd probably have to rework the whole thing. Strange how he was writing these stories down now, of all times. Why not a year ago, or two, when I first thought of them? Right now I should be writing about the sad sack who thought he was a superman, that's what I should be writing. Which is where I began.

On the other hand, this isn't the first time something like this has happened to me. And if I think hard and remember well, that's how it goes every single time. Which is exactly why it's impossible to write on command. You start writing a novel about Mr. President's youth, but what comes out is a story about a deserted island inhabited by weird apes who subsist not on bananas but on the thoughts of the shipwrecked . . . Here, though, the connection is immediately obvious. But, of course, it's always obvious. You just have to dig a little bit—but who's going to do that when they're craving a drink after two days of abstaining! I'll just mosey on downstairs; the concierge'll have something for me, he always does. Let me just finish this bun . . .

Victor shuddered and stopped chewing. From the black chasm outside his window, through the splashing of rain, came a noise like a hammer striking a wooden board. Shots fired, thought Victor with surprise. He strained his ears for a minute . . .

Well, OK, but what was the author's message in these stories of his? Why resurrect the difficult postwar era, a time when it was still possible to find the odd bedbug or loose woman? Was the author trying to depict the heroism and tenacity of the capital, which, under the leadership of His Excellency— No dice, Mr. Banev! We won't let you! The whole world knows that the owners of chemical production companies whose businesses pollute the air have been fined, according to the explicit decree of Mr. President, in the amount of . . . And that's just in the capital! The whole world knows that, thanks to Mr. President's tireless personal efforts, over one hundred thousand city children attend summer camp outside the city . . . That according to the Table of Ranks, those below the class of court councillor have no right to gather signatures on petitions . . .

Suddenly, the lights went out. "Oho!" Victor said aloud, and the lamp went on again but remained dim. "What the hell is this?" he asked, but the light grew no brighter. Victor waited a minute, then rang the concierge. No answer. I could call the electric company, but then I'd have to find the telephone book, and I have no idea where *that* is, and plus it's time for bed anyway. But first, I need a drink.

Victor stood up and suddenly heard a sort of rustling sound. Someone was dragging his hands over the surface of Victor's door. Then he began thrusting his body against it. "Who's there?" asked Victor, but no one answered. All he could hear was heavy breathing and pounding. Victor felt afraid. The walls, bathed in a reddish half-light, looked alien and odd; far too much shadow had gathered in the corners, and something large, stupid, and nonsentient was rummaging around just behind the door. What can I whack him with? thought Victor, looking around the room, but at that moment whoever was at the door said in a hoarse whisper, "Hey, Banev, you there?" *Idiot*, Victor said under his breath, then went into the entryway and turned the key.

R. Quadriga tumbled into the room. He was wearing a robe, his hair was rumpled, and his eyes rolled wildly. "Thank God, at least you're here," he chattered. "I was about to go insane with fear . . . Listen, Banev, it's time to split . . . Let's go, OK? Let's get out of here, Banev . . ." He grabbed Victor by the shirt and began pulling him into the hall. "Let's go, I can't take it anymore . . ."

"You're nuts," said Victor, tearing himself free. "Go to bed, you dotard. It's three in the morning."

But Quadriga nimbly seized Victor's shirt again, and Victor, to his amazement, discovered that the doctor *honoris causa* was completely sober—he didn't even smell of booze.

"No sleeping," said Quadriga. "We need to flee this accursed place. You see what's going on with the lights? We'll die here . . . We've got to get out of town. I have a car at my villa. Let's go. I'd do it alone, but I'm scared to go outside."

"Hold on, quit pawing at me," said Victor. "Calm down." He dragged Quadriga back into the room, sat him down, and went to the bathroom for a glass of water.

Quadriga immediately leaped up and ran after him. "You and I are the only ones left, everyone else is gone," he said. "No Golem, no doorman, no hotel director . . ."

Victor turned the tap. The pipes growled, producing a few drops.

"You want water?" said Quadriga. "Let's go, I have a whole bottle. But fast. And together."

Victor jiggled the tap. A couple more drops came out, and then the growling stopped. "What's happening?" asked Victor, feeling a chill. "War?"

Quadriga made a dismissive gesture. "What are you talking about? It's time to get away, before it's too late, and he's talking about war . . ."

"Get away how?"

"Real quick," said Quadriga, giggling idiotically.

Victor elbowed him aside, walked out of the room, and headed downstairs to find the concierge.

Quadriga minced along behind him. "Listen," he mumbled. "Let's go through the back . . . All we have to do is get outside, my car's right there. Tank's full, it's all packed up . . . I had a feeling, honest to God . . . We'll just have a nip of vodka and take off, 'cause there's no vodka left here."

The overhead lights in the hall shone dimly, like red dwarfs, but the stairwell was completely dark, as was the foyer—with the exception of a bulb glowing faintly above the concierge's desk. Someone was sitting there, but it wasn't the concierge.

"Let's go, let's go," Quadriga whispered, pulling Victor toward the exit. "Don't go over there, there's a bad thing. . ."

Victor shook Quadriga off and walked over to the desk. "What the hell is going on—" he began, but fell silent.

Behind the desk was Zurzmansor.

Zurzmansor sat in the concierge's seat, writing quickly in a thick notebook. "Banev," he said, without raising his head. "It's all over, Banev. Farewell. And don't forget what we talked about."

"I have no intention of leaving," Victor retorted. His voice cracked. "I'd like to know what's going on with the electricity and water. Are you responsible for this?"

Zurzmansor raised his yellow face. "No," he said. "We're closed, for good. Farewell, Banev." He stuck a gloved hand across the desk. Victor took the hand mechanically, felt it squeezing his own, and returned the squeeze. "That's life," said Zurzmansor. "The future is created by you, but not for you. But you probably already figured that out. Or you will shortly. It's really more your concern than ours. Farewell." He gave Victor a nod and resumed writing.

"Let's go!" Quadriga hissed into Victor's ear.

"This doesn't make any sense," said Victor loudly, his voice carrying across the whole vestibule. "What's going on here?"

He hated that the vestibule was quiet. He hated feeling like a stranger here. He wasn't the stranger, and Zurzmansor had no business sitting at the concierge's desk at three in the morning. And quit trying to scare me, I'm no Quadriga . . . But Zurzmansor didn't hear, or pretended not to hear. Victor shrugged demonstratively, turned on his heel, and headed into the restaurant, pausing in the doorway.

In the restaurant, the floor lamps, the chandelier, and the wall sconces were all dimly glowing—and it was a full house. Clammies sat at all the tables. They were all the same; only their poses differed. Some read, others slept, and many gazed fixedly into space, as if frozen. Bare skulls gleamed; it smelled of medicine and dampness. The windows were wide open, and dark puddles lay across the floor. There was no sound except the splashing of rain from outside.

Golem appeared in front of Victor, looking tense, preoccupied, and aged beyond his years. "What are you still doing here?" he asked, sotto voce. "Leave, you can't be here."

"What do you mean, I can't be here?" said Victor, getting angry again. "I want a drink."

"Shush," said Golem. "I thought you'd already left. I knocked on your door. Where will you go now?"

"Back to my room. I'll just grab a bottle and go back to my room."

"There's no alcohol here," said Golem.

Victor silently pointed at the bar, where rows of bottles gleamed dully.

Golem looked around. "No," he said. "Alas."

"I want a drink!" Victor repeated stubbornly.

But inside, he didn't feel stubborn at all. It was all bravado. The clammies were looking at him. The ones who'd been reading put down their books, the frozen ones turned their skulls in his direction, and only the sleepers continued as they were. Dozens of shining eyes stared at him, as though suspended in the reddish twilight.

"Don't go back to your room," said Golem. "Leave the hotel. Go to Lola's . . . or to the doctor's villa . . . Just make sure I know where you are. I'll come pick you up. Listen, Victor, don't dig in your heels, do what I say. There's no time to explain right now . . . and it wouldn't be appropriate, anyway. Too bad Diana's not here—she'd back me up."

"Where is Diana?"

Golem turned around again, this time to look at the clock. "At four . . . or five . . . she'll be at the Sunnygate bus station."

"And where is she now?"

"She's busy."

"I see," said Victor, and also looked at the clock. "So four or five at Sunnygate." He very much wanted to leave. He couldn't bear to keep standing there, the center of attention at this quiet gathering.

"Or maybe six," said Golem.

"Sunnygate . . ." Victor repeated. "Is that where the good doctor's villa is?"

"Exactly," said Golem. "Go to the villa and wait there."

"I feel like you're just trying to get rid of me," said Victor.

"Yes," said Golem. He looked at Victor's face with sudden interest. "Victoire, don't you want to get the hell out of here, even a little bit?"

"I want to go to sleep," said Victor carelessly. "I haven't slept for two nights." He grabbed Golem by a shirt button and led him out into the lobby. "Fine, I'll leave," he said. "But what's all the pandemonium? You having some kind of convention?"

"Yes," said Golem.

"Or is it a rebellion?"

"Yes," said Golem.

"Or maybe it's war?"

"Yes," said Golem. "Yes, yes, yes. Get *out* of here."

"Fine," said Victor. He turned to leave, but paused. "What about Diana?" he asked.

"She's in no danger," said Golem. "And neither am I. None of us are in any danger. Until six, at any rate. Or seven."

"I'm holding you personally responsible for Diana," said Victor quietly.

Golem took out his handkerchief and wiped the back of his neck. "I'm personally responsible for everything," he said.

"Oh yeah? I'd prefer it if you were just responsible for Diana."

"I'm sick of you," said Golem. "So very sick of you, you beautiful duckling. Diana is with the children. She is in absolutely no danger. Now leave. I have work to do."

Victor turned around and walked toward the stairs. Zurzmansor was no longer at the concierge's desk; all that remained was the light bulb, glowing faintly above a thick, oilcloth-bound notebook.

"Banev," R. Quadriga called from some dark corner. "Where are you going? Let's get out of here!"

"I can't just schlep around in the rain in my bedroom slippers!" Victor replied in irritation, without turning around. They've kicked us out, he thought. Out of the hotel . . . and maybe city hall, too. Maybe they've even kicked us out of the city. What's next?

Back in his room, he changed quickly, pulling on his raincoat. He kept tripping over Quadriga, who tailed him doggedly. "Is that how you're planning on going, in your robe?" asked Victor.

"It's warm," said Quadriga. "And I've got another one at home."

"Idiot, go get dressed."

"No way," said Quadriga firmly.

"Let's go together," offered Victor.

"No. I won't go together either. Don't worry, I'll be fine . . . I'm used to it."

Quadriga was like a poodle desperate for a walk. He jumped up and down, tried to catch Victor's eye, breathed heavily, plucked at his clothes, ran back and forth between Victor and the door. It was pointless to try to persuade him of anything. Victor threw him his old raincoat and paused, thinking. He took his identification papers and money out of the desk, distributed them among various pockets, shut the window, and turned off the light. Then he gave himself over to Quadriga's will.

The doctor *honoris causa*, head thrust forward, dragged him rapidly through the hallway, down the service stairs, past the dark, cold kitchen, and finally shoved him outside, into the pouring rain and pitch-black darkness, following close behind.

"We made it out, thank God!" he said. "Now let's run for it!"

But Quadriga was no good at running—he kept losing his breath; moreover, it was so dark that they had to move almost by feel, grasping at walls as they went. All they could discern in the light of dimmed streetlamps and the reddish glow filtering through the gaps in this or that curtained window was a general direction. The rain hammered on incessantly, but the streets were not entirely deserted. Here and there people spoke in hushed tones or an infant mewled; several heavy trucks drove by, and a cart clanged its metal rims against the pavement as it passed. "They're all fleeing," Quadriga mumbled. "Everyone's making a run for it, except us slowpokes."

Victor didn't answer. His feet squelched in the muck, his shoes were wet, lukewarm water dribbled down his face, and Quadriga clung to him like a tick. It was all so stupid, so ill advised; they would have to haul ass across the entire city with no end in sight.

He tripped over a water spout and something crunched underfoot. Quadriga released his arm and instantly gave a tearful howl, loud enough for the whole city to hear: "Banev! *Where are you?*"

As they fumbled around in wet darkness, searching for each other, a window banged open above their heads and a muffled voice inquired, "So what's going on?"

"It's dark, damn it all to hell . . ." answered Victor.

"Exactly!" the voice agreed enthusiastically. "And the water's out . . . Good thing we managed to fill up a basin."

"What's going to happen next?" asked Victor, holding back Quadriga, who kept lunging forward.

After a pause, the voice said, "They'll announce an evacuation, probably . . . What a life!" And the window slammed shut.

They dragged themselves onward. Quadriga, grabbing on to Victor with both hands, stammered out some story about waking up from sheer horror, going downstairs, and seeing that witches' sabbath . . . They stumbled onto a truck, groped their way around it, and promptly ran into a man carrying some kind of load. Quadriga screamed again.

"What's the problem?" asked Victor, enraged.

"He hit me!" Quadriga informed him indignantly. "Right in the liver. With his crate."

The sidewalks were littered with crookedly parked cars, discarded fridges and cupboards, whole thickets of potted plants. Quadriga managed to collide with the open door of a mirrored wardrobe, then got tangled in a bicycle. Victor felt fury welling up inside him.

As they approached yet another intersection, someone shined a flashlight in their faces, arresting their progress. Soldiers' helmets gleamed wetly as a brusque, southern-accented voice announced, "Military patrol. Papers, please." Quadriga, naturally, had none, and immediately began shouting that he was a doctor, a laureate, that he personally knew— The brusque voice said contemptuously, "Civilians. Let 'em through."

They crossed the city square. Cars clustered in front of the police station, headlights ablaze. Goldshirts rushed around senselessly, their coppery firemen's helmets blazing; there was a din of incomprehensible commands. It was clear that this was the very center of the panic. Car lights illuminated a short stretch of road near the station; after that, it was dark again.

Quadriga had quit mumbling; now he only wheezed and whimpered. He fell several times, dragging Victor down with him. They wallowed in the mud like pigs. Victor had gone completely numb and stopped swearing, a cloud of submissive apathy enveloping his brain. It was time to walk and walk, today and tomorrow, to shove aside unseen strangers, to lift Quadriga up by the collar of his waterlogged robe again and again. The one thing they couldn't do was stop. Nor could they turn back, under any circumstances.

Something kept nagging at him, something from the distant past, something shameful, bitter, unbelievable, except that back then the world was in flames, and the streets roiled with human hash, and there was thunderous crashing in the distance, and behind him was horror, and all around were deserted houses with windows crisscrossed with paper, and ash flew in his face, and the stench of burning paper, and a tall colonel in an elegant hussar's uniform stepped onto the porch of a stately mansion festooned with an enormous flag, removed his cap, and shot himself, and as for us—ragged, bloodied, sold out and betrayed, still wearing hussars' uniforms but no longer hussars, almost deserters—we started whistling, and shrieking with laughter, and whooping, and someone hurled his broken saber at the colonel's corpse . . .

"Halt!" whispered someone in the darkness, poking Victor in the chest with something awfully familiar. Mechanically, Victor put up his hands.

"How dare you!" squealed R. Quadriga, hiding behind Victor's back.

"Quiet, you," said the voice.

"Help!" bellowed Quadriga.

"Quiet, idiot," Victor told him. "I surrender," he said into the rifle-poking, heavy-breathing darkness.

"I'll shoot!" the voice warned, sounding frightened.

"Please don't," said Victor. "Can't you see we've surrendered?" His throat had gone dry.

"Get undressed, now!" the voice commanded.

"Excuse me?"

"Take off your shoes, your raincoat, your pants . . ."

"What for?"

"And hurry up!" the voice hissed.

Victor took a closer look, put down his hands, stepped to one side, grabbed the assault rifle, and shoved it upward. The robber squeaked and jerked away, but for some reason did not shoot. The two of them grunted with effort as they wreslted for the gun. "Banev! Where are you?" Quadriga howled in desperation. Judging by how he felt and smelled, the man with the assault rifle was a soldier. He was still putting up a fight, but Victor was much stronger.

"All right," Victor said through clenched teeth. "It's over. Now don't move, unless you want a punch in the face."

"Lemme go!" the soldier hissed, resisting weakly.

"What do you want my pants for? Who are you?"

But the soldier just panted. "Victor!" Quadriga howled, already far away. *"Aaaaah!"* A car turned the corner, its lights briefly illuminating a familiar, freckled face and, beneath a soldier's helmet, eyes rounded with fear. Then it sped away.

"Hey, I know you," said Victor. "What are you doing robbing people? Give me the gun."

The soldier obediently wriggled out of the strap, snagging his helmet on it in the process.

"So, what did you want with my pants?" asked Victor. "You deserting?"

The soldier only sniffed. He was a nice little soldier, all covered in freckles.

"Cat got your tongue?"

The soldier burst into high-pitched weeping, punctuated with short howls. "I don't care anymore," he mumbled. "They'll shoot me no matter what. I left my post. I ran away from my post, I abandoned it, where am I supposed to go now . . . Won't you let me go, sir? I didn't mean to, I'm not a bad guy, don't turn me in, please!"

He sniffled, and blew his nose, and, there in the darkness, probably wiped his snot on the sleeve of his overcoat—pitiful, like all deserters, frightened, like all deserters, and ready for anything.

"Fine," said Victor. "You'll come with us. We won't turn you in. We'll find you some clothes. Let's go, only don't fall behind."

He walked out in front, and the soldier dragged himself along behind him, still sobbing.

They found Quadriga by following his doglike howling. Victor was now strapped with an assault rifle, the sobbing little soldier clinging convulsively to his left arm and the quietly howling Quadriga clutching his right. It was like a fever dream. Of course, he could always return the unloaded gun to the boy and send the snot-nose packing. No, I'd feel bad for the snot-nose, and plus, the gun could still come in handy . . . We've consulted the people, and the consensus is that to disarm at this stage would be premature. The gun could prove useful in impending battles . . .

"Quit whining, both of you," said Victor. "The patrols will come running."

They quieted down, and five minutes later, when the dim lights of the bus station came into view, Quadriga pulled Victor toward the right, mumbling happily, "We made it, thank the sweet Lord . . ."

Quadriga had, of course, forgotten the key to his gate back at the hotel, in his pants pocket. Cursing, they climbed the fence; still cursing, they spent a while fighting their way through a tangle of wet lilac, nearly fell into the fountain, finally made it to the driveway, knocked down the front door, and tumbled into the great room. They flicked a switch, bathing the room in crimson half-light. Victor collapsed into the nearest armchair. While Quadriga ran around the house in search of towels and dry clothing, the little soldier quickly stripped to his underwear, balled up his uniform, and hid it under the sofa. This done, he calmed down some and stopped sobbing. Then Quadriga returned, and the three of them spent some time toweling off with savage intensity and changing.

Chaos reigned in the great room. Everything was overturned, scattered, and encrusted with mud. On the floor, books commingled with dusty rags and rolled-up canvases. Glass crunched underfoot, squeezed-out tubes of paint littered the ground, the television stared with its blank, rectangular eye, and the table was crammed with dirty dishes full of rotten leavings. All that was missing was excrement in the corners, and maybe that was there, too—it was hard to tell in the dark. The stench was so strong that Victor could not resist opening a window.

Quadriga began straightening up. First he lifted one end of the table and tipped it, sending everything crashing to the floor. Then he wiped the surface down with his wet robe, ran off somewhere, and returned with three beautiful old-fashioned crystal goblets and two square-shaped bottles. Bouncing around with impatience, he uncorked them and served up the liquor.

"To our health," he mumbled incoherently, then grabbed his goblet and pressed it greedily to his lips, rolling his eyes in anticipatory pleasure.

Victor gazed at him, smirking condescendingly and massaging a damp cigarette.

An expression of umbrage mixed with indescribable surprise suddenly appeared on Quadriga's face. "Not here, too . . ." he said in disgust.

"What's wrong?" asked Victor.

"It's water," the little soldier chimed in timidly. "Plain, cold water."

Victor took a sip. Yes, it was water—pure, cold, possibly even distilled. "What is this swill, Quadriga?" he asked.

Quadriga, without a word, grabbed the second bottle and took a swig. His face contorted. "My God!" he said, spitting, then hunched over and tiptoed out of the room. The little soldier gave another sob. Victor looked at the bottles: they were labeled Rum and Whisky. He took another sip from his goblet: water. Nothing to see here, just some run-of-the-mill devilry. Somewhere, the floorboards creaked of their own volition, and their flesh crawled under someone's intent gaze.

The little soldier buried his head in Quadriga's enormous sweater, sticking his arms deep inside the sleeves. He stared unblinkingly at Victor with round eyes. Victor asked, hoarsely, "What are you looking at?"

"What are *you* looking at?" whispered the little soldier.

"Nothing—why do you keep staring at me?"

"But why are you . . . You're scaring me . . . Stop it . . ."

Calm down, Victor said to himself. Nothing bad is happening. They're *supers*. This is nothing . . . they can do anything, my friend. Anything at all. Water into wine and back again. They just sit there in the hotel restaurant, transforming things. They're pulling the rug out, cracking the foundations. Goddamned teetotalers . . . "Scared?" he asked the little soldier. "Chickenshit."

"But it's scary!" said the little soldier, perking up. "You don't get it. You have no idea what I went through back there . . . There you are, on night watch, and all of a sudden one of 'em flies out of the zone, looks at you from way up there, then keeps going . . . One of the corporals even crapped himself . . . Our captain kept saying, get used to it, do your duty, you swore an oath, blah blah . . . But how can you get used to that shit? The other day some guy flew up, perched on the roof of the guardhouse, and just stared . . . with those inhuman eyes, you know, all red and glowing, and he's reeking of sulfur like you wouldn't believe . . ."

The little soldier pulled his hands out of his sweater sleeves and crossed himself.

Quadriga returned from the bowels of the villa, still hunched over and walking on tiptoe. "It's all just water," he said. "Victor, let's get the hell out of here. The car's in the garage, the tank's full, we can just get in and go—what do you say?"

"Don't panic," said Victor. "We can always cut and run . . . But you do what you want. I'm not going anywhere, but you be my guest. And take the kid with you."

"No," said Quadriga. "I'm not going without you."

"Then stop freaking out and bring us some grub," Victor commanded. "Your bread hasn't all turned to stone yet, has it?"

It had not. Similarly, the canned foods were still canned foods, and not bad ones at that. As they ate, the little soldier told them about the fear he'd endured in the last two days, about the flying clammies, about an invasion of earthworms, about little children who'd become adults in two days, about his friend, Private Krupman, a nineteen-year-old kid, who was so scared he shot himself just to get a discharge . . . He talked about how they tried to warm their dinner up in the guardhouse, how it sat on the stove for two hours but nothing happened, so they had to eat it cold . . . And then today I go on guard duty at eight in the evening, it's raining cats and dogs, and hailing, and out over the zone I see unauthorized lights, some kind of inhuman music's playing, and a voice is speaking—on and on and on, but you can't understand a single word. And then these whirlwinds roll out of the steppe and into the zone. And right then the gates opened, and out bursts Mr. Captain in his car. I didn't even have time to snap to attention, all I could see was Mr. Captain himself in the backseat, no cap, no raincoat, just whaling on the back of the driver's neck and screaming, "Go, you son of a bitch! Go!" Something snapped inside me, like someone said run, skedaddle, or you'll be sorry. So I skedaddled. I didn't take the road, I went right across the steppe, over the ravines, I even almost got stuck in a swamp once, lost my poncho out there somewhere . . . it was new, they'd just issued them the day before . . . anyway, I finally made it to the city. But it's swarming with patrols. They almost caught me once, and then they almost caught me again, but eventually I made it out to here, to the bus station, and I see all these people running . . . civilians can get through no problem, but when they see one of us they go, show us your pass. That's when I made up my mind . . .

Having finished his story, the little soldier curled up in his chair and fell immediately asleep. Quadriga, painfully sober, started in again about getting the hell out, right away. "This one," he kept repeating, pointing at the sleeping warrior with his fork, "this one gets it . . . You're a blockhead, Banev, an incorrigible blockhead. How can you not feel it, for me it's like a physical sensation, like something's pressing on me from the north. You have to believe me . . . I know you normally don't, but believe me now, I've said from the beginning: we can't stay here . . . Golem's taking you for a ride, that big-nosed drunk . . . Use your head: right now, the roads are clear, people are waiting for daylight, and then they'll clog up the bridges like back in '40 . . . You're a stubborn blockhead, Banev, you've always been that way, ever since we were in school . . ."

Victor told Quadriga to either go to sleep or get lost. Quadriga, sulking, finished his can of food and climbed onto the sofa, wrapping himself in a mohair blanket. For some time he tossed and turned, groaning and mumbling apocalyptic warnings, then quieted down. It was four in the morning.

At 4:10 the lights flickered and went out. Victor stretched out in his armchair, covered himself with random dry rags, and lay quietly, looking out into the darkness and straining his ears. The little soldier whimpered in his sleep; the utterly run-down doctor *honoris causa* gave an occasional snore. Somewhere out there—at the bus station, most likely—engines roared and hysterical voices shouted incoherently.

Victor tried to make sense of it all and concluded that the clammies had finally fallen out with General Pferd, kicked him out of the leprosarium, recklessly transferred their headquarters to the city, and convinced themselves that just because they know how to turn water into wine and scare the bejesus out of people, they'd be able to take on a modern army . . . or not even the army—the police alone can handle them. Idiots. They'll destroy the city and perish themselves, leaving people without a roof over their heads. And as for the children . . . They'll wipe them out, the bastards! And for what? What do they want? Is it really just another power struggle? Some supermen you are . . . So clever, so talented, but really you're the same shit as the rest of us. Yet another New World Order, and the newer the order, the worse it gets—that's common knowledge.

Irma . . . Diana . . . He jerked into motion, fumbled for the phone in the dark, and picked up the receiver. The line was dead . . . Yet again they're jockeying for some prize, while we who don't care about either side and want only to be left alone are yet again forced to leave our homes, to trample each other, to flee, to save ourselves, or worse, we're forced to pick a side without knowing or understanding anything—taking your word for it, or not even your word, just whatever scraps you happen to throw our way—forced to shoot at each other, chew each other to bits . . .

The usual thoughts in the usual vein. I've been down this road a thousand times. That's how I was raised, sir. From my very childhood. It's either hip, hip, hooray or go to hell—I don't believe any of you. Your problem, Mr. Banev, is that you're incapable of thought. Which is why you always oversimplify things. No matter what complex social movement you encounter on your path, you first and foremost strive to oversimplify it, by either believing or not believing in it. If you believe, it's to the point of slack-jawed, puppy-squealing loyalty. And if you don't, then you'll passionately spew your bile at all ideals, whether true or false.

Perry Mason used to say, evidence itself isn't the problem, the problem is wrong interpretations. The same is true of politics. Those crooks interpret things in their own favor, and we simpletons take up their ready-made interpretations. Because we're incapable of thought, we can't and won't think for ourselves. And when it's Banev's turn to interpret, Banev the dummy, Banev who's never in his life seen anything other than political crooks, he immediately makes a mess of things again, because he's illiterate, he's never been taught to think for real, and therefore, naturally, he can't interpret things except in crooked terms. New world, old world . . . and automatically, the old associations click into place: *neue Ordnung, alte Ordnung* . . .

Well, fine, but even dumb old Banev wasn't born yesterday—he's been around the block a few times, learned a thing of two. He's not totally senile, not yet. What about Diana, Zurzmansor, Golem? Why should I believe that fascist Pavor, or that snot-nosed village teenager, or the anomalously sober Quadriga? Why am I so sure it'll end in blood, pus, and filth? So the clammies have rebelled against Pferd. Fantastic! Good riddance to him. It's about time . . . And as for the children, the clammies won't let them come to harm, that wouldn't be like them . . . And after all, they're not rending their garments or calling anyone to national consciousness or disinhibiting any atavistic instincts . . . As we know, "it is precisely that which is most natural that least of all befits a man"—right you are, Bol-Kunatz, good man . . .

This could very well be a new world without a new world order. Is it scary? Is it alienating? Sure! But that's how it has to be. The future is created by you, but not for you. Look how hard I freaked out when I thought I'd broken out in "spots of the future"! How desperate I was to get back to my lampreys and my vodka . . . It turns my stomach to remember it . . . and yet, that's how it had to be. Yes, I hate the old world. I hate its stupidity, its indifference, its ignorance, its fascism. But what am I without all that? It is my bread and my water.

Cleanse the world around me, make it look the way I'd want it to, and it's all over for me. I'm no good at singing praises—I hate that stuff—and there won't be anything left to criticize or hate. And that means melancholy, and death. The new world is austere, just, clever, perfectly clean—but it's not a world that needs me; I'm a zero in it. It needed me when I fought for it . . . and if it doesn't need me, then I don't need it either. But if I don't need it, why am I fighting for it? I miss the good old days when you could spend your life building a new world, then die in the old one. Acceleration, man, it's everywhere . . . But how can you fight *against* without fighting *for*? Well, what can you do. If you set out to chop down a forest, the branch you're sitting on is bound to get the worst of it . . .

Somewhere in the enormous empty world a little girl was crying, saying over and over again in sorrow: I don't want it, I don't want it, it's unfair, it's cruel, who cares what's "best," then let it be not-best, let them stay, let them exist, is there really no way to make it so they can stay with us, it's so stupid, so pointless. Hey, that's Irma, thought Victor. "Irma!" he cried, and woke up.

Quadriga was snoring. The rain outside had ceased, and it seemed to be getting lighter. Victor brought his watch up to his eyes. The glowing hands showed quarter till five. A damp, freezing draft was blowing in—it was time to get up and close the window—but now he was finally warm, he didn't feel like moving, and his eyelids closed of their own accord.

In his dream, or in reality, cars drove somewhere nearby, one after the other, dragging themselves down the dirty, broken road, through the endless, dirty field, under a dirty gray sky, passing crooked telephone poles with severed wires, past a crushed cannon with upraised barrel, past a charred kitchen chimney, now a perch for well-fed crows, and the freezing damp penetrated the canvas and his coat, and he desperately wanted to sleep, but sleeping was out of the question, because Diana was supposed to drive by, and the gates are shut, the windows dark, and she thought I wasn't here and drove on, but he jumped out of the window and hightailed it after her, shouting till his veins nearly burst, but right then the tanks were passing, rumbling and rattling, and he couldn't hear his own voice, and Diana drove off to the river crossing, where everything was burning, where she'd be killed and he'd be left alone. And at that moment he heard the angry, piercing shriek of a bomb headed right for his skull, his very brain . . . Victor leaped into a ditch and tumbled out of his chair.

It was R. Quadriga who was shrieking. He was lying contorted in front of the open window, gazing into the sky and shrieking like a woman. The room was lit, but not by daylight: symmetrical rectangles of light lay on the trash-littered floor. Victor ran up to the window and looked out. The moon hung in the sky—icy, small, and blindingly bright. There was something unbearably terrifying about it; at first, Victor couldn't understand what it was. The sky was still shrouded in clouds, but into those clouds someone had cut an even, precise square. And at the center of that square was the moon.

Quadriga was no longer shrieking. He had gone limp from the effort and could only produce a faint creaking noise. Victor took a ragged breath and suddenly felt enraged. What the hell did they think this was—a circus? Who do they take me for?

Quadriga was still creaking. "Stop it!" barked Victor hatefully. "What, you've never seen a square before? You call yourself a painter, you shit . . . you bootlicker . . ." He grabbed Quadriga by his mohair blanket and shook him as hard as he could.

Quadriga tumbled to the floor and lay still. "All right," he said, his voice surprisingly clear and sharp. "I've had it." He got up on hands and knees and then, lunging like a sprinter, dashed away.

Victor looked out the window once more. In his heart of hearts, he had hoped he was hallucinating, but everything was exactly as before, and he could even make out a minuscule star in the square's lower right-hand corner, nearly drowned in moonlight. Everything stood out clearly: the wet lilac bushes, the inactive fountain with its allegorical marble fish, the latticework gates, and beyond them, the black ribbon of road. Victor sat on the windowsill and, stilling his trembling fingers, lit a cigarette. He noted in passing that the little soldier wasn't there anymore; he had either run off or hidden under the sofa and died of fright. At any rate, his assault rifle was where he'd left it.

Victor, comparing this pathetic hunk of metal with the force that had made the perfectly square hole in the clouds, gave a hysterical giggle. Some magicians they are. No, even if the new world perishes, it'll take the old one down with it . . . Still, it was nice to have an automatic weapon on hand. It's stupid how much calmer it makes me feel. On second thought, it's not stupid at all. It's obvious that there's an epic hustle brewing. It's in the air. And during an epic hustle it's best to stay on the sidelines with a weapon on hand.

An engine roared outside, and Quadriga's enormous, endlessly long limousine (a personal gift from Mr. President for selfless service with loyal brush) swerved around the corner. Seemingly unconcerned with direction, it careened toward the gate, crashed through it, and flew out onto the road. Turning, it disappeared from view.

"So he took off after all, the bastard," mumbled Victor, not without envy. He climbed down from the windowsill, slung the rifle over his shoulder, draped his raincoat on top, and called out to the little soldier. No answer. Victor looked under the sofa but saw only the gray, balled-up uniform.

Victor lit another cigarette and went outside. In the lilac bushes, next to the crumpled gate, he found an oddly shaped but very comfortable bench that, crucially, had an excellent view of the road. He sat down, crossed his legs, and wrapped himself tightly in his raincoat. At first the road was empty, but soon a car drove by, followed by a second and a third, and he knew that the epic hustle had begun.

The city had burst like a boil. The first to hustle off were the elite: the magistrates and the police, industry and trade, the court and the tax bureau, treasury and education, the post and the telegraph, the goldshirts—every last one. Off they went, shrouded in billows of exhaust, tailpipes rattling, bedraggled and aggressive, vicious and stupid, con men and strivers, servants of the people, fathers of the city, amid the howling of sirens and the hysterical moaning of car horns; the roar on the road was deafening, and the pus kept squeezing and squeezing out of the boil, and when it was done, the blood began to flow. Now the people were in motion: in trucks crammed to capacity, in lurching buses, in overburdened cars, on motorcycles and bicycles, in wagons and on foot, bent under the weight of bindles, pushing handcarts, empty handed, gloomy, silent, lost, leaving behind their homes, their bedbugs, their simple pleasures, their settled lives, their past and their future. And after the people came the army, in retreat. An all-terrain vehicle filled with officers crawled by, then an armored personnel carrier, then two trucks bearing soldiers and our world-famous field kitchens. The procession closed with a half-tracked armored car, its machine guns pointing backward.

It was growing lighter, the horrible square had melted away, and the clouds dissolved. Day was dawning. Victor waited for fifteen minutes or so—for no one, as it turned out—before venturing outside the gate. The pavement was strewn with dirty rags; someone's crushed suitcase lay on the ground, an obviously good suitcase, dropped there by some big boss; there was also a wagon wheel, and a little distance away, on the shoulder, was the wagon itself, with an old, threadbare sofa and a ficus inside. In the middle of the roadway, directly in front of the gate, lay a solitary galosh. The road was deserted. Victor looked in the direction of the bus station. There was nothing there either, neither car nor person.

Birds began chirping in the gardens, and then the sun came up—the sun that Victor hadn't seen for a fortnight, and the city for a couple of years. But now no one was around to see it. Then the air once again filled with the buzzing of a motor, and a bus appeared from around the bend. Victor stepped aside. It was the Kindred Spirits. They sailed past him, turning their blank, indifferent faces in unison to look at him. And that's that, thought Victor. I'd love a drink. Where could Diana be?

He began walking slowly toward the city.

The sun followed him on the right, now hiding behind the roof of a house, now peeking out from the gaps between buildings, spraying warm light through the branches of the half-rotted trees. The clouds had vanished, leaving the sky amazingly clear. A light mist rose from the soil. It was perfectly quiet, and Victor began to notice odd, almost inaudible sounds that seemed to come from underground—a sort of faint crackling, rustling, and swishing. Then he got used to it, and it slipped his mind. He was filled with a remarkable feeling of peace and security. He walked along as though drunk, looking constantly up at the sky. When he reached the Prospekt of the President, a jeep pulled up beside him.

"Get in," said Golem.

Golem was gray with fatigue and somehow depressed, and next to him sat Diana, also tired but still beautiful, the most beautiful of all tired women.

"The sun," said Victor, smiling at her. "Look at that sun."

"He won't go," said Diana. "I warned you, Golem."

"Why not?" Victor asked in surprise. "I'll go. But why hurry?"

He couldn't resist looking up again. He looked at the empty street behind, then at the empty street ahead. Everything was flooded with sunlight. Out in some field somewhere, refugees were staggering along, the retreating army clattering along beside them, the authorities were hustling away, traffic jam followed traffic jam, the air was thick with curses, and meaningless commands and threats were being screamed. Meanwhile, in the north, the conquerors were advancing on the city. Here, though, was an empty strip of peace and security, a few square miles of emptiness, and in that emptiness were three people and a car.

"So, Golem, is the new world a-comin'?"

"Yeah," said Golem, scrutinizing Victor through puffy lids.

"So where are your clammies? Traveling on foot?"

"There aren't any clammies," said Golem.

"What do you mean—no clammies?" asked Victor. He looked at Diana. Diana silently turned away.

"There are no clammies," repeated Golem. His voice sounded choked, and Victor suddenly got the impression that Golem was near tears. "You can assume they never existed. And never will."

"Well, great," said Victor. "Let's go for a walk."

"Are you coming or not?" Golem asked wearily.

"I would," said Victor, smiling. "But I have to stop by the hotel, grab my manuscripts . . . and have a look around . . . You know something, Golem, I like it here."

"I'm staying, too," said Diana abruptly. She climbed out of the car. "What would I do there?"

"But what will you do here?" asked Golem.

"I don't know," said Diana. "But now I have no one left except this man."

"Look, fine," said Golem. "Maybe he doesn't get it. But you do."

"He needs to take a look around, though," Diana objected. "You can't expect him to just up and leave without looking around."

"Exactly," Victor chimed in. "What the hell am I good for if I don't take a look around? That's my whole job—looking."

"Listen, kids," said Golem. "Do you even know what you're signing up for? Remember what they told you, Victor: if you want to do any good, be on your own side. Your own side!"

"I've spent my whole life on my own side," said Victor.

"You won't be able to do that here."

"We'll see," said Victor.

"Jesus," said Golem. "It's not like I wouldn't rather stay, too! But you've got to use your head! You have to be able to distinguish between *wants* and *musts* . . ." It was as though he was trying to convince himself. "What can I say . . . stay, if you must. Have a great time." He turned on the motor. "Where's the notebook, Diana? Ah, there it is. I'm going to keep it. You two certainly won't need it."

"Yes," said Diana. "That's what he would have wanted."

"Golem," said Victor, "why are you running away? You wanted this world."

"I'm not running," said Golem, sternly. "I'm driving. I'm leaving a place that no longer needs me for a place that still does. Not like you. Take care."

And he drove away. Diana and Victor, holding hands, began walking up the Prospekt of the President into the empty city, toward the advancing conquerors. They didn't speak but only breathed deeply of the unusually fresh, clean air, squinted in the sun, smiled at each other, and felt no fear. The city gazed at them with empty windows. It was amazing, this city: moldy, slimy, disintegrating, all covered in evil-looking stains, as if devoured by eczema, as if it had spent years rotting at the bottom of the sea until it was finally dragged to the surface to be mocked by the sun. And now the sun, having mocked its fill, began to destroy it.

Roofs were melting and evaporating; the tin and tile emitted rusty fumes and disappeared before their eyes. Entire chunks of wall thawed away, dissolved, revealing scratched-up wallpaper, peeling bed frames, wobbly furniture, and faded photos. Streetlamps broke softly into pieces and dwindled to nothing, kiosks and billboards dissolved into thin air. Everything around was crackling, hissing faintly, and rustling, turning porous and transparent, transforming into drifts of dirt, and disappearing. In the distance, the town hall tower changed shape, its outline blurring before merging into the blue sky. For a little while afterward, the tower's ancient clock hovered in the air, a thing apart, but then it too vanished . . .

There go my manuscripts, thought Victor joyfully. Around them the city was no more, except for an occasional stunted hedge or patch of green grass. Only in the distance, beyond the fog, could one make out the outlines of buildings, the remains of buildings, the ghosts of buildings, while a little ways from what had once been road, on a stone stoop leading nowhere, sat Teddy, stretching his wounded leg out in front of him. His crutches lay nearby.

"Hiya, Teddy," said Victor. "So you stayed, huh?"

"Yup," said Teddy.

"How come?"

"Eh, screw 'em," said Teddy. "Crammed themselves in like sardines in a can, there was no place to stretch out my leg. So I say to my daughter-in-law: you dumb bitch, what do you need a dish cupboard for? And she starts swearin' at me . . . So I said screw 'em, and stayed."

"Want to come with us?"

"Nah, you go on," said Teddy. "I'll stick around here. I'm no good for walking anymore, and whatever's going to happen can happen to me here."

They walked on. It was getting hot, so Victor let his useless raincoat fall to the ground, shook off the rusty remnants of the rifle, and laughed with relief. Diana kissed him and said "Great!" He didn't object.

They walked on and on under the blue sky, beneath the hot sun, over earth that was already green with new grass, and eventually came to where the hotel had once stood. It hadn't disappeared completely, but now it was a gray cube of rough, coarse concrete, and Victor thought it looked like a monument, or maybe a sign marking the border between the old world and the new.

And no sooner did he think this than a jet fighter slipped soundlessly from behind the concrete slab, Legion insignia on its hull, soundlessly flitted over their heads, and, still soundlessly, U-turned somewhere in the vicinity of the sun and vanished. Only then did a hellish, whistling roar descend on them, striking their ears, their faces, their souls, but Bol-Kunatz was already walking toward them, all grown up, broad shouldered, a sun-bleached mustache on his tanned face, and farther on walked Irma, also nearly grown, barefoot, wearing a light, simple dress and carrying a twig in her hand. She looked in the direction of the jet fighter, lifted the twig as though taking aim, and said, *"Khhkkhhhkh!"*

Diana burst out laughing. Victor looked at her and saw yet another Diana, a totally new one, one he'd never seen before. He'd never even suspected that such a Diana was possible—Diana the Joyous. And then he shook a finger at himself and thought, this is all well and good, but here's the thing—I'd better not forget to go back.

AFTERWORD

BY BORIS STRUGATSKY

The story of how we wrote this novel is unusual and rather complicated, and so, as I set out to tell it now, I'm experiencing some difficulty. I don't know where to begin or how best to order the events in question.

First, the title. We'd invented it long ago, intending it for a completely different work—a short novel "about a man it's dangerous to offend." We'd been thinking about that novel for many years. We came close to writing it many times, only to put it off again, seemingly forever, until finally Arkady wrote it himself, alone, under the pseudonym S. Yaroslavtsev and the title *The Devil Among Men*. That work's initial title, *Lame Fate*, then went to a novel about the Soviet writer Felix Sorokin and his dreary adventures in the world of "developed socialism."

The novel that would become *Lame Fate* was based on a fairly circumscribed idea: at a certain research institute, scientists are rapidly developing a fantastic apparatus called the Mensura Zoili, which is capable of measuring the *objective* value of a work of art.

We took the term *Mensura Zoili* from a little-known short story by Akutagawa; in translation, it means something like "Zoilus's Measure," where Zoilus is the ancient Greek philosopher made legendary by his especially caustic critique of Homer, so that his name eventually became shorthand for the excoriating, merciless, and unfriendly critic in general. In our work diary, the first mention of a piece by that name dates all the way back to November 1971, if you can believe it! Although at that point, we were considering writing a play rather than a novel.

According to that same diary, the very first detailed discussions of a novel, specifically, occurred only in November 1980. After that there was another nearly year-long break, until October 1981. Only in January 1982 did we start workshopping the draft in earnest. By that time, all the crucial situations and episodes had been decided, the plot was complete, and the literary task had been articulated: to depict Mikhail Bulgakov's Master in the 1980s—or, more specifically, not the Master himself but the endlessly talented and remarkably unfortunate writer Maksudov from Bulgakov's *Theatrical Novel*. How would he look, suffer, and create against the background of our slowly unfolding, "stagnant" 1980s? The prototype for F. Sorokin was Arkady himself, both in terms of personal biography and, to a large degree, in terms of fate, while the novel's working title was, at that point, *Dog Meat Peddlers* (which is a line from that same Akutagawa story: "Now that this thing has been invented, all those writers and artists who peddle dog meat and call it mutton—they're all finished!")

We completed the draft by October 1982, which is also when we renamed the novel *Lame Fate* and found an epigraph—a terribly sad and accurate haiku by the early-modern Japanese poet Raizan about the autumn of our years. (People tend not to realize that *Lame Fate* is, first and foremost, a novel about the merciless onset of an old age that brings neither joy nor salvation—it's a "confession of old age," if you will.)

Lame Fate is the second and final novel that we deliberately wrote "for the desk drawer," knowing full well that it had no chance of being published. The magazine version appeared only in 1986, in the Leningrad journal *Neva*. For us, this was the first miracle of intensifying perestroika, a sign of Big Changes to come, a portent of a New Era. It was at that point that we were first forced to confront a very particular problem, which seemed quite isolated in its way, but which nonetheless required a specific and final decision.

The issue was Felix Sorokin's Blue Folder, his darling, his favorite creation, painstakingly hidden away from everyone, possibly forever. When we were first working on the novel, we had, just to keep ourselves oriented, identified the contents of the Blue Folder with our own *Doomed City*, pieces of which we inserted into *Lame Fate* as Sorokin's direct quotations from, or scattered thoughts about, his secret manuscript. Of course, we understood that these brief references to a novel that, from the reader's perspective, didn't exist, were utterly inadequate at giving a full impression of our hero's double life—his real life, in a certain sense. It was clear that, ideally, we would need to flesh this "second" work out fully or at least produce two to three chapters that could be inserted into our main novel, along the lines of the "Pilate" sections of *The Master and Margarita*. But there didn't seem to be a suitable storyline—not even material for a couple of chapters. So at first we decided, with a heavy heart, to sacrifice the first two chapters of *The Doomed City* to this holy cause, putting them into *Lame Fate* as the contents of the Blue Folder. But that meant embellishing one novel (however good) at the cost of destroying another, which we loved tenderly and were carefully preserving for the future (however unattainably distant). Another option was to insert *The Doomed City* into *Lame Fate* IN ITS ENTIRETY, which would solve all our problems at once while simultaneously producing a composite text violating all possible norms of proportion. For in that case, the intertext would be three times longer than the frame text—an awkward solution at best.

It was then that we remembered an old novel of ours: *Ugly Swans*. We'd initially conceived it in April 1966—an incredibly long time ago; a whole age had passed since then—and written it down around the same time. By the early 1980s, it had already lived out its own, very typical fate—the fate of a samizdat manuscript proliferating in thousands of copies, illegally, without the authors' knowledge, published abroad and quite well known to the relevant authorities, who, to be fair, did not hunt it all that zealously, since they'd categorized it as "decadent" rather than anti-Soviet.

Ugly Swans had been written for a collection of our short works to be published by Young Guard.* That collection (*The Second Invasion from Mars* plus *Ugly Swans*) had even been announced in the publication plan for 1968, I believe, but it came out in altered form: instead of *Swans*, they put in *Space Apprentice*. *Swans* hadn't made it through. It was suffused with hopelessness and despair, and even if the authors had agreed to remove its numerous and utterly inextinguishable "allusions and associations," there was no way even our Soviet zoo could induce this leopard to change its spots (this line became something we said repeatedly about certain works of ours). It was simply impossible, even though the authors did try to dilute the darkness and despair in the final chapter, in which the Future, having swept away everything foul and unclean in the present, appears before the reader as a kind of *Homo novus*, omnipotent and merciful at once. (In the very first version, the novel had ended with that scene in the restaurant in which Golem says, "Poor beautiful duckling.")

The second and final version of *Ugly Swans* was completed in September 1967. Young Guard issued its final rejection in October, and no one else wanted it either. So the novel assumed its illegal status.

> 10/01/68—BS: People coming from Odessa say that [*Ugly Swans*] is being sold there, unofficially, for 5 rub. apiece. I have no idea how this happened. I only gave it to known and trusted people.

---

* Translator's Note: Young Guard was a Soviet publishing house, not to be confused with the monthly literary magazine of the same name.

I strongly suspected Arkady of insufficient vigilance and blamed him for the novel's illegal distribution, and he felt the same way about me. But the truth lay elsewhere: the manuscript was actually being illegally retyped in the very publishing houses where we were submitting it on quite official terms. That was how it multiplied and made its way "to the people." It took us a while to understand what was going on, but when we did, we remained unconcerned, continuing to submit the manuscript to more and more publishers—throwing it against the wall, so to speak, and hoping that somehow, somewhere, by the grace of God, it would stick.

It didn't. By now it's hard even to remember all the journals our manuscript visited. The only existing records are scattered references in our letters and diaries. For example, in the summer of 1970, the novel was apparently biding its time at *Novy Mir*.* By winter, it was at *Neva*.

> 01/09/71—BS: . . . The information that Yu. Dombrovsky gave a positive review of *US* turns out to be false. Izya Katzman saw Dombrovsky at New Year's, and Dombrovsky said that he had indeed been offered *US* to review, but refused because he "doesn't know the first thing about science fiction and cannot review something he doesn't understand." As for *Neva*, I haven't called them about *US* yet. . . .

> 02/10/71—BS: As we expected, it didn't work out with *US* at *Neva*. . . .

Our archive contains a couple of interesting informational exchanges pertaining to the possible publication of *Ugly Swans* in the journal *Yunost* (where Boris Polevoy was editor in chief at the time).†

---

* Translator's Note: *Novy Mir*, or *New World*, is a celebrated literary monthly, in print since 1925.

† Translator's Note: *Yunost*, or *Youth*, is a literary magazine in print since 1955.

09/30/71—AS: . . . Just before my departure, I stopped by the Central House of Writers and ran into Polevoy. He took me by the hand and said sternly, "We've been singing your praises. Submit something." I said insolently, "Sure, we'll submit something, but will you take it?" And that was the end of the conversation. He was whisked away before I could get another word in. What a comical situation. I've been thinking: What if we submitted a shortish novella, a spin-off starring Spiridon the octopus, 60 to 80 pp. long? Something about a trial of sperm whales, or about diplomacy, using characters from *MSoS*. . . .*

10/03/71—BS: . . . Polevoy's behavior is odd. . . . You know what I think? Let's submit *US*! At the end of the day, we risk nothing. Maybe some "journal" version of the thing will squeak by. And if not, then we'll submit the piece about Spiridon. . . . And what if *US* somehow makes it through? Their circulation is down, things aren't going too well for them, otherwise they'd never consider us in a million years. And in *US* we have a novel about the rotting of bourgeois morals, about capitalism destroying the future and all that. It's worth a try, I swear. . . .

10/06/71—AS: . . . The idea of giving *US* to Polevoy has occurred to me, but I rejected it as insufficiently insane. But fine, if you think that's the thing to do, I'll do it. We do have to change the title, though. *US* is bound to raise hackles. We should do something like *Stopping the Rain* or *When the Rain Stopped*. Send me your thoughts on a title. . . .

10/11/71—BS: . . . I offer you the following titles instead of *US*: *The Year of Rain*; *The Time of the Ark*; *Make for Yourself an Ark of Gopher Wood* (God's words to Noah); *Forty Days and Forty Nights* (that's how long it rained before the Flood); *A Time of Rain*. But really, the title isn't so important—if they accept the novel,

---

* TRANSLATOR'S NOTE: Spiridon was a character in *Tale of the Troika*, the 1968 sequel to the novel *Monday Starts on Saturday* (1964).

> we'll think of one that works. But it would be good to connect it with the Great Flood—the Great Flood of communism, so to speak, raining down on the head of the decrepit Noah of capitalist ideology. . . .
>
> 11/13/71—AS: . . . Handed in *US* (also known as *A Time of Rain*) under the most hilarious circumstances. Before I went down to Mayakovsky Street, where *Yunost* has its new offices, I stopped by our local spot for lunch. I'm standing there, looking for a place to sit, when all of a sudden someone tugs on my pant leg. I look, and it's Mary Lazarevna Ozerova, head of the fiction department at *Yunost*.
>
> "Where's that manuscript you promised?"
>
> "I have it. I just wanted to talk to Polevoy—"
>
> "Where is it? Do you have it on you?"
>
> "Yes, but I wanted to discuss—"
>
> "There's nothing to discuss. Give it here."
>
> "Here you go, but I need—"
>
> "Later. We'll give it a read, and then we can talk."
>
> And that's how it ended. She bore *US* (*ToR*) away in her predatory beak, promising to call me later. . . .

And that's where anything "hilarious" relating to *US* and *Yunost* ended once and for all. From then on, it was just tedious business as usual. Though really, what had happened was hardly unexpected.

> 01/29/72—AS: . . . Total debacle at *Yunost*. It passed with flying colors at the lower levels, but then Polevoy read it and announced that it was no good; he kept lecturing the lower levels about Marcuse and about the nonexistence of Nazism in West Germany. . . . Then Preobrazhensky chimed in and wrote that he agreed completely with [Polevoy]. A curious detail: no one at the lower level has ever seen Polevoy or Preobrazhensky's reviews in the flesh. Both reviews were created in a single copy and instantly handed over to accounting for purposes of

payment. I picked up the manuscript and put it on the shelf. Let it lie there for a while. . . .

And so the manuscript was shelved, definitively and for the long term. The authors immediately ceased flailing around and trying to submit it anywhere. They did not know yet that the fate of their novel had been decided for many years to come. In November 1972, Arkady sent me a letter, through a mutual acquaintance, that recounted his meeting with the notorious Comrade Ilyin, whom we had previously encountered in connection with *Tale of the Troika*. (Ilyin had been a KGB general, but was now the organizational secretary of the Moscow Writers' Union.)

11/24/72—AS: . . . On Monday the 13th I met with Ilyin. Just before (what a coincidence!) I had turned in a review to *Novy Mir*, whereupon Davis, smiling crookedly and avoiding eye contact, told me the following: a book exhibition took place in Frankfurt am Main, featuring the products of West German publishing houses—*Verlags*, they call 'em. The USSR was represented there by Melentyev (the current deputy chairman of the State Committee for Publishing), plus the heads of *Novy Mir* and Progress.* They walk up to the Possev booth and see five books on display:† Solzh.'s *August 1914*, a two-volume collection by Okudzhava, that Grossman novel you were interested in, *The Seven Days of Creation* by V. Maximov, and *US*, by You and Me. And on top of all that, there were blown-up portraits of all of the above authors, alongside the following text: "These Russian writers refused to compromise with the current regime." . . . Well,

---

* TRANSLATOR'S NOTE: Progress is a publishing house established in 1931, specializing in foreign-language and translated works.

† TRANSLATOR'S NOTE: Possev-Verlag is an émigré press established in 1945 by members of the National Alliance of Russian Solidarists (a group of anticommunist White émigrés formed in 1930) in the Mönchehof displaced persons camp, located near Kassel, Germany, which was then part of the American Zone of Occupation. By 1947, the publishing house had moved to Frankfurt, where it remains to this day.

> right after talking to Davis, I went on, crushed by fate, to see Ilyin, thinking that I was about to be shit on, and you and I pummeled. I couldn't have been more wrong! He greeted me, very friendly, even put an arm around my waist, sat me not on the other side of his desk but in an intimate little armchair in the corner, and began complaining about the enemies who had provoked us like that. He was extremely pleasant. Anyway, it all boils down to this: you and I need to distance ourselves, briefly, energetically, and with political clarity. You should draw up the relevant document, send it to me (in the normal way, since it's obviously not dangerous), and I, for my part, will take it to Ilyin and try to parlay it into something. . . .

(Strange to read this today, isn't it? A letter from another time, another planet. . . . To enhance that impression—I can't help myself!—here is another chunk, unrelated to literature, from the same letter: "As we now know for certain, Pyotr Yakir, having spent a month in prison on the Lubyanka, suddenly demanded to see his daughter and, when this request was granted, asked that they inform her that he had fundamentally changed his views and would like his former supporters to cease considering him a supporter of theirs. And after that, he denounced them *all*. I repeat: *all of them*. . . . Please keep this in mind and, if you have any cause for concern, draw the appropriate conclusions.")

Naturally, I immediately drafted and sent to Moscow a document in which we decisively distanced ourselves from an "act committed without the authors' knowledge or permission, obviously intended as a political provocation; a prime example of the most bald-faced literary gangsterism." Or something to that effect—I can't remember exactly what form it took by the time it appeared in the *Literary Gazette*, and only the earliest draft has been preserved in our archive.

It was on this hysterically high note that the *Ugly Swans* saga came to a well-deserved end. From this moment forth (and forever and ever, amen) its publication was entirely out of the question. It had now been permanently blacklisted and became taboo for any Soviet or Soviet-bloc publisher.

You will surely agree that a novel with such a biography was a good match for the role of the Blue Folder. *Ugly Swans* fit inside *Lame Fate* as comfortably and cleanly as a bullet in a magazine. It, too, was a story of a writer living in a totalitarian state. It was sufficiently fantastical while also being entirely realistic. And, in essence, it dealt with the very same questions and problems that tormented Felix Sorokin. It was exactly the work that Felix Sorokin would have written—as a person, as a writer, and as the hero of *Lame Fate*. And really, in a certain sense, he *did* write it.

The version of *Lame Fate* we submitted to the Leningrad journal *Neva* already included *Ugly Swans*. But this first attempt didn't really end up going anywhere. Of course, I felt obliged to explain the history of *Swans* to the journal's editor in chief, who promised to clarify the situation at the regional party committee. (It was very early 1986, perestroika was still all smoke and no fire, and no one knew anything—neither ordinary people nor anyone at the top. Anything was possible, including a 180-degree turn on a dime.) He was apparently unable to get a "yes," and so *Lame Fate* was published without the Blue Folder, on top of which it had been mangled in the dull cogwheels of Ligachyov's antialcohol campaign, then in full swing.

But then, in 1987, the journal *Daugava* took the risk of publishing *Swans* (even if it was under the mongrel title *A Time of Rain*) and nothing horrible happened—the skies didn't fall, no chastening lightning bolts smote the blasphemers. Times had finally changed, and what had previously been forbidden was now permitted. And—oh laughter of the gods!—the forbidden, having been permitted, immediately ceased to arouse anyone's interest. And so, when the unexpurgated version of *Lame Fate* appeared in 1989, in a magnificent edition by Sovetsky Pisatel,* it produced no uproar, no sensation. The reading public probably didn't even notice it. New times were suddenly upon us, and a new reader was born—

* Translator's Note: Sovetsky Pisatel, literally "Soviet Writer," was a press focusing on contemporary fiction, established in 1934.

coalescing almost instantaneously, like a solute precipitating in a saturated solution. And there was a demand for new literature, a literature of freedom and disdain, which was supposed to replace the literature "from under the rubble." But that new literature never arrived. We're still waiting for it to this day.

We wanted, in *Lame Fate*, to depict a person who is talented but hopelessly oppressed by his life circumstances; the "wolfhound age" has gripped him by the throat firmly and forever, and he has agreed to everything, almost fully acquiescing. But still, once in a while, he allows himself an indulgence—a secret one, enjoyed by candlelight behind well-sealed doors, because unlike Bulgakov's Maksudov, he knows perfectly well what is permitted here, now, today, and what isn't and never will be. . . . We saw Felix Sorokin as a kind of "hero of our time." Maybe he was that, in some sense, but time itself changed right before our eyes, taking many, many of our values along with it. The new heroes were totally different from our Felix Sorokin, who plunged into oblivion as a type, and as a hero. At least, I would very much like to think so.

Meanwhile, his novel *Ugly Swans* has lost none of its relevance today, because the problem of the future that thrusts its tentacles into the present remains unresolved, along with the practical issue of figuring out how to devote one's life to the future while managing to die in the present. The faster progress accelerates, the faster the future replaces the present, and the harder it becomes for Victor Banev to keep his balance in the surrounding world, given his state of unrelenting future shock. The New Horsemen of the Apocalypse—Irma, Bol-Kunatz, and Valerians—have already mounted their steeds. We can only hope that the Future will neither smite nor pardon, but simply continue on its way.